Sonia Perez

About the Author

Novelist and poet Zoé Valdés was born in Havana in 1959. *Dear First Love* is her third novel to appear in English translation, following *Yocandra in the Paradise of Nada* and *I Gave You All I Had*. Zoé Valdés lives in Paris with her daughter.

Dear First Love

A NOVEL

ZOÉ VALDÉS

Translated from the Spanish
by Andrew Hurley

Perennial

An Imprint of HarperCollins*Publishers*

Originally published as *Querido Primer Novio* by Editorial Planeta in Spain.

A hardcover edition of this book was published in 2002 by HarperCollins Publishers.

First Perennial edition published 2003.

Designed by Jackie McKee

The Library of Congress has catalogued the hardcover edition as follows:

Valdés, Zoé.
[Querido primer novio. English]
Dear first love : a novel / Zoé Valdés ; translated from the Spanish
by Andrew Hurley.
p. cm.
ISBN 0-06-019972-5
I. Hurley, Andrew. II. Title.
PQ7390.V342 Q4713   2002

863'.64—dc21   20022276254

ISBN 0-06-095909-6 (pbk.)

03 04 05 06 07 ❖ /RRD 10 9 8 7 6 5 4 3 2 1

To La Milagrosa

To Lázaro, for his fear of the Schools in the Country

To my sister Mary and my brother Gusty

To Ena, once again

To José Triana,
who makes me happy

Contents

To what shall I compare thee, dear bridegroom?

To a slender shoot, I most liken thee.

SAPPHO

But let her enjoy childhood

in the fleeting moment!

JUANA BORRERO

Dear First Love

THE FLEETING MOMENT

*W*HILE SHE WASHED the dishes stained and chipped by time and use, Danae created a winter landscape in her mind. Snow, miles and miles of snow, that was what she yearned for. Chunks of ice packed inside her skull, behind her eyes, a bathtub filled with frozen daiquiris she could sink into—the only thing that came close was one of those frozen cones of caramel-covered peanuts they were making these days, or maybe a snow cone. She dried her hands, and while they were temporarily free she repositioned her tortoiseshell comb and gathered up the two strands of hair that both called attention to her eyes and infected them, filling them with yellowy pus. She liked doing housework, padding around the house while her mind drifted off into absurd daydreams. She caught herself just as she was about to cut off the tip of her finger with the bread knife, the only knife she owned for cutting anything that needed to be cut. The kitchen was tiny, hardly enough space for her to turn around in and stand over the gas stove. She lost herself in watching the milk begin to boil; she loved to watch the cream on top suddenly rise up into a frothy dome. *Cream is the housewife's delight.* Suddenly there was the smell of scorched milk, and once again she let herself be transported; this time, it was the memory of the contact of her lips with the condensed milk boiled in a double boiler until it turned to "mud," that dessert they had in the Schools in the Country. She looked tired, even slovenly—it had been weeks since she'd felt like bathing, much less fixing herself up. Her hair kept slipping slowly but inexorably out of the comb, falling over her shoulders in greasy strands; her lips, dry and cracked and pale, resembled those desserts that Arabs made. There were wide brown circles under her eyes. Glassy, uninterested-looking eyes. She didn't eat; she cooked for the others but she had no appetite for any recipe she knew how to make. She went about making dinner the way she would have invested energy in preparing a performance, as though going through an aesthetic act. Her mind worked faster than her hands; all she did was think, and think some more. And that left her exhausted, drained, uninterested. She smoked a great deal, cigarettes or cigars.

But except for her, all the rest, everything around her, was sparkling clean. The apartment was of a size deemed suitable for a couple with a minimal monthly income and two daughters, yet her in-laws lived in it, too. At the moment they were on a trip, to Cincinnati, where her husband's brother lived. A living-dining room, a bathroom the same tiny size as the kitchen, two bedrooms, one for her, her husband, and the girls and the second for the in-laws. The furniture, even with its threadbare cotton upholstery, the flowers faded almost to invisibility, showed not the slightest sign of neglect; the wooden legs gleamed after being given a good dose of elbow grease and kerosene. The floor tiles, their surface pitted from the effects of the salt air and the lack of machine polishing, were nonetheless like mirrors, thanks to her constant work with the mop and the creoline. *Creoline is like a secretion of the mother's womb.* The mop was Danae's weapon of war. A woman wielding a mop is the heraldic device of any germ-obsessed mother battling to ensure that the floor gleams, to ensure that the smell of clean haunts the depths of her child's memory for the rest of that child's days. Two metal shelving units did duty as bookshelves—works on architecture, novels in the Huracán and Cocuyo series, plus one or two large-format volumes on the kind of art that hung in distant, unvisited museums, L'Hermitage, for example. At the windows, curtains made of a shimmery muslin fabric. Danae noticed that the hem had come out of one of them and she told herself that night she'd rehem it. In one corner reigned an antique sewing machine, a Singer, with a baby blue knit cover carefully draped over it. With a sense of pride and satisfaction her eyes took in the scene of domestic order, and when she returned to the dented aluminum canteen of milk on the stove she had to hurry, grab a kitchen towel so as not to burn herself when she took it off the fire. She laid a piece of window screen over the top to make sure a fly didn't fall in and set it on the windowsill, telling herself that the breeze would cool it. The doorbell rang, insistently. She went to the bathroom, tore a piece of toilet paper off the porcelain roller, and as she went to the door blew her nose several times.

"I'm coming, I'm coming! *Coño*, what's the hurry?"

She wadded the now slimy and disintegrating length of toilet paper and tossed it in a pressed-metal ashtray—how she wished instead of that ugly metal ashtray she had a Murano crystal one! She went to one of the drawers in the sewing machine, took out the house key, and opened the double lock. Before her stood Matilde, looking sweaty and pained, although from her earlobes there hung exotic and eye-catching earrings, fake opal dangling from wire twisted out of the aluminum-foil tops on yogurt cartons. From back when yogurt still came in cartons.

"How are you, how you bearing up in this heat, Danae, everything all right? In your life, I mean. Listen, is this a bad time? *Ay, chica*, I love the smell of boiled milk!" By now Matilde was standing in the middle of the living-dining room.

"I just took it off the fire. I won't offer you any, it's still scalding hot. Have a drop of coffee with me, though. Good timing—I finished straightening and cleaning up not half an hour ago."

"And you sacrifice your day off to do housework? Why don't you go to the movies?"

"I just can't seem to get excited about any of the new ones that are playing. Did you need something?" The younger woman sighed, smoothing her hair back from her forehead.

"*Ay, niña*, I came over to see if you could keep this package for me. Don't say anything to anybody about it. It's some letters, real important, from when poor Jacinto, may he rest in peace, was still alive and he had those problems with the law. Problem is, my nephews snoop through everything."

Danae took the rectangular package and locked it up in the sewing machine drawer.

"*Gracias, mi amiga.* Ay, this heat! I can't hardly breathe! Loan me all the air you can spare, hon, will you—down in my place the heat is worse than the bonfire of the Inquisition, *carajo*, so I came up for a little girl talk. My nephew broke one of the rockers off the rocking chair playing Zorro, I had to send it to a carpenter friend of Hilda's, my sister's? By the name of St. Popsicle, that apartment of mine is like a damn oven, the devil's cauldron, I tell you. Here, it being the third floor and all, why you've got this nice breeze through here, look how it just lifts those curtains right up, it's a blessing. So how are the girls? Off at school?"

Danae nodded and hummed an uh-huh as she spooned three spoons of coffee in the coffeepot. Then she beat the other woman to the inevitable question about her husband:

"And Andrés still on that construction job, laying concrete blocks, getting up earlier every morning. He's dying to finish that god-ugly, useless building."

"*Bueno, mi amor*, at least if he's working so hard he's not out getting into trouble!" Matilde took the steaming terra-cotta cup with its incomprehensible yellow and blue squiggles that Danae handed her and took a sip, burning the tip of her tongue. "Got a bullet? *Caballero*, you can't get a cigarette anywhere! They're practically extinct! So when are your in-laws due back?"

"Soon, sooner than I'd like to think, unfortunately."

She made her way into the bedroom, slip-slopping in her worn cotton espadrilles with the burlap-sack soles, the shoes so worn they'd become open-air sandals. Matilde noticed that her heels were caked with mud; the cleaning water had dried and crusted on her skin. A yellowish ring of old sweat marked the underarms of her T-shirt. *She may look like a street urchin but you could eat off this floor*, Matilde thought as she tried with a fingernail, and with something of a malicious, contemptuous look, to dislodge a clump of snot that had dried to her nose hair. Danae disappeared into the semidarkness of her room, pulled up a corner of the mattress, and stuck her hand in, groping around until she found the pack of cigarettes, the "bullets" that Matilde wanted. She came back with one between her lips, holding out the package to the other woman. Matilde lit the Veguero—the "round-trip ticket," as everybody called it, because of its size—and exhaled with her next words:

"Listen, you'll excuse me for asking but I've noticed a clear note of putre-faction in you lately. You're just not the same. Look at me, all sweaty from this heat, but I've just had a shower to cool off a little, I bathe twice a day, put on some nice cologne, try to win the battle of the heat. *Te digo, muchacha,* you need to spruce yourself up a little, buy yourself a hat or maybe a scarf, at the very least a net to hold those greasy locks of yours in place, pull on some nice stockings and climb up on a pair of spike heels. Women that don't wear heels lose all their cachet with the other gender, *querida,* and you know it. There's no reason to let yourself go, no reason to let adversity get you. I'll tell you, *I'm* not gonna let the sun turn me all wrinkled and lizard-skinned . . . no way . . . She sighed, and smoke issued in two identical puffs from her nostrils.

"Oh, how I'd love to have a *torreja* just dripping with honey! Tch"—Danae clucked "—I ought to get the hell outta here." She went to the refrig-erator, which was in the girls' room, opened the door, and fanned herself with it. "You're certainly right about this heat, pure hellfire."

Then she squatted down, pulled out the vegetable drawer, and took out a pair of tennis shoes, a blouse, and a pair of Bermuda shorts. Matilde was standing in the doorway now, looking on, smiling and shaking her head in disbelief.

"You still cooling your clothes in the fridge? I gave up on that—your clothes touch your body and in two minutes they're hot again. There's just no solution for it, girl. Where might you be escaping to, if I might ask?"

"Nowhere, I was just talking. Or maybe I will take a trip, somewhere way outside the city."

WAY OUTSIDE THE city what there was was country, but she longed to make that journey in reverse. The normal thing, or almost normal, was for a coun-try girl to want to move to the city. Not Danae. Danae longed for the coun-tryside, yearned to get away from all that bound her to her age, her family, her job, money. In the hall as she walked from one room to another, she was caressed by a breath of air, her face and bare arms were spattered with tiny salty drops of moisture. It called up that tornado cloud that had struck in the middle of the potato harvest. The group of girls scattering in panic—*It's coming, it's coming! A whirlwind! It'll kill us all!* La Milagrosa was right, they wouldn't live to tell about it. Danger was at least more fun. She wasn't afraid of danger—none of them were. Disappearing up into that black sleeve of cloud would've been a beautiful death. Fly off like Matías Pérez on that July 29, 1856, in the Plaza de la Fraternidad, hanging from a hot-air balloon—even that was romantic, if you asked her. Suddenly the glowering sky was pregnant with black lava, and a mantle of dirt had been blinded Danae's sight. Some girls had barely had the chance to throw themselves to the ground or take refuge under the heavy sacks full of potatoes. She had been swallowed up by the whirling cone of mud and swept away—she'd taken flight, like some suicidal kite, plunging to earth in a gust of uprooted tobacco plants. It all had been a roar, as though the whole world had crashed down out of a pine tree, and then utter and complete silence. After a while, a man she couldn't see stepped on her—she tried to call out, tell him that she was down there, breathing. A metal pole was stuck into her skin, into one of her ribs, but it didn't do her mortal harm, just a scratch out of which a rivulet of warm blood began to trickle, like the café-con-leche breakfasts that were all she could find time for when she was at home, being a mother. Luckily, the campesino kept poking around until a scrap of her clothing appeared. Minutes later she found herself in an improvised infirmary packed with survivors, none more than sixteen years old. There was a babble of voices calling out for Mercurochrome, nose drops, bandages, Band-Aids, tincture of arnica, antispasmodics, Milk of Magnesia, methylene blue. Methylene blue was very effective in treating pinworm, those parasites that schools found in schoolkids' asses, little white worms that took up residence in the pleats and puckers of a kid's anus, and when they scratched down there deep in their crack they picked up the eggs on their fingernails and a minute or so later, when they stuck their fingers in their mouth, they infected themself again. It's extremely effective to take one of those cotton-tipped swabs for getting the earwax out of your ears and wet it with methylene blue and slip it up into a kid's ass—it poisons the worms on the spot . . . They were also calling for kaolin to stop all the shitting. One guy too polite to use bad words gave the one that was talking about all the shitting a poke in the ribs—hey, listen, it's *diarrhea, diarrhea,* you hear, they try to teach you but some people just refuse to learn. But then it was like the tornado had never happened—it was like turning the page in a book and starting a new chapter. That was when the jokes, the laughing, and the nightmares started—the fleeting things that happen to young, insolent people whose only reaction, after they've cheated death, is to think they're above it, that it can't touch them.

SHE LIED TO MATILDE, said she had an appointment with the gynecologist. The butt of that deception didn't worry herself about the other woman's health because it just sounded like Danae wanted to get rid of her. She'd been noticing that along with Danae's letting herself go there was a constant attitude of avoidance about the woman, a holding-back, a recoiling from companionship that didn't gibe with the cheeriness she'd once so admired in her neighbor. Even so, she followed the young woman down to the corner and there said her goodbyes, telling her that if she needed anything, anything at all . . . confession, affection . . . she could count on her, that's what neighbors were for. Danae barely thanked her, she just said she was sorry, she was going to be late for the doctor's appointment. Matilde waddled away, her thighs brushing against each other; she couldn't wait to reach the door of her apartment, hoping she still had a pinch of cornstarch to soothe the chapped skin—the skin rubbed raw—between her legs.

Danae, pausing under the neighborhood's spreading flamboyán tree, waited for the other woman to disappear around the corner. She tried to cheer herself, tried to be happy, attempted to call up some pleasant memory to make herself smile. She tried to laugh—even for no reason, just to do it, force it if she had to. She tried to make up some joke to tell herself, make herself laugh so hard she'd have to throw herself on the ground with her toes pointed up at the sky, straight for the clouds, and vomit out a stream of laughter. But she couldn't do it. Laughter . . . Salvation lay in laughter, she knew that. Two men crossed the street, each carrying his end of a huge mirror. In its silver surface she saw herself shattered into fragments, reflected back as girl and woman at the same time, as though she had gone out looking for something—help, salvation, a man to marry, looking to buy some kisses, as the old saying went. *Fresh out,* said the first stranger. *None for you today,* the second one said sarcastically. Fresh out of kisses, and if they had any, they wouldn't be for you. Behind the jigsaw puzzle of her silhouette in the mirror she saw the red-specked foliage of the flamboyán tree; its spreading branches resembled a low cloud, or the explosion of that atomic bomb in the picture. The flamboyán was her fetish tree, anachronistic in its elegance, ghostlike in its lightness. Trying to forget the ceiba tree and the royal palm, the usual trees of magic and power, she consoled herself by telling herself that it gave you good luck. She suddenly felt ambiguous—in the midst of her desolation, protected like some figure from an earlier century standing in the shade of the leafy branches. Out of a hole in the red-colored mud there emerged an army of little ants, in single file, rhythmically climbing up her shins, then quickly, swiftly, half crazily running down again, unable to understand this new territory, so unaccountably and uncustomarily smooth, that they had trod upon. She slapped at her ankles to shoo the bugs away and then began to walk, conscious of her own automatism . . . *I yearn and I seek,* she murmured, quoting a verse from Sappho.

She had no idea where she might go, yet indecision was all that seemed to comfort her. She walked and walked and walked, taking no notice of the streets' symbolic names, thinking of nothing, looking down at her own feet, her eyes fixed on the white glare of the pavement. At number 162 Calle Trocadero, Danae stopped before the bluish gray building with the two serpentine columns at the entrance. It was one of those buildings that were so common—one door for the person who lived downstairs on the first floor and another opening onto a stairway for those who lived on the floors above. Without realizing it, she had come to the poet's house. She read the plaque that gave his date of birth and death, and then, above the lintel, she spelled out to herself the sign that was hanging there: *The Writer's Library.* Danae stuck her head in, through the wrought-iron bars at the window. Not one piece of furniture, not one painting, not one knickknack or figurine—nothing that had once belonged to the obese writer. All there was inside were some bookshelves made of squeezed-out sugarcane stalks, painted a metallic white (that wounding white of hospital cabinets), books all lined up tidily on the shelves but in no apparent order—politics, economics, technology. Danae wanted to go in; she gently pushed at the none-too-well-cared-for front door. It was locked. She stepped back, over to the window, and called out:

"Hello! Anybody there?"

From the hallway that led back to the back patio came the nasal voice of a girl—a crude, snotty girl.

"We're closed till week after next!" She didn't even show her face.

Danae drummed her fingers on the window's wooden sill.

"Can I ask you a question?"

"That'd be two, because you just asked the first one!" came the shrill, invisible, impertinent reply from out of the dimness.

"Could you come up here, please?" Danae had to shout her plea because at just that second a deafening bus roared by, its engine laboring, its exhaust pipe spewing black smoke into the pearly light of the morning.

"Jesus Christ, you can't even eat a piece of two-day-old bread in peace around here!"

The young woman came through the door that led into the patio, a door painted that same bluish gray as the house and pitted with termite holes. She was wearing a dress made of gauze dyed with tea. She was very thin, with dark chestnut hair, and she was wearing sandals that were silver shoelaces woven together. Her legs were dark with the stubble of black, badly shaved hair.

"How can I help you?" she asked as she pushed the last hunk of bread into her mouth and brushed the spit-wet crumbs off her, first her hands and then the front of her dress.

One of the girl's eyes was paying attention but the other one was gathering wool somewhere. She was as cockeyed as a train wreck in the middle of the desert. And everybody knew that cockeyed people were shifty, deceitful, hypocritical.

"What did they do with the writer's belongings? I'm asking because his furniture, books, paintings—"

"Let me make this clear so you don't get the wrong idea, *cariño*, all right? This is not a museum, it's a library. I don't have the slightest idea what they did with his stuff. By the time I got here this place had been cleared out already. People say they're going to bring the stuff back, and that if it's not the original it'll be copies, which amounts to the same thing, right? Anything else?"

Danae felt she was being watched by two eyes that weren't getting along, a pair of pupils that couldn't come to an understanding, that would each prefer to go its own way, so she shook her head, thanked the girl, and left the window. She crossed the street, stopped on the sidewalk opposite, gave the house one last look, and began to walk away. As she retraced her steps, the young woman remained standing at the window, her hand on the burglar bars. Danae bit her lip, then said so softly to the girl as almost to seem to be talking to herself:

"I met him, years ago . . . it was totally by chance. Every so often, while he was taking his afternoon walk—it was not easy for him—he would pass by under the balcony of my building, where I lived. A girlfriend of mine and I would make fun of how fat he was, we'd yell out, *Here comes Old Blubberbucket! Here comes Mr. Inner Tube!* Of course at the time we had no idea that he was a brilliant man, a genius. But one day I was in the Avellaneda bookstore on Calle Reina and I discovered him. I opened one of his books of poetry. Nobody discovered him to me, or for me. I discovered him all by myself. And it was also by chance—concurrent chance, maybe—that I had the fortune to meet his widow, years later. She was sitting in front of that . . . that imaginary . . ." She sighed, pointing to the center of the living room, where there had once been the big armchair that the poet would sprawl in as he composed his verses. "He would sit there and look out at the world with those eyes, like some Pascalian mystic, in love with the word *knowledge*, as the critics and his own widow tell us."

"Big deal. You're not the only one, you know," the librarian spat out contemptuously, releasing the iron bars to study her long, lilac-painted fingernails, filed off square at the ends. Danae figured she was so full of herself she saw twenty fingernails instead of a mere ten.

"I was a librarian, too—for years . . . I owe my name to him—those ideas my grandmother would get in her head. My grandmother was a good friend of their maid's—in fact it was Nelly, the maid, that insisted I introduce myself to his widow. . . Remember that line? . . . Remember that first line of that book?"

"Which one, *mi amor*?" And at that, her pupils rolled away and hid in the corners of her eyes, leaving only white in the eye sockets.

"*Danae weaves the hours gilded by the Nile* . . ."

"Uh-huh, of course, cute line. I don't imagine it's easy to carry around a name like that, so, so . . . with that . . . I dunno, something so weird about it . . . But . . . your face reminds me of somebody—didn't we go to high school together? You don't remember me, you may not recognize me because I got all disfigured in an accident, a train wreck in Santiago, my face is reconstructed. For aesthetic reasons, you understand . . . You're . . . you're Danae Duckbill Lips! We were in that School in the Country together, La Fe . . ." And her pupils swung back to focus on the bridge of her nose.

A coincidence. Her voice was like Salome the Satrap's, but Danae didn't want to find out for sure.

"No, I'm not the person you're looking for."

"Looking for? I'm not looking for anybody. You're the one that came here, ya know."

She nodded, and then there was nothing to do but say goodbye, a banal enough goodbye. And well deserved, she thought, for expecting too much. She walked along counting columns, playing with the Chinese-like shadows. Suddenly she stopped; she remembered that playwright she'd met when she was young, in the School in the Country. He said his name was Ruperto, but as hard as she tried to find him years later, she'd never heard another word about him. Ruperto had been a friend of the poet's, too, and he asked a favor of Danae: when she got to be as old as he was then, forty-five years old, he wanted her to think hard about him. She crossed the street, toward the Paseo del Prado, and with a little clearer idea now of what her anxieties were asking of her, she walked straight to the entrance of the tunnel that connected the center of the city to parts east. A trip, she needed a trip. When she came to the Casablanca pier she took her wallet out of her backpack and checked to be sure she had enough money to take the train.

Soon it would be her birthday.

The milk train wouldn't be leaving that day or for several days after. So she took the ferry across the bay again. She walked along the wall of the Malecón until it turned into the wall bordering the customhouse. She came to the Alameda de Paula and came to rest finally at the train station.

I, the narrator, the time of the city, had dragged on long enough to let her dream.

SITTING ON A crossbar of filthy, dark wood in the train station while she awaited the arrival of the shabby old train car pulled by a locomotive that dated back to the thirties but promised to take her to the town of La Fe, Danae fretfully pictured what the faces of her daughters would be like when her husband told them that their mother had run away from home. That *she*, their own mother, had abandoned them in the most cowardly way—for no reason, with no explanation, without so much as a goodbye. The girls wouldn't cry because they wouldn't understand, or maybe they would, but Danae preferred to think that they wouldn't shed a single tear. That indifference, born of the incredulity of innocence, made her smile. He, on the other hand, overcome with rage, blind with jealousy and powerlessness, would break things, she was almost sure. During their last argument he had smashed his fist into a bookcase and knocked it over, turning it into a pile of wood shelving with the planks' ends all cracked and split. In that same outburst he had broken her nose and fractured one of her ribs when he gave her a karate kick. *¡Qué bestialidad!* —every breath for months had been a stabbing pain.

I, the time of the city, the narrator, was holding out possible means of flight to her. She no longer believed in me or anything else—not seconds, not minutes, not hours gained or lost. She detested me, too, because she saw me as but one more of her harassers, yet another of the things that hounded her and would not let her rest. One of the things that accused her. Many times women suddenly lose their trust in time. In its ability to do good, to make things right.

Big drops of sweat ran from the top of her skull down her temples, the rivulets at one point beginning to follow the lines of her veins. They left wet tracks down her forehead, and from there ran down her cheeks. One drop hung suspended from the tip of her nose—she wiped it away with the back of her hand and passed her dry tongue over her lips and tasted the salty spatters caught by the almost microscopic blond down on her upper lip. She had walked far, her feet were dusty, swollen, her underarms sticky with sweat. There were rings of wet dirt in the wrinkles of her neck. She felt perverse; she felt like a bad woman, a common tramp that hurts those she loves most, the girls, her husband, her home—the conventional things, those things most true and valuable, into which a woman channels her libido the moment she takes the step of marrying. But just then, hunger (yearning) and weariness were stronger than conscience. The sternness of her sense of guilt struck her just now as more than a little boring.

She was leaving for Pinar del Río; she'd persuaded a street vendor with flyblown merchandise to sell her his round-trip ticket. She needed to look once again upon the greenness of those *mogotes* in the Valle de Viñales, the huge pillars of limestone, covered with trees and bushes, that made the most haunting and beautiful landscape in the world, in a certain person's opinion. She told herself that although it was very lovely, if you compared it with other landscapes she had seen as she leafed through books, it was nothing out of this world. She thought about her past and gave an ironic little smile—a pretty stupid little life. At that, several passengers looked at her warily, some out of the corner of their eyes, their ears perking up—they thought she was mad. Her life bore some resemblance to the life of a character in a certain American novel she remembered fondly; she was proud to recognize that detail. How could such a simple existence be, on account of that very simplicity, so complicated? She yawned without trying to hide the rude noise of the yawn, without putting her hand over her mouth. She needed sleep, longed for sleep; for years, ever since her first daughter was born, she hadn't been able to really let herself go and sleep the deep, soothing sleep she needed. And then, when she woke up, it would be nice to have a big fresh white fillet of fish for lunch, with lemon, and lots of vegetables—beans, grated carrots, mashed yucca with garlic and olive oil, tomatoes, lettuce, cabbage, watercress, cucumber, every kind of bean and green imaginable. And she would love a glass of white wine, very cold and dry. Then afterward, if that whole dream had been possible, she'd have loved to read a novel about love, or leaf through magazines with pictures of people different from her. People with money, things—luxuries.

An old beggar was making his way, person by person, through the station, trying to sell merchandise hidden deep inside a grimy, smelly burlap sack. Stubbornly, he stopped in front of Danae. Suppurating eyelids being eaten away by a fleshy reddish yellow excrescence, a nose covered with blackheads, long gray sideburns, hair yellowing and greasy, bare, filthy feet. And yet his eyes were gay. From the bag he extracted a handful of homemade strawberry lollipops, elongated red cones wrapped in brown paper.

"*Pirulís,*" he said, "a peso each," virtually convinced that she wouldn't buy one.

Danae shook her head, but with an attempt at pleasantness. The old man stuck his scabby hand back in the bag and felt around inside. This time it was wax and clay reproductions of saints and virgins. When he saw the woman's inexpressiveness, her lack of enthusiasm to buy, he didn't even bother to tell her the price.

"I also have taffy . . ." But he didn't put his hand in the sack.

"Taffy? I'll take some taffy. How much is it?" The old man hurried to comply—or rather, to satisfy the salivating gluttony shown by a fat woman as stubby as a whale, accompanied by three children who also looked like starving little chubby walruses. "I bet I haven't had any taffy in a hundred years— I've even forgotten what it tastes like."

In the waiting room, a seat became vacant next to the *iyawó,* the bride of the *santo,* who was dressed head to toe in airy white tulle, with a white turban, white shoes, white stockings; on her wrist she wore gold bracelets, and around her neck, brightly colored necklaces. The snowy whiteness shimmered and glinted like something in those old black-and-white movies. The initiate motioned to Danae, offering her the seat; she saved it by setting her shopping bag, woven of fishing line, in it. Danae realized that it was strange that she herself should be carrying only a backpack, unlike the piles of baggage carried by all the other passengers. The woman in white who had offered her the seat with interest and concern—her appearance marking her as an adept, an initiate in the secrets of santería, *una hija de las Mercedes—* was dying to talk; that was why she had saved the seat for Danae, so that she'd owe her at least some chitchat.

"Thank you, and may God repay you with a son," was all that Danae said, though she was immediately sorry she'd said it, and the *iyaguoná* took advantage of that opening to launch into an endless rushing stream of babble about the lateness of trains, the lack of consideration for the passengers shown by those responsible. Instantly, to Danae's ears the woman's words became a rhythmic din, a distant drumming that from time to time underwent bizarre yet barely perceptible rises and falls.

And without its being clear in her own mind that really, she'd rather go on thinking than have a conversation, she sat there in a kind of daze, her eyes filling with tears. They were fixed on a distant point somewhere beyond the peeling window, out there in that cemetery for dead trains where many years ago some far-out-of-the-mainstream filmmakers had shot a movie. The movie, in black and white, which she had seen by chance on one of those nights when she'd gone out wandering through the city, had left her catatonic. It was during the film festival, in December, and she'd gone into the Yara without noticing what was showing, and it had been that strange movie about two characters waiting for a third one. They were in a cemetery for trains; it was a variation on Samuel Beckett's *Waiting for Godot*. And now here she was on location for that film again, imprisoned yet breathing free air, filled with that psychiatric-hospital sensation that train station waiting rooms give, waiting for the train for La Fe. Suddenly her weariness disappeared, she forgot she was hungry and thirsty and that she would have given her life for a book or one of those magazines that would keep her abreast of how other people, in distant *other* places, lived. The vision of the landscape brought to her memory paintings she had read about ... *No one escaped love, nor will escape it, while beauty exists and there are eyes to see it.* That was from *Daphnis and Chloe,* by Longus of Lesbos. The sudden upswelling of that quotation from somewhere deep inside her made her want so much to be young again and read the books that one reads in one's youth, and to live with the same innocence, the same naiveté, and still be a virgin to knowledge of the world. But there was no going back. No returning. And immediately she devoted her time—that is, me, the time of the city, the narrator—to toying with her memory, touching, feeling, caressing recollections, mixing up the chronology of things on purpose, to make it all less hurtful. Things looked less bizarre and anachronistic that way.

Where was she just then—in a train station or a madhouse? Had she just had a conversation with a traveler or with a nurse? Were those buzzing currents running through the invisible labyrinths of her brain emotional spasms or just electroshocks? What zone of memory had she come to anchor in?

Dear Husband,

I am not writing this letter on paper yet, but I am writing it in my mind, while I wait to take the train. Every so often I feel the need for a train; this is not something that will take you by surprise, since I've always talked to you about my passion for trains. Imagining that I am going to take a train to some unknown or unfamiliar place, or even just thinking about the platform at the station, gives me butterflies in my stomach. It thrills me that my gaze travels as swiftly as the landscape, that it does not fix on my destination. I have taken a train only a few times, however. My trips could be counted on both hands, with several fingers left over, and they have never been long. I have never taken a plane. I don't like planes, but I am drawn terribly to trains, because you can admire the imperceptible trembling of the land, not to mention the spiritual vibrations of the trees, the peace of the animals in the countryside. Sometimes, all of a sudden, a river will loom up, and the ocean. The sky seems to melt and run down over my head, depending on my perspective. You have never invited me on a train ride. And that is what in the long run I hold against you, knowing that you could have given me the best gift of my life had you just bought two train tickets—or four, counting the girls—but you never gave me that happiness. Nor did it ever occur to you to give me that pleasure, not even if it was such an everyday sort of wish to have, and so easily granted. It's that in our relationship it's always been me that's thought of others, me that's made the sacrifices. You think you deserve everything. In your opinion, I have a right to almost nothing.

Listen, Andrés, I love you—you better than anyone know how much I love you—but I'm tired. I don't give more because I can't give any more than I've already given. Nobody gives what they don't have. I've tried everything I know to break your silences. I've lost the desire to enjoy even the little things. I am obsessed with you, with our daughters, with your peace of mind, yet I never think of myself. I live exclusively for the three of you. Every waking hour, you might say. And I cannot go on in this torture of self-denial and self-renunciation. I have to acknowledge myself. I have to live for myself much more than I've been living. Look at myself in the mirror the way I used to do, even if I don't look the same, feel that some part of my body is beautiful. I've developed a phobia for mirrors. I can't bear my own flesh, because it's no longer skin—I feel that I'm more like some horrid floury, greasy, lumpy meatball. My surface is as cracked and fissured as the flanks of a volcano. But there's no fire inside me. I feel ugly inside, and that is the worst part, more unbearable than having to exhibit my outward putrefaction. I need some distance from the three of you because I sense that I'm destroying myself, and that in the blink of an eye I will be gone. If I go on living more for your lives than my own, I am going to wind up dissolved into your personalities, and my own will be annihilated. A heroic variant of suicide. I know that I'm giving you the news too abruptly, too unpreparedly, but I have no other option. I wouldn't know how to do it any other way, and you would keep me from going. I am not myself—I am very much not myself. I haven't been since that time you didn't come home and didn't send word, I don't even know how many days ago that was, an eternity. You didn't come home, and the hours dragged on, and the three of us, the girls and I, looking for you in the hospitals, at police stations, at your friends' houses, your enemies' houses. I don't want to think about that. Yet something strange happens to my emotions—I don't like to suffer, like other women do, feeling some sadomasochistic pleasure in heartbreak. Even though I might experience my sufferings physically, that's simply evidence that my salvation will come by my being conscious of them, by my coming to know that I can control them and even nourish them. For example, I know that the doctor has forbidden me to indulge my obsessive need to eat spoonfuls of sugar, but every time I think about that ban I go like a robot to the sugar bowl, stick a spoon in, and bring it to my mouth. And then I chew the sugar until it dissolves in my saliva—it's at that moment that I can control myself, realize that I'm poisoning myself. It's strange, explaining what I suffer from. I suffer from horror and hatred of myself for abandoning the three of you.

But at the same time I'm afraid of missing the train.

What about the girls, Danae? What do I do with them? you'll be asking in desperation, although you'll just pretend, as though I were there listening to you. The girls will understand. Isn't that what men say when they leave their wives and children? I know it's not often that it's the woman who decides to go. Much less this way. Without saying a word. Without telling anyone she's leaving. Without even an argument to set it in motion. Because I want it to be clear that I'm not leaving on some pretext, something other than ourselves. There's no one in my life but you and the girls. My love has never known anybody but yours. I don't have a lover—I don't even meet with friends unless you're there. Not that that's so healthy, either. I'm leaving because I can't take the day in, day out rudeness and inconsiderateness of you three. Period. It would be silly to try to explain every single reason. When I think about them, those apparently unimportant things, it seems idiotic to leave because of such trivialities. So I'd better not think about it anymore—I might change my mind, turn around and come back home.

Besides, I don't want you to think that my decision to leave is final. I'll be back in three months. I think I deserve three months of rest. Maybe I'll be able to live with the bare necessities in the country. Breathing some new air will do me good, cure this anxiety that the city, among other things, produces in me. The hysterical presence of the city's inhabitants, our lack of control over our own lives, combined with our total control by outside forces, that human rupture that exacerbates this unbearable malaise of mine. I know, I know, Andrés, you're going to say that it's unheard of for a woman to do such a thing, that it's not "proper," that this only happens in movies that later get the Oscar. You're going to argue that leaving one's family is not something that decent, sensible women do. But how many women are wanting to do that very thing right now, yet will go on, hypocritically bearing up under the pressures of "homemaking"? A woman, just like a man, no less than a man, can feel oppressed by her surroundings, her daily life. And there's no reason she has to be tied hand and foot and made to bear it. A woman can yearn to free herself from the responsibilities of motherhood. We need vacations for a while, to disconnect from routine. What right do you men have to be the only ones that are allowed to come back, while if we women go away we can never be forgiven?

As for the girls, I'll write to them, and I'm sure they'll understand— though of course they'll need your help. Consider that things might have been the other way around, that you might have been the one to leave—yet again—and then I'd be the one who'd be responsible for making them understand, for "supporting" you, for making sure your image as a father wasn't tarnished, making sure they kept loving you until you came back, making sure they understood that daddies—or in this case mommies—have the right to a little bit of independent life. I don't even know myself how to explain it! I feel deeply selfish, feel that I've descended into the lowest, worst sort of behavior. A mother fleeing from her children! Because no one would heap the same scorn if it were the husband that ran away. Yes, I suppose I've read about this happening in certain cases before, a woman photographer, an Italian, I think, who decided to run away and wander the earth and came back only when her daughters were grown. One of them never forgave her, the other one admires her for her courage, even became a photographer like her mother. It's unpredictable.

You and I, Andrés, haven't talked much. We've known each other since we were teenagers, and I think if we've said twenty important things to each other it's a lot. You were my first boyfriend and my only husband. Marrying your first boyfriend is not a good idea, my mother used to say. We met at that School in the Country, remember? Of course you do, how could you not! It seems like yesterday. We'd run into each other a few times in the city; I'd just started junior high school and you were in the eighth grade, a year ahead of me. I'd be thirteen my next birthday and you fourteen—a couple of inexperienced kids. You were my first boyfriend, but not my first love. I fell in love with you little by little. Ours was not love at first sight. Like all girls, I wanted to have a boyfriend. No, you weren't my first love—it's something I've never had the courage to confess to you. I wasn't sure you'd be ready to understand. I'm still not sure you'll accept it when I explain. We'll talk about it later. If I get the courage. Now what's important is saying goodbye to each other, even if only temporarily.

Note: I now realize that you've never said *I love you*. Not once, never, *jamais*.

"*Je t'aime.*"

"*Moi non plus.*"

Thank goodness there'll always be a song that makes life livable. What did Serge Gainsbourg mean with that "me neither"?

When you told me you loved me and wanted me to be your girlfriend—although I think it was actually me that rushed things a bit, it bored me to stand on ceremony—you were pretty much obliged to confess that I turned you on—*you turn me on,* you said, *and I want you.* That was it, and I thought it was enough. We turned each other on, although we'd never experimented with desire, never even tested it. We hadn't had time to feel true desire, to suffer from or because of it, to renounce and make sacrifices for it. Later, two or three times, at the most important moments of our lives, you've said *te quiero. Te quiero,* but never *te amo.* When Ibis was born, when Frances was born, when the dog died. You've never once said you're sorry for your excesses, or asked forgiveness—nor might it be said that you've ever made the slightest gesture of remorse. And you *have* hurt me, if you want to know! But

I'm not going to start dragging out our dirty laundry, because it's not the accumulated shit that's made me decide to pull away from the family. Or maybe it *is* because of the mountain of humiliations to which your conscience can also add those insults, those slights, those sudden beatings that I won't enumerate—more out of a desire to forget them than out of any sense of pride.

I need to go back to the country. Pavement offends my sensibilities. And to think that one of the things I like best is watching the rain fall on asphalt melted by the heat, or smelling the wetness mixed with the salt air, listening to the rushing of the sewers, watching the steam rise off the streets. But it bores me to be moved every day by the same things. From watching the pavement so much, watching my feet, I don't seem to be able to concentrate my energy on where I'm going anymore. My friends have noticed that I walk with my eyes on the ground, counting the cracks in the sidewalk, as though all I cared about were burying my personality in the concrete.

I'm not sad. I'm not even sad. What I feel is estranged. Alienated. "Out of it." I've lost all confidence in myself. I'm not a person anymore, I've been replaced by a thing, a useful piece of furniture or some piece of equipment that must not forget that one of its functions is decorative. And I had expected so much of my energy, my impulses! I think I expected more of us. Of you, my husband. Of myself with you, beside you. Maybe—a terrible maybe—I didn't know how to be a wife. Maybe I'm not a good woman or a tender mother. Because a mother doesn't just run off like this, "just because," for three months or more, without even saying goodbye. But I have to go—I have to find myself, my true self. Unearth it. That self covered with mud.

Have you really, truly loved me, Andrés? Why have I never heard the word *love* from your lips as you've looked into my eyes?

Why has it been me to get up and be the first one to think about making the bed, why am I the one that's had to lay out the girls' clothes? (It's true that you take them to school. It's your only responsibility, the only "chore" you do.) Why do I have to wash the dishes after dinner, sort the clothes for the washer, clean the bathroom and the rest of the house on weekends, cook good food, make delicious desserts? If it depended on you, we'd eat pizza day and night. Why is it me that has to fill out all the paperwork in the world, mail the letters, be the one responsible for every possible detail, large or small? For example, when we have a visitor I have to be the one to suggest coffee, water, beer (if we have those things). Nobody breaks the ice if I don't start the conversation. Why don't you see, the way I do, that a person has to be nice to guests in your own house? Your answer will always be the same: *I don't know how to do that, Danae.* And who do you think taught me? I learned it all by myself, watching movies, walking down the street, living. I learned. Was it through tradition, habit, genes? Get real!

Why, husband, do you have more of a right to things than I do? And to top it off, I have to have a job, too, because I can't *not* work. It's not who I am. I can't stand forced "rest." I imagine you'll ask yourself many questions about me. I'm filled with doubts, too. Like what will I do from now on? Well, the psychiatrist has given me sick leave. I'm exhausted, I can never get rid of these headaches, my legs shake, no pill helps my insomnia, all I think about is eating. You didn't even know I was seeing a psychiatrist—I hid the tests. Stress, the doctor said. *All you need is love.* And it occurred to me that that was the title of a Beatles song in English, the title in Spanish of a hyperrealist painting I'd seen in the Fine Arts Museum.

"All you need is love, señora; that's why you're so ill emotionally."

But I didn't need to be told that. I knew my head had been out of whack for some time already—everybody saw it. Everybody but you. *All you need is love . . .* Afterward I had that song in my head all day. Even the girls noticed that I was a wreck. Mamá, lie down, rest, *ay, por favor, Mami,* don't faint without Papá here. Poor things, sometimes they'd drive me crazy with their whining. The girls can be hard to take sometimes; if they want to, they can even be cruel. Do you know how many times they've told me to go away, to leave them alone with you? *Don't stick your nose in, Mamá, this is between Papá and us. Go on, go away now, Mamá, we love our daddy best.* I know, I know that that's just talk, that they weren't trying to hurt me. I'm really not blaming them at all, for anything. Have you seen me acting like a fool? Well, now I feel like a fool.

Anyway, it's too much work, and I don't think you've realized it. Do you know how many times I've wanted to kill myself, so that when you were the only one to take care of them you'd realize, having to take it all on yourself, the weight, the importance, of my work? How often I've wanted to die, just to teach you a lesson. But I'd rather just leave, take the train and close my eyes. By the time I open them again, I'll be back home. For me, a second will have passed, an eternity. I've already thought that you probably won't be able to find the patience to wait, and you'll want to divorce me, accuse me of abandoning you and my children. That's your right. This, though, is the only thing that you can allege against me. If you put yourself in my position, I think you'll see that this is the way a woman would act, and yours is the way a man would *re*act.

Do whatever you think best. I'll see my daughters again anyway, nobody can prevent me from doing that, and if you're willing, I'll see you too. I swear I love them. I insist on that, insist that I'll write Ibis and Frances. I hope they'll understand it as well as they can, hope they'll be able to wait for their mother without too much resentment or anger. At ten and twelve, children can begin to be kind, generous with their parents. Although I wasn't with my mother. Ibis will soon be a young woman; I'll be there to advise her, I don't suppose I'll be away long, though I don't know, I'm very confused, very disturbed . . . I've left her a letter explaining things—I took a few hours out for that. Nothing will take her by surprise—although becoming a woman doesn't happen without quite a fuss on the part of nature and some on one's own part, too. I do think sometimes we're guilty of exaggerating our femaleness.

But let's talk about you and me. We began this relationship when we were both young and tender, Andrés, but we've exhausted our hope in arguing over trivialities. It's time we learned to give importance to things that are really important, to look at the things that are essential. We must delve into the essence of our problems, their origins, but also into the potential of the mysteries. I have the impression that I have lived with you only the routine side of my emotions, that we have worn each other away in juggling matches of words that have gotten us exactly nowhere. Still, I love you as a lover, although I sense that you don't feel the same for me. We have been faithful to one another. At least I have been to you. Do you see me as a mother, as an older sister? Or is it that your way of experiencing love is more distant and therefore more elegant than mine, since it's less "committed"? We've been boyfriend and girlfriend since we were fourteen. We've lived under the same roof since I was eighteen and you were nineteen. Financially, your parents and my mother supported us until we started working. We got married after the first girl starting kicking in my belly. I'd just turned twenty. Everybody around us thought we were so much in love. I think we may have been, in a way. In a very strange, very simple way. In the distance, I see such disparate events, unfolding as though in a silent movie—so unlike my later decisions, even so unlike who I was, what I was. Sometimes I suspect that we were never in love *enough*. It was a great performance by two confused adolescents. Or if that tingling, tickling sensation that heralds love did occur, we were too young, too irresponsible, and the love ran between our fingers—our desires. Or have I evolved while you've remained behind? Or vice-versa? Am I simply more selfish?

No. I despise selfishness. When I was a girl I gave away the things I liked the most. I like to be generous. Giving of myself to others is how I've survived so far. And that's why I want to try another way, giving of myself to myself, small but intense pleasures. Letting myself be caressed by the sun whenever I damn well feel like it, drink dirty water from the watering trough or the irrigation pipe, bathe under the sprinklers or in the lake, sleep under the nets that cover the fields planted with tobacco, or hide in the big wooden tobacco-drying sheds, all drowsy and curled up in a basket where the fresh leaves are kept. I'd give anything to watch the sun come up while I was lying in grass wet with dew. Alone. Without you and the girls. I am sick and tired of watching myself drag myself through the house in that chaotic multiple exposure reflected in the floor tiles in the kitchen. I am dis-couraged, dis-heartened, dis-souled. Exactly as you have been on so, so many occasions. You've left and I've always stayed behind. Now it's my turn. It's my turn to run off and find adventure—or one more helping of boredom. Who knows what awaits me?

Someday I'll tell you about that love that finally went nowhere; at the time it happened, I didn't even know that that could be love. We'll sit down together and recall that obsession that I thought was past. We'll do it just to entertain ourselves; I don't think it's worth your while to take it seriously. You existed only vaguely in my life. You see, I have been faithful to that first episode of love without ever ceasing to love you. A woman can love two people at the same time. But, I repeat, have no fear—the only person I could live with is you three, my family. I do so wish I could say something sweet to you. Nothing impels me to the words, though. What was it that broke—or that *we* broke? Maybe I shouldn't think anymore. I wouldn't want to miss the train.

In a little while I'll send along some suggestions, advice, that sort of thing, certain strategies to use with the girls. I hope you haven't forgotten that it's

Ibis that doesn't like warm milk for breakfast, and that for Frances you have to strain the skin off the milk after you heat it. But that Ibis loves the skin when it's cooled off, with a little salt—you can spread it on her bread. And don't even think about combing their hair the same way; they hate seeing themselves in each other, each one has her own very clear character, and I have no idea how to explain which one of them is more complicated. I am not blinded by love—they are imperfect daughters, fortunately. You demand things of them without looking at yourself. I do, too. But what's the point of making a list of defects and shortcomings? We all have our share, but the key is to know how to spoon them out in small doses. Of course if we did, we'd be even more foolish in the long run.

Frances coughs a lot early in the morning, before the sun comes up—her back gets cold. The minute she starts, give her a spoonful of Benadryl. Make Ibis put on her glasses to read or watch television; she's got a complex because those comedians at school call her "Four Eyes" or "Coke Bottle Eyes." I know what it is to be humiliated in front of the boys—I was never a beauty. She, as you must know, is very vain. Frances, on the other hand, doesn't like to wash her hair, you'll have to watch her because she'll tell you she washed it and come out of the bathroom dripping water but I'll bet anything she'll be fibbing. It's that she's terrified the shampoo will get in her eyes and make them burn. She says she dreamed that I was washing my hair, scrubbing it real hard, and that my eyeballs rolled out of their sockets from the suds. She tried to catch them, so they wouldn't hit the floor, but she missed and they exploded on the tiles. She woke up sobbing, looking at her hands to see the shards of glass from my eyeballs. Ibis clings to me more, she's more the mamma's girl. She's certainly the more fragile of the two—this separation will not be easy for her at all. Don't neglect them for a second, Andrés—it kills me to think that something might happen to them while I'm away. Look who's talking! It's me, after all, that's wanted to get away from you three, free myself of you. I feel like shit, but I can't back out now. Now—will you accept my going away? Please, I beg you, try to be understanding—let's be calm about this, let's be adults, I can't go on feeling so unappreciated.

Why don't you act and think at the same level and the same speed as I do?

I'm coming to the train station. The trains look so lovely there in the distance, beached in the weeds and grass, all rusty; some even painted rust red.

They are old trains; it will take them days to reach the country; they stop at every little town. Inside, they're still made of wood—they were among the first trains made. I bought the ticket on the black market, not expensive at all, I saved more than twenty pesos by exposing myself to the risk. The reseller looked at me and smiled perplexedly, as though he'd heard about my contemptible behavior. I still am not sure whether I want to run off to that place where I experienced my first emotions. That place where we met, Andrés, in the midst of nature. But as I told you, that first passion, that first tingling sensation in my center of gravity, around my navel, was not caused by your presence alone. There was another person, even though you already existed. I don't know whether there's any value in going on writing this mind-letter, because although I'm already sitting in a seat upholstered in hundred-year-old leather smelling of bitter sweat, tanned by all those backs and backsides, I don't know whether I can find the heart to take out my notebook and write what I'm now tormented by.

The train has started moving. My mind is wandering, it's roaming aimlessly through my memories, and so I disconsolately enter the landscape; the faces on the platform have disappeared from my visual plane. The faces of the three of you fade and pass away like a passing second. I am unscrupulous, I admit that forgetting so quickly is absolutely superficial and disgusting.

But the greenness of the countryside gleams and shines in my eyes. I still don't know the names of certain trees, or I've forgotten them, and yet I gradually make out others, and this brings me incomparable happiness. I hear the exclamations of those absurd tourists who have decided to undertake this long journey under subhuman conditions in order to feel closer to *the real Cuba*. I hate that word *real,* as I hate the word *autochthonous* that everyone uses nowadays. It contains the sense of exclusion. Indigenous, native—which is just another way of saying *worthless rubbish*. The train makes a terrible noise as it chomps its coal, and the screeching of the wheels gives the impression that it's squeezing blood from the rails as it tries to pull them under and behind it. It is a phantasmagoric shriek, a horrific moaning sound that adds a spectacular power to my departure. The palm trees move me, though not so much as those thick trees that look like hanging roots are growing out of their trunks and branches—I know they aren't weeping willows, but that's what they look like. I've seen pictures of weeping willows in books. I see no flowers, no crops, no irrigation ditches. Once in a while a group of very poor-looking huts appears, and an aerial battalion of butterflies of all colors. Out of the thick vegetation bony cows emerge, grazing in broad grasslands. Or cropping the fresh green of a field recently sprayed with insecticide. They'll poison themselves! But that's their problem, they must know what they're eating. Besides, these cows are for decoration, since their milk is not nutritional and their meat is inedible. There are the horses, their glossy manes and withers gleaming as though they were sweating beer and the sun's rays were making the golden bubbles sparkle. The horses' motionless gaze is fixed on the train, on my window, on me—as I yearn to swing astride one of them, ride off into the undergrowth, never look back even for one second.

Then all of a sudden the gigantic red sun looms up from behind a hill. It looks like a ball of fire melting chunks of ice, the clouds. The sky itself has turned red—or a Flemish rose color, rather. I stick my head out the window. We're moving slowly if you compare this train with European trains today, but it gives me pleasure to think that I might be picked up by a hard gust of wind and sent flying off into the super-electronic song of the goldfinch, a warbling that thins the air, fills it with complaints, with campesino idolatry. I feel a tickling in my throat, I am breathing red dust—it smells like the vomit of a mangy dog or the guts of a skinned goat. There is a sweet stench of dried blood on the hardwood ties, clots hanging off the dry branches of a locust tree like bags containing ancient spiritual treasure desecrated by the Spanish soldiers during the war of independence. One can sense, hear the presence of the mambises in that phantasmagoric galloping, souls in torment declaring their love to anonymous heroines, defending themselves in the battles fought with machetes—for dignity, for freedom, and for all of those other things that have no place in our world today.

A fluttering, a cackling, and I am forced to look around at my fellow travelers. The car is full of women, men, old people, children with dirty faces; the baggage they are all carrying is suspicious-looking bundles. Here, having a suitcase has always been reason enough to bring an investigation down on you. There are lots of fowl, the noise and persistent smell of barnyard. The sweaty children try to smile at little just-hatched chicks in cardboard boxes with holes punched in them, but what their lips produce is a grimace that growls like a cave. The chicks have pip, and the kids hope the country air will cure it. The women, feeling like they're about to faint, pull out fans made of limp cardboard, with tongue-depressor handles. It's clear that the fans were all made by the same craftsman. One of the women has a tame crocodile in her lap, and she's petting and stroking it; she remarks that she's planning to trade it to a guajiro for a little pig. The men try to sleep. Their heads nod, then they suddenly wake up, fearful of passing their station. They all lie, in loud voices, that they're going to cut sugarcane, but it's a secret to no one that they're on their way to bet the last penny of their miserable fortunes on the cockfights. The old men read newspapers from last century.

Back there, at the far end of the car, a girl's mind has wandered—or she's doing it on purpose—and her legs are spread. Her knees are too dark; they're filthy and there are old scabs from suppurating pustules. From her knees down, her skin is a road map of eruptions, pimples, green with infection, like drooling volcano craters. She realizes that I'm looking and I think she waves; it's an indecisive gesture, and her hand, too, is covered with those fish-eye sores. And there is a cluster of glistening sties on her eyelids. Her face, though, is pretty, her lips smooth and full, her teeth large, her forehead broad and prominent. She has the face of an inoffensive, insipid sort of girl, but something about her gives her the look of one of those girls that feigns inno-cence—the "still water runs deep" (especially in carnal matters) type. She spreads her thighs even wider and pulls her caramel-colored skirt up higher. I'm not sure it's me she's trying to flash, so I turn my head and realize that the show is not for me, it's not me she's been flirting with, or trying to seduce by showing me the most secret parts of her half-washed body—it's the mastodon sitting behind me, dizzy with desire to caress her, a guy with crude features, lizard skin—by the way, would you like to be swapped for a pig? His eyes are gray, his hair dark and gleaming with that nasty, smelly brilliantine from big pint jars. He reminds me of those guajiros that Servando Cabrera Moreno was always painting. The guy is holding a fighting cock under his arm, a good-looking bird with a red crest transparent in the light, its beak the color of fine ivory or pearl, its spurs filed sharp. The young woman goes on stoking his fires, to the *choo-choo, choo-choo* of the train.

I try to turn my eyes to the landscape again, but now it's a blur slipping past, brushing my ear, keeping me from entering my forced daydreaming rapture. The goliath behind me has freed the cock, and it's on purpose—I hear him siccing it on: *Sic, Solito!* "Solito" must be the bird's name. And Solito has headed straight for the girl's spread legs, has begun to wriggle between them. The girl spreads her legs a little more and now the animal has begun to peck—not exactly at what birds generally peck at, which is birdshit, but rather there, in the dark triangle, right at the tiny head of the girl's clitoris. At every peck, the clitoris grows, and its owner arches in her seat, before the eyes of her fellow travelers, who pretend that nothing's happening. She begins a concert of moans, the rooster pecks and pecks and pecks, and behind me the man begins to breathe more heavily, heating the back of my neck with his wet panting. I can hear the rhythmic rustle of his hand rubbing at the crotch of his trousers—or at least that's what I imagine it is, you don't have to have the gift of second sight to tell what's going on. The girl roars out when Solito attacks, trying to tear off that other crest, as red as its own. The guajiro is still lost in the thick haze of his jerk-off, abusing that veiny third-class passenger lying resentfully along his thigh, now ready to explode in lustful fury.

This erotic joust lasts for half an hour. The atmosphere has become dense; only the two of them, lost to the world, still palpitate. The rest are dozing, hypnotized by the *clackety-clack* of the train, which plunges everyone into a dull dreamland. But they're also sick of what they consider a spectacle that's *too* vulgar this time, for although everyone is accustomed to this kind of exhibitionism—it's not in the least out of the ordinary to be riding a bus and have somebody lay a thick, throbbing penis, like some rubbery bar to be pounded, on the anvil of your shoulder and fill your ear with cum, a string of it arcing out the window and bathing the face of an old lady trying to eat a lemon ice as she crosses the street at the corner of Neptuno and Belascoaín—this one is not the usual local-color jerk-off.

But I am not sleeping, or pretending to; I want to see this Rabelaisian comic opera—which is more like the traditional porno soap opera, actually—through to its final spasm. The guy has gotten up out of his seat, steadying himself on my shoulder. His hot, callused hand scratches my skin; it is a boxer's hand, or an oxcart driver's, rather. Like a charging bull, he heads for the possessed woman's seat, weaving and stumbling back and forth with the swaying of the train. He snatches the fighting cock from the throbbing pudendum and wrings its neck, remarkably like a jealous husband taking revenge on a lover. Immediately he grabs the porn queen by the neck and, with a gesture like Robert Mitchum throwing a calf in *The Lusty Men,* flings the brazen damsel onto the filthy carpet in the aisle. And there he "has his way with her," though from the looks of things it's *her* way, too. Brings her low with one blow of his belaying-pin. Deflowers her, in a word, with one quick shove. Not far away, the fighting cock gasps, jerking and quivering in the aftermath of the murder. I feel a new tickling in my throat, perhaps the urge to sing some elegant, eloquent song. Such as

> *My sweet sharecropper lass, what have you done*
> *with our happy home . . .*

Dazed with embarrassment and vaginal chills, I let my eyelids fall; when I open them again, the two of them have returned to their seats. The girl, now quite prim, savors the weariness, lays her head to one side, cozies her neck into the faded, threadbare cushion of the seat back. The man, hedonist, voluptuary, swine to the end, has not renounced his grossness; he has lit up a cigar as thick and prepossessing as his member—I see this when I turn around, pretending to look for something that I've dropped. In a wicker basket lies the body of Solito, sculptor of corollas of salty, delicious flesh. Elegguá has received his sacrifice.

It is then, dear Andrés, that I reach into my backpack for my notebook and begin to write two letters, one for you and the other for the girls. I don't know how faithful to these reflections I can make them. And although in the Schools in the Country I distinguished myself as the camp scribe, since all my bunk mates pleaded with me to write poems to their boyfriends for them, I've never been happy with my own letters. Though I've never written one to you. Not that you've ever written me a love letter, either. Or even a phrase tied to a bunch of flowers. Or a note left under my coffee cup in the morning before you went off to lay bricks. You see, Andrés, the small details that slowly wear love away when they're not there? I think we should have tried a little harder. Maybe I should call you instead, when we come to one of the next stops.

Geography of a Letter Delayed

*T*HE CEMENT WAS THERE, like the lava of a live volcano, throwing up fat slow bubbles—*plp flp plf plf plp*. If he didn't hurry it would start stiffening, hardening, he would have to stop and mix it again—a royal pain in the ass. A man thirty-something years old, pushing forty, was laying one block on top of another—out of my *way*, I'm coming *through*, out of my *way*, I'm coming *through*, out of my *way*, I'm coming *through*—that was the phrase, the rhythm, that had come into his mind to entertain his neurons. The cement was threatening to turn into formless rock and go to shit. Andrés whistled shrilly and then yelled:

"Gizzard, *mi compay*, bring a bucket of water and get over here and stick a hoe in this cement before it goes sedimentary on me!"

Swan was coming toward him, pushing a dirty, beat-up wheelbarrow piled almost to toppling-over with gray cinder blocks. As potbellied Gizzard was crossing the wheelbarrow's path, his leg caught the side of the heavy bucket of water he was carrying and he lost his balance and stumbled. And as he did, Swan ran the wheelbarrow's front wheel over the toe of his boot. Swan was called Swan for good reason—that long, skinny neck of his, which was in glaring contrast to his body covered in graying fuzz, like some overgrown baby bird fattened on keg beer. At first, of course, he hadn't liked the nickname at all, but he was used to it by now.

"Holy fuckin' ratshit, Swan, don't you ever look where you're going? Shee-ee-it! You fucking *murdered* my toe, man!"

Gizzard had dropped the bucket and was lying on the ground, holding his foot, writhing in pain. Swan hurried over to help his friend.

"Take it easy, *compadre*, that boot is two sizes too big for you and I just caught the toe of it."

Swan pulled off Gizzard's boot to expose the foot, covered in a thick green sock. A broad area around the toe was turning a deep shit-brown color from the blood, and the stain was widening.

Swan yanked the sock off in one quick tug, and with it came the toenail off Gizzard's big toe.

"Aaagh! Jesus Christ! Take it easy! You're gonna make me faint, goddammit—call a doctor!"

"Oh man, I'm sorry! Jesus!"

Immediately Swan lent his shoulder to help Gizzard to his feet—or to his *foot,* rather, because once he was up he had to hop along on his good foot as the blood spurted from his injured toe. Andrés rushed over to the two of them, jumping over the debris of the construction site. He pulled off his heavy gloves and as he gave Gizzard support from the other side, he started yelling:

"Call an ambulance, Mulatto, a taxi, something—quick!"

Another man with a good-natured face and the slow authority of a reluctant boss came around the corner of the building. Nothing about his expression changed when he saw the situation before him; he kept his cool as he played with a piece of a palo vencedor root he had between his teeth.

"Let's not be alarmists, here, men—it doesn't look to me like he's in danger of bleeding to death," he drawled impassively.

"He's in pain, man, that toe's ground beef and you're sucking on that goddamn stick. It could've been worse, but shit, man . . . " Andrés scolded as he left his friends on the sidewalk to run into the middle of the street and flag down a passing vehicle.

Which he managed to do by stepping directly between an army jeep and its intended future. Swan and Gizzard climbed aboard as fast as the circumstances allowed while Andrés ordered the driver to get them to the hospital. As the Willy took off in a cloud of suffocating black smoke, Andrés slapped the fender.

"Put that slow-motion mind of yours in gear and see what you can invent for that cement and that mess of blocks over there. Those two gone, plus the five that never showed—I'm short seven men. You can probably pick up the slack on these two, at least—we've gotta kick ass here, *compay,* because if we keep on like this, between having to stop because there's not any building materials and not being able to make any progress for all these injuries, this building won't be finished by the middle of the third millennium. When we die, *compay,* our heirs will have to keep working on this thing and our great-great-great-grandchildren will finally get to live in it. At this rate, no way in hell *I'll* be around to," the foreman grumbled, shaking his head.

"Okay, okay, I'll see what I can do, but I've only got two hands, *mi cúmbila.* None of my mama's children grew up to be octopuses."

In a huge square overlooking the sea stood this razed lot covered in concrete, sand, cinder blocks, and battered and salt-air-blasted machinery dedicated to the construction of large buildings. In the center of it all rose a gray phallus of rough-skinned stone some fifteen stories tall. Square holes heralded the possibility of windows, and hallways, or mazes, could be inferred from zigzags of half-erected panels. Clouds of opaline dust hung in the air, polluting the day's natural honey-colored light. The man with the skin covered with scars from an unyielding and disfiguring case of adolescent acne, his seminude torso resembling a statue cast in bronze, pulled on his gloves again and covered his close-cropped head with a white hard hat; he was wearing a T-shirt that was full of holes and too short for him, so it revealed his navel and the black fur of his muscular belly. His legs, like tree trunks or steel columns, moved with powerful elegance, and they were clothed in an old pair of jeans torn at the knee and across the butt. His face and moustache were covered with a fine sifting of white cement dust, and every time he blinked, his eyelashes seemed to sprinkle stardust. Sweat, black with grime, dripped from his thick biceps and triceps. He coughed several times, cleared his throat, and hocked—his distance was as good as one of those experts that could knock a flower off a bush at ten feet with a well-aimed oyster of phlegm. He moved with long strides across the construction yard, and when he had taken up his station at the wall, he set about mixing the cement again, leaving the bucket of water close by to wet down the mixture from time to time. Then he picked up his trowel and returned to his block-laying.

It's a shame there're no bricks; the building would look a lot better, have a lot more class with bricks, he thought. *Whssh, plp; whssh, plp; whssh, plp; whssh, plp.* Out of my *way,* I'm coming *through,* out of my *way,* I'm coming *through,* out of my *way,* I'm coming *through* . . . He felt a rivulet of sweat rolling from the base of his spine down the crack of his ass, and from there, as he bent over, to the base of his scrotum, and then down the back of his thigh to his ankles, to come finally to the heel of his foot, ill clothed in a sock riddled with holes. Sweat stung the blisters on his feet. His boots were rough, stiff, unbending, although he'd worn them often. He had been breaking them in for two years.

He moved his tongue across the roof of his mouth and tasted, half disgustedly, half heroically, the dryness of it. His saliva was gluey and his tongue smacked against his palate. He closed his eyes and, never halting as he laid one block atop another, called up the image of a pineapple sliced into juicy rings; a cooling sensation of pineapple juice descended his throat, bringing relief to his tonsils—which were as gravelly and prickly as the wall he was building. Or an ice cold lemonade with chunks of ice his wife had broken up in a dishtowel with a hammer. And pieces of the lemon peel, or even seeds, mashed and crushed, making his mouth pucker, the cold, as it passed over the fillings in his back teeth, the ones you used the most to chew with, producing an ache in the whole side of his head. He swallowed, dry, and made an effort to turn his thoughts away from such illusory temptations.

"Man, you are one slow mother-lover—you need to get a move on!" The boss woke him with a bellow that came more from the exercise of power than from enthusiasm for it.

Fuck you and your goatee, thought Andrés, smiling and saying nothing.

The foreman had recently grown a beard, a goatee, actually, the one generally known, for obvious reasons, as a keyhole. When the other builders snickered at him, he argued proudly that it was the latest thing in Mexico, a pointed beard like the philosophers wore at the end of the nineteenth century. And what a mistake that was! Andrés razzed him unmercifully—Mulatto, you look just *like* Trotsky, man, I'd say your mother and Trotsky were *very* good friends, dude. But the other man took it well, you'd have to give him that—"You oughta try one, Andrés, the girls go crazy over hairy chins, man, they can just *feel* that goatee tickling their twats, *compay.*"

The block-layer's hands were swollen from mixing and heaving cement. His mind, swollen, too, with memories, wandered off into the archives, pulling images out of its file drawers of erotica. Danae, her body just slipping from adolescence into womanhood, naked. White from her neck to halfway down her thighs, while her arms, knees, and legs were bronzed from the sun and her skin was scratched in long trails from the pigweed, pangola grass, and other sharp-leaved weeds. They had made a date to meet that afternoon in a field of plantains, when the day's work was done. Andrés had waited anxiously, shivering like a colt. Not to mention that he was soaking wet, because he had gone by the river first, to wash off the stink of B.O. and the fields. About an hour passed; he'd known it was an hour by the movement of the shadow of a stick he'd stuck in the ground, his own personal sundial.

"I never felt so dependent on the sun before," he'd murmured.

After all those minutes, so many and so slow, he had heard footsteps swishing through the weeds and underbrush—*Danae weaves the hours gilded by the Nile*, he'd whispered, and she whispered it back to him. That was their password. Then she'd broken through the dense vegetation with a smile that made her eyes crinkle into Chinese slits. Tall and proud (arrogant), from a modesty she couldn't quite conceal. She had gotten rid of her Soviet-commune kerchief, and her chestnut hair was parted down the middle, pulled back tight, and gathered into a little bun at the base of her skull. She was wearing a flowered blouse and a pair of shorts the color of red clay—or were they covered with mud? The legs of the shorts were rolled up a good three inches above her knee. She was barefoot, and her feet were muddy. In each hand she was carrying a boot filled with guavas, so many that when she set them down, some of the fruit spilled out and rolled along the ground. A necklace of beads made to look like lapis lazuli was around her neck, and from it hung the key to her wooden suitcase. Focused, decided, determined, she'd thrown herself against the body of the youngster and planted a quick peck upon his lips. He hadn't even had time to close his eyes. Then, "Are you already here?" she asked, as though she hadn't seen him.

"Andy, they called from the hospital!" the foreman bellowed, startling the laborer from his daydream. "Gizzard's never going to dance again, man—he lost his toe. He's a diabetic!"

Cumbaquín, quin quin, cumbacán; cumbaquín, quin quin, cumbacán; cumbaquín, cumbacán, baquín, bacán. From a distance came the sound of a rumba, several young men using their lips and mouths to imitate the beating of drums, the sounds of a guaguancó. The chorus was coming from the Casa de la Requidia. People said that over there in that old mansion, its once Pompeian-green paint faded and peeling, some lowlifes and decadent perverts had made a porno movie—totally amateur, with a movie camera that dated from the fifties, and totally clandestine, naturally. Requidia was the pseudonym the woman who owned the house used for her romantic poems. Andrés had never seen one of those films, but he was curious, to say the least, to see one. He pulled a wadded handkerchief out of his pocket and wiped the sweat from his neck and chest. What fuckin' luck, man—Gizzard losing a toe, and the week before, his buddy Bolt had lost an eye. The ironies of life, huh?—it was a bolt that flew off and hit Bolt in the eye. Andrés shook his head and tried to refocus his mind, but suddenly he sensed the presence of his boss, standing behind him.

"That's something, Gizzard's toe, huh?" the foreman said, his voice breaking. He may have been the boss, but deep down, all the way down to China if you wanted to be precise about it, he was a marshmallow.

Andrés put the handkerchief back in his pocket and turned and picked up a cinder block, without even looking at his interlocutor.

"So Gizzard loses a toe and you go deaf on me, or what? Did you hear what I said?"

"I heard you, *compay,* clear as a bell. But what's to think? Another combat casualty."

"Tomorrow they're sending him home to his old lady. It's not so serious—well, that's what they're saying. But he'll be on medical leave for a long time, and they'll take him off the top of the list to get housing."

"Losing the apartment isn't so bad when you consider he lost a toe." Andrés, bending over as he worked the mix of clay, sand, and cement, looked up straight and hard at his foreman, his mouth set in a half-defiant smile.

"Shit, *compay*, of course! He-e-e-e-y, don't get your back up with me, *mi asere* . . . What's the story?"

"I don't have my back up. Nothin'—it just pisses me off. It's not easy to dream about your own place and all of a sudden they tell you where to shove it, send you off on medical leave with a nub of a toe for a war decoration." Andrés stood up. The older man patted him on his stomach, winked sympathetically, and walked away, pushing Swan's wheelbarrow.

What might Danae be doing right about now? Andrés wondered, still feeling the tickle of the foreman's touch on his belly. It was her day off. He returned to his thoughts where he'd left them. It had taken some persuasion to get the girl to agree to meet him out in that plantain field. But Danae had been the one to come up with the password, that phrase they were supposed to use when they met. It's a line of poetry from a great poet, she insisted. Her parents had given her that name because her grandmother had been a friend of the poet's maid. What the fuck did he care about poets? When he pressed his lips to the girl's skin, it tasted like tamarind. Slippery tamarind, sucked tamarind, my sweet succulent tamarind, my head full of tamarind, tamarind dreams. Then Danae, acting on her emotions, had whispered in his ear that they had to hurry, she didn't want the brigade leader to miss her. And she'd vanished behind the curtain of plantain trees. By the time he'd found her she was already naked. Her body marked out with the two colors, as though she were two girls in one . . . A centaur-woman, or a mermaid. One part made of brown sugar and the other of cream custard. At first he didn't like her nipples, which looked like berries, too hard, too small against such large, firm, upright breasts. Danae fooled you—with her clothes on, her breasts didn't look that big. Her pelvis was broad and bony. His eyes hadn't lingered on her pubis, but he had seen a small triangle of curly hair much darker than the hair on her head. And he hadn't seen, or hadn't wanted to see, more; she'd stepped toward him and helped him get his clothes off, quickly, piece by piece, and then she'd pulled him down, made him kneel with her. Their bodies touched. Sinking deeper and deeper into the baroque landscape reflected in his eyes, she had softly pushed Andrés' body toward the ground. Lying in the furrow, on a carpet of inoffensive ants and weeds, the only thing they'd done was kiss—nothing more sinful for their age. When she caressed his testicles, he ejaculated on her thigh. She leapt up, pulled off a plantain leaf, and wiped herself clean. The dark gray stain from the leaf remained on her thigh for weeks. Then she hurriedly pulled her clothes on and gave the encounter as much dramatic meaning as she could.

"You know, Andy, this is the first time I've ever been to bed with a man. I need you to tell me whether I can consider myself your girlfriend or not."

He was still lying on the ground, enjoying the afterglow. He nodded. She straddled her new boyfriend's chest and leaned down to give him a peck, this time more to tease than out of innocence. Andrés pulled her to him.

"Me neither, Danae, I've never—"

"Sssh, hush," and she silenced the boy with a hard, full-lipped kiss.

Then she ran off at full speed, almost laughing out loud with glee, toward the sunny open field nearby, where the camp was. Back then she was the happiest of teenage girls, just one step this side of childhood, the tiniest jump. That had happened in the third week of the School in the Country; there were still days and days before they returned to the city.

Today, as a woman, she was not so happy; when she was not grumbling and scolding about some little thing she would fall into a nerve-racking silence that could last for weeks. It drove him crazy. He wasn't sure when the transformation had taken place—little by little, maybe, and he hadn't known how to stop it. He'd had plenty of chances to cheat on her, plenty, but he was lazy even in that—plus, he loved her. And there were the girls. He had no interest in becoming a cliché. Cheating, separation, divorce, hatred, suffering . . . what a waste, letting your life go down that road.

The fact was, he wasn't always as tough on himself as he thought. Once he had gone out with another woman, but he was so used to the way Danae smelled, that tamarind taste she had, that he was repulsed by the other woman's perfume. As far as he was concerned, all women should smell exactly like his wife. The "affair" never went far. But the Other Woman, as his friends called her, expected more, and she started pushing it.

"*Chico, ven acá*, are you married, or what? Something's going on with you that I don't copy. You better put some serious move on me pretty soon now, because a girl gets tired of this mummy routine of yours. Any chance you're not fully licensed by the Department of Heterosexuality?"

Andrés played his role as heterosexual male very superficially—a lot of groping and heavy breathing but no real getting it on. The farthest he took things was getting the woman horizontal late one night on the grass in the park.

"If you're tapped out I can pay for a room," the Other Woman offered. "You can pay me back when you get paid next month."

He couldn't do it, even though she was ready to roll, even in the park—she was "easy," his friends would've said. And on top of being good-looking and fully primed for action, she bragged that she was an actress and a dancer, and that someday she'd be going on tour, leaving Cuba and going abroad. She was a natural redhead, and Andrés had a thing for redheads. But Belinda—that was her name, Belinda—started pressuring him—and not just him; she'd call his house at three in the morning. She'd gotten his phone number by making up a story for the office Andrés worked out of. That was the mistake, giving her the address of his jailer when he had that job as an accountant at the People's Savings Bank in the Focsa building. With the number in her possession, she passed herself off as a distant cousin of his, and she called the office when she knew he had the day off, saying that she'd lost the address book she had her cousin's home phone number in, that she'd gotten his work phone from a girlfriend of hers, a waitress at the El Emperador, which was right next door to the bank. The person that talked to her swallowed the story like a greased banana and gave her all the personal information on Andrés that was available anywhere in Havana. Belinda dialed the antique Bakelite contraption and thank goodness it was Andrés that answered that day, because it was usually Danae.

"So, *mi amor*, when can I see you? I don't think I can live another day," she cooed.

Andrés stammered out a *How are you?* that sounded like it came from beyond the grave. A few feet away, his wife was ironing their daughters' school uniforms.

"Whoa, baby . . . did I get the ice machine?"

"Listen, I'm busy right now and I can't really talk. I'll call you back in an hour or so, okay? No, no, I'll call *you.*"

Danae set down the iron and looked in puzzlement at her husband. Fortunately, at that exact instant Matilde started yelling from downstairs:

"Danita, I just made some coffee! Come down!"

Andrés wound and unwound the cord as he muttered *mm-hm, uh-huh, uh-uh, uh-uh* into the receiver. *Uh-huh. Uh-huh.* Danae was apparently so eager to take a break from her ironing and have a hot cup of coffee that she left without a word and slammed the door behind her. She was beginning to feel little ant bites of doubt up and down her back.

Suddenly there was a gust of wind and rain, and the smell of the ocean flooded the room.

"Don't call me here anymore, Belinda. You don't want me to get jammed up here, do you, baby?"

"Don't you baby *me*, Andrés. You don't have to draw me a picture, I can see it as clear as day—you're married, aren't you, papi?" On the other end of the line, deafening silence. "No big trauma, papá, you call me when you decide to spring yourself from that baby-making jail you got yourself into, okay?"

The stupidest thing he did was just that—call her. They decided to meet in the Parque Central.

"The pitching sucked big-time today," Andrés heard as he passed by the Corner Where It Happening, which had moved here from Twelfth and Twenty-third. The Happening, as people called it, was where baseball fans would sometimes get into huge brawls over their favorite clubs and players.

She was waiting for him with her hands on her hips, tapping her foot impatiently on the gravel of one of the walks.

"How's life treating you, then, papito? Smiling with you or laughing *at* you?" she asked sarcastically, then put her arm through his. "It's kids, isn't it?"

He nodded tragically.

"Listen, if there's anything in this country that's easy, it's divorce. Ten pesos a month to the kids—*pff!*—what's ten pesos?" she cheered him.

Andrés shook his head; the inside of his skull sounded like maracas to him.

"Say something, *chico,* don't stand there like you've got lockjaw or something, acting offended—the only one here that has the right to be offended's me."

They didn't talk about it for the rest of the night; they walked around and around the Torreón de la Flota, along Calle Obispo, down to the harbor. It was one of those cool nostalgic winter nights; it was January. Andrés remembers that she was wearing a red sweater, no collar, with bright gold buttons. He complimented her on it.

"*Ay, mi amor,* it's from the colonial days. I inherited it from my god-mother."

He slowed, then stopped. His face was tragic, his mouth turned down at the corners, and he turned his eyes away from her. She found his idiotic male clumsiness sexy, no matter what was coming next.

"Belinda," he announced, "I don't think we should see each other any-more."

"What? What are you talking about? Listen, don't think I'm going to take this like some little nobody. You can't humiliate and insult me and think I'm going to just dry up and blow away."

"Goodbye, Belinda, I love you and . . . well, I don't know what else to say."

"That tongue of yours never did anything for me anyway," she snapped, yanking her hand from his arm and turning to walk quickly down Calle Mercaderes, as though she were headed for the old Hotel Cueto, where Mercaderes turns into Inquisidor.

He never saw her again, but she made a point of taking her hurt pride out on Danae. She telephoned early the next morning, before daybreak.

"I slept with your husband. I'm still lying here enjoying all that cream I milked out of him, mamita. I didn't leave a drop for you. I milked that man of yours dry."

Danae had taken all that a woman who considers herself reasonable could take.

"Andrés, you have Another Woman." And from that moment on, when-ever there was discussion of the Other Woman, the words were pronounced in the uppercase.

"No I don't, I absolutely do not, I swear to you on what I love most."

"Do you swear on the girls?"

Taking refuge in his habitual taciturnity, he tried to combine hesitancy with a caress. She pulled away.

"Tell me the truth, Andrés, be honest. I'd rather know the truth. It won't change anything, I won't do anything, but I can't live with the uncertainty."

"Nothing happened."

"So why won't you swear on the girls?"

"Please, Danae, don't be ridiculous."

"If you don't tell me the truth, then I *will* file for divorce."

"There was nothing—nothing happened. She's the cousin of a guy at the bank that's been after me, but I ended it," he lied, and the lie opened the door to a misinterpretation.

"If you say you ended it, then you must have started it."

"How long are you going to keep on with this nonsense?"

"Oooh, I see what's happening . . . A guy at the bank that's been after you . . . Shit, Andrés, I thought I was living with a man, not with a goddammed closet queen. Why don't you want to tell me? Was it with a man? You cheated on me with a faggot?!"

"What! Why, I'll . . . I'll . . ." and he drew back his hand as though to backhand her, but she dodged away. He did not follow through, though. "Just leave me alone, you're going to make me do something I'll regret."

"Leave you alone! Me here taking your shit moods every day and you out there fucky-fucky. Out there coochy-coochy with who knows what. You've got balls! What I ought to do is take the girls and get my ass to Timbuktu, get as far away from you as I can! They told me I ought to keep an eye on you, that you were out running around with a bunch of faggots. Although I'd rather have you cheat on me with a queer than with some cheap whore."

"All right, that's it! You're making me crazy! I'm the one that's leaving, before I knock your teeth into next Friday! I've had enough of this!"

He disappeared for seventy-three days. He wandered aimlessly, staying in friends' houses, and even enemies'. By the time he came back she had lost weight; she looked drawn and skinny. The girls were spoiled, cranky, and would cry over anything. But he had never cheated on Danae, or at least never consummated his adultery in a bed. But definitely even before the Belinda episode, his wife had changed.

"The side effects of childbirth," Jacinto, Andrés' father, assured him. "The bad mood will go away in time."

"Yeah? How many years exactly?"

Because life is years. And he had no intention of spending his life in a state of unrelieved bitterness, waiting for a miracle to give his Danae back to him whole and untouched, the way she once was, a happy teenager with not a care in the world.

"Sign up for a microbrigade, son. Try to get away from us a little. She's dying to live with you, just the two of you."

"I'm sure you're right, but she also likes the fact that you and mamá take care of the girls."

"Well, we *are* the grandparents, eh? And it was you that insisted on coming to live with your mother and me—she really wanted to live in her mother's house! I know there was not as much space as here. But still, she went with what you wanted."

Not long after, Andrés took a job in construction and Danae was transferred—she went from librarian to clerk in the Palacio de Matrimonios. She put in her time there despite the fact that she was excited about the idea of signing up for the same microbrigade her husband was in. It was the last time Andrés had seen her excited about something. After trying everything, pulling all the strings possible, and after futile visit after futile visit to all the offices, Danae gave up. Nor was Andrés at all sure why she'd gone to all the trouble, where all the desire had come from, if it all ended this way, in weary resignation. If there was one thing that alarmed him, it was that he could not figure out what was going through his wife's mind, he didn't understand the least part of her uneasiness or her suffering. Nor did he intend to ask, or try to convince her of his innocence. She should *want* to confide in him. A husband had no call to be begging his wife to share her problems with him. He was willing to wait, patiently, and he would not lift a finger until Danae took the initiative.

Cumbaquín, quin quin, cumbacán; cumbaquín, quin quin, cumbacán; cumbaquín, cumbacán, baquín, bacán. The music makers had congaed out of the Casa de la Requidia and were approaching the corner, encouraging passersby to join in the revelry, sweeping all before them like raging, lecherous beasts. They'd been drinking, and from the mouths and noses of the dragon monster issued the fires of rum and beer. One of the carousers was carrying a pine suitcase painted brown. With his trowel, Andrés cut the droop of cement off the last cinder block of the afternoon, pulled his wristwatch out of his front pocket, and confirmed his suspicion that it was time to close up shop.

There were no showers on the site. Inside a dilapidated shed, he ran a grimy towel over his sweaty body and changed out of his work clothes into a clean set Danae had put in his backpack for him that morning. He certainly felt like joining the singers and merrymakers, who had pulled up under the balcony overhang next door to the bodega; they opened a wooden table and spilled the dominoes out on it.

"Gina, turn on this lightbulb down here! It's getting so dark we can't even catch 'em cheating!" yelled a black man, using his hands as a megaphone and shouting up at the second floor.

"I don't want dominoes down there till all hours, now—Raymundo's gall bladder's bad again and the top's about to blow off the thermometer! Why don't you go keep them up all night over on Teja's corner?" a woman answered from inside. But as she finished, the light flickered on and a cone of radiance lit the tabletop.

"Because Teja's corner hasn't got the *swing* this corner's got! Don't give me no Teja's corner, woman!"

The group shouted its approval. Andrés told himself that if he weren't so dog-tired he'd love to stay and play a serious game or two—serious enough to end in a fistfight and black eyes and enough cop cars to take half the street off to jail. Forty-eight hours in stir wouldn't be half bad, he could actually use the rest. But he continued on toward home. He was beat, beat to shit; he'd have something to eat, then run himself under that rusty pipe they still called a shower out of patriotic respect for the past, and then—bang!—hit the sack.

JUST AS HIS FOOT reached the top step and he started inside, the sky seemed to split open. A thunderstorm exploded with so much lightning and thunder that you'd have thought it was a load of iron rails falling from the sky. It was one of those tropical downpours that seem like they'll never end. Lucky to make it home before *that* started, he thought. *San Isidro, water giver, take away the water and turn on the sun.* Although he immediately added a few more words to the thought: his wife wasn't going to speak to him, she'd try to avoid looking at him; she might even avoid his physical presence, go into the bedroom when he came into the kitchen and vice versa, because he was coming in late. Once she'd even told him that the way he walked bothered her. Was he supposed to explain that he'd walked home, depressed by the loss of Gizzard's toe? What for? Words that would fall into the frozen and indifferent abyss of that stubborn ear—she probably wouldn't so much as react. And there would be other things: the girls would already have had their baths and dinners and they would probably be sitting openmouthed in front of the TV, hypnotized by whatever idiotic soap opera was on. It would be hard to persuade them to let him watch the ball game. He climbed the three flights with back bent, feet heavy. He stank—he could actually distinguish between the smell of the apartment house and his own B.O. He didn't feel the blisters on his swollen hands, the calluses as he touched the wall on his way up; his hands had gone to sleep on him, even tingled. Finally he reached his floor. Beneranda's door was wide open; strange—she never left her private life so exposed for all to see. He said *Buenas noches* to a shadowy figure with its back to him, rocking in a rocking chair with one leg hanging over the wooden arm, the chair placed directly in front of the black-and-white screen of a vintage television set, the figure in ironed pajama top and bottom. Must be the husband, or the son, he said to himself; he moved on, quickly, bewildered at not seeing any light under the door to his apartment or through the shutters of the living-room window that opened onto the hallway.

"Andrés." His name, spoken by Beneranda's soft voice, sent a shiver of dread down his back.

"What happened? Is it the girls? Why isn't anybody home?" The gray matter was working furiously, his eyes trying to read Beneranda's face. He sensed something terribly wrong.

"Nothing, your girls are in my bedroom—Norberto is watching the baseball game and I told them to do their homework. They already ate. But they haven't had their baths yet . . . they haven't been able to get in, they don't have the key . . ."

"Where's Danae?"

The woman's face suddenly took on an expression of *Well, if you don't know, how am I supposed to? You're her husband, aren't you.* The bad feeling started to feel more and more justified.

"They don't have any idea where she might be either. They were sitting out here on the stairs, and since I saw that neither one of you had gotten home, I brought them in and fed them . . ."

Andrés waited for the girls to come out of the bedroom, and while they were getting their things together Norberto offered him a cold beer. The game had just started; it was tempting. He turned down the beer; for the first time, he was denying himself that welcome reward after such a hard day. His daughters gave him a kiss on the cheek, as usual, and then they asked where their mother was. *How the fuck do I know?* he wanted to answer, but he controlled himself. She's been looking for a way to get back at me, and now she thinks she's got it. Son of a bitch, she thinks she's so smart. Take that, mister, now you're going to find out what it feels like—you'll see, I can come in at all hours, too. No, she wasn't like that, this wasn't some kind of vulgar revenge. He shepherded the girls to the apartment. He opened the door: darkness, and a smell of bleach and muriatic acid, clothes put away with camphor and naphthalene, assailed his nose. He turned on the light and saw that as usual, everything was in perfect order. Puzzled that the windows were hermetically closed, he looked to see if he could see fingerprints or smudges before he opened them. He threw one open and a gust of salty air washed across his face. Frances went into the bedroom. Ibis was in the bathroom; speaking very slowly and deliberately, she reported her findings:

"Mami's toothbrush is not here, or her comb, either . . . I think Mami left."

It took Andrés a few seconds to reach the door of the bathroom. He leaned against the salmon-colored doorframe. The little girl, scared, looked up at her father's face. He smiled, feigning confidence, and turned away, on the pretext of opening the rest of the windows. His other daughter ran into the bathroom, too, and their whispering drilled into the man's brain. Then they went into the bedroom, to look for their mother's belongings. With relief, he heard them say that nothing else was missing; at least they didn't discover anything else of any importance.

"She must have gone to Grandmother's house, or is off visiting a friend; she'll turn up . . ." Andrés murmured as he tried to fix a curtain that had come loose.

The girls thought it was strange that he said *Grandmother* and not *her mother* or *that crazy old bat,* as he usually referred to Danae's mother.

After they had each had their shower, he put them to bed. It was still pouring. When he thought the girls were probably asleep, Andrés picked up the receiver of the old Bakelite telephone and dialed his mother-in-law's number. The old lady said she hadn't heard from her daughter for several days. She asked whether they'd had a fight; he said no, and he tried to reassure her by telling her that now that he thought of it, Danae had said something about going to sign up for a night class in English. His mother-in-law said Danae had mentioned something about an English class the last time they talked—that was probably where she was.

He saw that there were pots on the stove, and when he opened them he found that before she had left she had made arroz con pollo, then some more arroz con pollo, and a slightly wilted tomato salad. Why had she made salad so many hours ahead of time? Why hadn't she left a note saying where she was going? Why didn't she call now? He looked up some of her friends' telephone numbers in the address book. None of them had heard from her recently, but they all seemed pretty unconcerned to be told that Danae might possibly have disappeared. The truth was, he had a hard time believing that such a thing had happened, too; he was as calm as his nerves allowed, and even joked about his wife running away.

He was exhausted, ready to drop. He would have a shower and watch the baseball game. She would show up, explain, say she was sorry, kiss the girls, lie down with him in their bed, screw better than ever. He would remain firm, unyielding, distant, aloof to her blandishments for several days, just to get back at her a little, then he'd put it aside for the sake of domestic tranquillity and marital contentment.

The water refreshed his dry skin, washed away the sweat and grime. He came out of the bathroom fully dressed—pants, shoes, and clean T-shirt—he couldn't quite bring himself to put on his pajamas. He'd have liked to walk around the streets for awhile to see if he could find her, but he turned on the TV. He had trouble focusing, though; he had no idea what was on the screen. He'd count to ten and the key would turn in the lock, she'd come back and he'd be willing to forgive her, no questions asked. Ten, eleven, twelve, thirteen, fourteen, fifteen . . . a hundred . . . She didn't appear.

As the hours dragged by, his ears strained to hear sounds announcing her arrival; downstairs, in the interior patio, he heard Matilde putting out traps and poison for the rats. He didn't want to yell down at her so he telephoned; he could hear the *rring-rring, rring-rring* in the other apartment. Why was it taking so long? The stupid woman was not answering. Finally he could hear her slip-slopping into the dining room, over to the black table with wrought-iron legs where she kept the telephone, on top of a stack of old dog-eared telephone books. He heard her answer, and the echo in his ear. He asked whether she'd seen his wife as though he were making inquiries about a cadaver over at Forensic Medicine.

"I was with her today. It was hot down here so I went upstairs to your house to see if it was cooler up there. I borrowed a cigarette from her . . ." Andrés thought it was a good thing the telephone line was between them, because if he'd had her in front of him he'd have strangled her—she was taking all the time she could, talking nonsense, giving him all these idiotic details on purpose. "Oh yeah, I remember—she said she had an appointment with the gynecologist, she was going over to the hospital to the doctor's office . . ."

While Matilde went on chattering, he found among other papers on the telephone table a piece of paper from the hospital; the appointment had been yesterday, there was the evidence, the doctor's signature, the release from treatment. There before his eyes was the proof—she didn't have any parasites or anything else, she was healthy, there was nothing that would take her back to the gynecologist. He cut the conversation short, hung up, and from down below he could hear Matilde swearing, pissed at the interruption, and then returning with housewifely zeal to her rattraps, *slp, slp, slp, slp* across the floor.

He went back to the challenge of convincing himself that he was absorbed in the baseball game. He was surprised to find his eyes glued to the test pattern; the day's programming was over, and he hadn't even seen whether his team had won or not. He went to the refrigerator, avoided looking at the kitchen clock, poured himself a glass of milk. When he lifted the glass to drink, his eyes caught the clock's hands. Hour hand, minute hand, even second hand . . . Three o'clock in the morning. He put the glass in the sink. He started to turn on the tap, but thought better of it—let her wash it when she comes home, when she has the decency to remember that she's got a family waiting for her.

In the doorway of the kitchen he was overcome by a flood of rage, and he felt as though he were about to faint. He bit his hand, his teeth sank into the flesh, and then he smashed his fist into the wall. He brought his hand to his mouth again, but this time to suck the blood off his knuckles. He didn't want to wake the girls, didn't want to scare them. He would just have to bear up. She'd have to come back. Why did those words *come back* sound so gloomy, so impossible? What if she didn't? He'd wait until it was time to take the girls to school, then he'd go to the police, file a report on her disappearance. How could she just vanish, just disappear like that? What would he say? What if something had happened to her, an accident of some kind? What if she'd gotten run over by a car? No, the news of a tragedy like that travels fast. Finally he decided to call his friend Swan.

"Swan, *viejo*, it's me, Andy . . ."

"I was surprised you hadn't called. You can imagine how I feel—it's all my fault Gizzard lost his toe, man, I've gone through two bottles of rum, I'm wasted, wasted . . . I feel so bad, *mi hermano*, I tell you, this fucking sucks."

"I know, man, but don't blame yourself. Things just happen . . . Listen, I'm having a bad night, too, I'm going kinda nuts here—I got home and the girls were over in Beneranda's apartment, the neighbor, you know? . . ." He waited for the other man to say something, but the only response he got was heavy alcoholic breathing, phlegm-vibrating sighs . . . Finally, from the other end of the line, his friend said something:

"Uh-huh?"

"Uh-huh?! Whaddaya mean 'uh-huh'? I don't know where Danae is—she took her toothbrush and comb. Three o'clock in the morning and no sign of her . . ."

"You think she's out at a bar somewhere putting the horns on you, *compay*?"

"She doesn't have the ovaries for that, and if she did, she's not the type. I don't know whether to go down to the police station or what . . . And I'm here by myself with the girls, to boot."

Swan's voice cleared:

"Get Beneranda to watch them and get down to the police station right now. I won't go with you because with the amount of ethyl I've pumped tonight, they might decide to throw me in a cell for my own good . . . And listen, if you find out anything or need anything, you can call anytime, any hour, man, you know that . . ."

"I think Danae's slipped a gear here lately is what I think, *compay*. She barely talks, you know, just the minimum necessary, and her hands shake, she quit taking baths. She's still nuts about keeping the house clean, she does do that, all the fucking time as a matter of fact, but herself—forget it. Sometimes she actually *smells,* man, and I haven't said anything to her because I kinda, I don't know, I hated to . . ."

"You know my cousin Kiss-Ass, the son of that stupid guajiro from La Fe? He works in Mazorra, he's a shrink at the Psychiatric. If you want me to, I'll brief him on your case."

"I don't think we need to go *that* far, man." But his tone of voice was unsure.

He barely heard Swan's last words. He pulled on a shirt and went out into the hall, stood before Beneranda's door, hesitated. He didn't think Beneranda, as a good neighbor, would refuse to take care of the girls. He had to ask her. But before his knuckles could touch the wood, Beneranda's face, alarmed but still half asleep, met him.

"I was on my way to see you. Your wife called. She wanted to know how you and the girls were. Come in, come in . . ."

"Where is she? No, I can't come in, I left the door open and the girls sleeping. I was coming over to see if you'd look after them while I went to the police. Where'd she call from?"

Beneranda pushed Andrés a few steps into the apartment, trying to keep the two of them from being overheard. Norberto, in silence, was boiling water for some linden tea. He wasn't the least bit happy about his wife getting involved in this kind of situation, but she, on the other hand, was delighted. She loved this being in the middle of a tragedy—she could finally feel important, needed, the center of things. In just a couple of hours Norberto would have to put on his mechanic's overalls and go to work.

"Danae? She could hardly talk she was crying so hard. She called when the train stopped in some little town where there was a telephone on the platform—and it was working, can you imagine! She covered it up pretty good, but you could tell how torn up she was—she tried to keep from showing she was crying but I could hear it in her voice. Two or three times she could just barely talk, you know? get the words out. She said she had a cold. Anyway, she said to tell you that she couldn't take it anymore, but she didn't have the courage to call you. She figured the girls would be here, with me, since you always come in late. She went off to the country for a while, out in Pinar del Río somewhere, she said. She said she'd be back, but she needs to think about things, get away . . ."

Andrés' tense muscles began to relax, and his legs gave way on him. He had to pull over a chair and sit down. Thank goodness she was safe and sound, thank goodness she'd just run away, had an attack of hysteria. He even had to make an effort to keep himself from smiling in relief.

"When is she coming back?" he asked, sure that a precise answer would be coming.

Beneranda already had her lips to the edge of the steaming cup of linden tea that her husband had handed her, so she just shrugged her shoulders. Andrés took the second cup, but he held it for several seconds before sipping.

"Are you sure she didn't say when?"

She nodded, as though her mouth were stuck forever to the fiery lip of the cup.

"Why did she leave?"

"She didn't say a word about that. She seemed nervous, though, really nervous."

"She's with some guy," he muttered angrily, making the sign of horns with his index and little finger.

"No, she's not with anybody, she's by herself. Give her time, I'll help you with the girls, I promised her . . . She doesn't want to get her mother involved in this. Now take this pill and go to bed. You just get some sleep."

Andrés obediently put the diazepam tablet under his tongue, drank down the rest of the tea, thanked Beneranda and Norberto sincerely, and went back to his apartment. He'd hardly gotten inside the door when he butted his head, like a cornered wild boar, into the china cabinet. Not only did he destroy the glass doors; the shards and slivers of glass cut his forehead and cheeks and the noise woke the girls. And when they saw their father with his bloody face they started screaming, calling for their mother. Ibis was the one most upset. Suddenly Frances whirled and ran off for the Mercurochrome and a bandage, to put on the cuts. There was none of either in the medicine cabinet, so she wet a dishtowel with rubbing alcohol. She tried to calm her father, get him to sit on the couch. When she touched his cuts he bellowed, but she cleaned the wounds the best she could. Ibis was still sobbing and asking for her mother. Where was her mother, when would she be back? she asked over and over.

"Hush! Your mother is a bitch! She left, the bitch, she left you, you and your sister!" he burst out, pushing Frances away brusquely.

Ibis stomped on the floor, her chest rose and fell; she was crying so hard that she could hardly breathe and her hiccups were becoming more and more arrhythmic. Her father put his head between his hands. Frances managed to get up off the floor, where she'd fallen when her father pushed her away, and went over to him. He seemed to be trying to crush his skull with his bare hands. She tried to pull his hands away, tugging with all her strength, but once again, furious, he pushed her away. Her sobbing was not as uncontrolled as her sister's, but she felt devastated, and she paced the living room. Her father finally stood and with even more force threw himself against a bookcase; he then saw the old Singer sewing machine and immediately thought of heaving it over his head and throwing it out the window. At first it didn't want to move, and as he wrestled with it a drawer came open and the contents scattered across the floor—among them, the package that Danae had been holding for Matilde. Wrapped tight in brown wrapping paper and then in plastic, the package looked immediately suspicious to Andrés, who took a pair of scissors and plunged them into the packet. The point came out covered in white powder. Andrés smelled, tasted—he couldn't believe it. Cocaine! This was cocaine! Had the bitch gone crazy?! The girls stopped him by hanging onto him desperately. He picked up the package and hid it in the oven.

Beneranda heard the screaming and the noise, the breaking of glass and the crashing of heavy objects. She didn't have time to put on her house slippers, she just ran out half-dressed to save her neighbor's daughters. She knocked softly, not wanting to seem too aggressive—by the sound of it, you'd think the devil was in there breaking up the place. When no one came to the door, she started banging.

"Andrés, open up! Open the door, dammit!"

Lights started coming on in apartments up and down the hall, and people started yelling at them to shut up. The more curious stuck their heads out, or gathered in groups in the hallway, or even went to Norberto to ask what was going on.

"Don't ask me, I got nothing to do with this—in fact, I gotta get my ass in gear and get to work." And he ran down the stairs, pulling on a transparent plastic rain cape as he went, leaving the neighbors puzzled, wanting to know the reason for such a strange reaction.

It had not stopped raining all night. In his haste to get out of the building, Norberto slipped on the outside steps, his feet flew out from under him, and he fell, hard, his back hitting the hard bullnose of one of the steps. He cursed the mother of the tomatoes— "I could have been paralyzed," he said, rubbing his back, "in a wheelchair for the rest of my fucking life. I practically kill myself and it's all because of that woman that calls herself a mother but runs off and leaves her husband and two daughters. I tell you, before this shit gets any better, it's gonna get a lot worse!"

The most courageous, or curious, neighbors were moving, little by little, toward the scene of the disaster. Inside, the noise was finally abating.

In the apartment, Frances was doing her best to bring the situation under control by covering her father's face with kisses and whispering soothing words in his ear. Ibis, taking advantage of a moment of affectionate distraction on the part of her sister and her father, ran and opened the door. Beneranda rushed in, sprinkling the three with holy water out of a bottle another neighbor had handed her. She was here to restore order. And soon the room grew quiet, with only the sound of isolated sobs. That was when Matilde appeared, looking nervous, wringing her hands; she had come to get a little package she'd left with Danae.

"Did any of you by any chance see a little package, about this size, wrapped in brown paper and a piece of plastic?"

Andrés hesitated.

"No, get out of here! We haven't found anything! Get out of here or I'll break your neck!"

Matilde shivered and turned on her heel like an automaton. The gossips returned to their beds or their usual morning activities. Beneranda began to straighten up the room, pick up the debris. Andrés was still clutching his younger daughter. The older one, her voice shaking, her lower lip quivering, went to ask Beneranda where her mother was. And Beneranda put her finger over the little girl's soft lips, to indicate that she would explain later.

She went back to her apartment to look in the medicine cabinet for something to put on Andrés' cuts—all there was was household remedies, some *yerba amansaguapo*, mainly. The cuts were not serious, just scratches really. After a while she begged Andrés to talk to the girls before she did—it was his job. His summary of the situation was short and sweet.

"All right, you know your mother left. She'll be back after she has a while to think. She needs time. That's all, now . . . . Or . . . well, I love her . . . I hope this passes."

Ashamed of his violence, he asked the girls to forgive him. Then he slunk off to the bathroom; he needed another shower. He came out in his pajamas, went straight to his bedroom, and climbed into the bed that still bore the smell of Danae. When he buried his face in the pillow, her perfume, the fragrance of lily of the valley, filled his nostrils. He wanted to groan, but the fragrance left him so disconcerted that he simply sighed; the grief had subsided into something more fleeting. At the moment he was so exhausted, so bone tired, that there was no energy inside him for remorse or anger. He closed his eyes and fell instantly asleep.

The two girls and Beneranda set about cleaning up the mess. They threw out the twisted bookcase, the broken figurines and plates, and did their best to erase the traces of fury and desolation. Beneranda made breakfast. Sitting with her elbows on the table, she explained to the girls, in her own way, the reasons for their mother's flight. The girls chewed their bread, their eyes vacant, fixed on the table's oilcloth with its wreaths of flowers twining absurdly about Egyptian friezes. The woman did what she could to reassure them, even telling them that Danae had called late last night, that she'd promised to write them, and promised also to come back. She said she hoped they'd try to understand their mother—she needed a rest. Ibis didn't so much as blink, but her eyes grew wider and wider, redder and redder with panic, and soon big tears were rolling down her face, dropping into the bowl in front of her. Her sister looked at her contemptuously, backhanded her shoulder gently with her fingertips, and said between gritted teeth:

"Get over it."

"Poor Mamá."

"Poor Mamá? What do you mean 'poor Mamá'? She shouldn't be doing this to us, it's not fair. Look how papá is—" Her voice rose; clearly Frances had taken her father's side in this.

"She did what she had to do, and that's all there is to it, now. We're not going to talk about this anymore right now. Come on, let's go, put your uniforms on, don't think you're gonna get out of going to school today," Beneranda interrupted.

"You're not the boss of us, and I'm not going to school. I don't have to mind you. Do you think I'm going to leave Papá here by himself?" And she jerked her head toward the bedroom.

The telephone rang, then rang again, but then it stopped. Apparently Andrés had grabbed it in the bedroom. In the living room, they all froze in suspense.

The first ring had interrupted a dream in which he, a teenager again, was playing with a manatee. He was in a river, splashing about naked, and all of a sudden he felt something soft and warm rub up against his legs. At first he jumped back, but then he decided to dive under to see what it was that had so tenderly caressed his legs. The manatee and he looked at each other, face to face. Then the animal opened its mouth to speak, and bubbles of air came out.

"You're in love."

"I'm not sure . . ." Andrés replied, and air bubbles came out of his mouth, too.

The second ring broke the oneiric vision.

"Hello." His voice was flat, uninflected. His mouth was tacky.

"It's me."

"Where are you? When are you coming back? Why did you have to call Beneranda's house and not here, not me?" He cleared his throat, then reached over to the night table and picked up a glass and took a sip of the lukewarm water that was left from the night before.

"How are the girls?"

"*Coño*, what the fuck's with you? Are you not going to tell me what the fuck is going on?"

"I'm tired, Andrés—sick and tired. I need to get away. I don't know for sure how long, probably not long. I love you, I swear I do, and I love the girls, but I need to breathe. You suffocate me, your parents suffocate me, my mother suffocates me, even the girls suffocate me . . ."

"Just tell me one thing—are you involved with another man? Because I couldn't take that."

"Please. Is that the only thing you could figure it might be? I'm not with anybody, I'm by myself, my*self*. I'm going to see a girlfriend I haven't seen in a long time. You can tell yourself I've gone on a vacation. I'm sorry that this has been so spur-of-the-moment and all, that I didn't let you know before-hand. I didn't say anything because if I had, I wouldn't have gone through with it. I love you, Andrés, I love you."

"I love you too, but I don't understand why the fuck you had to go off this way. Your daughters are really, really upset . . ."

"And what about you?" She waited, to see whether he would finally tell her how much he missed her.

"Well, now that you've called, I'm better. I thought something had happened to you, you'd had an accident or something. I went crazy when you called Beneranda and not me—I put my head through your china cabinet, smashed it to shit. And if it had been *you* standing there in front of me, I'd have done it to you . . ."

"Is that all?"

"Yes. What else?"

"Let me talk to the girls."

"Listen, stop this craziness, Danae. Don't be so pigheaded. Come back."

"Let me talk to Ibis, please."

Danae spoke to her older daughter, trying to reassure her by telling her, only partly untruthfully, that she had a very important job to do in the country, something very important to her that might take a few days but might take months—the people in charge hadn't told her exactly what it was. On the other end of the line, the silence grew; this attempt at a white lie, not even a young girl was naive enough to believe. Danae also explained that there were some problems between her and their father, they didn't always understand each other—the girls, remember? had seen several arguments. So this separation was in hopes of saving the relationship; she and her sister shouldn't worry, things would get better, their father and she would work things out. She was taking advantage of the new job to get away, temporarily of course, so it would be easier for both of them to think about things. Ibis, her mind somewhat more comforted, asked her if she wanted to talk to Andrés again, but Danae said no, put Frances on the phone, so she handed the receiver to her younger sister, after blowing her mother a big kiss. Danae tried to explain to her, too, just as she had to Ibis. But Frances was not so easy:

"Don't worry, I believe you, but I've never heard of a mother that left her own kids. It's always the fathers. I'm not mad or anything; we'll wait. And don't worry, I'll take care of Papi." Livid, she hung up.

Danae had to hurry; the train whistle was blowing to announce the train's departure. She climbed aboard, her eyes filled with tears, feeling very much her mother's daughter, very little her daughters' mother, yet at the same time less upset after talking to her husband and the girls—the fruits of her and Andrés' love? And also after seeing once again that her husband would never change, not with this separation or any other, no matter how temporary or final it was.

In the living room, Andrés saw Beneranda to the door; he was almost at a loss for words, he didn't know how to thank her, she'd been so good to them, how could he . . .

"And I'll see they get to school, don't worry," he said, still not understanding in the slightest the emotions his wife had wanted to communicate during the call, or the confession she'd wanted to hear from him.

Cumbaquín, quin quin, cumbacán; cumbaquín, quin quin, cumbacán; cumbaquín, cumbacán, baquín, bacán. The music of the city can be very cruel, and if we are not prepared for the violence we might die of a heart attack in the attempt to get our revenge. Vengeance should be swifter than the wind, like the pistols of Billy the Kid. I am the music that accompanied Andrés in those last moments when he was more alone than a stray dog. I'd have preferred to poison him, preferred even that he take matters into his own hands and commit suicide. But he was so fragile, so wiped out, that he didn't even have the spunk to realize that his existence was worth less than a drunk's vomit, less than a drunk's *burp*. I, the music of the streets, a rumba beat out on the top of a cardboard box, I love these down-and-out guys, these miserable, unhappy, sad guys, the saps that women make lower than spit. Those poor damned unlucky sons of bitches sometimes get so negative that they'd be capable of murdering anybody that gets in their way. And they can sing guaguancós that would make you want to throw up, they're such tearjerkers. You can get a lot of mileage out of guys like that.

Cumbaquín, quin quin, cumbacán; cumbaquín, quin quin, cumbacán; cumbaquín, cumbacán, baquín, bacán. Andrés felt a rage deep, deep inside himself, and a blind desire to have his revenge. If Danae had walked through that door, he wouldn't have known whether to kiss her or cut her throat. But there were the girls—why do people have children if all they're gonna do is make them suffer? There were Frances and Ibis, whom he would also be happy to just drown, in a swimming pool, say. Bitches-to-be, conceived in the womb of that snake-woman! A snake-woman, yes, and yet he loved her.

Cumbaquín, quin quin, cumbacán; cumbaquín, quin quin, cumbacán; cumbaquín, cumbacán, baquín, bacán. The telephone woke him up again— who could it be at this hour of the morning? Danae? No, it was Swan. Great. Swan whispered to Andrés that he was bad, man, from the . . . the . . . you know, the booze, that he was still drinking because he was a born drinker, man, that hitting one back was just the best thing there was, man, you know? "But hey, listen, buddy, what I called you about— did your old lady come back home again or wha'?"

"Leave me alone, Swan, man, let me get some sleep. Don't fuck up my night, man, or what's left of it. Danae left me—left us. So now you know, okay? Happy now?"

"What am I gonna be happy about shit like that, man? That's way bad, man."

Cumbaquín, quin quin, cumbacán; cumbaquín, quin quin, cumbacán; cumbaquín, cumbacán, baquín, bacán. Kill her like a dog, *mi compay,* she doesn't deserve you, the bitch—the whore!—wring her neck like a chicken! Women are all alike—putas, man, and I can tell the world—PU-U-U-TAS! Pornoputas.

Swan, man, do you know what time it is?

No, no, *¿porqué mi cúmbila, mi hermano?* don't you have a minute for your buddy, *mi asere?*

Swan, I'm bad, man, I'm really feeling bad here, don't screw with me now, just let me get some z's, that's what I really need, man—okay? You're not going to the site tomorrow? Well, get some sleep, then, have a cold shower.

Women (and that one in particular) are a bunch of pornographic bitches, pornomothas, pornohags, pornoworkersinthevanguard, pornonurses, pornopoliticians, pornoteachers, pornolawyers, pornohousewives, pornomusicians, pornopainters, pornofortunetellers, pornowitches, pornoshits, pornofuckingshits, pornoparachutists, pornopilots, pornocampesinas, pornoilliterates, pornoactresses, pornowriters, pornograndmas, pornoaunts, pornowaitresses, pornowasherwomen, pornopharmacists, pornobankclerks, pornoaccountants, pornobusdrivers, pornomatrons, pornoprosecutors, pornostreetsweepers, pornotruckdrivers, pornotaxidrivers, pornonuns, pornoforeigners, pornobricklayers, pornowhores, pornotechnicians, pornofatsos, pornoflatasses, pornoanorexics, pornoaviators, pornotrainconductors, pornopastrychefs, pornocooks, pornojunkies, pornoalcoholics, pornoteetotalers, pornoreaders, pornojournalists, pornophotographers, pornopornographers, pornoeditors, pornofuckheads, pornosculptors, pornosingers, pornodaughters, pornogranddaughters, pornofrigidbitches, pornobowleggedbitches, pornodeafbitches, pornoblindbitches, pornodecadents, pornodinosaurs, pornodeadbitches, pornofuckedbitches, pornoscientists, pornoanalysts, pornospies, pornonarcs, pornovictims, pornodancers, pornoballerinas, pornomechanics, pornodoctors, pornolawyers, pornoqueens, pornopresidents, pornohypochondriacs, pornotravelingsaleswomen, pornonewspapersaleswomen, pornohotelkeepers, pornobooksellers, pornomonsters, pornoexecutioners, pornotalkers, pornoperfumedbitches, pornopaintedupbitches, pornorafters, pornohungerstrikers, pornoprisoners, pornotraitors, pornoovarians, pornosurgeons, pornobigtittedbitches, pornobigassedbitches, pornosideshowstars, pornomissuniverses, pornosupermodels, pornosweeties, pornobitchybitches, pornoexiles, pornopoliticalrefugees, pornoshits . . . And he'd go on if he didn't hear you snoring on the other end of the line. Andrés! Andy, wake up, I haven't finished!

Cumbaquín, quin quin, cumbacán; cumbaquín, quin quin, cumbacán; cumbaquín, cumbacán, baquín, bacán.

I am the music, the guaguancó of the barrio, and I was not going to allow my good cúmbila Andrés to stay so whupped, no sir. Damn woman, the abakuás here in my prenda demand vengeance. Not for nothing is a man a man. And the abakuás must be respected. *Men* are the ones that get the last word around here. Fall to your knees—kneel, woman, and kiss my white loafers. Wash these white clothes. Put it to her!

THE ARBORESCENT SUITCASE

I am the suitcase, listening to the woman who owns me. Before being a plank that later became a suitcase, I was a tree. Trees listen. Wood never loses its poetic properties. I am a happy suitcase, though sorrowful as well, because I suffer from an excess of emotion—an *extreme* excess sometimes. I am that thing that listens:

At eleven, I'd known no world but the city. I had never set foot in pure, authentic nature. Before she died, my grandmother had pleaded with my mother not to let me go to the Schools in the Country. I hated that selfish side of La Milagrosa. Which was what the whole neighborhood called that lady who had given birth to Gloriosa Paz and who was thus, transitively, my grandmother. Although the best part of my life had been her, La Milagrosa, the Miraculous One, still . . . I hated her.

Before she vomited up her last torment, that black, hairy ball—her goiter is what it was, if you ask me—La Milagrosa pulled my mother down to her and with her last strength she told her: *Don't let the girl go; it's dangerous. People say terrible things happen out there. She won't be looked after, and you've worked too hard for that girl to have them come in one day and, just like that, tell you that something's happened to your daughter, or to bring you her body. Don't give her permission. Promise me, please.* My mother told me this to see what my opinion of it was, to find out whether I still insisted on going. I hadn't gotten over La Milagrosa's death yet and I already had to "give my opinion" about this. Around here, there's no time for being sad.

It's not that I'm just dying to go, I told her; it's that if I don't, they'll all make fun of me. I had to do it, I had no choice. If she wanted to see me go to the university someday, I couldn't back out. Plus I wanted to do the same things the other kids were doing—make my contribution, leave home, feel independent of my mother, Gloriosa Paz, cut the umbilical cord. I didn't really use these last two reasons on her, of course. I hated La Milagrosa with such a physical hate that I was terrified of my own hatred; my ribs turned soft from the tension, and if she'd been alive I might have had the nerve to smother her with her own pillow—and all for having vomited up that last speech against what I saw as my freedom, the denial of my entire future. Wasn't she dying? Why did she have to stick her nose in *my* life? Couldn't she devote a little more time and energy to observing her own death? Old people are selfish meddlers, I thought at the time. I don't think that today. Old people are scared—and it's the same fear as newborns have when, at the tender age of nine months, they have to leave their mother's sheltering warmth—although old people know more, a little more, about mistakes. When an old person and a five-year-old kid meet, they discover that they possess the same degree—same *high* degree—of wisdom. After the burial, my mother never brought the matter up again. I figured that authorized me to go and get to know the country. I was a big baby raised on sea spray and asphalt. I needed some soil, some earth. Nobody had ever talked to me about trees, their fine-sounding names, those mysteries held within in the forest. I yearned to breathe new air, invent secrets. Dig into the entrails of nature until my fingernails were bleeding.

The passage from sixth to seventh grade was decisive. I was suddenly transformed into a teenager, enjoying to the fullest the painful throbbings of puberty. The first symptoms made me laugh out loud and smell myself all over. Effluvia began to ooze from my body, and there was nothing pleasant about them, especially under my arms. I had to start wearing deodorant, an entertaining new habit. Long hairs started sprouting from my pubis, on my legs, and also under my arms, although it was sparse and very fine at first, soft, delicate, hardly visible at all—and that bothered me a lot, because I needed other people not to have the slightest doubt that I was growing up. I had always wanted to grow up, get older. Now I regret that—which is logical. I'm on my way to old age. At that moment I was beautiful, but I didn't know it. Mirrors disappointed me. Today I have another kind of beauty, maybe, though I still don't know how to recognize it; tomorrow I'll regret not having accepted the beauty I have today. There's no hope for it—I've moved on into the land of aches and pains. And I'm on my way to old age—the *real* old age. The lasting, lovely end. I still have some time left, but the lack of dreams, of grand ambitions for "what you wanna be when you grow up," cuts the balls off youth.

When we started seventh grade, one of the first things the teachers and guides told us about was the period we'd be spending at the School in the Country. Forty-five days in the hot sun, working right alongside the campesinos—that last part truly made my heart beat faster. I was fascinated by the guajiros in the newspapers; all I knew about them were the pictures of rustic but friendly-looking faces. All lords of olden times, because "guajiros" was what the lords of Yucatán were known as. The sun I already knew—at least the sun of the beach, the ocean, the city. Because the sun is not the same everywhere. There's the sun up on the roof where you hang the clothes, the sun of the balcony, the sun of the sidewalk, the café, the shop, the sun of "Run, baby girl, don't let the bogeyman get you!" Here in the city it's the sun and his kids and his whole family, dozens of them, a battalion of regular suns and little suns and great big sunny suns. The sun even slips into movie theaters, and I don't know how it can roast you alive like a piece of meat on the griddle while you're sitting in your seat at the picture show, but it does. But what I also didn't know, didn't have the experience of, was that sun of the country, the sun from one edge of the sky to the other, sun up to sun down, with no escape, no way out, and no choice in the matter, either. The teachers gave us an orientation on the kind of work we'd be doing, and they led us to believe that we would be an essential part of it. When I got home I discussed it with Gloriosa Paz, my mother, who did not share that opinion.

"You'll go to the country because it's a requirement for getting into the university, period—I don't want to hear any speeches. I'm not going to swallow

some story, not for one second, about without you kids out there in the country it would all go to rack and ruin and rot on the vine or whatever—what are
those campesinos for, anyway? Are they some kind of painted scenery or
something? Since when is it not honorable to be a campesino? What I don't
understand is why they want to turn city kids into campesinos and
campesinos into city dwellers. If you ask me, it's turning the world upside
down—and it's stupid, to boot. But I'll accept it—not too happily, but I'll
accept it—because it's your future that's on the line."

A waiter at the Polynesian gave her the address of a carpenter who made
good solid suitcases, out of pine, especially for the Schools in the Country.
First I had to go by the restaurant to get the address. I went in and asked for
Gervasio.

"He's out in the kitchen," the maître d' told me. "*Espérate aquí, chiquita.*"
So I waited.

At the tables, people were eating chicken roasted over charcoal. It smelled
like that Chinese sauce mixed with rancid butter, and still my mouth
watered—I hadn't had a bite to eat all day. At the time, however, I didn't like
chicken, hated it with a passion—now I love it. As you get older, your taste
changes, it turns strict, simple, conservative.

Gervasio came out of the kitchen carrying a trayful of beer bottles without any labels. With amazing skillfulness he set the glasses down on the table
after he'd poured them full of the frothy liquid, without dripping a drop.
Then he kind of winked at me, motioning me to follow him, and he took me
by the hand and led me into the kitchen and from there we went out to the
back of the place.

"Next time, come in the back door, I don't want to attract attention.
Much less get my ass booted out of here—I've got five mouths to feed. Wait
here—I'll be back in a few minutes."

Gervasio was queer, you could see that a mile away, but he was married
and had four kids. Cover, my mother, Gloriosa Paz, called it. Gervasio was
beautiful; he didn't deserve to be working as a waiter. In any other country, I
thought, he'd have been an actor or a model or a poet—because that was the
way I pictured poets, starving but beautiful, and that was before I'd ever seen
a picture of Verlaine. Or learned that all over the world there are boys as
pretty, or even a thousand times more mouthwatering and seductive than

Gervasio, who are still waiters or anything else, just to work without losing their dignity. Sure enough, Gervasio was back in less than ten minutes.

"Here you go, *niña,* the carpenter's address, and a chicken, too, so you girls can eat like queens tonight." The chicken was wrapped in the editorial page of the newspaper, and the grease had started to turn it transparent.

When I got home, Gloriosa Paz, my mother, practically jumped up and down with happiness, clapping and cackling like she'd gotten news that she'd won an alarm clock for her merits at the work center.

"Chicken—chicken, at last!" she exclaimed, like she'd found a diamond. She tucked the torn-off piece of paper with the carpenter's name on it into her brassiere.

It's important for a girl to remember the first suitcase she ever had. A suitcase is the positive symbol of your destination. You will put your belongings in that suitcase and carry them to your first far-off place. Your first journey. You should never forget it. It is the memory of your first desire for freedom. I can still close my eyes and call up the way that suitcase smelled. It smelled like pine, of course, and then down underneath it had the fragrance of paper written in that black ink that comes from Persia—not India like everybody says. I didn't know anything about the Persians or the Indians or anything then, or about their ink, or their poetry. Several years would have to pass and one afternoon in the middle of a hurricane—Frederic, they called that one— I was reading a poem by Gastón Baquero and I got interested in the Persians and their poetry and the aroma of the ink manufactured by them. *An inno- cent—no, innocent even of innocence, awakening innocence. I do not know how to write, I have no notion of the Persian language. What person who does not know Persian can know anything?* I not only knew nothing about Persia and the Persians; I had never seen a fish face to face, and as for the city, in spite of living in it, I was only beginning to have any sort of definite idea of it when I read another poem by Baquero. In my case, it's poetry that's taught me every- thing I know. Poetry has shown me the world; I owe a debt of gratitude to poetry for the love I feel for nature, the earth, the trees, the ocean. Before I had read any poetry I resembled nothing so much as a blind woman—and a mute one, too, because I had no idea how to put my thoughts in order, no idea how to speak, the words wouldn't come. Poetry taught me how to talk. That suitcase for the School in the Country smelled like pine—that was its *superficial* smell. But then, as I said, it gave forth the fragrance of Persian poetry.

My mother asked the carpenter if he could paint it the closest color he could get to dirt. *Since it's bound to get dirt all over it,* she said, *we'll just save some time and work here.* And so my suitcase was painted a dirt color that I thought was horrible, but of course when I got to know dirt I had no choice but to take my hat off to the carpenter, who had reproduced its color and texture perfectly—no one could have done it better. That was why whenever anybody in the School in the Country saw me carrying the suitcase, they couldn't seem to keep themselves from yelling at me:

"Hey, you! Schizophrenic! Where you going with that big clod you're carrying there?" At least until they got used to the fact that it was a suitcase.

The suitcase, as I was saying, was all smooth and polished inside, and I loved to stick my head in and inhale, inhale, inhale that aroma. The carpenter had taken some tacks and tacked in a piece of flour sack for a big pocket or compartment where I could keep my underwear, socks, and other smaller things. I can't say that the handle of my suitcase was comfortable—the thick rope tied to two eyebolts cut into my hand—but it had a beauty of its own. Now, looking back, it's funny to remember the blisters it gave me. The afternoon Gloriosa Paz, my mother, came in with that suitcase was a red-letter day for me. She was ranting and raving: *It's highway robbery to charge a single mother who's got a daughter to bring up twenty pesos for four pieces of wood hammered together!* I picked up the suitcase and sensed that it would make my soul vibrate the day I used it for the first time—a delicious electric buzz ran from my fingers to my funny bone.

I got to my room and swung the suitcase up on the bed. I opened it. Inside, as I said, it was all smooth and polished. It was as though a labyrinth, or Ali Baba's cave full of treasures, had opened before me. I felt an incomparable thrill of pleasure as I looked at that promising emptiness. My suitcase was like me inside, empty—it knew not a thing about the country, or about nature. For weeks all I could think about was going home from school or wherever to look into that box painted terra-cotta, the color of trees way down deep inside the earth. For weeks I imagined what I'd fill it with, since a suitcase is supposed to be crammed full of stuff—personal, secret utensils of all kinds. When I thought about how poor I was, the fact that among my possessions I could not count even enough imagination to invent things to fill my suitcase with, I got depressed. I owned nothing—not secrets, not books, not even real desires. The suitcase became a monster, some sinister animal that demanded victims to devour, to fill its implacable belly with. I held back from it for a while, until I managed to reconcile my spirit with the enigma that it was. It is so pretty inside, Mamá; it's a shame to have to put garbage in it, I said. Don't be silly, child, we'll find things to put in it—you're just going to the country, not to a ball to dance a waltz on the red carpet in the prince's castle in *Cinderella*.

We filled the suitcase with the help of neighbors and some of my mother's friends. We found some old plastic boots that had been worn by some iceman somewhere—way too big for me—some capri pants that had belonged to my mother, Gloriosa Paz, in the fifties, two olive green shirts, two long-sleeved white flannel shirts, three pairs of socks knit out of kite string— kite string dyed aqua, that is. We also found some Venus cold cream, a huge imitation tortoise-shell comb, a canteen of heavy aluminum that my mother had my whole name, given name and both last names, engraved on in big Gothic letters. A pair of plastic sandals that made your feet sweat like anything and when the sweat mixed with mud gave off these awful gargling, farting sounds. Plus a bottle of violet water; a sheet made out of scraps of colored fabric like a quilt; a pillowcase made the same way; a silver tube of toothpaste; another tube, green this time, of deodorant; a roll of toilet paper; some hair clips and bobby pins; a straw hat to keep me from getting sunburned; two head scarves, one green with gold threads and the other one red with metallic threads in it, too, but silver and other colors; a change of nicer clothes for the Sunday visits and holidays, consisting of a work shirt made out of khaki material but light gray and shiny, a pair of dark brown pants made out of that same shiny cotton drill, and a pair of red tennis shoes with white soles—too big for me, of course. There was a white cotton T-shirt and a white blouse with a floral pattern on it and a nice collar, a bottle of green Fiesta shampoo for oily hair, several pairs of jersey panties with my name embroidered on them because my mother had decided to mark every single article of clothing I took with me so they wouldn't get stolen or in case there was an accident and she had to identify me. I carried three cans of condensed milk, two jelly rolls, a bar of chocolate, a package of café-con-leche-flavored hard candies, six packages of Africana cookies, the crunchy ones like fingers covered with chocolate, one for each day of the first week, and a plastic bag of María cookies. My suitcase was full in no time, which led to the second problem—finding a lock to keep thieves from getting in and taking anything they wanted. (I insist that all you heard was that in the Schools in the Country there were thieves everywhere—scooping up stuff like kids playing marbles, but with both hands at once.) My mother hit on the solution. She took the lock off the latch of the room we lived in, muttering that she'd see to the thieves in the neighborhood—everything we had of any value was in the suitcase, anyway. She found a blue shoelace, strung the key and some blue beads on it—imitation lapis lazuli—and hung it around my neck. That was my necklace for the forty-five days of my first experience as an agricultural worker in the country. In fact, it was my first necklace.

We were supposed to be at the Parque de la Fraternidad at two in the afternoon. It was a day when the sun was so bright it blinded you. My mother didn't want me to carry the suitcase, so she practically dragged it from Calle Tejadillo to the park—the Parque de la Fraternidad, as I say, with its magnificent ceiba tree, although in those days I didn't care about ceibas or any other trees. I could barely make out my mother's teary eyes, which were as red as my grandmother's white rabbit's. My mother was nervous, depressed, because we had never been separated before, but she didn't say a word about the state of her emotions. I pretended that I sensed that she was what my grandmother had always called "despondent"; my grandmother had always said a person might die of that, so I figured that was what this was. My mother was quiet, except when it came time to put the suitcase up on the truck—because the luggage went on a truck, not on the bus with us, so I had to write my name on the wood of the suitcase with a black eyebrow pencil of my mother's. It was then that my mother finally spoke. She reminded me that my grandmother, if she were alive, would be so upset with this mess, this going off to the country. I shrugged my shoulders and told her that first, it was no big thing and, second, my grandmother was dead and buried. It was not very nice of me to use such a hard phrase; after all, it was her mother we were talking about, and my grandmother. It never occurred to me that my mother might get old and die some day.

In a while my classmates started straggling in. I should mention that my mother and I were always extremely punctual. I never liked to be the first person anywhere, but my mother, Gloriosa Paz, would get frantic if she thought we were going to be late, no matter where. My friends came over to us; except for two or three, no relatives or anybody had come with them. The only ones whose parents came were the nerds. I was so embarrassed. In a desperate whisper I pleaded with my mother, Gloriosa Paz, *Go, go, get out of here, I don't want you to stay*; but she kept saying *No, no, I'm staying now, so hush.* She wasn't leaving until the bus pulled away. A school bus—a rattletrap. *Go, go, you're making me look stupid, I don't want you to hug me or kiss me! Please don't make one of those icky scenes, Mother, I don't want any melodrama— please!* And she insisted that she was *not* leaving, because until she saw that bus drive away with her own eyes, saw to it that I was going off to the School in the Country and not somewhere else, her mind would not be at peace.

Where did she think I was going, the Kaguama Hotel in Varadero?

Finally the teacher in charge of the group called the roll; almost all of us were present, except for two apathetic cases who from that moment on would be considered slackers, and their respective records sullied and filled with insults. I got on the bus. As soon as I was inside, I rushed to sit by a window. With my arms hanging outside the window frame of banged-up aluminum, I picked my mother out of the mass of gawkers and students' parents. Her eyelids were so swollen that her eyes looked like two little peas, and in the blinding light she didn't see me. I waved at her madly, half my body hanging out the window. She made a huge effort and opened her eyes as wide as she could; she looked adrift, like a drowning woman. Then she ran over toward my window, tripped over her own feet, almost killed herself, and finally made it, red-faced and panting, to the metal rim of the window where, standing on her very highest tiptoes and reaching as high as she could, she took my hands. Hers were like ice, and covered with sweat. *Please, m'ijita, take care of yourself. You're all I've got in the whole world. Don't do anything dangerous. I beg you to be careful, responsible. Put on warm clothes when they get you up at dawn— because they'll be getting you up before sunrise—and when you have to work after dark. Don't go around barefoot. And I put in some Kotex in case you become a woman, you know, while you're there. If you get the cramps, get a bottle of water and ask them to heat it up in a double boiler in the kitchen for you, or if there's hot water just fill it up from the tap with the hottest water you can get and rub down here with it, like you were kneading bread.* All this advice she was giving me while the bus was slowly starting to pull away. Her hands slipped off the window frame. She stood talking to herself in the middle of all the people and the noise and the glare, her mouth moving like in the silent movies, thinking I guess that I could still hear her, but the bus's engine was making a deafening racket and my mother slowly turned into a talking dot, back there in the distance, without me, embarrassing me to death with all her little pieces of advice. Finally, her spirits as bedraggled as a wet hen, she turned her back and disappeared in a cloud of dust and blue exhaust.

She'd said I was all she had in the world. I was horrified by the idea of being possessed that way. I was clueless. I've always been clueless about my own life. And other people's lives, too. Until that day, I'd never imagined the possibility that my mother, Gloriosa Paz, might die. It's a terrible image that's invaded my mind and my nightmares since that day. I know that the day she dies, my childhood will be over. Yet the way she sees it, since the day I was born I've been working against her life. Every time she gets a headache it's my fault; I've come to the conclusion that I've been more a torment to her, a misfortune, than a daughter. I even have the feeling that she's sorry she ever gave birth to me. She might even wish I wasn't alive, that I'd never been born. That may be unfair; these thoughts may be nothing but nasty, egotistical ramblings. When you're young, it never occurs to you that you could die just crossing the street.

I got on the bus like a girl climbing astride a shooting star. Once in my seat, though, I started to feel like crying, too. My eyes got all watery. Crying is pretty contagious. And I wasn't the only one—sitting beside me, Irma the Albino was weeping and moaning for all she was worth, and Renata the Physical in the seat ahead of us. She was called "the Physical" because she was more concerned with the physical appearance of people than with their human qualities. She herself was a pretty girl with wavy light brown hair, streaked with gold, that fell halfway down her back, green almond-shaped eyes, a long neck with a constellation of black beauty marks—oh, and she was developed, too! She had firm breasts, and she smelled like a woman at the full of the moon.

Most of the teenage girls were sniffling in silence. Only a very few took a more hardened view of things, making fun of the sentimental ones wiping our noses on our sleeves—but even they were mostly putting on a show of being above it all, as you could see from their trembly lips. Makeup was streaming down cheeks—some of us were wearing our first makeup that day—and the shoe-polish mascara ran off our eyelashes right down to our spastic lips. I turned my head toward the back of the bus. Sitting in one of the back seats was the teacher-guide—because in the country they weren't just teachers, they were "guides"; God knows what they were going to guide us to, or through. Her name was Margot, and we had given her the surname Wrangling; she was our snotty math teacher. Whenever there was a problem at school, a fight or something, the first thing she did was call the parents in for a meeting. She'd wave her hands around, or that copper calendar of hers, and arms akimbo, she'd say, "Let's see what we're going to do about this, then! But let me just say one thing—I won't have any wrangling! Don't think anybody can get away with that with me!"

Wrangling to her meant problems, misunderstandings, gossip, fights—in a word, intolerance.

From time to time she would write something down in a notebook. She was a big, heavyset, light-footed woman with huge arms, a bored look on her face, and a bitter rictus on her lips. Her eyes looked like they'd been injected with egg yolk. You could tell she was not thrilled about having to spend forty-five days with us in the country. She had explained that the camp would be mixed—which meant that there would be one barracks for girls and another one for boys. She threatened everything she could think of if she caught any of us breaking the rigid rules of discipline she was sent to enforce. From that moment on, our motto was to be *Long live the three V's: volunteerism, vanguardism, and virginity!* In a little while, Brigida the Imperfect worked up the spirit to sing—she clapped her hands, trying to get us to join her. That was just when the city was beginning to give way to another kind of landscape, the pavement to turn into highways covered with huge potholes, the houses to become squat to the ground and farther apart.

What's the matter with this driver, why's he driving so darn slow? And what's the matter with this bus, is this as fast as it'll go? we sang as we swiped at our faces to dry the tears. Louder! shouted Brigida the Imperfect, louder! *Light a fire under this thing, man, see if you can speed it up—maybe what this driver needs is a cold beer in a cup!* The driver smiled, pleased that we had taken notice of his innocuous presence by singing songs handed down from generation to generation, from the first Schools in the Country to today. He gave us a look of sympathy.

The countryside became larger and broader, marble buildings gave way to modest houses of concrete and finally to wooden shacks sitting in the middle of broad acres of crops or, on the contrary, in the middle of vacant lots. The campesinos looked at us in bewilderment, their mouths slack, studying us almost resentfully, as though we were some kind of funny-looking insects they'd never seen before. *Here come those people from Havana!* It was like watching the devil drive by in a school bus. Little by little I forgot about my mother, forgot that I had a home, put aside the twinges of conscience about my grandmother's opposition to this journey. I disdained and renounced everything connected with my family and my past. My family, from that moment on, was to be all these girls (who were also homesick with memories, sitting sniffling and wiping away tears) and the camp would be my new and only home.

I suppose I've always asked uncomfortable questions. Even when nobody else thought about a thing, I did, in a split second. What sense did it make to go off and work in the country, leave our true families? Immediately I had an answer for myself: Make contact with nature, prepare ourselves for the future, toughen ourselves against the harsh realities of life, pay for our education with work and sacrifice—this last one I hardly dared to bring up, even if it was a direct quotation from our teachers. Suddenly I had a moment of panic when I thought of dying without seeing my mother, Gloriosa Paz, again. Or of her disappearing behind a mountain or into the depths of a river. I mentioned that horrible impression a few minutes ago—or was it years ago? I thought about my grandmother lying there dying. What if it was my mother that was dying? I saw myself returning from the countryside, opening the door to our room and finding her bloody body lying on the floor, in a state of decomposition, her head split down the middle with a hatchet. I have always had visions of murder. It's something I can't help. I couldn't stand it if she was dead. Although everything seemed to point to the fact that I was the greatest misfortune of her life. Although to her way of thinking I had betrayed her love. Sitting in that bus, unable to get out, accompanied by my classmates, on the way to the country, to the earth, I couldn't stand to think of the death of that creature who had conceived me so that I might, among other calamities, perversely toy with such idiotic ideas, that defenseless creature who bore me only to come to hate me, abhor me, or bear my abhorrence. But at the time, my weapon against that pain was to think even worse of her and not feel obligated for anything—instead, hold her in venomous contempt for having wanted to bear a child, for not having had the courage to eliminate that fetus before it was too late. Before my birth.

The lavish green of nature began to gain ground—sprawling, open spaces that I compared, much too naively I now realize, to infinity. Looking out through the grimy window, I wanted to lose myself in that tangled undergrowth, among those unfamiliar trees, the animals that I figured had to be dangerous, as though the infinite depended not on something out there but on me, my fears and anxieties. The road began to become harder for the bus to navigate, the badly paved highway became a wide ribbon of dust and stones. The tires crunched over huge crusty rocks, and tiny fragments of them were thrown up into our eyes. My hands and mouth were dry, and they felt parchmentlike, feverish, with a delicious stickiness. There was something disgusting about my body that distanced me from myself, from my *previous* self. I was sweating like a stevedore, and the smell, a mouthwatering, incomparable stench that issued from my body, thrilled me. I thought I would swoon.

The trip lasted for hours—hours that seemed like years. Even today, in my memory, it's a journey that is still going on—an endless, delightful jaunt punctuated by stands of palm trees and rebellious jungle. Irma the Albino had fallen asleep, exhausted from all the useless crying. I studied her carefully. She was not exactly an albino, but she was very, very white, almost transparent, with fragile-looking skin, her eyelids crisscrossed with blue veins. Her pink, half-open mouth revealed yellow, melted teeth, from which a string of saliva hung, darkening the khaki-colored fabric of her shirt, turning it chickenshit brown. She was so blond and her hair so fine that her head made you think of an ear of corn. I had a feeling that Irma the Albino would be one of the ones that did not totally enjoy our stay at the School in the Country—

quite the contrary, in fact, she wouldn't be able to stand it. Two seconds later, she started violently shaking, quivering, and from out of a nightmare she began to shriek:

"Mami, Mami, I don't want to go, I don't want to be separated from you! Papi, save me!" Her voice was like a tin whistle, shrill and piercing, or a katydid. "You have to go, you can't not go!" And this time her voice became a deep male rumbling. She was either delirious or a dead person was speaking through her.

The teacher-guide of brigade number 9, Margot Wrangling, started down the aisle, staggering from side to side from the lurching and bumping of the bus through the potholes. When she got to where we were sitting, she took Irma the Albino by the arms and shook her. Then, furious about such behavior, which she considered unforgivable weakness, she slapped her. We were petrified. I could feel the rage in the denseness of the atmosphere, a thick stew of mixed emotions that you could cut with a knife. Irma jerked erect, her eyes bugging out of her head, paler than ever in terror, and she stammered, through the hiccups that racked her chest: "And who do you think you are, hitting me like that?"

"I'm the boss, young lady, and you'd best start getting used to my idea of discipline. You there, what are you girls whispering about? Start singing! I want to see smiles, lots of smiles—vanguard smiles! Come on, you rattle-brains!"

Renata the Physical and Brigida the Imperfect started clapping again, though at first just barely. One, two, three claps. The muscles in Renata the Physical's face were tight, rigid, and her cheeks and temples were flaming red. She stared at the teacher with the hatred of a madwoman and the obsession of a murderess. Yet her lips somehow softened, and slowly, at first just barely, they parted. We all were dying for her to start the song, teach us the lyrics, since Renata the Physical had older sisters who'd already had six years' experience in the Schools in the Country—and had fortunately gotten into the university—so it was they who had copied out the lyrics of all these ridiculous songs, anthems to brutality and stupidity, fully worthy of the occasion and totally humiliating. I fixed my gaze once more on the landscape outside. We were driving down an alley of tall, tall trees whose trunks were utterly and completely new to me. The vision of that line of trees calmed me, and my respiration slowed. The green-yellow mantle hypnotized my mind, the wet smell of the land was like a soothing balm. Renata's voice was intoning the following song, sad and stupid at the same time, whose message could not have been more trivial or clichéd:

> It was a night of full and silver moon, with lightning and with thunder, that a fine and cultured gentleman set out with his coach and coachman. He was dressed in white from head to toe . . .

A cold chill ran from my scalp to my belly, and there it lodged, making a bitter, gooey swamp. I realized that Gloriosa Paz, my mother, would not be there to brush away my anxieties and protect my life. I had to learn to defend my rights alone, and despite the uncertainty, I couldn't manage to avoid a sinking feeling I had never felt before. It was doubt and loneliness—but I wasn't ready yet to give those experiences a name.

I didn't know the names of the trees—branches, leaves, vast tracts of green, a dance of fallen leaves across the ground. The wind, like a tenor recalling accidental encounters, tragic love affairs, broadcast its plaint upon the air. The origins of the countryside's perfumes were alien to me. I was seized with a desire to lie in the grass and weeds and impregnate myself with its fragrance. What immediately seduced me was the sensation that I could not control that space, even if I'd wanted to. Quite the contrary—as I followed its many rises and drop-offs my desire was steered hither and thither with a delight I'd never felt before. I was a babe in diapers so far as the essential details of that vegetation were concerned. And so I was clumsy, unskilled, unlearned . . . How can we human beings survive for so long in such a state of alienation from the mystery, and indifference to it?

The suitcase which had once been a tree heard and spoke. The suitcase was the link between the city and the country. The suitcase, the savior. Through me, the arborescent suitcase, we adapted better and more quickly to the many accidents of youth.

The school bus made its way along the path, leaving the print of its enormous tires in the red mud. It was hard going on that road that ran so bumpily between the lines of trees at each side of the road, and the bus swayed and bobbled like a metal mule—a drunk and stupid mule, at that. The members of brigade number 9 immediately sat up straighter in their seats, lost their sleepiness at the driver's news that they were almost there. Renata the Physical was so nervous she started stuttering. Irma the Albino couldn't stop sneezing and blowing her nose with a tiny linen handkerchief bordered with lace, while she mentally calculated how many hours there were in the forty-five days she had to live with that monster of a teacher who'd slapped her. The square of cloth could hold no more, it was sopping wet and gooey with snot, the result of the emotional allergy brought on by the surprise arrival. Sitting behind Danae was Alicia Machine-Gun Tongue—that was the nickname of the skinny-legged teenager with a body too well developed for her age and a shock of thick tangled hair standing out all over her head, "more hair than brains," the others would say mockingly. The name had been given to her because of the incredible number of words that could pour out of her mouth (a mouth deformed by long buck teeth, which she'd got from being allowed to suck her thumb too long) in no time. Sometimes, in fact, they also called her Twenty-four Per Second, which was the number of frames per second in the movies. Since Alicia Machine-Gun Tongue chattered constantly, trying to seem better educated and more cultured than the rest of her classmates, she could come out with some of the worst gobbledygook imaginable, although nobody ever noticed (she wasn't even listening, herself) because it was like some kind of generalized environmental rattling—but sometimes she managed to string together endless *coherent* speeches, which meant that the teachers had to stay on their toes with her. In any school it's dangerous to have a student that talks all the time, because practice makes perfect, so by staying in shape in the talking department, it'll be that student that arrives at the truth—or *creates* it—before the others. Alicia Machine-Gun Tongue pulled a tiny nail file out of the pocket of her shirt and started filing her thumbnail, at the same time, not seeing more fields planted, asking in a puzzled tone:

"That's it? Potatoes and tomatoes? I don't get it. They should have told us. I do not share the erroneous opinion that we will be of any use in this anonymous enterprise." Her saliva methodically spattered Danae's ear.

"Hush," her friend replied, furiously scratching her neck and scooting away from Alicia Machine-Gun Tongue, which meant squeezing her bulging asthmatic rib cage and round, widely separated breasts closer against the window.

She inhaled the cool breeze of evening, and the smell of the moist plants made her nostrils vibrate as though a little tree swallow were fluttering inside her head, trying to escape. In the distance, a horse appeared, galloping swiftly, with an indistinct rider. She squinted her eyes, trying to see more clearly. It wasn't a man, it looked more like a boy, but it was hard to make out his face because he had a huge palm-frond hat pulled down tight over his ears, not to mention that the speed at which the horse was moving blurred his features. A ray of opaline light made him seem more like a heavenly presence than a living creature. He was dressed in the clothes of a campesino, with dark colors. Then suddenly he was gone, disappearing behind one of the three big whitewashed barracks buildings.

"That must've been Big Foot!" excitedly whispered Alicia Machine-Gun Tongue.

"And who is this Big Foot?" Danae turned, intrigued, toward her classmate.

"A ghost that haunts the camps . . ."

"Oh bullshit. Don't start with the 'camp ghost' shit!"

"I swear by any saint you want to name that it's true. They told me it's this horny ghost that feels up the girls. It sneaks into the barracks at night and while the girls are sleeping it starts getting fresh, pinching nipples and even *down there*."

"Well, don't tell the Albino; she won't get five minutes' sleep for six weeks," Danae scoffed.

"The Albino is a big baby. A dry husk of poor and ludicrous existence. She'll never amount to anything." Alicia Machine-Gun Tongue adjusted her enormous breasts in her one-size-smaller-than-appropriate brassiere. "Plus look at her. She's a fucking ironing board. I'll bet my bumpers she stuffs something in there, because sometimes you can see the outline of something pooching up under her T-shirt."

"All right, girls! Let's get ready for work! Two minutes to touchdown!" cried out the driver joyously.

Brigida the Imperfect made faces at the driver's high-spirited clichés. Renata the Physical, sitting up straight in her seat and then hanging on the handrail that ran the length of the bus, looked as though she were about to go into orbit from happiness and excitement, that obscene pleasure you see in spectators at soccer matches. The rest of the group began to applaud excitedly:

"We're here! We're here! We're finally here!" they cheered.

"All right, listen to me now!" And Renata the Physical, one degree away from having no voice at all, again began to sing that song she had copied out for each of her classmates, so they could learn it by heart:

> It was a night of full and silver moon, with lightning and with thunder, that a fine and cultured gentleman set out with his coach and coachman. He was dressed in white from head to toe, with a medal on his breast, and as he passed the four corners he was stabbed three times in the chest.

The bus parked directly in front of the girls' barracks. On a huge galvanized-metal panel glaring in the sun, the camp's name was written in red, amateurish letters painted with a broad housepainter's brush:

LA FE

What caught Danae's eye, though, was the fabulous tree that stood across from the three buildings. She observed the strong ridged buttresses—they resembled hammocks or cribs sculpted into the thick trunk. The leaves and branches climbed and spread, embroidering the sky with glowing leaves like the flames of sacred candelabra. Danae told herself that that tree looked like a queen, a goddess, all the beauty in the universe combined. Like her suitcase with its smell of Persian calligraphy. Like me, that is, the suitcase that listens to its owner. And she was on the verge of falling to her knees before the image that flooded her eyes with purity and filled her soul, made the hair on her arms and the back of her neck stand up—sent her a message in her very deepest darkest depths, in her soul, perhaps.

"That's a ceiba tree—you must have seen one like it in Havana. There's the one at the Bandstand and the other one in Parque de la Fraternidad," the driver said to her, seeing the interest the young woman had taken in it.

But she didn't recall ever seeing a tree of such elegance and incomparable majesty.

The girls' barracks was to the left as you came into the camp on the highway; it was clear that the building in the center would be the mess hall and also where group activities of any kind would take place—studies, recreation, politics, whatever. The big building to the right was the boys' barracks; the boys were to arrive late that night, several hours after the girls. In a few minutes the other buses began arriving, with the other brigades. The drivers and teacher-guides set about unloading the baggage that had been brought in the buses' luggage compartments; that took about an hour. Meantime the girls had been ordered not to get off the buses, so they sat in their seats, absorbed in their own slightly frantic reactions, the reactions of inexperienced, inexpert creatures, endlessly repeating mottoes learned at school or expressing their emotions through the latest hits they'd been hearing on the radio. Sometimes one brigade would taunt another with a slogan handed down, like the songs, from generation to generation: *What does brigade 1 want? To sleep all day! What does our brigade want? To pay our own way!* Or the slogan might be self-promotion: *What does 9 have? What it takes! And what is it that 9 gives? Better than it takes!*

The bags were set out on the ground or on top of long tables in the mess hall, the drivers got on their vehicles, and the director of the camp, a stylized, muscular man as black and shiny as a lump of coal, blew his whistle to call for the girls' attention. The director's last name was Puga and he was a teacher of literature. Besides being a cheerful, winning young fellow, his four front teeth were cast in Russian gold. An excellent dancer, he'd promised the students that on weekends, at the end of the visiting day for their families, he'd let them have parties with bands, and he told them that he'd even packed a tape player and his own personal tapes in his foot locker. But as great a guy as he was, he could also be the most demanding, rigid disciplinarian in the world. Even so, it was clear that the youngsters felt admiration, respect, and affection for him. He was the typical teacher on the same wavelength as his kids, since he himself didn't look a day over thirty, and the best part of it was that he wasn't some half-ass—he had a degree in computer science, with a transcript of nothing but excellent grades, and even though he could have gotten a position more in keeping with his talents, and much better paying, he had decided (the government hadn't decided for him) to dedicate his skills and knowledge to teaching, and to go into the humanities. He enjoyed the same high esteem among his colleagues, with the exception of certain mediocre teachers who saw him as a threat to the communication, so to speak, between the authorities and the student body, since Puga defended the individual opinions and viewpoints of his students with might and main, and in the teachers' meetings fought hard to obtain the best teaching and learning conditions possible for them. Those who disdained and hated him—among them the school principals in the city—had appointed him director of a mixed camp at a School in the Country because they knew that it was one of the hardest jobs in the world to handle and they were dying for him to make a mess of it so they'd be able to get rid of him once and for all.

Camp director Puga blew his whistle three times, and then, smiling, he shouted out:

"All right, it's not getting any earlier around here! From now on, at the third whistle you people tumble out of wherever you are and fall in, right here!"

The nine groups rushed to follow his orders. Each brigade was made up of twenty-five or thirty girls. At the command of *Fall in!* they all scrambled to form up into military-looking ranks in front of the barracks building that would be their home from that moment on, as their respective guides had explained to them during the journey. Each teacher stood before the group he or she was leading. Except for the camp director, who stood before them all in a clear posture of command. He coughed and cleared his throat and a silence fell that was broken only by the swish of tree branches and the early song of a night bird, a blue grosbeak that had been shaken from its usual routine by the tumult of the girls' arrival .

"Now listen up, you fire ants." The director began his speech, the oily skin of his high cheekbones glistening in the bluish light of the evening. "This is Camp La Fe, and this will be our home for the next six weeks. Every morning we will fall in for morning formation right here, where you're standing now. Reveille will be at five a.m., as you all know . . ."

There was a general murmur of disapproval. Irma the Albino suffered the first dizzy spell; she was about to faint—sweat was pouring even out of her ears, and she hated herself for being the only one feeling hungry and exhausted. Brigida the Imperfect hated her because she was a weakling and because she pretended to be better than everybody else, and she made up her mind to leave a wet booger in her hair the first chance she got and the Albino wasn't looking.

"What's the problem? Don't tell me this is the first you've heard! And while we're on the schedule— every morning we will make our beds, wash our faces, and get dressed as quickly as possible—no more than half an hour. That's not much time, given how few washbasins and toilets there are—twelve for the girls and twelve for the boys. At five forty-five we'll begin to fall in in front of the barracks with our canteens in our hands, so we can be finished with our morning chat here at six on the dot. From here we'll go to breakfast, which will last an hour. It's as little time as possible, since there will only be three compañeras helping us to serve the milk or the cereal and bread. At ten minutes after seven you'll board the buses that will take you to the field your brigade has been assigned to that day. Some of the fields are close to the camp, so the brigades assigned to those fields will march to them . . ."

Another murmur, which the director quickly cut off:

"Won't we, my little workers in the vanguard!"

And at that, what could the girls do but cheer? "Ye-e-es!"

"Naturally, we'll have a rotation for this. The objective is for all of us to share the work equally. Sometimes we'll be going to a field a few meters away, sometimes a few kilometers. We'll all work at a little bit of everything, but mostly it will be in the tobacco—picking, stripping the leaves, stripping the flowers, drying, and sewing it into bundles. It's delicate work, but don't worry, the field leaders and agronomists will explain everything. As for the potatoes, tomatoes, cabbage, weeding is the easiest; it just takes enthusiasm and discipline. For the tobacco you've got to give it not just enthusiasm but also some brainpower. Everybody understand?"

"Yes-s-s-s s-s-sir!"

Irma the Albino couldn't conceal her distaste for the shouting and carrying-on, and she stuck her fingers in her ears.

Danae was standing behind Brigida the Imperfect, who was behind the Albino. She didn't have to move her head much to see Irma's shirt sticking to her back, the marks of sweat making bizarre patterns, like an abstract painting.

Then Irma the Albino raised a limp hand, and then the rest of her went rubbery. Danae was there before Brigida was, catching Irma and hooking her hands under her armpits to hold her up. Irma the Albino turned her pale face toward Danae and made a grateful, goofy grimace that tried to be a smile. Her eyes were glowing feverishly, like two milky blue aggies that kids knuckled down to play marbles with. Puga's lecture continued.

"All right, the boys will be coming late tonight . . ."

"Like always, teach!" cried out a voice camouflaged with a feigned cough from one of the last rows. There were titters and outright laughter and a few feminist exclamations such as *girls rule!* The director smiled, too, then moistened his teeth and lips with the tip of his tongue.

"Not 'teach,' *di-rec-tor,* is that clear? . . . I don't want to add fuel to the fire, but I should make it clear that it's not their fault. We have serious problems with the transportation, so the same buses that brought you here are going back now for the boys. When they get back, we're going to give a big round of applause to the compañero drivers who have been so generous and taken a double shift. We'll invite them to eat with us, so the ration will be reduced. I know you'll understand, all right?"

Murmurs of approval rippled across the formation field.

"So, to make this short, this same formation will be held tonight for the boys, but I wanted to go ahead and have it with you girls so you'd have more time to put on your makeup and get out the sequins . . ." —another wave of hilarity— "The exact time we start work is eight o'clock, no excuses, and we stop at exactly twelve. Lunch will be from twelve-thirty to one forty-five, and then there will be a ten-minute siesta. At two-thirty we start work again in our respective fields or assignments, until five-thirty. Baths from six to seven-thirty. At eight we will have dinner, until ten. Between ten-fifteen and eleven, it's lights-out and rest. As you can see, it's a tight schedule, so we have to stay on it exactly. Any student who disobeys the teacher-guide or the head of the brigade will force us to give demerits. Three demerits means you clean latrines; more than three and depending on the seriousness of the offense, you can lose your right to go to the parties or have your Sunday visits. Tomorrow at the break we'll elect those who meet the criteria to be head of the brigades. Oh yes, I forgot—during each of the two sessions of work in the fields, we'll have a ten-minute break!"

He finished and there was applause mixed with exclamations of several sorts—more hypocritical comments in favor than sincere ones against. The trip had been long and stomachs were demanding nourishment. The director gave them permission to break ranks and go find their luggage. There was a stampede to the mess hall and the teachers tried to impose order too late. Danae was one of the first to find her suitcase, the brown-painted wooden suitcase in the midst of the tumult of other baggage . . .

The suitcase that hears and tells the story, the suitcase still imbued with the time and speed of the city yet already noticeably less stressed-out in the country. The suitcase that was once a tree.

Once she'd dragged it over to one side, she went back to help the Albino, who was half blind from the crying and the big drops of sweat that were dripping from her hair into her face. She was stumbling over every bag that stood between her and her anxiety to recover her suitcase, falling over the other girls, who seized the opportunity to play shove-the-Albino with her white, slippery body. Danae felt sorry for her, so she asked, ladies, for a little compassion for poor Irma, who's not feeling so well, come on, girls, she almost keeled over out there in the welcome party. The other girls, too busy trying to find their bags to bother picking on the alleged sick girl, slacked off.

"Irma, what does your suitcase look like? Come on, tell me so I can try to find it," Danae pleaded.

"I can't . . . I don't remember . . . Look, look, I think it's that one, the one painted blue . . ."

"Did you put your name on it? They're almost all blue."

"Of course. I mean I think I did . . . No, it's not that one," she said more assuredly when she saw that Pancha Flatfoot was wrestling with the one she had pointed out as hers. "Maybe, let's see . . . let's see . . . no, it's not that one either . . . Listen, don't worry about me, you go on, you got yours already, so—"

"I'll tell you, Corn Head, we'll just wait. The last suitcase will be yours. That's the easiest way; come over here, sit down, you need to rest. You look as limp as a wet loaf of bread."

And so it was—when all there was was a single suitcase with streaks of the most boring blue on the planet, the paint just slapped on and the bag battered and lumpy from being tossed around for years, Irma claimed it as her own. Even so, she had to use her fingernail on one corner to be sure her name was still there, written in little near-unreadable yellow letters. Danae, ill humored, tried to hurry the Albino, telling her they needed to get a move on—she had asked her stunned-seeming classmate a thousand times if that one there belonged to her, before it sat solitary and unclaimed and lost-looking. She had always said no, so sure of herself—that couldn't be it, nothing like mine, mine is brighter blue, or maybe not quite as blue, or maybe not as bright. To finally wind up with that bag and none other. A disaster, poor Irma, so skinny, so out of it, so helpless. They got in one of the lines, Danae dragging both her suitcase and her semi-invalid friend's. From the mess hall the girls went in order of their brigade numbers to the camp's barracks number 1.

Inside, there was a damp cold that smelled of rotting burlap and long-settled dust. The floor was unpolished and the girls' feet dragged and scuffed on the sharp, rocky droppings of dried cement, the irregularities in the rough floor. Several years earlier, the place had been a farm for prisoners doing forced labor. On the walls there were still traces of love messages, hearts pierced by arrows: *Loly, stay true. If you make it with another man, I'll commit harikari.* Another one said, *My life has no meaning without you, I don't know why I killed you.* One was in blood: *Adry, I write your name with my heart in my hands.* It was signed *The eternal fugitive.* The newcomers warily studied all these personals from the underworld, but the worst impression was caused by the bunks they were supposed to sleep in: hammered together from rough branches cut out of the trees, they were no more than four sticks stood upright and four laid out longways horizontally, two on the top bunk and two on the bottom. Across the horizontals were strung rectangular fragments of stiff, porous, raggedy burlap for a mattress, though the cots had been used for so long they were more like big loose pockets—that is, the body of the person who slept on the top bunk hung down onto the person on the bottom, and the back and buttocks of the person on the bottom dragged on the floor. They didn't promise much comfort, and the concentrated filth became evident the minute someone brushed against the thick, primitive uprights or put even the lightest object on the "cot"; dust would rise in reddish clouds and hang in the air.

The female teacher-guides took the cots in the center of the barracks so they could maintain better surveillance over the two doors. But then from heavy canvas tarpaulins they constructed a kind of tent that isolated them from their charges. The male teachers—because some of them were males—would live in the boys' barracks, of course. Brigade number 9 was assigned to the very end of the barracks, right next to the door that opened onto the toilets and the showers. Danae managed to get a bunk next to the door, and she also had the good fortune to have the head of her bed against a window. I need to make clear that the architecture of these barracks was that of the old tobacco sheds—that is, the place that had once been used for sewing, hanging, and drying the tobacco leaves. Irma the Albino tried to light on the bunk next to Danae but a small protest broke out when Renata the Physical objected. Finally Irma had to content herself with putting her things underneath Danae, who of course had chosen the advantageous upper bunk. In the next bunk Renata was on top and Alicia Machine-Gun Tongue was on the bottom; they didn't have a window. Not that they minded—in fact, they preferred to have as little contact with the outside as possible, for fear of rats.

Rolled up at the foot of each cot was a ticking mattress, most with the cotton stuffing poking out here and there, and all stained with food, the ejaculations of decades, diarrhea, and, apparently, menstruation—that, at least, was what the girls imagined, so as not to have to sleep in a bed where somebody's throat had been slashed. The "campers" unrolled the disgusting affairs and not without a wince or a grimace fitted their sheets to them—crisp sheets redolent of lye, yellow laundry soap, and the rooftop sun they'd been hung in to dry. The biggest problem was the luggage; there was no space for it. Renata the Physical, brimming over with expertise transmitted to her by her sisters before her, suggested to the girls who were going to sleep on the top bunk that they wedge their suitcases at their feet, between the bedposts, and that those on the bottom put theirs under the bunks, on the floor—it was that easy. In the midst of fights, laughing, pushing and shoving, and some hair-pulling—some in jest, some serious—each camper found a place for her suitcase as best she could. Danae was one of the first to put her space in order. She jumped up onto her bunk and sank into it like a frog in a stagnant pond. She realized that if she covered herself with her blanket from head to foot, the bed would look as though it were perfectly made and she wasn't there. It occurred to her that she had found an excellent hiding place, especially for a little privacy. As usual, she had begun to weave a little secret. She lay there unmoving for minutes, absorbed in the sound of her own breathing, and she might have managed to fall asleep had it not been for Irma the Albino, underneath her, who was making so damn much noise with her bottles and jars, the cans of condensed milk, the things she dropped and the muttered swearing that went with them. Renata the Physical was also kicking up some dust. She had turned on a portable radio, a model so sophisticated that it practically begged to be stolen, and was turning the knob from one station to the next, refusing to be content to listen to just one. After going from one end of the dial to the other about a hundred times, she chose a program of campesino music, but she began to make fun of the rural sounds of Coralia and Ramón Veloz, which were, according to her, her grandfather's favorites on those long Sunday afternoons of his. Alicia Machine-Gun Tongue—this was strange—hadn't made a sound for minutes now, not a single syllable. She was concentrating on sewing up the seat of her pants, which she'd torn as she'd walked past a barbed-wire fence and caught her pants on it when she pushed somebody out of the way in her scramble to be the first to get to the barracks. Her mouth was busy not talking but whistling the theme song of a French movie not suitable for minors. Brigida the Imperfect was dragging and pushing her stuff into place far from her friends, who could see her at a distance over there, in a huge set-to with a big ugly overgrown girl that looked like a weight lifter. They were fighting over a can of evaporated milk that the other girl had instinctively tried to swipe. On the other side of the room, Migdalia Fake Eyelashes and Carmucha Women's Shelter were arguing over a pair of flip-flops that had suddenly vanished from under their owner's nose—Migdalia, that is, who was accusing Carmucha of swiping them just to bug her—because that was all she ever did, go around bugging people. Carmucha was protesting that the last thing in the world she'd swipe would be a pair of sandals that smelled of eighteenth-century toe jam. And besides, they were like ten sizes too big for her.

After a while, Danae felt a terrible heat that seemed to be coming up through the mattress. From the chorus of crickets and the splashing of the turtles in the pond that she was beginning to hear, and the rumbling sound of the school buses and excited yelling of male voices that suddenly came from outside, she realized that it was getting late.

"The males have landed!" Pancha Flatfoot called out, with a certain repressed desire to descend to the boys' level.

"About time. I hope we can eat now, finally—I'll tell you, my belly button's stuck to my spinal cord," complained Irma the Albino, ending her speech with a long sigh of exasperation.

Danae uncovered her face. From the rafters, a rat the size of a cat was looking down on the activities of the new arrivals. When it realized that it was being watched, it ran for a hole between the beams and disappeared. Danae threw the blanket to one side and jumped down to the floor. She was about to yell *Rats! Rats! There are rats in here!* but she opted for silence when she bumped into the questioning, terrified, ready-to-panic-at-any-moment face of Irma the Albino, who had sensed that something was amiss—that something *horrible* had happened to scare her friend.

"What!? What did you see? What's happening?!"

"Nothing, goofball, nothing. Don't be such a wuss."

"If you don't want me to have a heart attack, in the future do me the fucking favor of climbing down with a little less energy, then—you looked like somebody was after you with a knife."

The director gave the male brigades their arrival briefing, and the boys picked up their bags and set themselves up in their respective bunks the way the girls had hours earlier. Puga stood at the entrance to the women's barracks, carefully averting his eyes so as not to look inside; he wouldn't want to catch some young woman in her underwear. His gold Russian teeth gleamed, and Margot Wrangling took that as a green light to order her female charges to form up in front of barracks number 1.

"All right, you rattlebrains, fall in! Let's get a move on, we haven't got all night! Fall in and be quick about it, you guppies—shake those tail fins! One more minute and there'll be no dinner for you tonight, one more minute and I'll be giving every girl a demerit. Let's move!"

The teacher was shrieking, obsessed with the infinitesimal power bestowed upon her by destiny. She was a deformer of personalities, a demeaner of spirits, a guillotine of all inspiration in these girls' teenage years, a wing-cutter, a woman frustrated and therefore a frustrator of others' talents, a woman ashamed of her miserable past, sick of her gray present, and eternally distrustful of her future, which was lacking in any promise whatsoever.

Behind Margot Wrangling, Mara, the chemistry teacher, leapt to her feet. She was a slender, ethereal woman with an enormous head and curly, burned, brittle hair standing up all over it—the result of a permanent gone bad. Her green eyes, bulging out of their sockets, were sure signs of a serious thyroid problem, and the skin of her long face looked as though it had been smeared with mustard and pepper. She was a fright. The girls called her Mara Medusa, for obvious reasons. She had short arms and legs and a long torso, a low-slung ass, and a tiny, tiny waist—she looked as though somebody had tried to pinch her in two. She had such a terrible underbite that when she talked you thought her chin was going to hit her nose. On top of all this, she bit her nails, and she liked to drum her stumplike fingers on the desk while she attacked her students with impenetrable oral exams—*cutaraba, tibiri tabara, tibi lacutaraba, cutabara, tabara,* went the drumming fingertips maddeningly.

For some time there had been much talk, spread by both teachers and students, that Mara Medusa was an old maid, while there were others who said that she'd been married twice but that both husbands had died on her. The truth was, she'd have them know, she had married five different bums of one stripe or another—not all at the same time, of course. Tired of all the rumors, she decided one day to take the five photo albums of the various weddings to school. How did the woman manage to camouflage her defects (she was a walking disaster area) long enough to catch such beauties? Or maybe her Medusa looks had frozen them in their tracks. All five of the catches had the following features: they were tall, dark, with blue eyes, sensual lips, muscles here and muscles there, hairy where they should have been and smooth where they should have been, and judging by their smiles, nice guys—and all of them in love with her, the ugliest woman that ever walked the earth! Plus, she made it very clear that she never let them leave her—it was always her that asked for the divorce. Had she ever gotten pregnant? Of course she had! The last time, seven years ago, her fifth husband had gotten her pregnant while she was still working at the school before this one. She was proud of the twin boys her first husband had given her, the daughter from her second, the boy from the third. The fourth husband told her he was sterile, but he managed to give her a pair of Siamese twins joined at the head, the forehead to be exact, a problem they were trying to solve through delicate surgery, since one of them wanted to be a dancer and the other one a stewardess. From her union with the fifth husband, poor thing, she gave birth to an ear. Uh-huh, when she went to have the baby, what came out was an ear twenty inches long and weighing eight pounds four ounces, with two little legs and two little arms. Period. That was it. No little eyes to see with or a little mouth, even a crooked one, to smile at its mami with, or a little behind to smack when it misbehaved. As though an ear could misbehave. She had really wanted to coo to the ear, so the first words it heard would be from her, but the neonatologist, a very circumspect man, said, *Señora, I'm sorry to tell you this, but you'll have to yell—it's deaf.*

So that was why Mara Medusa had turned so bitter and mistrustful. And she was a good mother, she really was. So self-sacrificing that during the Schools in the Country, when she had to do her patriotic duty, she left her children, entrusting to her mother the care of the Siamese twins Amor and Deseo, names she had given them because they had been conceived out of love and in a mad frenzy of desire, and the Ear, which had been christened Fina. The other children, the twins Rótulo and Reto and the others, Usnavy and Estálin, were sent to their respective fathers. It was hard on her, because she had asked over and over again to be allowed to attend the camps at least with the handicapped children, but the request was denied, due to their physical impediments. She accepted the decision without a word, though her heart was broken—a phrase she borrowed from high-ranking politicians who were closet queens and pseudocultivated. On weekends Mara the Wheezer, as she was also called, due to her chronic asthma, would request a pass and go off to the city to give her brood the care that only she, their true mother, could.

Anyway, the Medusa leapt up at the first shouts and handclaps from Margot Wrangling.

"Let's go, ladies, get a wiggle on there! The chow's getting cold!"

Despite the fact that the girls could not bear the teacher's embittered personality, they felt sorry for her because of all the misfortunes—one right on top of another, it seemed—that she had suffered, and they jumped to obey her orders. Then came two other teachers—English and biology—whose personal lives were pretty tame in comparison but who overacted dramatically (to compensate for their usual extraordinary passivity) when it came time to perk up their charges or correct them for improper behavior.

"Think you girls can move any slower?" sneered one, the English teacher, whom the girls called Tícher. She had her work cut out for her in a country where English was considered the language of the enemy.

Danae banged her spoon on the bottom of her aluminum canteen cup, more to imitate her schoolmates than out of any particular desire to make noise. Renata the Physical couldn't sing; her laryngitis had gotten progressively worse. Alicia Machine-Gun Tongue was busy mentally sculpting her next speech; Migdalia False Eyelashes and Carmucha Women's Shelter were still arguing, although not about the flip-flops anymore, since they had turned up some time ago in Migdalia's own suitcase. The subject of the new argument was the sleeping arrangements. They were trying to figure out some way one of them could sleep a little longer one day, the other the next. Migdalia would begin by making both beds and the next day Carmucha would, while Migdalia gained a few minutes of extra sleep—or so Carmucha had decided.

"And why do I go first?" Migdalia (with her Maybelline-blue eyelashes) asked.

"Aren't you the one with the great idea? So you go first!" Carmucha shot back, and the logic of it momentarily rendered Migdalia speechless.

Then she leaned into Carmucha's ear and whispered, "Well, that's right—it was my idea, so you go first or forget about it!" And to punctuate her right to the first turn, she reached up and pinched the other girl's neck.

And so they went on, back and forth, until they stepped out into the shocking chill of the night.

The darkness was filled with a fragrance of flowers or fruit whose names Danae did not yet know. Over there, and there, and there beyond, the shimmering shadows of dancing tree limbs, bushes, vines twisting and bobbing in the wind. She opened her mouth and sucked in the wetness of the air, and then she stepped off the concrete step and her foot sank almost to the ankle into soft mud. She found her place in line, after Irma the Albino—she was next to last, Emma was behind her. Emma the Menace, they called her. Although Danae got along well with her, Emma, unlike Alicia Machine-Gun Tongue, was shy, almost skittish; she never felt like talking to anybody, much less early in the morning. She spent her life avoiding looking in people's eyes; she didn't like anybody—everybody was half-assed, mediocre. All she wanted was for people to leave her alone. (In that, she could have been Brigida the Imperfect's twin sister.) The other thing she wanted was to sleep; she *lived* to sleep. There would be moments when she'd wake up and join the general cheeriness, sing along with the others, even laugh, but then something would trip her switch and she'd turn off like a light, fall into a silence that could last for two or three days. But she never failed to answer Danae if Danae asked her something or said something to her. She would even converse, almost, with her—not much, but at least she'd talk, even if it was to complain and say how bored she was. Emma came up dragging an old leather jacket that had belonged to her Basque father when he was in the army in Africa. The Chaw, she called it, because it was so tattered and beat up and raggedy that when she put it on she felt like she was putting on the chewed-up stub of a cigar, or the butt end of a plug of chewing tobacco. That night wasn't especially cold, not cold enough for such a heavy coat, but Emma was determined to ward off the "evil eye," protect herself from people's envy, mean-spiritedness, spells, and witchcraft, and the Chaw was her shield, her amulet, the symbol of her defense. Plus the buttons were made out of real jet.

"Danae, look, look at the sky—look at all those stars! All running together, practically! It's like scrambled eggs made out of stars!" she whispered—since surely it wasn't the Chaw that was talking.

Several minutes earlier Puga had launched into a new speech thanking the bus drivers, who had gone the extra mile (he said, oblivious to his own metaphors) and worked double shifts to bring the rest of the students out to the School in the Country here. He asked for applause for the drivers; there was a round of robotic clapping. He invited the drivers to eat in the mess hall with the students. The faces of the kings of the road did not betray any great enthusiasm for the idea; it was obvious that they were expecting a more metallic form of recompense—which there was no denying they deserved. Not to mention that the cooks had intimated that since it was the first night, there would be white rice with peas and papaya slices in syrup, and that was it. Oh, and the soft drink, that stuff that tasted like medicine, B complex with iron, to be exact. Tasted like medicine, maybe, but as a matter of fact it was actually brake fluid, just the thing for a thirsty bus driver! A tribute almost on purpose, you might say. Not even drunks drank that stuff, but when you're thirsty even ditchwater tastes good.

Puga had turned into a talking machine. He was now saying something about the importance of symbols and raising the flag. Emma the Menace and Danae were barely listening; they stood in wonder, their eyes fixed on the immensity of the bluish-black night sky with its sparkling, glinting stars above their heads, their feet covered with icky mud and ants, their keys hanging around their necks, giving a chill to that hollow between their breasts still unexplored by hands tingling with lust. The full moon was three times brighter than the lights on the barracks roof. A country moon, rounder and closer than any city moon had ever been. The crickets' concert grew louder and the frogs chimed in with their part. Danae thought, at least, that they were frogs, since she'd never heard such melodious belches in her life.

"That's frogs, bullfrogs," Emma whispered in her ear, her eyes still exploring the stellar labyrinths.

"Would somebody tell me what item those two students have lost up in the stratosphere?"

The voice broke into the girls' extraterrestrial fascination, but they realized it was them Puga was referring to only when a wave of giggles drowned out not only the director's voice but the chorus of frogs and crickets as well. Puga saw that his remonstrance had had its effect when the two girls' surprised eyes locked on him—or pretended to look at him when in fact a curtain of stars clouded their retinas.

After a while, they were able to look at the director without listening to him. Emma the Menace kicked Danae's right heel as a prelude to an announcement hissed between her teeth:

"In the seventh row of boys, the fourth one from the back—he's the one for you."

Danae answered *uh-huh* without moving her lips, since the director never took his eyes off her.

"It's Andrés Crater Face . . . I know him, he's in my brother's room at school," Emma added.

Andrés Crater Face would always joke with her that he could eat her alive, just like a girl sandwich, with garlic, onion, pickles, ketchup, and mustard. Andrés Crater Face was called Andrés Crater Face because his face was covered with pimples filled with yellow pus, ready to explode. Andrés, with or without the craters, was not a boy Danae could be interested in. He lifted weights, no doubt about that, at least judging by the muscles in his arms and the fact that his neck was thicker than his waist. One of those cavemen types, scholars of the Charles Atlas School and suntans on the rooftops, probably a good dancer and even well endowed between the legs. But she was looking for something else—words, poetry, difference. She totally looked the other way; she didn't want anything to do with jocks, she knew them by heart already. Lots of coochy-coochy but not an inch of intellect, not a pinch of romance, not the slightest dollop of real sensitivity. What did she want with a sweet-talking brute, an insensitive octopus?

Emma the Menace gave her a shove, to get her to move as the line formed for the mess hall. The speech was over and the brigades were beginning to march off in order, alternating one file of girls and one of boys. Andrés never took his eyes off her; their gazes met and he grinned. To top it off he thought he was hot stuff; he was not just a jock, he thought of himself as a girl magnet. That's why he was a bodybuilder; he built up his ego with bones and muscles and tendons and arteries.

BEFORE THEY ENTERED the mess hall they had to cross an ocean of mud; inside their shoes they all now carried pounds and pounds of warm, wet, gooey muck. Danae's toes stuck together, and she felt like there was some kind of porous fabric between each one. Her feet felt webbed—like ducks' feet. The mess hall was another big remodeled tobacco drying shed—or reclaimed, since there was no remodeling to it; running along on each side was a line of three gigantic tables with rough plank bases and gray, unpolished marble tops. At the rear of the building a counter had been set up, with three huge cooking pots, and standing behind them were three old campesino women who served the food up on trays. It would be a while before Danae's turn came, and from the rear of the line she could see towers of aluminum trays piled one atop another; beside them was a can, also of aluminum, though dark with age and dirt, with the eating utensils. The trays were warped out of shape and banged up from years of use, slippery from accumulated grease; the knife, fork, and spoon handles were bent, the forks' tines twisted, and all were encrusted with dried food. From one of the gigantic cauldrons steam rose off the rice, a gray-colored mass that looked like wallpaper paste. Somebody said there were weevils in it, too. In another there was hot pea soup, without any seasoning whatever. One of the teachers called the women who were ladling out the food *tías,* aunts, with false kindness. The *tía* at the rice pot would spoon up a ladleful of the rice and plop it down in the well on the left side of the tray; the sound it made was like cow flop hitting the bottom of a ravine. The *tía* with the pea soup turned out a ladle of greenish mush in the middle section. The third one was serving up a reddish-looking substance they said was "papaya in syrup." Smashed papaya. Each student was supposed to stick their hand into a wet burlap sack for the bread. The water was straight out of the faucet, lukewarm, and tasting of mossy pipe. So the information broadcast by Radio Grapevine to the effect that there would be guava paste and brake fluid had been false, slightly.

The mess hall with its swarm of youngsters reminded you of a prison movie, thought Danae. She sat between Irma the Albino and Emma the Menace, who was not mute, as we all know, but did fall into long periods of deep taciturnity. Across from them sat Salome the Satrap, Pancha Flatfoot, and Venus Putrefaction. Salome the Satrap was a climber, envious of everybody and as calculating as they come; she dreamed of marrying some famous somebody, it didn't matter much who, and living in a mansion with servants—oops, sorry, with *compañeras and compañeros that worked in the house with her*—taking long trips and actually becoming famous herself, no matter what the cost, even if she had to write bad poems and worse novels about shoe stores, because she had a thing, as everybody knew, for shoes, and besides, she thought it was presumptuous to call yourself a poet. Pancha Flatfoot was good people, really good people, but foulmouthed—a mulatto girl with broad shoulders, her hair dyed dirty blond with Batey soap, hydrogen peroxide, and days up in the limbs of a yagrumo tree, hoping the sun would bleach out that monster head of hair of hers. But if she lost track of time and stayed up there too long, she ran the risk that her kinky hair would turn out as silvery as the backside of those very yagrumo leaves. She had the biggest feet in the school, and she used Micocilen powder to counteract the terrible smell of moldy blue cheese that they gave off. Venus Putrefaction had become famous not for any external disintegration or decay but rather for her farts. As anyone who had ever smelled one could tell you, her intestines were clearly filled with pus and gangrene. She had terrible digestion, she said, and because of her constant constipation, she always had a little tip of shit just peeking out her asshole, which produced farts that would put out candles at ten feet and smelled like utter putrefaction. There was a plant, Venus' belly button, that was famous for calming inflammations, scrofula, that sort of thing, drying up running sores, and soothing stomach pains; the leaves and roots were said to break up stones—not the philosopher's kind, but in the kidneys—so you could pee like new again; it was also recommended for fathering sons. Well, someday Venus' anus will be famous, too, but for environmental pollution.

The din of the three-hundred-something spoons and forks banging against the metal trays, plus the conversations, the yelling, and the laughter, was deafening. The teachers were the last to find their seats and dig in to dinner, and they huddled together over at one corner of the last table that was free. And no matter how much Puga, with a piece of bread in his hand and spoonfuls of rice and pea soup in his mouth, waved at people to try to get them to keep it down, nobody paid him the slightest attention. Irma the Albino finished before anyone else, and she polished her tray with a little piece of bread she'd saved till the last. Then she stuck her face in it and smiled to contemplate her cheery face, her cheeks red from the heat of the trip, her smile from the sense of well-being the mess had brought to her insides.

"Don't push those weevils to the side, now; think of them as the protein in our diet, girls . . . Listen, Danae, don't think I didn't notice that you've got an admirer," said Salome the Satrap slyly, licking her spoon. "I saw the way Andy Crater Face was licking his chops over you, girl."

With her fingertips she smoothed her hair down tight over her temples.

"I find him totally unfloginistic," Danae said, which meant what it sounded like it meant.

"Oh, please, *niña,* don't give me that bullshit—you don't got such a face on you that you can be so choosy, you know," the Satrap insisted.

Irma the Albino smelled a storm on the horizon and she slinked up out of her seat, pretending that she was going to rinse off her tray. Pancha

Flatfoot also sidled off, but she headed for the pots in case there might be a chance of a second helping. Emma the Menace was gnawing at a piece of gristly bone she had swiped from the girl sitting beside her, and she was playing dumb, her eyes and thoughts apparently focused on the far, empty spaces of the Other Side. Danae refused to rise to the bait. There are days when you need to let the pimple come to a full head before you pop it. She fixed her eyes on a file of coconut-palm cockroaches that were marching in lockstep past the table, as though they were in a world of their own. Finally one of the girls gave the cry of alarm:

"No, it's not the dessert walking off all by itself, it's not guava slices or rivers of papaya! It's the King Kongs of cockroaches, girls! Watch out!"

And the table emptied as though by magic. The boys crept over, boots raised, to squash the filthy creatures and watch their guts explode all over the floor. They crushed the roaches' carapaces under their heavy rubber boot soles, and within seconds the entire army of coconut-palm cockroaches was yellow and green pulp.

In the camp, everything was in lines and files and rows. Rows of bunks, a line of tired youngsters to get in to eat, stacks of trays, a row of faucets to rinse the trays off with. The trash cans were also in neat rows—a line of cans set in concrete in the open air. Another row of lightbulbs, barely glowing. For lack of detergent, the trays were washed in water and scraped with fingers to dissolve the grease. Viscous yellowish pools of greasy water formed in the clogged drains. Anyone who turned their tray in with bits of food left on it would receive a demerit, Margot Wrangling assured them. The *tías* burnished the cauldrons with charcoal ash. Once Danae had stacked her tray on the leaning tower, she hurried off to find her toothbrush. She tiptoed into the barracks building to keep from getting the floor muddy, and returned to the sinks to brush her teeth, since there were no washbasins anywhere. She went around the back to return to the barracks so she could rinse off her feet in the showers, wash away the clumps of dirt stuck to the bottom of her shoes and even inside them, on her heels and ankles, the arch of her foot, even between her toes. She walked back barefoot, balancing on the top of a low brick wall that bordered the walkway.

She rummaged around inside her suitcase to find her work clothes. She brought her nose down close and was thrilled with the delicate fragrance of papyrus, of Persian poetry. I held her spellbound for several seconds. Dressed as though she were ready to weed tomatoes or pick potatoes, she sank into the mattress; she shut her eyes and pretended to be asleep. She heard the other girls as they ran into the room—all as danaidic as she herself. Lots of talk about how little food there was, and how awful it was—not just the way it was cooked, but *it,* you know, *what* it was, yech—or listen, didn't anybody want to go out and rap a little with those males over there? Let's go outside and sing, you guys—don't be such sticks in the mud! Tomorrow morning there's no *way* I'm getting up at daybreak! Oh god, *niña,* I miss my bed! Not me, I don't miss a thing, not a thing—here at least I can do anything I feel like doing! Could I borrow some toothpaste? I left mine on the television, at home. Oh great, I knew it—I *hate* it when people want to borrow my stuff! I can't decide whether to take a shower tonight or tomorrow morning. Well, at least wash those feet and smelly armpits of yours—and down *there,* too, if you'll be so kind. With that fish smell and all that grit all over you there's no way you're sleeping anywhere *near* me. Okay—which one of you comedians hid my radio? Ohmygod, these roaches are the size of a tiger—the rats must be like elephants. Shut up—nobody wants to hear your whining! I think I'm getting a cavity . . . I think *I'm* getting asthma, I can feel it coming on. So go to the infirmary. The medic hasn't gotten here yet; he's supposed to come tomorrow. A medic? Oooh! Yeah, and I hear he's *very* sexy—makes you so hot you feel faint every fifteen minutes. I heard Tícher drooling over him when she was telling Mara Medusa about him. Did you see how skinny the Medusa's gotten? She definitely looks like somebody ate the chicken and left the bones. I'd say she's wasting away; it's probably that consumption of hers. Instead of Mara Medusa we need to start calling her Mara the Wheezer. Ha, ha, ha! That's great. Shh! They're going to hear us. I was asking around, and the town is not far—just go across that tobacco field back there behind us. When are we going to do it? Do what? Go to town, stupid. Oh. Not yet, it's too soon. And besides, we need to get some of the boys to go with us. Andy Crater Face and Adenoids. Andrés has the hots for Danae, you can tell already. Bullshit! And speaking of Danae Duckbill Lips, where *is* that girl, anyway? She must be around somewhere, the doofus. No, you're all wrong, Irma the Albino said serenely, she's right here, under the bedspread, AWOL, sound asleep. Emma the Menace, likewise sunk deep into the hollow of her cot, was meditating. Renata the Physical was copying new lines of poetry into her personal poetry album, which she called the Autograph. Alicia Machine-Gun Tongue was explaining, though nobody was listening to her, the reasons a person should act honestly, simply, and humbly in living her life. *The reasons are the following,* she was saying. *It's not worth it to get people to notice you, there's no reason to put yourself out so people will point their fingers at you, there's no reason to stand out from the crowd. If you're unassuming nobody will notice you and it'll be easy for people to like you, you'll get what you want without having to make a big issue out of everything, and you won't arouse people's envy. Thinking that you're superior, that you're better than everybody else, is hard on the nerves, not to mention that it doesn't let you concentrate on your own personal, individual dreams and desires—you waste energy competing with everybody. Things ought to be done with honesty, without pretensions— that way, in the long run, you come to like yourself. Because the goal is your own self. If you achieve humility, your nervous system will be strong and immune to disease; nothing will be able to harm it. You shouldn't chatter all the time; I talk too much, I know it, I need to learn to shut up once in a while, to be modest and quiet.* And on and on she went, chattering like a parrot, totally out of touch with the moment, all the while making and unmaking her bed, trying unsuccessfully to get the sheet to lie absolutely tight and flat. The noise in the big room subsided considerably when one large group decided to go outside and sit under the trees and another to go over to the mess hall to hang out with the boys and watch television.

That night the Cubavisión channel was showing *Historia del Cine,* and the girls were dying to sink their teeth into the announcer, whom the girls all called Eyedrops because he was so soothing to the eyes, a suavely handsome, maybe even pretty type that they also called Tropicola, the Pause that Refreshes, and also Antilles Ecstasy. That night Antilles Ecstasy would be presenting and commenting on the third in a series of westerns. Nobody gave a shit about westerns or John Huston or anything else, so they turned down the volume and sat back to watch the announcer's virile gestures. But he was so vain that he kept a surreptitious eye on the studio monitor every second; he was constantly pulling up a sock so that his fans at home could see that it matched his shirt—not that it mattered, since back then TV was still in black and white. Or he would smooth down his sideburns, then delicately pull at his nose, using just the very tips of his index finger and thumb. To change the channel the girls had to go through the boys; the boys, though, were conflicted, because despite their innate love of westerns, they were desperate to see a baseball game that night, between the Industrials and the Hempmakers. Tele-Rebel would surely show it. Oh, no doubt there'd be a fight over which channel to watch.

The window at the head of Danae's bunk was open. She put her arms out behind her head and her hands were bathed in the night's coolness. She smiled because she suddenly felt she'd entered a Gothic novel; she expected that when she opened her hands, dew from the starry heavens would fall upon them. She sensed the nearness of a royal palm, its tresses tousled by the night breeze; she sensed the nearness of a sweet mystery. And as she was playing at that game of catching at the uncatchable she fell into a trance and then, within a few minutes, lulled by a guajiro melody, a profound sleep.

> *I love you as a Cuban, tierra libre,*
> *and as a campesino, naturally,*
> *I love you as a Cuban, patria libre,*
> *and as a campesino, naturally.*
> *How beautiful the new-plowed fields*
> *bathed by the summer's heat, vida mía.*
> *I love to see my brother, tierra libre,*
> *with his campesino ways,*
> *assaulting fields of weeds, vida mía,*
> *as though on a battlefield,*
> *wresting from the earth, vida mía,*
> *its natural wealth, tierra mía.*

I, the arborescent suitcase, who up until now had listened and recounted, at that moment made contact with the labyrinths of her mind. I managed to express my melancholy amazement through Danae's dream and her revelation.

And she dreamed about you—she didn't know yet who you were, but she dreamed of your faceless silhouette. Outlines, shapes, nothing more. Not you, Andrés—she still didn't know you well enough. She did not yet know that you would become her first boyfriend, or that she would love you without ever thinking seriously about love, or that you two would get married and have two daughters. She dreamed of a *you* that wasn't quite you, but rather an unnamed, unnamable *you*, a *you* that I was about to invent when your *you*, the *you* of Andrés, showed up. She dreamed of hands that were not yours and that took hers, held them. They were long, and delicate, extremely delicate in their courting. Yet firm—they tried to pull her out into the dense darkness of the night. They were *determined* to pull her out of her bunk, and they were as hot and fevered as ocean waves in August. Danae was not naked, yet she suddenly felt a current of cold and her skin turned to gooseflesh. But the hands warmed her. *It's Big Foot,* she told herself, struggling to wake up. It was the ghost of Big Foot who'd come to touch her body as she slept. But they weren't a man's hands, much less the ice cold hands of mischievous spirits. These were warm hands, as I said, and with their index fingers they began to tickle her palms, the hollows of her hands. She knew that was the way boys invited girls to do a little coochy-coochy with them—they tickled girls there where the lines of the hands made an M—an M for *madre,* an M for *muerte,* and for so many other superimportant things whose first letter was M.

No matter how much she struggled, she couldn't manage to break the dream. The hands' owner—she suspected it was a woman, or a girl or a little boy, because they were so soft and warm—whispered, *Soon you will know who I am. —Are you going to kill me?* she dreamed or thought. She heard giggling, or really more like tittering—tiny shards of laughter, tinkling like pieces of a broken pitcher of fine crystal as they pittered down on her eyelids. Inside the dream, I was very stupid. A dumb old suitcase that watched things. Danae was not named Danae anymore; she had the name of a plant, which slithered out of our memory the moment we emerged from the dream and awoke. In the dream, as I recall, I hated being me and she repudiated herself. Or was it she and I trying to give ourselves away? Who wants to be us? Come on, all of you, catch our I's, catch them. And I pitched that absurd *I* to see who'd run their ass off to catch it.

I am certain that that sense of intense pleasure from hands protecting, kneading hers lasted for a long time, yet the dream was over quickly. She awoke with her face ice cold; she could barely open her eyes—her eyelashes were stuck together with some icky, gooey substance that smelled of mint and medicine. Those fucking bitches in the barracks had squeezed a whole tube of toothpaste onto her face! It looked like meringue on the top of a face pie. The giggles at her confusion when she woke up confirmed that she was the victim of a nasty practical joke. Plus, her feet had been tied to the bedposts, so when she tried to get up she fell headlong off the bunk and hung there with her skull two inches off the floor. *Guffaws!* Emma the Menace and Irma the Albino helped Danae get up and in the cot again, and then they untied the rope that was cutting off the circulation to her feet. Irma ran to the bathroom to wet a towel and clean off her face. Laughter echoed in the cavernous barracks. Irma the Albino hurried back nervously and wiped at the skin as though she were a nurse and Danae a wounded soldier in the Second World War.

Then Danae looked down at her sticky hands; she smelled them, licked them—it was honey. This was no dream. Some real person had covered Danae's hands with honey. She leaned back and stretched her neck until her head was out the window; she saw no one, but she heard a horse galloping away. Emma the Menace startled the jokers by picking up a bucket full of piss and swinging it back and forth, threatening to sling it all over them. The other girls ran to find the boys and tell them about their latest achievement.

"We put toothpaste on Danae Duckbill Lips! And she didn't do a thing! What a loser, a rattlebrain, a wuss!"

"If you want to hear the chamber pot's song, toorala toorala tooralalee . . . then you just give a listen to what I say, toorala toorala tooralalee . . . When you sit down to shit and it's time to clean your rear, toorala toorala tooralalee . . . don't wipe with newspaper 'cause your ass will learn to read," sang Brigida the Imperfect.

Irma the Albino insisted that Danae go back to sleep, that she'd watch out for the other girls, the unsleeping beauties—she wasn't the least bit sleepy, she suffered from insomnia.

"I'm afraid to go to sleep," she said, "because I sleepwalk and I'm terrified of winding up on the roof, on the eaves up there without knowing it. I could fall off and break my neck, I could kill myself, or worse, I could wind up in a wheelchair."

Danae announced that she was going to the latrine.

"No, here, pee in this bucket, that's what it's for. I suggest that you not go back into the back part of the camp at night—it's darker than a wolf's gullet back there."

"Bah, nothing'll happen."

A wolf's gullet would be as bright as day in comparison with what Danae walked into. She groped her way into the latrine, and with the tip of her right foot she blazed a trail inside. At last she came to one of the plastic curtains and held it aside and stepped in, into the starry-ceilinged stall. She spread her legs and squatted, taking a guess at where the hole in the ground was. First all that emerged was a few timid drops, the smallest trickle, but finally she became braver and a strong stream of pee fell into the hole, sounding like a serpent uncoiling in reverse. Down below she heard the rustling of fragile but rapid-moving bodies; at the bottom, a living carpet of maggots waited impatiently, like starving baby birds, for the anus up there to open and a rain of turds or diarrhetic slush to fall upon them—manna from heaven for them, though for Danae simple excrement. Balancing acrobatically, grabbing onto the curtain, she leapt out of the latrine onto the brick walkway. On the rod from which the curtain hung she made out a dozen or so motionless bullfrog silhouettes. They were breathing, making a sound like snoring, waiting to ambush any insect prey that passed that way.

Danae did not return to the barracks; she went around the side and came up to the front. There was a wooden bench under the ceiba tree, whose trunk and branches, she now noticed, were covered in silvery-leaved epiphytes, bromeliads, some with gorgeous flowers emerging from their central cups, some tiny, spidery, like stars sprinkled throughout the branches. Sitting on the bench were Renata the Physical, Pancha Flatfoot, Alicia Machine-Gun Tongue, Salome the Satrap, Venus Putrefaction, Andy Crater Face, Fermín Adenoids, the Mummy Casimiro, Mario the Tender, Luis the Licentious, Tin the Man, Noel the Nuisance, and Eduardo Busy Hands, who was sidling up to Venus Putrefaction in pretended lechery:

"Come on, my little fart-flower, gimme a break. Let's head out to those fields out there and do some night-plowing, whatcha say, honeybunch?"

"Get outta here, you. You think it's that easy to cut through this chastity belt I'm wearing? Whaddaya think you are, a blowtorch? Besides, it takes a longer stick than you got, dude, to stir up my virginal . . . emotions." And she kicked his shin to get him to move over.

The ceiba rose queenlike, enormous, towering, rising so precipitously skyward that she seemed to be seen from directly below, her trunk thick and deeply grooved, the fluting of centuries of growth, of rubbings and caresses—the countless signs of devotion. If you walk around a ceiba tree three times without ever taking your hand off its trunk, it'll grant you three wishes. But the ceiba must not be neglected; it must be sprinkled with coins, offerings must be made to it—hens fattened with sweet corn and a red ribbon tied round their feet, bunches of black-ripe plantains. The ceiba will protect you if you show your love for it. The ceiba will take care of you, and pamper you. You are ceiba's daughter. Blessed Iroko.

Pancha Flatfoot, sometimes known as Captain Storm because of her macho mannerisms, was the one who first noted Danae's presence.

"And here, ladies and gentlemen, Miss Mint Pie, Miss Toothpaste Face, hee, hee, hee."

And everyone but Andrés started singing a toothpaste jingle . . . Andy Crater Face sneered perversely and even his pimples started popping, one by one, *plf plp plf plp.* Salome the Satrap pulled a cigarette out of her bra and tried to light it, but Alicia Machine-Gun Tongue slapped the match away— Are you *nuts?* Didn't you see Puga wandering around, just looking for somebody coloring outside the lines?! Don't be rebelling without a cause, *chica!* Then she turned and smiled and beckoned Danae over, as though wanting Miss Toothpaste Face to come over and be her best friend. But she froze, stiffer than a plaster mannequin, when she realized that Danae was stalking furiously toward them. She glanced over toward the mess hall; some kids were sitting in groups, talking and laughing, paying no attention to the TV program, while others sat hypnotized before the swiftly changing images of the movie, their heads bobbing and jerking up again from time to time as sleep got the better of them. Sitting on a low wall made out of rocks at the entrance to the boys' barracks were a bunch of retardos trying to see who could hold their breath the longest.

"Which one was it?" Danae asked in a neutral, even friendly tone of voice.

"Which one was what?" inquired Eduardo Busy Hands, playing dumb.

"I wasn't talking to you, booger-breath. Which one of you squeezed a tube of toothpaste on my face?" And she pointed at them, her finger going down the line of girls, one by one.

"Ee-e-ei! Looks like somebody's in for it! Watch out, girls!" mocked Eduardo Explorer Hands, but Alicia Machine-Gun Tongue interrupted his raillery.

"That little practical joke? I swear by all that's sacred, *mi amiguita,* that it wasn't any of us. Right, Renata—we didn't have anything to do with that toothpaste?" Renata the Physical put her hand over her mouth, openly muzzling her laughter, acknowledging the collective guilt.

Luis the Licentious picked up a rock and threw it into the darkness of the furrowed field. Tin the Man was chewing on a weed stalk, savoring its bitter taste. Noel the Nuisance was telling them about his plan to become very, very famous so he could get in Salome the Satrap's pants—although his dreams led him to imagine that someday he would marry a wealthy Frenchwoman who would lead him to the staircase of the Opéra de Paris and help him become a tenor envied by Plácido Domingo, José Carreras, and Luciano Pavarotti, or maybe the first great opera singer to win a gold medal for figure skating. He was so brainlessly vain that his life's greatest ambition was to be envied by multitudes. Of course he had never heard an aria from a single opera or read a single line of a book on the subject, because he considered that a waste of time— for Noel the Nuisance saw himself as an innate genius of *bel canto.* Of course he was gravel-voiced—the gift seemed to be definitely lacking.

"Sorry, 'twas I—it was my idea." Pancha the Flatfoot put her thick hand out to Danae, like the schoolyard bully who's decided to be nice to her worst enemy.

Mario the Tender was shaking his head back and forth, as though saying, *Oh come on, you two, still acting like little kids, I can't believe it—you lie down with babies, you get up with piss all over you.*

"Okay, that's what I wanted to know. But now I owe you one. And I assure you, all of you, that the payback won't be in honey." And she turned and walked away with an ostentatious swagger, making certain to give the impression of a person who was to be dealt with, who wouldn't take this shit lying down.

Andy Crater Face ran after her, and before he'd quite overtaken her he reached out and caught her wrist, pressing it lightly between finger and thumb as though taking her pulse—trying a little too early, if you ask me, to start something between them.

"Stop right there, ugly, I wanna suck a little face . . ."

Before you go, I need to ask you why . . . we let so many things come between you and I. I know the moon isn't moon anymore . . . that there are only memories of what we had before . . . But anyway, I want to talk to you, to ask you . . . whether you . . . are as lonely-y-y-y . . . as me-e-e-e . . . It was Emma the Menace that had broken out in song, the melody emerging from the thick darkness. We were all surprised that she of all people, the quietest of all the girls, had started belting out that old standard like that. Naturally, the others followed along, trying to put a comic spin on the theatrical atmosphere created by Andrés. He, in turn, was unfazed by the razzing; he was still dogging Danae's heels. She walked on, pretending to pay not the slightest attention to the young man's foolishness, pulling her head back whenever he tried to bring his lips, his whispery breath, to her ear, until the others got bored and ignored them—they were incorrigible, anyway. Just as Danae was about to enter the barracks, he jumped in front of her. Pus flowed from his pimples; little clumps of coagulated yellow matter clung to the center of several of the tiny craters. Danae realized intuitively that if she rejected him, he would be the butt of humiliation for the rest of their days there. Pity works miracles, and out of pity she stood there, out of pity puckered her lips comically, to give him confidence. Out of pity she pretended. And out of pity certain even grander amorous adventures have begun. She accepted, rather than rejected, his daring and goofy advance.

"All right, let's get this over with—and listen, I don't wanna hear any declarations of love . . ."

"I don't know about gettin' this over with, but it's okay with me if we start . . ."

She leaned forward to plant a kiss on his cheek, but she was repulsed by the pimples, so she rerouted it to his lips. Then, with an expression of idiotic surprise, she pronounced a scared *See ya* and disappeared into the barracks. Danae never dared ask him whether he slept like a holy imbecile that night. When she got to her bunk, she got the feeling that Irma the Albino was quickly hiding some rare treasure under her pillow. Some tiny, warm packages the size of thimbles. Pink, meaty thimbles. Palpitating, slippery-looking.

She had no time to witness anything else; by the time she hit the bunk, she was out. We both dreamed of butterflies. I, the suitcase that listened, and she, the teenager who believed she was in a Gothic tale. Butterflies with wrinkled cheeks; old, decrepit butterflies. Butterflies with greasy faces smudged with black ash from the wood cookstove. Butterflies with translucent wings and eyelids that oozed yellow matter when they fluttered. A Cuban, menopausal Greta descending out of the moist, throbbing leaves and branches. Nocturnal wings beating. Butterflies sucking at flowers as they leaned on tiny canes. Cannibal larvae, intense blue-green and red. The chameleons had a feast as they balanced on the seesaw swings of fresh green bouncy branches. A monarch with gigantic yellow-and-black wings was fluttering from chest to chest, as though trying to pin decorations on dying orphans. Dreaming of butterflies is bad luck; dreaming of butterflies can attract Death. She put her hands out the window again, hoping the mysterious encounter would happen again. And she pulled the cover of night toward her. She waited, filled with emotion, her heart beating in her tonsils—and nothing happened. The girls' dreams started jostling each other, bumping into each other. Irma saw centipedes everywhere, ready to suck blood from the veins in her neck. Emma prophesied murders and hurricanes and drank goat's blood from a calabash. At Danae's head, hundreds of naked spirits, the spirits of the night, wood and river spirits, dwarflike sprites, were licking each other's navels, which tasted like ripe guava. The night spirits resembled Indians; she later learned they were called *güijes* and that they were the spirits of aboriginal people, the souls of the countryside and of history. Inoffensive water sprites.

"Souls . . . in purgatory and in perdition," Alicia Machine-Gun Tongue groaned in the midst of her nightmare.

The teenager's skull began to tingle, gooseflesh began to creep across it, with the coldness of the night. Maracas, drums, and güiros began to sound: *chiquichín, chacachán, cumbaquín, quin, quin, cumbacán; chiquichín, chacachán, cumbaquín, quin, quin, cumbacán . . . It was a night of full and silver moon, with lightning and with thunder, that a fine and cultured gentleman set out with his coach and coachman. He was dressed in white from head to toe, with a medal on his breast, and as he passed the four corners he was stabbed three times in the chest. "Open the door, my darling, for I am wounded to the heart; three times the man has stabbed me, and this life I must soon depart. It is a hard thing he has done, and a hard thing I must do, for I leave you here to weep alone, and our unborn baby too."* . . . The guaguancó flooded the vastness of the countryside, and the countryside grew larger and larger, spread wider and wider. Shadows like fruit adhering to a mirage. A Cuban still life. A few steps from the door of a thatched-roof dwelling, the ambiguous rider took the saddle off the horse that was the same color as the moon, a kind of luminous metallic white color. The rider was not a young man, but one could not quite say that it was a girl dressed as a boy, either. It—whether he or she—went on singing, and its asexual voice had the timbre of an animal moan, or something very much like the plaintive cry of a Paganiniesque violin.

WHAT FOLLOWS OCCURRED about a quarter of a mile away, behind the camp. Tucked away in a clearing stood a group of human dwellings—huts, or shacks, or hovels, but not quite "houses"—and the little circle of dwellings gave the impression of having fallen from another planet. It looked so poor that no one would ever have thought that such a place existed here, in this countryside, in this century. It was like something out of the distant past, something that had emerged from and never moved beyond the war of liberation. The batey, as I will call it, because it resembled the circle of thatched huts built by the Indians in the days before Columbus came, and that was their name for their settlements, had some twenty bohíos—which is also an Indian word, the word used for those very huts I just mentioned. The bohíos in this clearing here tonight were built out of rough wood planks; their roofs were of palm fronds or homemade roof tiles shaped on the thighs of the dwellings' inhabitants, as people did back in the days when there were slaves. There was no electricity; they were lit by what the inhabitants of these dwellings called "wax lamps," that is, improvised homemade candles, a wick floating in grease or oil in a clay bowl. The rider hung the saddle and bridle on a pole, tied up the horse, kissed it under its orange-colored, almost fiery eye, and passed a thin but rough, callused hand over the sweaty mane. The rider's eye then caught the light of a blue flame approaching the door from the dark interior of the bohío.

"Tierra Fortuna Munda? Tierra? . . . Is that you? . . . Where the devil have you been, child? . . . Your father has been out in the woods . . . looking for you . . . for hours." At each group of words, spoken in short staccato bursts, the candle flickered and almost died, but then it revived again after each pause or attempt to peer out into the darkness. The voice went randomly, as though without recognizing the difference, from the informal *tú* to the formal *usted*. "Answer me—is that you? You pigheaded flibbertigibbet—you're going to be the death of me . . ." she muttered at the end.

The rider dodged one slap, and then another that grazed her back. Then she—because now we know that it was Tierra Fortuna Munda—went directly to a cot and without taking off her clothes threw herself down on its mattress made of still-green palm fronds.

Danae felt a strong attraction to that figure, which was neither Andrés Fuck Face nor herself in disguise within my stuffed-suitcase dream—for this was not my dream; those oneiric turbulences, those confused dreams and nightmares of all those daughters of fortune in that gloomy camp did not belong to me.

The woman holding the clay bowl knelt beside the cot, put her hand on the forehead hidden under the weedy curtain of wiry hair.

"You've gotten another sunstroke . . . Until that stupid father of yours puts his machete to the heart of that accursed horse of yours, you're never going to stop . . . Will the princess have something to eat? Boiled sweet potato with pork drippings—come on, I'll heat it up for you—do you want some or not? Answer me, Tierra Fortuna Munda, you willful creature!!" *Tú*s and *usted*es intermingled in the woman's speech.

"Mamá, just let me sleep. Papá is going to come in in a minute, I heard him behind me—but with that nag of his he couldn't catch me! Go to bed, Mamá—we'll see about eating in the morning."

The woman's body resembled a mango—a tiny head set on a body that bulged outward toward the sides. The hair of her bangs, which fell over her forehead in locks somewhere between dirty blond and gray, gave the impression of a thatched roof. The skin of her hands and forearms was covered in scaly excrescences and she had sties on all four eyes—because she had an extra eye in the hollow of each cheek, so that each time she smiled they would wink and tears would come to them. The rider, as I have said, was named Tierra Fortuna Munda, and she spoke grudgingly, rejecting the woman's attentions—*unwanted* attentions; at that hour nobody could stand such sweet talk. Tierra Fortuna Munda was female, but an urchinlike nymph at best, a tomboy, a rapscallion, a hellion—judging by her behavior, she was more or less the same age as Danae. Their characters and personalities, though, were nothing alike.

At the party for the lollipops, the gumdrops aren't invited, the gumdrops aren't invited, the gumdrops aren't invited!

In the distance there was the sound of the conga drums, the raucous singing of the youngsters in the barracks. Had Danae dreamed or lived it? She was at that age when dreams and adventures are often confused.

Landscape Under the Gravitational Influence of the Ceiba Tree

I cannot deny that it was not just the youngsters, interrupted in their first night's sleep away from home, who leapt up, panic-stricken, on their teetering bunks—if those rickety contraptions of iron and sticks could be called bunks. I, too, despite being a ceiba tree, got a terrible scare when I heard the rumbling voice of that human being, sometimes glowing, sometimes dark, who insisted that he be called "Director Puga" here and "Director Puga" there and "Director Puga" whenever anybody spoke to him. A man as black and shiny as his spit-shined shoes. I had barely slept a wink, thanks to the tickling I'd been getting from that restless owl the livelong night, with her talons in my branches. Plus those hutias—I don't know what had gotten into them, they were usually such sleepyheads. I suppose they were nervous with so many people around, but anyway they were up and down my trunk all night, carrying food back and forth and scurrying around and tucking the dead little animals they'd caught into every furrow of my skin.

Not a few dead people, too, all riled up, ancestors upset with all the carrying-on. Pretty soon they got wound up and started in with a whoop-de-doo like you never heard, arguing over this and over that and over this other thing over here. Two of the most prominent were the venerable San Cristóbal and the wise naturalist Tranquilino Sandalio de Noda y Martínez, from the town of Vueltabajo. There was Sanfancón, the mysterious Chinese deity that Lydia Cabrera wrote about, who was roiling around with his tail feathers in a tizzy, not to mention the saints of all my religions, African and Catholic both, who were shrieking and yowling about this *outrage*. The only one that behaved like a gentleman, which is what he always was, by the way—very calm, very peaceable—was the translucent spirit of Andrés Facundo Cristo de los Dolores Petit, the famous kimbisa or Abakuá sorcerer, an elegant blond-haired, blue-eyed, light-skinned, fine-featured Negro fellow who had the supreme power of turning the sun off and on whenever he wanted, changing water into milk, and turning his eyes back in their sockets and telling the future. He was dressed the way he always was—the way he'd required that all the other members of the sect dress, too, for more than half the nineteenth century—in a black frock coat, white pants, leather sandals, and a walking stick. Very much the Abakuá lord. Andrés Petit was the man who introduced me, hundreds of years later, to my very dear and irreplaceable friend Lydia Cabrera, who, the first thing she did was whisper in my ear, *In Lucumí: Iggi Olorun. In Congo: mother Nganga. Musina Nsambia. Ceiba, you are my mother, give me shade.*

Oh, and that night another spirit came, the no less scientific spirit of Felipe Poey, reciting some lines of poetry that gave me a shiver that made me think I was delivering a baby right there, as the saying goes:

> *Now rest: A place well furnished*
> *filled with cooling shade*
> *the trunk of this ceiba does present us:*
> *from here you can see, spirit delighted,*
> *the birds as they fly,*
> *the calf as it plays in the meadow.*

I finally managed to get to sleep around daybreak; I kept having nightmares, though—because I want to make it clear that we trees suffer from terrible nervous disorders, too. But the racket the youngsters made when they got up made me forget the exact contents of my bad dreams.

"Ma-a-a-le ba-a-a-a-a-racks! On your fe-e-e-et!" yelled Puga the Patent Leather Captain at the door of the boys' barracks.

Dressed in overalls, he next went over to the girls' barracks and screamed the same thing, at the top of his lungs again, as if they had to get up no matter what it cost them, as though the world was coming to an end and you had to take off running as fast as you could for your heavenly bomb shelter. That Patent Leather Captain had turned out to be a royal pain in the sunrise.

"Aaaagh. What are we, astronauts?" yawned Emma the Menace contemptuously.

"One demerit for the comedian!" barked Mara Medusa. "And if I'm not mistaken, it was you, Renata."

"No, teacher—don't take it out on me. It wasn't me—but I'm not going to rat on the one that did it."

Mara the Wheezer knew when she couldn't win one, so she started straightening her assigned space, all the time thinking of her two—no, three—freakish children. (Do Siamese twins count as one or two?)

The lights were turned on and the babble began to resolve into a prayer, more than a song—*Soft and beautiful are the mornings sung by King David for the handmaidens.* From my vantage point I was able to keep every movement under observation. We ceibas are ubiquitous, despite the fact that our roots are very deep and cling tightly to the entrails of the earth. We can move about with our senses; the older we are, the more acute they become, just as the growing power of our branches and hoofs is infinite. We ceiba trees are great walkers, and even fliers. I know one ceiba tree—we were raised together, as a matter of fact—whose roots expanded so far that they finally wound up in China—one day they just sprouted up out of the ground down there. The Chinese couldn't believe their eyes when they saw that trunk that was more solid than walls and revolutions.

It was still pitch dark, probably no more than five o'clock in the morning, and fog everywhere, when the barracks began coming to life. It was cold, because in the country it's an unwritten law that mornings are freezing cold, there's just no two ways about it. But in the midst of all that rude gape-mouthed yawning, heavy-lidded groaning, and stiff stretching and moaning, the sheets on the bunks were pulled tight by the girls before you knew it. The ones that hadn't slept in their work clothes started getting dressed for a day as farmers, and within a few minutes a long line had formed for the latrines. The boys made their beds any way they felt like it, with a lick and a promise, you might say. Since I had overheard certain conversations that had occurred the night before just a few yards from my feet, I mean my roots, I had learned several of their names. Not to mention that, as I said before, I possess certain abilities—I have the power to set in motion machinery, "occult powers," some people call them, although there's nothing occult about them, by which I can move from one place to another, either through the air or on land, and I can also hear things—absolutely everything, in fact—for miles around.

By the light of day, Danae saw that she had peed into an ocean of little yellow maggots almost the size of her little finger, squirming in the mud mixed with shit that dated back to the nineteenth century. The pee would shower down and the maggots would threaten to practically climb up the filthy walls of the latrines—hard to tell whether they were fleeing the yellow Niagara or dying of thirst and therefore euphoric with that warm, nauseating rain that was falling on them, like a liquid rope to shinny. Irma the Albino retched, gagged, retched again; she wasn't sure she'd have the stomach to eat breakfast after such a scatological sight. Alicia Machine-Gun Tongue told her that the best thing to do was not look down; they'd just have to do their duty blindly, so to speak, and keep their eyes on the higher prize. And hold their noses, naturally—the stench was unbearable, and as the weeks went on it would just get worse, since there was no way to sanitize the toilets, which were no more than burrows, rabbit holes dug out of the soft ground. A squadron of bluebottle flies landed on the girls' wide-spread haunches. But it was worse with the boys: the flies lighted on their pricks, which were wrinkled and shriveled from the cold, and kept them from concentrating, so the pee would almost never start flowing. For a ceiba tree, this was all quite a spectacle, even though for hundreds of years I have witnessed countless personages pass through this place. In the last few years alone I have seen, not counting the people who actually live in the area, prisoners, religious leaders, intellectuals and artists of all kinds, doctors, lawyers, and, among other groups of depressed persons, suicides, murderers, innocents, and a whole raft of etceteras. This time I must admit I was surprised by the youthfulness of the group, virtually school-childlike in gray matter and therefore extremely naive with regard to nature. For example, it took quite some time before they realized who I was. At first, no one but Danae, who had already felt tremendous curiosity about me and to whom the bus driver had muttered my name, was the slightest bit interested in knowing who or what I might be.

Save for the instantly recognizable royal palm, as far as they were concerned all we trees were just alike and I was just another one—majestic, maybe, due to my age, and possessing a certain solemnity in comparison with the rest, whose thick, cooling foliage served as shelter during their rest periods—which I can tell you were not many. To them, I was basically no more than a tree protected and watched over by a bench—a none-too-well-constructed bench, I might add, and made out of hard, vulgar jiquí wood. But after a few days, one of the *tías* in the mess hall explained to the students that they ought to be a little more respectful to me, be sure not to hurt me or injure me in any way, no carving hearts and arrows on my trunk, because I experienced the same pain as humans, and bled just like they did. She told them that if people behaved decently toward me and made me an offering of sixteen eggs cooked on a cross made out of cocoa butter, smeared with bálsamo tranquilo and almond oil with some old coins thrown in, I would see that the vows made to me were well rewarded, because I could grant wishes, *just alike the old folks tell,* she said in her misspelled way. *And the books, too,* she said on second thought.

She went on to tell the youngsters that I was a blessed tree, the Virgin Mary, the most wonderful, holy thing in this whole world, that I symbolized holy love and power and that not even hurricanes could knock me over and that I had so much power that lightning didn't dare strike me. She added that they ought to come to me to find out what names the guajiros, which is what we call our campesinos hereabouts, had baptized me with—Niña Linda or Fortuna Mundo. I should note, in all modesty, that the mess-hall lady was not exaggerating; she was right, even if I had probably never given her any proof of my mystery. There are those who truly deserve the greatest respect and admiration for the mission of love that they carry out on this planet. I did what I always do—I listened and I watched, with all the discretion that is my nature.

I should confess that it didn't take long for the new arrivals to earn my hats-off, and in time my deep affection. After all, I am a very sentimental sort of Mamá Fumbe, Iggi Olorun, tree of god. This time I sniffled and sniffed a little, then I cried buckets—crying not because of the bad things that trouble me so much for no reason, but rather the good things, and deep emotion. I am very sensitive to demonstrations of tenderness, although if people treat me badly I can punish, let me tell you, and without looking back.

That dawn was characterized by total and absolute disorganization—the teachers telling the youngsters to hurry up, moving them along but at the same time giving them orders that were too strict to follow, plus the threats of demerits that would keep them from participating in the recreational activities that were all any of them had to look forward to. The kids came out of the latrines half dressed, carrying their canteens and their toothbrushes with the toothpaste from the night before all dry and sticky on them—because Renata the Physical had been told by her older sisters, supposedly experienced in these matters, that she should do as much as she could beforehand, such as leaving her toothbrush ready with the toothpaste already squeezed out onto it, but of course covered with a piece of plastic so the rats wouldn't be drawn to it by the minty-fresh smell. Crowds of morning-grouchy boys and girls formed around the washtubs that served as wash-basins, and the youngsters would brush their teeth and rinse so hurriedly that they would run out to their formations with rings of froth around their mouths. It was hard to believe how much scurrying around there was, totally helter-skelter, with some of the boys buttoning their flies all crooked, or forgetting to altogether, which of course gave rise to endless hooting and laughing. In the case of the girls, it tended to be blouses buttoned wrong, or just one side tucked in. Their boots or high-tops sank into the mud, which had been softened even further by the morning mist, and the youngsters looked like inexperienced high-wire artists as they tried to pull their feet out of the soft, sucking muck.

Finally the sun rose, the sky turned light, and the day dawned, and all those youngsters from the city marveled at the beauty of the sky—blue as blue can be, but streaked and smeared with sunrise orange. I wanted to laugh out loud at how *new*, how *green* they were. But I had to contain myself, because we ceibas laugh so loud and so heartily that we've been known to scare people. What for me was an everyday occurrence for them took on immeasurable importance—one would have thought they were standing before some famous painter's painting in one of those European museums where people say even we, even we ceiba trees, are exhibited, the central motif of certain landscapes that date back hundreds of years. It's true that way back when, lots and lots of people painted us; today very few are interested in immortalizing us in that way. Although I can't really say that in the olden days things were better than they are now; I can never forget how many trees of my species, and others, too, from different families, were criminally cut down and trimmed and deported, no more than moribund trunks, and sent off to distant lands, as far away as Europe, where they were used to build maybe those very museums, which once were palaces but now contain portrayals of our real existence. Cutting down a ceiba tree is a crime for which there is no absolution. Anyone who fells a ceiba tree destroys the seed of the mystery. And the punishment shall come, sooner or later. Preferably sooner.

Once the youngsters were in formation, all in nice straight rows, the Patent Leather Director started in on a speech about obligations and duties that was unbelievably boring—even for him, certainly for me, and I suppose for the rest of nature, because with my own millions of eyes I saw the boredom in the droopy vegetation all around and in the stampede of lizards, chameleons, majá snakes, birds, hummingbirds, hutias, a nigh-extinct manatee (poor endangered thing), bees, butterflies, moths, cockroaches, and even rats (fleeing as though this were a sinking ship), the plantain owl, and other inhabitants of the woody wilderness. And when he had taken his morning dump—because this was verbal diarrhea if ever I heard it—he gave the order for all the boys and girls to march in order, by brigades, to the mess hall for breakfast. This morning they would begin with brigade number 1, tomorrow brigade number 2, and so on, taking turns, so that each brigade would receive the benefit of a breakfast at a decent temperature. There was no hope for the last breakfasters; they would invariably be served food that was lukewarm and tasteless and in all other ways in terrible condition because of the time it had sat there waiting to be served and the heat that made even the air of the mess hall acrid.

The burned milk—which was also watered-down and smoky-smelling—and the hard, black bread with threads of burlap cooked into the dough did not meet with general approval. Of course as the days went by, the youngsters' palates adapted, and when they came in really hungry they had no choice but to wolf down what at first had seemed to them a repellent, nauseating, disgusting, *vomitative* mess (not for nothing was it called a "mess hall"), food for pigs and birds and hardened criminals in prisons—bread and water— but had finally come to seem like food for the gods. It was the boys, this time, who were first to be served.

After washing off their breakfast utensils they all snapped back into formation so the brigades could be assigned their jobs for the day. Some of them would be driven off in trucks to the nurseries or the tobacco fields; there, the campesinos would impart to them the full wealth of their wisdom with respect to the stages the plants had to go through in order to reach the lips of all the smokers of the world. To judge by what I could see, the brigades were assigned at random, because apparently none of them had any knowledge whatsoever of how to weed the plants, strip off the flowers and suckers to keep them from sapping the plants' strength, or strip the leaves off the plants to harvest them. They had never sewed the leaves into sheaves and bundles, and not a one had the remotest idea how to get the sheaves up into the roof of the drying shed and suspend them from the rafters to dry in the hot air, away from the dews and wets of the open and also to keep the blue mold from getting into it. Nobody knew how they were supposed to stack the leaves to transport them to the factories. The boys' brigade number 7, the brigade that Andy Crater Face belonged to, was one of the ones chosen for that first day in the tobacco fields.

Danae said a silent prayer that her brigade not be sent to the same place. And she got lucky—or God heard her plea; I had passed on the message. The members of brigade number 9, girls who tended to be somewhat undisciplined to say the least, were ordered up on a rickety old oxcart pulled by a tractor; they were to be driven to a fabulous plain that stretched for miles and miles and was planted with tomatoes and then farther on with potatoes, then beets, then cabbage. In the middle of the immense field there was an irrigation feeder pipe that brought water to the crops from the place it had been taken, one of the several streams that fed into a river nearby—a relatively unknown river that nobody had ever heard of before, but that was in fact very important: the Cuyaguateje. The girls helped one another up into the cart, boosting each other from underneath, both hands on patched rear ends. They were lovely to look at—full of energy, some wearing kerchiefs with bright-colored designs, others in baseball caps, some with their hair pulled back, others with braids or hair wrapped in little buns, wanting to keep the sun from drying out their glossy Havana hair. The boys threw kisses at them, yelled insults or insinuations (some actually almost complimentary if you consider gross sex complimentary), or challenged the girls to contests related to the farmwork or romance—these last, based on puns, double entendres, so the teachers wouldn't catch on to what they were "proposing," as you might say. The girls shot back as good as they got, making it clear to the boys that there'd be none of that, nothing off base or off color, not one thing "fresh." I confess that their slang shocked me even when I got a good laugh out of it.

The vehicles drove off in their various directions; my attention was drawn to an unusual sort of conversation, mysteriously linked to one of the dreams a girl named Danae had had the night before. Almost immediately after brigade number 9's oxcart began to move, its wheels bogged down in the spongy mud and the cart threatened to turn over at any moment—which made the girls shriek so loud that it would make an owl's feathers stand on end—but the brigade leader, one Margot Wrangling, told the girls to hush, not to scream like that, and then she told them she was going to give them a piece of information that would be very useful to them all. She explained that right behind the camp, not half a mile away, there was a collective, and the members of this collective were pretty strange, and it just so happened, imagine their miserable damn luck, that one of the heads of one of the weird families was the guajiro who was to be in charge of the field the girls were going to work in—and when she said guajiros she meant *gua-ji-ros,* ladies. Her eyes popped out and her lips pursed as she carefully pronounced each syllable of the word.

"Which means," she rasped, "people who are apparently simple country bumpkins, just as friendly as they can be—but never, ever, to be trusted. You don't want to ever, that is, get in a cage with them." She said that to be cruel, because she knew she was turning those people into animals in a zoo.

For reasons of security, the best thing would be not to visit them or have anything at all to do with them, she insisted. People said they were standoff-ish anyway, a kind of untouchable, maybe; she didn't trust them because all signs pointed to the fact that due to their low level of education and culture—culture in general, she meant—they believed all kinds of strange things and practiced weird rituals, maybe even the worship of evil spirits, and *some* people even said they mated with one another.

"Excuse me, teacher, but don't you use 'mate' for animals?" asked Alicia Machine-Gun Tongue, more sure of herself than doubtful.

"Why . . . yes, you do. And what exactly is your point? You know, miss, it's rude to correct people in public; you could have spoken to me in private. But of course that's neither here nor there; I mean what I said: they *mate,* because according to what I've been told, they do things *worse* than animals."

Danae had become thoughtful. Then, suddenly, she made the mistake of thinking out loud:

"That's wrong, it's not exactly *several* families, it's just one. They live in fear, they've cut themselves off from the other people in the area because they're afraid of them. People have threatened them with extinction."

In the girl's enlightened mind I could read and decipher her dream, or her adventure, the presence of the secret rider entering the batey in the dark hours of the night, pursued by the father, greeted by the mother with a candle as the only light. The half-mischievous, half-sad face of Tierra rose before me. The beloved Tierra Fortuna Munda, whom I guarded, watched over, and protected. My goddaughter and my friend.

Fortunately, the heavyset woman with the boxer's arms possessed no powers and so could not possibly see the same visions I could. So she hardly paid Danae any mind; she probably just thought the girl was making fun of her.

"We'll leave the mysteries for the campfire, Danae. I'm not having any of your funny business if you please. And there's a whole bookful of demerits here in my pocket if you don't believe me." But just as she was finishing her threat, the front wheel of the cart lodged against a boulder in the path and the teacher fell backward, splat on her backside, a mass of quivering flesh.

Howls of laughter followed the accident, until the butt of the hilarity punished the lack of humanity in her charges with demerits all around. Then Danae sank once again into her own thoughts, until Renata the Physical clapped her on the back, urging her to join the inevitable group sing-along. The girls piled out of the cart, hanging on the uprights of the sideboards and the rope that feebly prevented them from falling and cracking their skulls.

Their eyes roamed across the heart-stopping, crushing expanse of plain, its broad, endless green beauty. Its countless tints and hues of hope.

> *It was a night of full and silver moon, with lightning and with thunder, that a fine and cultured gentleman set out with his coach and coachman. He was dressed in white from head to toe, with a medal on his breast, and as he passed the four corners he was stabbed three times in the chest. "Open the door, my darling, for I am wounded to the heart; three times the man has stabbed me, and this life I must soon depart. It is a hard thing he has done, and a hard thing I must do, for I leave you here to weep alone, and our unborn baby too. Two things only, I ask of you, two things you must promise me: If the babe be born a girl child, then of Santa Clara she must be; or if it be a boy child, a dandy such as me. And then, my darling, when I die, in Havana make my tomb, and on my gravestone carve these words for the cruel world: 'Under this cold earth, my friends, there lies a wretched man. He died not of cowardice, or pain in the side, but the knife of his best friend.' Mother, I no longer have a friend, for he has murdered me; Mother, I no longer have a friend, for he's taken my friend from me. My best friend did betray me and stab me through the heart, my best friend did murder me, and this life I now depart. But Mother, I beg you, don't you cry, it is too late for a tear. Ay, Mother, don't you cry, and always wear your brassiere."*

The girls' guaguancó ended in gales of laughter and ripples of gleeful chatter, and then the laughter segued into another song of the same girls'-camp genre, and then into a third, this one less melodious, until the promised eternity of the landscape began to flow into them, quieting them, hushing them, forcing them to confront the enchantment of an unsuspected thing.

I flew to the head of my goddaughter's bed. Tierra Fortuna Munda had healed, her fever had passed, but she was still in bed. She had no desire to get up; her eyes were fixed on the morning light that filtered through the primitive, off-square window. Tierra was aware that some time ago her father had gone off to the field; she suspected that her mother was out feeding slop to the pigs and that her brothers and sisters were outside, running around with slingshots, shooting the heads off mockingbirds or garter snakes or those big majá boas. She'd told herself that after she had a big breakfast—because she was now beginning to get really hungry—she would get on her horse Sunny and "go climb trees," as she put it to herself, maraud through the woods and wilderness awhile, and then bathe in the river.

Tierra Fortuna Munda was named Tierra Fortuna Munda because it was just when her mother was helping a sow, Marie Antoinette it was, give birth to all her little piglets that the labor pains began with Tierra Fortuna. Santa stayed with the sow, bearing up under her labor pains, her legs wet from her own broken water, until the last little piglet had emerged into the light. And when she saw that the animal was out of danger, she left her to go tell her husband that she, too, was about to give birth.

"Bejerano," she cried, "*alabao*, it's come! Run for the midwife!"

The woods gave back the turbulent echo of Santa's voice. Despite the fact that Bejerano was far from the house, he took off running madly, swam rivers and lakes, climbed up hills and precipices and then down again, and at last came to the bohío belonging to Salustiana Rubio, who (according to her own reckoning) was descended from the famed Cuban patriot Isabel Rubio. As indeed she was. But Bejerano found Salustiana busy birthing a set of triplets.

"I can't come now, Bejerano. That Santa of yours is something, deciding to have hers at the same time as Estelvina. Couldn't she have squeezed her legs together a little while longer?"

Her hands, covered with slime and gore, emerged from the gaping orifice, waved about in a sign of desperation, and plunged once more into the red tunnel. The woman in labor, Estelvina, never stopped groaning, but from time to time the groans crescendoed into shrieks and bellows of pain. To the man standing by, the woman's face, twisted by pain, looked like a mare's.

Bejerano wasted not another second. He turned and began running again, toward home. Santa had barely managed to reach my trunk; she leaned against it, puffing, blowing, panting, her mouth dry. Then, inspired by nature herself, she squatted, low to the ground. I spread my thick roots and opened a soft cradle in among the best, the softest of my entrails. And then, in one long, constant push, the little thing was born. Her skull hit the rocky red ground, but nothing really happened except she got a pointy little knot on her head—her head always was harder than an ironwood tree. Right there and then she started suckling at me, nursing from my sap—aaah, her little mouth sucking at my bark. With the placenta I made myself a necklace, because I happen to be a ceiba tree that likes to make herself look nice. Santa, relieved, managed a smile, she grabbed the baby by one foot and pulled her toward her, toward her breast. But without false modesty I believe I can state without fear of contradiction that the first to nurse that child was me.

"I'm going to call you Tierra, yes, you pretty little thing, I'm going to call you Tierra Fortuna Munda, in gratitude to that queen of all trees, and I'm going to ask this ceiba to be your godmother."

Just then Bejerano ran up. He was panting and sweating and well nigh exhausted, and I thought for a second he was going to collapse. But he looked down on that scene with tears of joy and relief in his eyes and he gathered up some leaves from in among my roots and rubbed the baby's body. He loved the name his wife had chosen for their daughter. And he also nodded, most respectfully and proudly, when she told him of her decision to ask me to be the child's godmother. I agreed immediately, because, as I said, I'm a very sentimental ceiba tree. And of course no one can deny that a little living creature would be the tenderest and sweetest offering that anyone could ever dedicate to me.

Santa counted: the baby had six fingers on each hand and six toes on each foot, but there was something unusual—the baby had six nipples, three down each side of her chest. An honest-to-goodness mammal. The couple knew that there had to be such things in their offspring; according to the witches and sorcerers in the country, the family had been blessed (according to some) or cursed (according to others) for generations upon generations. In one of the versions, they all descended from the Guanahacabibe Indians, who in turn were the last survivors of the Guanahatabeyes, Guanatabibes, or Guanatabeyes, as their name was variously recorded. In order to survive the slaughter that was visited upon the Indians, one brother and one sister hid up in the highest branches of the trees; there, they grew into adulthood, there they bore children, and there, in consequence, something of that prehistory about which so little knowledge remained was saved. A second version had it that one of their ancestors had been ostracized, a punishment he had brought upon himself because of a crime whose exact nature has been forgotten, for it happened hundreds and hundreds of years ago. In his loneliness and banishment, he was not able to keep himself from falling in love with his sister. The two had children, many children, and those children, it was said, were the ancestors of Tierra's parents.

Therefore, no matter which legend was to be believed, Santa and Bejerano were the children of a brother and sister, who were themselves the children of brother and sister grandparents, who were in turn the children of brother and sister great-grandparents. And they themselves, Bejerano and Santa, were brother and sister. They belonged to a large family of blood-only relations, and so their offspring were fated to be born as freaks. Their oldest son had been born with twelve fingers and twelve toes, three eyes, and two navels; his name was Chivirico Vista Alegre. Then came Silvina Reina Sabiduría, who possessed the same number of digits, hand and foot, but no ears, just holes on each side of her head. Their third child was Tierra Fortuna Munda. In addition to her six nipples and the six fingers on each hand and six toes on each foot, she had one further remarkable feature: from her navel oozed a liquid with the smell and taste of guava jam. The children that followed her, all sons, had countless magical stigmata: Felipón de la Caridad had the tail of an ape, a red backside like a chimpanzee's, and was deaf and dumb; Carlos Quinto was born with an arm in the middle of his chest; Quixote Panza's jaw was the shape of a pelican's bill; and Fernando Liviano had three legs, although the one in the middle wasn't exactly a leg.

Physicians, sociologists, politicians, experts in parapsychology, in the study of remarkable physical characteristics ("freakologists," the family called them), visited and even stalked the family, hounding them unmercifully, insisting that they be isolated, not allowed to come in contact with persons unrelated to them. The family never yielded to this, but they didn't flee these people, either; they resisted as best they could. They were then left alone, written off as "uncooperative," "stubborn," "recalcitrant," because if the investigators persisted they ran the risk that the case of this insignificant community might reach the ears of another, more important community, the international community, and *then* these creatures would become altogether too significant, and the only option would be "cleansing," extermination, genocide.

Analyzing the situation in the clear light of day, the authorities arrived at the conclusion that these "aberrations" (sexually speaking, if not in many other ways) were, for the moment, doing harm to no one, and that in fact they might be kept under observation and perhaps even, in the not too distant future, be turned into a circus attraction or relocated to a site that tourists might be persuaded to visit. Naturally some advantage, some benefit, had to be extracted from those poor miserable wretches. So the investigators mused as they stood before a cluster of spavined and dilapidated huts with their doors hermetically plastered shut against them. No big deal, the land they worked didn't belong to them, it had been expropriated. Let the old folks keep working; that didn't hurt anybody but the old ones themselves, who persuaded themselves that they were still the owners of that ridiculous, unimportant piece of land. Just leave them alone, let them rot, stew in their own juices till they were good and cooked. What did anybody care about a bunch of perverted freaks?

"Monstrosities! Incestuous pigs!" exclaimed the Higher-Ups in the region before they marched away in contempt and outraged piety.

Ever since she was just a tiny baby, Tierra Fortuna Munda has communicated with me. At first she sent me just short little thoughts, but then it was the cutest gurgling sounds. I was always attentive, always replied very explicitly to whatever she might ask, because I have never been one to ignore children, or leave their little questions unanswered, especially the mental questions they don't say out loud. Tierra loves me and I love her; as far as she's concerned, I'm a member of the family. She was so used to freaks that she never thought it was strange that a ceiba tree should be a relative of hers. One day she asked whether someday she would fall in love with one of her brothers. I explained that it wasn't obligatory, but the poor creature got all panicky, she was so terrified of coming in contact with some stranger who didn't understand her emotions, didn't understand the way she and her family lived their lives outside society. Tierra knew that to outsiders, her grandparents, parents, brothers and sisters, and all her other relatives were "odd," and she feared that she would never find anyone to fall in love with her, since she had already observed that normal human beings have only ten fingers, ten toes, and two nipples, and that none of them had guava jam coming out their navels. And that they were a lot more stubborn yet a lot more gullible than her and her whole family put together.

Hard clumps of sleep were sticking to her eyelashes; she carefully peeled and rolled them off, then entertained herself by kneading them and the dried mucus she picked out of the inside of her nostrils into balls, then throwing the little balls out the window. After a while she went to the stove, wet a finger and stuck it into the ashes, and then, picking up a can of water, walked out into the yard to wash her teeth. The sun, still pallid from its long night out, was rising about as full of energy as she was, and there was a low fog along the ground. She cursed the cold; she hated to feel cold on her back. After scrubbing her teeth with her index finger she went back to get another can of water, for her face. Just then Santa, drying her hands on her apron, passed her daughter.

"Come have breakfast. Your father went off before light; he's in the field over by the lake and he's mad as a hornet with you, *muchacha*. Chivirico Vista Alegre started working with him today. Ave María, how I wish you children could go to school!" She sighed, then clucked despairingly.

Tierra had already served herself raw milk in a clay calabash. She picked up a piece of white cassava bread and smeared it across the iron skillet greased with pork fat. With her mouth full, still chewing, she raised the calabash to her lips, took a drink of the thick, warm liquid, and then, giving her mother, who was poking up the fire in the stove, a defiant look out of the corner of her eye, she said:

"But, Mamitica, you're mighty changeable in your mind. What do we need to go to school for? Don't you know they make fun of us, and don't you know we don't learn a thing? . . . Now that I remember, I need to talk to Papaíto, because yesterday I was over in the town, and I went in that bar of Maximino's, the Make It a Double? And with my hat on and as dirty and all as I was, they didn't recognize me, and I heard 'em saying that the bosses are intending to take our animals away from us and throw us off the land. They say we're living too close to that camp with all the students over there . . . that we're a danger and a bad example for 'em."

Santa served the girl coffee in a gourd calabash.

"Those scholarship students the government brings in, you mean?" She picked up a duster made of strands of unraveled rope and started dusting the rickety chairs, an old table made out of linden wood, worn and unstable. "Your uncle Efigenio needs to come glue this table again; it's not much better'n a seesaw."

"They're not scholarship students, Mamá. They're like those other ones, from before. They're just schoolkids from Havana that they bring in for forty-five days to work in the fields."

"I don't know, we barely had time to get to know the ones they brought in before, and then they moved 'em out again, and thank goodness they didn't move us out with 'em."

"Well, I'm not moving away from here, and they can just start getting used to it, Mamá."

"Don't worry, child, the Higher-Ups are all talk and no do. No do at all."

"But what if one day they decide to do what they keep talking about?"

"Those are things best left to us grown-ups, girl. You children have no need to be worrying about such things as that, so you just be quiet now and go on. A person keeps her mouth shut, she doesn't catch any flies, you know that."

The floor of the house was of the same poor quality of concrete as the floor in the camp, and the plywood walls were crumbling and buckling, layers of them peeling away like wet crackers. Tierra looked up at the roof and told herself that they needed to start thinking about drying some palm fronds to restore it; you could see the sky through certain sections, sure hope it doesn't rain. The furnishings in the house were in keeping with the poverty of its inhabitants: in the living-dining room there was the table that I mentioned, and around it four wooden stools, of linden wood also, their seats upholstered with goatskin; there was a low, armless rocking chair that was rickety and unsafe even to sit in and an armchair with a woven hemp-rope seat. Reigning over one of the walls was a round mirror in a frame that five hundred years ago had been gilt; the glass was covered with flyspecks and its silvering was spotted and cloudy. Tierra inspected herself without much enthusiasm and told herself that she was without a doubt the ugliest person in the world. She tried to comb back her hair; her hair was thick, wavy, like the Indians', but it was stiff and tangled, so she gave up. She sniffed at her armpits; she smelled. She couldn't go another day, she had to get herself to the lake or the river, the only bathtub the family had, since they had no resources for showers and toilets and such facilities. It was just fifty or sixty people, anyway.

In her parents' room there was a bed with springs about to give up the ghost and a mattress with stuffing coming out everywhere, and a chest of drawers painted blue with two cracked mirrors. In her and her brothers and sisters' room, there were rusty bunks with palm frond mattresses for the girls and burlap hammocks for the boys; the remainder of the furnishings consisted of wooden crates sent in by Harvest, meant for the tomatoes the family picked but held back to keep their few articles of clothing in. Tierra poked around in the crate that belonged to her; everything in it was dirty.

"Mamá! What have you been doing, for me not to have any clean clothes?"

The woman called back from the porch, her voice feigning irritation:

"What have I been doing!? *Alabao!* You best watch your mouth, young lady. I've been working like a mule, and you're a big girl now, so you can go down to the river and wash your own clothes! You go down there often enough to jump in and cool off that crack between those legs of yours!"

The woman looked out at the other bohíos, which belonged to her parents, aunts and uncles, brothers and sisters, nieces and nephews. No, surely they wouldn't have the nerve to throw them out. Besides, the Higher-Ups had their smidgen of respect for what they called the Backward Ones. Tierra found a clean change of clothes in her brother Felipón de la Caridad's crate; she surreptitiously stuffed it in a little plastic bag—one of the bags they planted the coffee in—and threw it over her shoulder. She walked out past Santa on her way to saddle and untie her bright bay, Sunny.

"Are you off running around like a tomboy again astraddle that blasted beast?"

Doors in the neighboring dwellings had begun opening and kids were streaking into the clearing like little balls of lightning, running off to play on the lands that bordered the batey.

"What's up, cousin?" Santa called out to Cornelia, the daughter of one of her father's sisters and also her sister-in-law, since she lived with one of Santa's brothers.

The hunchbacked cousin remarked on her creaky joints and the weather report she'd just heard on her portable radio, how uncertain the weather promised to be—they couldn't tell whether the heat was going to be normal today or scorching. During the day, those were the only two possible variations in the weather; it was only at night and in the wee hours of the morning that it got any cooler. Tierra took advantage of the distraction, the confusion of greetings and the yelling of the kids, to leap astride her horse. Santa reacted:

"Tierra Fortuna Munda"—her mother called her by her whole name when she tried to impose a little authority— "you still haven't told me where it is you're off to." It was funny to hear the woman switch from *usted* to *tú* and back again.

"Over yonder, to see Papá." The girl kicked at the horse's flank with her bony ankles and the horse began to trot off toward the path that led out of the clearing.

"Be good, and don't you be bothering those people—I don't want one of those teacher-women in here complaining about you!"

"Don't worry, Mamá!" Tierra shouted over her shoulder as she disappeared into the thick stand of high grass, only to reappear galloping cross-country at full speed, tiny in the distance, like some magic sprite in those fairy tales about enchanted forests.

Meanwhile brigade number 9 had begun its agricultural labors under the tutelage of Bejerano and his son Chivirico Vista Alegre, who had introduced themselves to the teacher and students that the guajiros had been waiting for since before dawn. The teenagers would never forget that first sight of the field—at last they stood with their faces to the sun and their backsides to the city.

Before them opened a huge expanse of moist earth, covered in what looked like a blanket of soft white silk embroidered with transparent bugle beads—that was the image called to mind by the morning fog lying low to the ground, the plant's leaves glistening with drops of dewy mist. The hillocks appeared to the girls and their teacher alike as endless rows of green shoots rising out of the ground, waving their gleaming golden sabers in the air. They seemed to go on forever; they faded in the distance, behind a little rise in the ground—no more than the *hint* of a rise, really. At three blasts from Margot Wrangling's whistle the girls had jumped out of the cart. The guajiros were waiting for them. The girls' eyes were immediately drawn to the men's physical abnormalities—the father had more fingers than he should have (I forgot to point out that Santa also had four ears) and Chivirico Vista Alegre, forget it, his hands were like bunches of bananas, he had three eyes and two navels, though none of the girls managed to see the navels because they were covered by a blue T-shirt that hung to within a couple of inches above his knees.

The teacher had said good morning with her eyes averted from the men. The guajiros were used to people not wanting to commit their eyes to such strangeness. Bejerano was escorted by two German shepherds; despite the nobility of their faces, their intelligent eyes and warm noses, the dogs' size and physical strength commanded respect. The campesino ordered the animals to go to the shade, and then he began to explain how the work was to be done, while Chivirico Vista Alegre, with his hands and body, demonstrated. The girls were hardly listening; they were still mesmerized by the golden glow of the open fields shimmering before them. In a while they returned to reality, and it was then that the giggles and perverse remarks about the campesinos' bizarre physical features began.

"Whoever made those two put some extra effort in it, I'd say."

"They've got spare parts built in. I think in the military they call that redundancy."

"Hush, you girls! The poor things seem like they're real nice people."

Bejerano, however, went on explaining that they would begin by weeding the tomato plants; that is, pulling up all the pangola grass, which is what he called this particular weed—a weed, he pointed out, that cattle loved to feed on. Once they'd reached the unseen end of these rows, way down there in the distance, where this field met a field of plantains, they were to turn around and start back, along the rows that nobody had worked, and when they got back here to the beginning they would each pick up one of those empty oil cans that Harvest had brought in and start picking the tomatoes that were ripe. If one of them fell too far behind, then when it was time to go one of the others should start out from the other end of the row and meet up with her, because they were not to leave any of the rows half done. Without uttering a single syllable, Chivirico Vista Alegre would jump from one row of plants to another, pulling up weeds by the roots and then running back up the row to show the girls exactly what kind of weeds they were supposed to get rid of— and they were to leave them in the furrows, lying on the ground, waiting for sacks to be brought in to pick them up and throw them out or give them to the cattle.

A few yards away, a fifty-five-gallon drum had been unloaded. It was covered with a round wooden top and it held drinking water; a soup ladle hung from the edge. Migdalia Fake Eyelashes got herself named water girl (water *carrier;* the Revolution did not discriminate on the basis of sex), alleging a pain in her side that she'd waked up with that morning, she had no idea where it came from. Of course this was a huge lie, but she signaled to Carmucha Women's Shelter that she was not about to sink her long pearl-white-painted fingernails in all that dirt. She'd rather run back and forth, chattering for all she was worth, carrying water to quench the other girls' thirst—that would allow her to spend quite a bit of time in the shade and also trade gossip with her compañeras once in a while. More while than once, let it be noted.

The girls, including their teacher, were sitting or squatting at their respective workstations, ready to start weeding, and Bejerano asked if there were any questions. No one seemed to have any, so Margot Wrangling gave the order to start. The sky was a glorious deep blue, the fog and mist had burned away, and the landscape absorbed the light as though it had just been painted in oils.

The girls' feet sank into the red earth. As their torsos bent down to the plants, they discovered new muscles to have cramps in. Their hands eagerly patted around the stalks of the tomato plants, seeking out and eliminating any parasitic weed they found. They began with utmost care, trying at every moment, every step forward to discover positive, productive knowledge that would inform their lives, and therefore making hardly any progress, moving at a snail's pace. Margot Wrangling decided to lay it to them:

"Come on, you rattlebrains, move it! At the rate you're going we're never going to get to the other end before noon! Put some muscle in it, girls!"

Danae hated that word "rattlebrains." The idiotic teacher-guide used it even for going to the latrine, especially to humiliate other people and make herself feel superior. The girls started moving faster, charging at the rows of plants, and of course in their hurry they uprooted not only the weeds but the precious tomato plants as well, and then they would scrabble holes in the dirt, stick the plants in the ground again, and throw some dirt on the roots, planting them with a lick and a promise. Within a half hour their hands were numb, their backs stiff, their feet killing them, and their stomachs rumbling, because work and the country air were giving them a voracious appetite. The sun beat down on their thick khaki work shirts and the quilted jackets some of them were wearing, and in combination with the streams of sweat running down the creases in their skin the girls felt like armies of little ants were marching over them, biting here and tickling there. They began pulling off their shirts and jackets, and since they didn't have anywhere to leave them they knotted the sleeves around their waists, exposing their pale, transparent city skin, barely covered with T-shirts, light blouses, or tube tops, to the hot morning sun.

Bejerano and Chivirico worked at the head of the caravan, absorbed in their labors, not even straightening up for brief breaks. I might note that Bejerano was still a strong, able-looking man, somewhere around fifty years old, although due to his long exposure to the sun and the aridity of the countryside he appeared older. The girls' T-shirts were revealing, some very low cut, and neither of the men wanted to raise their eyes, to avoid misunderstandings. The sun began to burn the girls' delicate epidermis. For the time being, all they thought about was how nice it would be to return to the camp all suntanned, to flaunt their sexy bronzed skin before the boys.

The furrow Danae was working was next to Emma the Menace's. Emma couldn't stand her leather jacket, the Chaw, which she had tied around her waist, a second longer, so she asked permission to leave it by the water tank. On the other side of Emma was Irma the Albino, but she was straggling; in fact, she was the last of all the girls. The hot sun had started by frying her eyelids to a crisp—they looked like sautéed onions. She was so red that she looked like lobster salad with mayonnaise, because she was sweating lakes of talcum powder and Venus cold cream. Her eyes squinted, her eyelashes were blonder than ever, her lips were dry and cracked and covered with flakes of dead skin, her teeth were melted and yellow and covered with a viscous drool that blurred their edges, so when she opened her mouth it looked like she had one broad denture made out of some kind of off-white plastic. Irma stood up, and she once again felt a sharp shooting pain in the area of her kidneys. She was hit by a wave of pleasant dizziness, her head buzzed. She blinked, and drops of sweat dripped onto her cheeks. *I can't take this anymore,* she told herself; *I can't go on,* she muttered to herself; she had to get back to the barracks that very minute, gather up her stuff and head for home nonstop, get back to her family, her bed, and shade, beautiful shade.

"Irma! *Irma!* Wake up, you lazy thing! Stop that goofing off over there!

Aren't you ashamed of yourself, you slacker?" Margot Wrangling yanked her out of her daydream like a weed.

Farther on, Renata the Physical was inventing a new and improved way of moving along the rows; sitting on her backside in the furrow, she was scooting along, dragging her butt along beside the little hillocks of earth.

"Oh, that's cute, you bitch! Can't you see that you're fucking up my row?" scolded Brigida the Imperfect, hands on her hips.

But then she, too, sat down and stretched out her legs in front of her and dragged herself along the row. Soon others were imitating her, to the wrath and displeasure of Margot Wrangling.

The teacher was about to make another of her scenes when suddenly there was the sound of an engine, a sound very much like that of a helicopter. Halting in their tracks, the girls looked up, visoring their eyes with their hands; the sun gave them crow's-feet in the corners of their eyes, their mouths hung open, and their teeth glistened in grimaces or shy smiles. And sure enough, it was a helicopter, which came in flying almost at treetop level. A man leaned out and waved with a gloved hand. The girls waved back mechanically, all the while groping the wet earth with the fingers of their other hands, pretending to still be weeding. The dogs, hypersensitive, sensing that this was a bad omen, growled at the apparition. Chivirico reassured them by whispering baby talk and making an exception, this one time only, and giving them each a lump of brown sugar.

The helicopter made a second pass over the field, then came back and hovered directly over the girls' heads. The man leaned out again, and they could see that he was holding a big box of something in his lap. He pulled his hand out of the box and began scattering handfuls of little brightly colored objects that fluttered to the ground. At first, the girls weren't sure how to react. And then they realized that the sky was raining candy, and they threw themselves on it like Huns pillaging a defenseless village—it was a piñata at a poor kid's birthday party. Nor was Margot Wrangling far behind them this time. Bejerano and Chivirico stood stunned by this spectacle, their eyes like saucers, but they didn't move a muscle. The girls ran, hair and clothes flying, their hands full of hard candies wrapped in gold, silver, and colored paper. They filled their pockets with the treasure—the sweet payola—and when they had picked the field as clean as an army of locusts might have, they returned to their stations.

"Who are those people, Bejerano?" Danae asked. In a fit of vanguardism she had outdistanced the rest and screeched to a halt just before she ran into the two campesinos.

Before answering, the man raised his eyes and studied the expression on the teacher's face, which was at more or less the same height as his.

"Whatever you want to know, you need to direct your question to me, all right, Danae?" Margot Wrangling said officiously, and Bejerano lowered his head. The girl understood.

"I asked him, not you. What I want to know, I ask anybody I think might know enough to answer my question. Bejerano teaches us to work, I don't see why I can't speak to him without going through somebody else. I'm sure he can answer my question better than you can. We speak the same language; so far as I know, I don't need an interpreter."

"That's true. And I have no idea who those people in the helicopter were. Which doesn't mean you haven't earned yourself a demerit for insubordination." The woman had no pedagogical retort, but she couldn't keep herself from using revenge against the girl, who was so often standing up to her. "Could you tell us, compañero Bejerano, who those individuals in the helicopter were? Big shots, huh, more big shots?"

"*Ekelequá*, the Higher-Ups, miss," Bejerano said, but not to the teacher. His eyes had turned to Danae, who quickly thanked him, quite loudly and with a note of kindness, to be sure the others heard her.

"You have good manners, Beje, even if some people don't," she added.

Now a white Fiat, spattered with mud and dented around the headlights and fenders, was driving into the field from the highway at the end of the rows. It stopped and three men piled out. The driver remained inside the car. One of the men, a big, heavyset type in a military uniform, signaled to the girls to gather round him. The girls, curious, ran to greet the men, thinking that they must be very high up Higher-Ups. The heavyset one, they thought, must be the big boss, Brutus Escoria himself. His skin, whiter even than the girls', sweated something that looked like the water that separates out of yogurt, and his cheeks were a bright, false pink—as though he'd smeared rouge on them. The second one was Bejerano's boss, that is, the boss of the field bosses, Brutus Escoria's second-in-command and personal brownnose, and the third one was a studious-looking black man, the agronomist, loaded down with file folders, of course, and smiling uncomfortably. The dogs stepped out of the shade and breeze at the edge of the woods and trailed the visitors, growling softly. Brutus Escoria, naturally, spoke first:

"I'll bet you can't guess who it was throwing candy down out of the sky a few minutes ago! I'll eat my hat if it wasn't Papá Díos! Ha! Ha! Ha! Ha!" He laughed like a man in some third-rate clown act.

The girls weren't such an easy crowd, though, and the only ones that allowed themselves to find the laugh infectious were two or three opportunists and the teacher. Not even Bejerano and Chivirico Vista Alegre; in fact, they had practically ignored the group's arrival, and were still weeding.

"Bejerano, come over here and say hello, you old bastard, you guajiro leper, you!" yelled Brutus Escoria.

Bejerano hesitated a moment, thought about it, and told himself it would be best if he didn't trifle with this blustering bigmouth. So he went over, held out his hand, his eyes humble. Chivirico Vista Alegre followed his father's lead and made the same gesture, but Brutus Escoria, seeing his unnatural fingers, made a gesture of revulsion and pulled his hand back, raising it to his head instead and scratching his scalp. Then, regretting his squeamishness, he shook the young man's hand, although afterward he wiped his fingers off on his pants leg.

"Your son, eh? I think we met once before."

"Yep, my son. You've met him several times, but it's like you don't have much recollection of it."

Then Brutus Escoria acted like *Who? Me?* and turned his expression of knowing innocence toward the girls, trying to make them see him as kindly and understanding.

"You're always forgetting to call me compañero, Bejerano . . . So these girls stop working anytime some stranger comes along and tosses candy at 'em? Tsk, tsk, an undisciplined bunch, this one, eh, Bejerano? But I suppose we'll have to forgive them, since this is their first offense . . . So tell me, girls, are you tired? You look kinda wilted to me."

"Yes-s-s-s!" they chorused.

"Well, you'll just have to find some energy somewhere, then, because you've got one shitload of days left here, not counting the rest of today. But I'm sure all of you will pull up your socks and see this through, won't you?"

"Yes-s-s-s-s-s!" they all chorused again. "Who's the greatest? Who's the greatest? Number 9! Number 9! Number 9! Hoo-ra-a-a-ay!"

"All right, you go back to what you were doing now. We need to talk to Bejerano a minute here."

Brutus Escoria laid his arm over the campesino's stooped shoulder. The girls returned to their labors. The Higher-Ups, standing in a circle a short distance from Danae, tried to keep from being heard but the wind carried their conversation. Brownnose spoke first.

"Beje, *compay*, you don't wanna make me look bad, do you? You've got to move, compañero, there's no other option. This is life or death."

"You're here with that again? I don't understand how it is that you can put me to work with these scholarship students one day and the next day come in here with this mess about the batey being too close to the camp, it's a bad example for the girls. *Caray,* you need to decide which one it is . . ."

"Those are two different things, Bejerano. In the first place the batey is, it's true, close to the barracks. The parents don't like it even a little bit that their children are so close, running the risk of being influenced by you people. But we could get around that; we already did it once by moving the kids over to Río Verde, but we can't do that now, we haven't got the capacity, we'd have to send them off to another province, and I'll tell you, *compay* . . ." Brownnose's voice trailed off as he cleared his throat noisily and hacked up a dark wad of phlegm, which he spat out, turning his head half away. "But in the second place, and the most pressing issue, you see, is that we're about to build a luxury hotel here. You've gotta go, you can't stay there . . . Oh, and they're not scholarship students. I keep tellin' you, they're students who come out to the country temporarily, like the last time . . ."

Brutus Escoria interrupted, attempting to persuade more guilefully:

"You'll be given a new place to live in town, in a microbrigade building. . ."

"Don't think I was born yesterday. I know what a cooperative is—it's a sewer. No, I said, no!" The old man turned stiff and angry. The dogs perked up their ears, on alert, showing their teeth and growling more audibly.

"Are we going to have to use force, Bejerano? Don't make us do that . . ." Brutus Escoria was watching the dogs out of the corner of his eye.

"*Caballeros,* leave him be now. He needs to think about this situation." It was the agronomist stepping in. "You can't just shove it down their throats like that. Let up a little, all right?"

"And who invited you to this party? You just see to your beets and tomatoes and don't be sticking your nose in where it doesn't belong. *Alabao,* the blacks are doing so well in this country they think they can have opinions." And Brutus Escoria smiled broadly, patting the agronomist's back half threateningly, half-jokingly.

The professional slipped away from the big man.

"All right, *ekobio,* let me do my job, then." Turning to Bejerano, he asked, "Is the brigade working for you all right, the girls understand about the weeding?" The guajiro nodded, his face suddenly lighting up with gratitude for the fact that someone was asking his opinion in a positive way.

"What do you mean 'working for *you*'? Nobody works for him or anybody else here. Goddammit, let's get this straight, he's just the head of a shitty tomato field . . ." protested Brutus Escoria.

The agronomist went on without paying the man's words any attention. He rested his hand on the campesino's shoulder in a gesture of friendliness.

"Listen, now, I'm not sure yet, I haven't received the latest information, but I think tomorrow we won't be in this field, we'll be going to the beets, or maybe the potatoes or sweet potatoes—or even the tobacco."

"Then what brigade am I supposed to have tomorrow? Because the beets and the potatoes and the sweet potatoes belong to me, but the tobacco, only a piece of it is mine, not all of it. I say 'mine' because they put me out here to work on it, not because it's actually mine . . ." His eyes, squinting in the sunlight, glanced mischievously over at Brutus Escoria's hypocritical face.

"Don't worry. I just got through saying that you'll be staying with brigade 9 till the end," the agronomist announced.

"I think you need to be careful what you promise here, *compañero.* Programming who works with what brigade where, and when, around here—I'm the one that decides that," Brownnose cut in, his tone bullying and vulgar, "since I'm the head of the field bosses. As far as I know I'm still in charge here."

"And as the agronomist, I'm telling you that I want Bejerano to instruct this brigade. He has the most experience of anyone around here, he's taught the members of his batey. It's knowledge that's come down for generations. He loves the land, and that's what I care about—I want the girls to learn to cultivate, but also to love the land, because that, you can't force anybody to do, it's not a question of wham, bam, thank you ma'am. In two minutes we could destroy all these crops . . . Look, look how they've trampled those plants out there, running after that goddamn candy of yours—a disaster. The tomatoes are ruined, they've burst all over the place. And if this gets fucked up out here, the one that pays the consequences, from the point of view of getting the work done in the most efficient way and most profitably, is me, my friend—so you just go write that up in your report."

There was the sound of a horse galloping at full speed. The rider emerged out of the dense shadows of the woods, coming like a streak of dark lightning; the horse jumped the hood of the car, slowed as it reached the furrows, passed alongside Danae, and pulled up short just as it reached the circle of men. The horse pranced nervously around the group. It was Tierra Fortuna Munda, her hair blown wild, her forehead furrowed, her mouth set in fury, her fists, white-knuckled, grasping the horse's reins.

"We'll discuss this later, with the officials upstairs, at the appropriate levels," said Brownnose, uneasy at the presence of my goddaughter, wanting to end the argument.

"Don't forget about that housing, you old leper." Brutus Escoria poked his finger in Bejerano's chest. Chivirico Vista Alegre stepped forward a pace or two and firmly pushed his hand away. Brutus Escoria guffawed again, as he had at first, a laugh of feigned victory. "Ha! Ha! Ha! *Caramba,* this one's a tough guy, *mira,* this son of his is a tough one, by god!"

"Papá, tell him no, we aren't leaving, and they're not going to cut down the ceiba tree either! They'll have to kill me first!" Tierra was shouting and the horse reared up, its eyes wild.

I felt a wave of tremendous pride, seeing my goddaughter come to my defense that way, but I already had plans for teaching those men a lesson. Bejerano was keeping the dogs under control; they were riled, barking and snarling to put fear into any man, and ready to sink their teeth into somebody. Brutus Escoria looked at Tierra Fortuna Munda with a mixture of lechery and contempt.

"You can shut your mouth, girl. Nobody's going to cut down the ceiba tree. You think we're idiots? By the way, I didn't know bitches could talk . . . *Oye, muñeca,* tell me something. People around here say you've got six nipples. 'S that true?"

This time Brutus Escoria had crossed a line, and Chivirico Vista Alegre couldn't control his rage; he charged the blustering windbag. The dogs leapt forward, too, in defense of the offended brother, but Bejerano threw his arms around their necks, his hands just under their ravening jaws, and held them back. At a sharp word from him, the dogs sat, but their eyes were fixed on what was happening. Chivirico Vista Alegre was hanging on Brutus Escoria's back and not letting go. Seconds later Bejerano left the dogs and went over to put an improvised headlock on his son and pull him off the boss. His ill-cared-for mouth spat out the only warning he would give, straight in Brutus Escoria's face:

"I'm not looking to hurt you, but let this be the last time you insult a member of my family. You tell her you're sorry or I'll skin you right here, like a sheep." The father was still holding Chivirico Vista Alegre with one hand, but with the other he pulled a hunting knife out of his belt.

"I don't want trouble either, but the next time that half-witted son of yours as much as looks cross-eyed at me, I'll have him in court, or give him another kind of lesson he won't soon forget . . . You don't know who you're fucking with, I'm not scared a nobody. My fambá is the most powerful one there is, my prenda gives me tremendous protection . . . But I won't press the matter, Beje, just so we're all happy here, I'll apologize.—I apologize, Tierra." The words came out grudgingly, from between Brutus Escoria's clenched teeth. Then, not content to leave things as they were, he looked at her with contempt and lechery again and said with unmistakable insinuation, "You know, your name suits you." Then he and Brownnose laughed obscenely again; the agronomist smiled, but not vulgarly.

In a while they went away, without saying goodbye to the teacher, who had moved on ahead in her furrow just enough to be able to pretend that she hadn't heard a thing, so she could get out of testifying if it came to that. Danae, on the the other hand, had stayed back on purpose, intending to take part indirectly as a witness to the argument.

The car's engine started but the wheels spun futilely, spraying mud in every direction. Brownnose and the agronomist had to get out and push;

they managed to extricate the machine and then ran and jumped in as the car moved away, as though they were in some old Western, robbing a stagecoach while being pursued by savage Indians. The dogs, back in the shade, lay down and rested, their mattery eyes blinking watchfully, looking from one side to another.

However, Danae's attention was on the rider and her horse, galloping off frenziedly, the noise of the horse's hooves louder than the car engine, toward the plantain fields at the other end of the parcel they were working. The girl's curiosity was piqued, and she had an urge to follow the rider, escape with her, know more about her life.

Bejerano and Chivirico Vista Alegre hurried back to get started weeding again. Emma the Menace wanted to take a rest, so she took a moment to approach her friend Danae Duckbill Lips with two tomatoes, cleaning the dried mud off them carefully with her shirt tail. When they were lustrously clean, she bit into one of them and extended the other one toward Danae. These were "kitchen tomatoes," as they were called, with pointed ends, Romas, perfect for making paste with, or sauces. They were delicious—what a treat, the taste of tomatoes picked fresh off the vine! There was no flavor like it. The two girls' taste buds reveled as their mouths filled with the sweet-acid tang.

"I need to get permission to go pee," whispered Danae, sucking at the skin of the red fruit.

"You won't get it. Margot's got the rag on today serious. Plus it's just fifteen minutes till break," Emma answered, pointing at the wristwatch that hung from the strap of her T-shirt.

The other girl shrugged her shoulders, devoured the rest of the tomato, and, cleaning her hands off on her pants, leaving tiny yellow seeds and specks of reddish pulp, walked off resolutely, stepping over rows of tomato plants, toward the teacher-guide.

"Uh, I need to go attend to my physiological necessities," she said. She might have said "use the bathroom" or, more precisely, "do number one" or "number two," but she preferred to leave the time it would take in doubt, use a more refined-sounding and ambiguous phrase so as to ingratiate herself with the teacher and make getting the permission easier.

"You can wait; it's just a few minutes to the break." The teacher did not deign even to look at her.

"I can't. I gotta go. I already waited long enough to get cancer of the kidneys and intestines. My, uh, bowels are not in great shape."

"*Vaya, muchacha,* you're certainly a gotta-do-it-now girl, aren't you? Go on, then, but hurry up. It's not the *runs* these rattlebrains suffer from, it's wanting to run off!" And she watched the girl dart away, scorning her for being young, for being a student, for being brave—or rather, for being a girl who knew what she wanted.

Danae ran, ran, ran toward the curtain of green, the plantain field she had seen my goddaughter Tierra Fortuna Munda disappear into a few minutes ago. She was going to look for her. Her feet sank into the wet doughy red mud, and despite the fact that she tried to step in the hollows and not on the crops, there were moments when she could not avoid squashing fresh tomatoes. The juice and red pulp spattered and stuck to her ankles; the heat of the day dried the pulp, and soon it began to rot. She could hardly breathe, from the running and the emotion. Her chest heaved because she sensed that it must mean something, something profound, when the rider was a teenager named Tierra, which was pretty mysterious in itself, who had actually appeared to her in her dreams. That, from the point of view of reality, was *very* weird. As she ran she could feel the looks the other girls were giving her, imagine the questions they were asking themselves and each other. They'd be figuring that the last thing she would be doing in the next few minutes was emptying her bladder or her bowels. Thin dark lines of sweat began to show on the fabric of her T-shirt; the quilted jacket tied around her waist cumbered her, but she went on at full speed until she was deep in the thick stand of sticky, aromatic leaves with their unmistakable smell of ripe fruit.

At first she experienced no fear, but as she went farther and farther in, the plantain field began to swallow her, suck her into it. Finally she came to a point at which the lush, broad leaves prevented her from seeing the sky. The humidity, mixed with the sticky sap that oozed from the leaves, covered not just her clothes but her hair, her entire body. She noticed that it was beginning to be hard to open her lips; her skin was slowly turning gray from the stains left by the plantain leaves. She could hardly move forward anymore; she stuck to the stalks. She didn't know how far she had come; she looked all around her and realized she also didn't know which way she'd come from or which way she was going, she had lost her sense of direction. If she took a few steps one way, she wondered whether she might not actually be going back the way she'd come; if she struck out forward, she thought she was swerving off to one side, going off at an angle. She made the fleeting mistake of stopping, and then she didn't know what to do. And to top it off, inside the forest of plants it felt as though night was about to fall. If she hadn't been sure of the time, sure that it was still before noon, she could have sworn that it would soon be pitch-dark night. The vapor given off by the earth inflamed her lungs. I, the powerful ceiba tree, was witnessing an adventure that I knew beforehand was inevitable. I, in fact, had added certain elements of my own creation to it. That girl deserved to discover the mysteries, live from this moment on differently than those who'd come here with her. Tierra Fortuna Munda, on the other hand, *knew* the mysteries; she had lived in a world of presentiments and premonitions since the day she was born. Would the ending be tragic? Oh, unquestionably, like all respectable endings. Or perhaps not, but happiness in these cases of fortuitous encounters is highly unlikely.

I don't know whether it was my breathing that infected Danae with the sweet dream or just a breeze that swept over her eyelids. She let herself drop to the ground; taking care that her clothes lasted a whole week, until her mother came on Sunday with clean ones, wasn't worth the effort anymore. But some inner alarm told her that she couldn't allow herself to sleep; she knew she was lost, and that made her afraid. So she'd no sooner lain down than she slowly stood up again and with difficulty, stretching her body, her joints cracking, she carefully contemplated the weedy ground. Instead of looking for her own footprints, she put her hand to the ground and felt the countless prints of countless shoes, boots, horseshoes, and naked feet, stamped one on top of another. She put her ear to the layer that covered the phreatic mantle and listened—she had read about doing this in some novel or seen it in some Technicolor movie. It made her feel better to hear a sort of murmur, a buzzing, throbbing sound, a sound like that of some endless monastic labyrinth in which the nuns muttered intermingling prayers. Of course she had also never seen a real-life nun, just one in a movie in which a little boy was orphaned. Wait—was it a nun or a priest, a little boy or a little girl? What difference did it make? She was getting ready to call out when she heard a horse snorting, breathing heavily nearby, then a rustling sound, like a fire devouring the vegetation, an eerie noise; it also seemed to be an animal singed by the flames, snorting, hanging between life and death. Something or someone was coming, leveling anything that stood in its path.

Tierra Fortuna Munda stopped, panting, still waving the machete, sniffing the air. Affirmative! She smelled a person, panic, a person from the city or the nearby town. The scaredy-cat people from the city breathed in a particular way, different, heavy, thick as whipping cream, and from the oils that melted out of human fat there emanated a whole spectrum of fragrances smeared on at different times. She could smell everything from cologne put on several days ago to the residue of whitewash from walls, drops of gasoline, paint, traces of several meals, eggs, fried potatoes, pizza, soap . . . all those essences, diluted in an oversecretion of adrenaline, filled the air, tainting the purity of nature's own incense. Tierra was convinced—with her free hand she pushed aside a large leaf, and she was not surprised by the presence of a face whose muscles were contracted in uncertainty, a body absolutely rigid yet trembling uncontrollably. The two girls looked at each other for what seemed like several seconds, and then my goddaughter decided to move on. Danae, still a bundle of nerves, grabbed Tierra by the wrist, holding her, but Tierra yanked her hand away.

"Wait! . . . I got lost looking for you . . . My name is Danae and the girls in my class call me Duckbill Lips," she said in a tone of supplication, trying so hard to make Tierra like her.

The girl with the wild hair signaled to her to follow her—she'd show her the way out.

"Wait, I don't want to go back so soon . . ." replied Danae.

Tierra Fortuna Munda's red eyes showed that she had been crying, and there were smears of clean skin showing through the dirt on her face where she had wiped away the tears of rage and the mucus from her runny nose with the back of her hand. She quickly turned her eyes away when they met Danae's. It was Danae who decided to make herself comfortable among the plants. Tierra hung back when Danae tugged at her hand to come down and sit with her; she was skittish, like a cat, and she picked a stalk of *aguañusongo*, the grass of the sacred river wherein lives Tanze, the great sacred fish.

And then I, her godmother ceiba tree, foresaw her fate in the tenderness of her heart. She was going to sit down next to the newcome girl; the girl represented salvation, or at least would open for Tierra the doors of flight.

Although the flight might be long in coming, it would imply the departure, final and definitive, for another world. Flight before that, early flight—ah, then it would be Tierra Fortuna Munda who had to make that decision. She had two options: escape soon or escape late, but the inevitable result would be flight, flight from the beloved place of childhood, from the heart and soul and entrails of her origins.

Though they sat beside one another, it took the girls a long while to begin to talk. Silence reigned for excruciatingly long minutes. Because of the excitement, Tierra Fortuna Munda's navel began to ooze a guava liquor. Danae Duckbill Lips pretended not to notice, but her mouth began to water; she loved guava jam, guava paste, guava made into any sweet at all, especially with slices of soft white cheese. Lying on her back, Tierra could contain some of the torrent that flowed from her navel, but only temporarily; first a puddle formed, then a pool, then a lake. Danae, lying back also, closed her eyes and imagined that the other girl had become a fruity beach. She moved her elbow and brushed against the Other, and Tierra shrank back instantly, startled and afraid.

"I got permission to go to the bathroom." They both smiled. "But I really wanted to find out about you. There's no reason for me to get involved, but I didn't like the way those people treated you and your family . . . The Higher-Ups, right?"

"The Lowest of the Low. The Slitherers. The Drag Their Potbellies on the Ground . . . One night they'll set fire to the batey, they'll burn it down and kill us all . . . I don't trust them, at all at all, they're all a bunch of sons of bitches."

"What's your name?"

"Tierra Fortuna Munda."

Danae reached out for Tierra's hand, and this time Tierra did not draw back. Their fingers intertwined and I made sure to thrill them with a shiver they had never felt before, a tickle, the pleasure of strangers coming together, nothing banal, nothing to spoil this moment. A half inch from becoming *niñas malditas*—bad girls, perhaps even damned.

"Is God a man or a woman?" Tierra Fortuna Munda asked in that hoarse, standoffish boy's voice of hers.

"A man, of course," said the city girl, by rote.

"What do you know? You don't know nothing! Nobody's ever seen him. I kinda like to think that he's a woman . . ."

"?" The silence hummed softly, like a question hovering in the air. Danae shrugged her shoulders and looked away; a file of ants was marching past with an infantry's worth of bits and crumbs of bread. "God a woman, what an idea! Can you imagine God having a period, and breasts?"

"We women are stronger, we can do more than men—I see it in my Mamá, she's smarter than Papá . . . I understand everything before my brothers do . . . And even before Papá . . ."

"I don't want to burst your bubble or anything, but that doesn't mean a thing. Everything's organized so God is, and always will be, a man."

"Why not disorganize things?"

"Disorganize what?" The girls' hands were perspiring with emotion. Danae was losing interest in her own argument.

"That 'everything' that makes us believe that God is a man . . . Although, come to think of it . . . nobody's ever asked what sex the Holy Spirit is, right? The Holy Spirit might be a woman."

"The what? Nobody changes the world, the universe, history . . . don't be stupid."

Tierra Fortuna Munda reacted by hitting the other girl, hard.

"Don't ever call me stupid again! I'm normal, do you hear! Normal!"

Danae realized that she had made a mistake; the other girl probably had all kinds of complexes on account of her physical defects.

"I quit going to school because of those damn insults. The others would never stop calling me stupid, retard, monster, freak . . . !" She had turned and was lying with her body against the ground, hiding her face among the stones and grass.

"I'm sorry, I didn't mean anything like that . . . I didn't mean to hurt your feelings." She took the other girl's head in her hands and turned it toward her. Her lips touched the muddy cheek.

Tierra wept, kicked, sobbed. Danae didn't know what to do to console her. She started crying, too. They both cried so much that they never knew exactly when their lips met, the way two cherries hanging from branches on two separate trees, blown together by the wind, kiss, or two pieces of papaya, swimming in a bowl filled with nectar, find each other, rub together, longing to be whole again. Their bodies clung tightly to each other, and they hardly understood the pulse of desire, its throbbing; they lay quietly, still dressed, the six erect nipples of the campesino girl, like the pink-colored flesh of genip fruits, rubbing against Danae's chest, their pelvises rubbing against each other softly, their fingers intertwined. Danae noticed that the other girl's skin was like sandpaper, rough. She liked it. Should they stay like that, in that position? One of them did not know it was forbidden; the other one did, but didn't care.

Voices coming from the tomato field woke them from their languorous spell. Everyone was out searching for Danae. Concern, uneasiness were in the shrieking calls of Bejerano and Chivirico Vista Alegre. The teacher-guide gave the order to comb the plantain field, though the guajiro stopped the searchers, saying that more girls might just get lost. Danae and Tierra smiled mischievously, and their smiles culminated in peals of laughter, muffled in the hollows of their hands. Danae pleaded with Tierra to come with her, she wanted to introduce her new friend to the other girls. The girl with the wild, knotted hair shook her head. Danae Duckbill Lips insisted:

"Come on, shoot, don't be that way. Don't let them get you down."

"Not today, I'm too upset. I think my head is going to explode, I'm so mad."

They promised, then, to meet that night, at the foot of the ceiba tree; that is, at my roots, or maybe in a more isolated place, the nearest tobacco-drying shed, or in the batey, or in the fields of high grass near the barracks. There wasn't time to be specific, so my goddaughter offered to come for the other girl, at the barracks. Meantime she led her through the plantain field for a while, until she could show her how to get out. When they said goodbye, the halo of my magic still lay over them. Tierra Fortuna Munda's skin sucked up the shower of dewdrops that sprinkled over her as she ducked back into the thick vegetation. Danae stepped out into the brutal sunshine, and she looked as though her body were absorbing all its rays.

"Where have you been, rattlebrain? You had us scared to death!" Margot Wrangling flew like an arrow to shake the girl and humiliate her, but I managed to halt her in her tracks by seeing that hundreds of cockleburs stuck to her varicose legs. "Ay-ay-ay! Aiieee!"

"I got lost. Fortunately, I found his daughter"—she gestured toward Bejerano— "and she helped me find the way back."

"We had to hold the meeting without you. We elected Brigida the Imperfect brigade leader . . ." said Margot W., while with her long fingernails she tried to pick off the almost invisible but extremely sharp spines of the little burrs.

"You didn't miss anything much. I'll bet my bumpers you had a *good* time out there—your eyes are sparkling like little diamonds, girl." Emma the Menace could always see right through her.

"*Caballeros,* look, they've turned on the water for irrigation—come on! Let's have a bath! And over there, look! The sprinkler's on!" Renata the Physical was always at the head of the class when it came to culture and recreation; she had no equal in spotting entertainment, even a mile away.

"You're not going anywhere—don't even *think* about it! (Cough, cough, cough!) . . . Ugh, I don't know what's wrong with me . . . (cough, cough, cough) . . . I think I inhaled one of those fucking thorns (cough, cough, cough)." Margot Wrangling tried to stop the girls by waving her arms at them. Salome the Satrap took advantage of her helplessness to beat her on the back several times, pretending to want to clear her lungs.

Chivirico Vista Alegre ran to the head of the rows to get some water for the teacher. He ran back with the water in an empty milk can, but by the time he got there there were only two or three sips left; in his haste, half the water had sloshed out of the can. The teacher drank it down, never so much as thanking the young man.

About a hundred yards away, the girls were bathing under the spray from the irrigation feeder pipe, splashing mud, playing with the controls, and trying to shoot water on each other. Laughing and giggling, they would hold their mouths open and swallow the pearly water, and the streams of water would make gurgling sounds as it ran into their mouths and down their throats. Even Irma the Albino, usually so withdrawn and uninterested, had been swept up in the collective euphoria. Songs trilled forth like the water itself, and the girls followed the course of the water until, perching on one end of the aqueduct, they slid down the length of the channel, pushed along by the force of the water, finally reaching a small tank that served as a drinking trough for the animals. There they grabbed the edge of the cement walls, because a dangerous vortex formed at the drain and they ran the risk of being dragged down and carried to the depths of a communal well.

Far from the noise and merrymaking, Tierra Fortuna Munda looked on at the spectacle of her nature being usurped by a bunch of girls made giddy by any silly thing that happened. Deep down, she was angry; she would have liked to be one of those city girls without a care in the world, although she was sure that she would never be able to live anywhere but the country, or with her family, or her horse—not to mention me, the godmother ceiba tree! That made me feel very proud . . .

She was frightened by all those unknown emotions. She had never felt anything like them before, a pleasant tickling sensation, an itch that made her feel vulnerable. Her chest, what she called "the box of whimsy," was now beating hard, in turmoil. She observed the tiny silhouette of Danae, dancing around in an improvised shower of silver droplets. She believed the girl had forgotten her, judging by her change of mood—just then she looked so much happier, so unconcerned about anything except irrigation pipes and the sprayer making its rhythmic silver circle.

"No . . . there's no way she's forgotten you," I whispered in Tierra Fortuna Munda's ear. "Danae would love for you to join them. Right now she's asking herself what the flavor of sunrise might be if she were in your company."

Tierra smiled, cocked her head to one side, tenderly closed her eyes, and with her cheek caressed the breeze that slipped between the skin of her face and the smooth ridge of her shoulder. That was our secret code, our exquisite, sweet way of caressing each other. That was the way she showed her affection. The love between a girl and a ceiba tree.

Brigade number 9 ended its day's labors at seven that night. The teacher-guide was not satisfied with the day's work, although she qualified that—for the first day, it wasn't bad. While Bejerano was totting up the number of furrows weeded and the cans of tomatoes picked, trying to reconcile his list with Margot Wrangling's, the girls lay in the bed of the cart and rested. If it weren't that they were singing and waving their legs up at the sky, it might have looked like this was one of those terrible carts piled with the bodies of the dead, like in war movies. Bejerano, for his part, took his hat off to the girls' tremendous effort that day, although his kind words to them did nothing to soften the nasty teacher-guide's attitude toward the campesino. Chivirico Vista Alegre had decided to go off with the dogs to give them some scraps or maybe let them catch one of the little siskins that flew around close to the ground.

The cart bumped and lumbered along the dirt road between the fields; with all the bouncing, it was a wonder one of the girls wasn't bounced out. When they reached the camp, Danae was the first to jump down and take off running, so she could be first in line for the showers; fortunately, brigade number 9 had arrived before all the others and the showers were empty. Positioning herself in front of the black plastic curtain, she waited impatiently for a second person to come in, to hold her place for her. While the second person bathed, she'd run back and get the things she needed out of her suitcase. Renata the Physical came in, dragging the heels of her wood-soled sandals. She sounded like a one-girl rhythm section for a rumba band—*clack, clack, clackity-clack, clack, clack, clack-clack!*

"You go on in while I get my soap and towel," Danae said, stepping aside for her and then running back to her bunk. Each person was allowed five minutes under the shower—or the dribble, rather.

A large group was gathering along the cement hallway that led to the latrines. As Danae came back, she ran into Renata the Physical as she was coming out, her hair wet, her body clean, and without the clods of red clayey soil that had spotted it. When she saw Danae, she smiled uncomfortably.

"Listen, Duckbill Lips, I couldn't save your place—you know what a pain in the ass Pancha Flatfoot is, she came in like somebody had run her tit through the wringer, and she was ready for a fight—if she was number one in line, she said, then she was number one in the shower, and nobody got ahead of her. You know how she gets. So I had to let her in."

"What about the rest of these people?" Danae pointed to the enormous crowd waiting behind Pancha Flatfoot. "Didn't they do anything? Didn't anybody protest? What are they, for decoration around here?"

Renata the Physical just shrugged her shoulders.

"They're terrified of the monster-girl. Adversity, *mi amiga,* adversity."

Danae pushed her way to the head of the line and yanked the curtain away so violently that it came down, rod and all.

"Eeeeh! What bug's in your britches, bitch? What are you looking at me for, are you a dyke or did you just never see the Winged Victory of Samothrace with her head on?"

The hilarity was general over the sarcasm and feigned surprise shown by the girl, whose dark hair had been bleached blond with laundry soap and hydrogen peroxide and days in the sun as the girl sat in the branches of a yagrumo tree. She went on soaping her underarms, with no modesty whatever at exhibiting a pubic triangle of reddish hair that extended far to each side, then above that a double roll of belly fat marked by a vertical red line from her navel to her sex, like the scar of a caesarean, though she'd never had children. Her breasts hung like two bags, with enormous round nipples that pointed down toward the ground. The inside of the bathroom gave off an unbearable smell of B.O., piss, and vaginal secretions, with a hint of groin-sweat and ass encrusted with dry vomit.

"Don't just stand there! Close your mouth and put that curtain back! Move it!"

Danae picked the curtain up off the floor and set the rod back in its bracket.

"All right, that's the way I li-i-ike it, a little re-*spect!*" crowed Pancha Flatfoot at the girl's submissive gesture.

When she came out, she stepped up to Danae, lifted her chin and looked down her nose at her, and burned her with her dragon's breath.

"So—you got a problem?"

"Me? Nah, nah . . ." and she stepped into the shower to cool off, her spirit quashed by the hoots and laughter of the girls behind her.

In two shakes she had soaped down and scrubbed her body, which was shivering with cold and embarrassment. What she wanted more than anything in the world was for night to come. At ten, when the camp director called for lights out, her new friend would come to get her. She tried to negotiate a decent place in the mess hall; that second night, the food was worse than the first: rice with mashed sweet potatoes. She devoured the gross mixture and wiped her tray with a piece of days-old bread. Then she hurried off to wash the warped rectangle of aluminum, ran to the barracks for her toothbrush, came back, and carefully brushed her teeth—she hated the taste and texture of the goo left in her mouth, between her teeth, by the tough bread and guava jelly.

Andrés Crater Face, "her" Andy, stepped between the barracks door and her.

"You look like you're in a hurry, princess—where's the fire?"

"Give me a break, I'm dead, I'm going to bed." She knocked aside the arm that was blocking her way.

"If you need some company . . . or if you decide it's too boring to sleep with the angels, you could try it with a little devil . . ."

Inside the barracks, she came upon Irma the Albino playing with some little pink creatures—newborn rats—wriggling and squirming on top of her pillow.

"Ech! That's disgusting!"

"No, Danae, look how cute they are; they're so defenseless. You know how squeamish I am, and my heart just melted when I saw them. I can't just throw them out of my mattress, can I? Aren't they sweet? Look how clean they are, too! See, aren't they cute! Answer me, *chica*."

"Like something out of a bad dream, especially when they grow up and turn into great big sewer rats."

"There're none of those here . . ."

"Wha-a-a-at?!"

"Sewers, *chica*, sewers—you forget we're in the middle of nowhere. All there are is rats, period, and they don't hurt anybody. I say live and let live . . ."

"You can let them live if you want to, but I don't want to see those things near my bed again, so you get rid of 'em, and I don't want to know how. Ech, I think I'm gonna throw up. You're nuts, you know?"

Irma the Albino made a nest for the animals in the cups of her brassiere, while Danae, dressed in a nightgown made of sheer cotton embroidered like a Nicaraguan wuipil, stood openmouthed, stunned.

At ten on the dot the camp's lights were turned off. Danae struggled against sleep, and just as she was about to lose the battle she thought she heard three taps on the window behind her bunk. Careful not to make a sound, she crept to the window, put out her hand, and opened it, but no one was there. The pink-tinged night, still colored by the waning sun, danced before the girl's eyes, more beautiful than any she'd ever seen before—in fact, this was only the second time in her life that she'd realized that night truly existed. A night with moon and sun at the same time. The crackle of footsteps on the wooden suitcases made the sleeping, hardworking beauties stir in their sleep. Danae put her right hand out, into the darkness of the aisle that ran down the center of the barracks, and her fingers touched the face of Tierra Fortuna Munda.

"Let's go out your window, hurry!" my goddaughter whispered.

Two shadows emerged from the Lethean mist, scurrying to reach the wetness of the path that ran into the fields of tall tobacco bordering the camp.

"Wait, Tierra, stop—aagh, what a pain, I can't wait . . ." Danae walked a few steps, doubled over with pain. "It's the sweet potatoes—oh god."

She had time to get her pants down, but not her panties; the rice with mashed sweet potato had given her diarrhea.

"I've gotta stop, I can't . . . here it comes—oh god, oh god, diarrhea. You'll have to go on without me; I'm going to have to go back and wash, change . . ."

"Did you get it on your pants?"

"No."

"Well, then, throw away the panties, wash off in the latrine—I'll wait for you here. Run, hurry!"

So she ran. One thing about Tierra, she made you want to have adventures—made you want to follow her lead, follow *her*. Danae took off her pants, being careful not to get them dirty. She wrapped her feces in the panties and threw the bundle into the immensity of the constellation-sprinkled darkness. She loved the idea of shooting that bundle of shit like a cannonball into the night, a nuclear-shit projectile aimed at the stars. She grinned. But only because she couldn't laugh out loud—somebody might hear her—although laughing out loud was what she really felt like doing. Running through the high grass, laughing, shouting at the top of her lungs that she was free, buck-ass naked—at last she had managed to run away from everything and everybody. Running through the night with a shit-covered ass fanned by the cool air down near a river ought to be one of the greatest ambitions of every human being. Although we're not *human* beings, she thought, we're *Cuban* beings. She entered the latrines, picked up a can, and splashed water on her backside. The starving maggots immediately went on the alert. In the drain channel stood a puddle of lice dip, milky, fetid. That evening, all their heads had had to file through and be treated, to avoid a general contagion.

"You smell like dead meat—we'll bathe in the lake, okay?"

Danae nodded.

"Then we'll go steal Sunny, that's my horse—my Papá won't let me ride him at this time of night. I'll show you the hills, the *mogotes*, the manatee . . . You'll get to see the only surviving manatee! And if you feel brave enough, I'll take you into town and we'll go to the bar, Maximino's place. You'll have to put on my brother Chivirico Vista Alegre's hat so they won't recognize you for a woman . . . It's a bar for drunks and sons a bitches."

Danae was delighted; she followed the girl with admiration in her eyes. Her gaze never left the girl's back, the wild hair, the face which every once in a while turned back toward her, bestowing upon her a smile so white it looked like the milky tail of the star that guided the three wise men in the drawings in those old books her mother kept in the rickety bookshelves in the little apartment in the city where she lived. Her house came to her just then like a flash of lightning, but she immediately wiped it out.

They cooled their naked bodies in the lake, which was full of silvery mollies and cichlids, frogs, minnows, and waterworms. Danae was afraid of the darkness of the water at first, afraid of putting her foot into that blackness, but the way Tierra fearlessly splashed around gave her courage. She looked at the other girl's body, inspected it as best she could, but the covering lent by the shadows of night conspired against her curiosity. Tierra was very thin, but strong, and Danae could actually make out the three pairs of nipples along her torso, like a cat's.

The weeds and grass around the lake were filled with little green lights blinking slowly on and off—fireflies, lightning bugs. And a boa, more lecherous than ever, wound about the trunk of a nearby tree. Out of the branches poured a mob of tiny fragile-looking dwarves, strange creatures, elves with glittering eyes. Their navels secreted guava juice and their heads were pointed, like a straw-thatched roof, like the bohíos where Tierra Fortuna Munda's family lived.

"Oh, look, come dance with the *güijes*." Danae hung back but Tierra went over to her and tugged at her hand. "They love to party!"

"But they're spirits!"

"Of course they are! What did you think, they were baseball players or macheteros in the vanguard?"

"We're naked!"

"So are they. But they keep their sexual parts in their pocket, in their minds."

The *güijes* sang and the girls danced, wiggling their hips and backsides, wriggling down and twisting back up again, down and up, like the blade on a milk-shake mixer. A fragrance of guava and soursop permeated the countryside. And then the manatee appeared, gliding along the surface of the water, its skin smooth and glistening. It swam past Tierra and she touched the elegant cetacean tenderly. Then the girls laughed out loud and sang that song by Guillermo Portabales—

> *In the palm grove down in the hollow*
> *There's a bohío covered with flowers*
> *Waiting for that cinnamon girl of mine*
> *The cinnamon girl that dreams of me at night*
> *If she dreams of love . . .*

As the *güijes* said good night they sprinkled the girls with a shower of luminous mist, which turned to honey as it touched the dewy ground. Danae and Tierra thanked the *güijes* for that gift with effusive words and gestures. Then they pulled their clothes on and ran to find Sunny, the horse Bejerano had given his daughter.

In the circle of dwellings, everyone was asleep. The girls crept forward silently, and while Danae watched for the slightest stirring, Tierra saddled her horse, murmuring sweet words in its ear so it wouldn't whinny or wake the others as she untied it and led it out of the batey. The animal understood that it needed to behave itself. Some two hundred yards away, the teenager leapt astride the horse and put out her hand, motioning for Danae to swing up behind her.

"You're crazy, I've never even ridden a mule."

"It's time you did." And in one strong motion she pulled her up behind her, astride the horse's hot muscular rump. "Hold tight, against my back, and don't let go even if they tell you you've won the best bull at the rodeo."

Tierra kept the horse at an easy gait for a good while, until they could get far enough away from the batey not to be heard. In town, at the bar, the Make It a Double, they went in disguised as men, with their hats pulled down over their eyes.

"Rum for us both," Tierra said to the weather-beaten bartender in a hoarse voice, her hand on the handle of her machete.

The rest of the men in the place were so drunk they barely took notice of the two newcomers and their strange behavior—one kicking his head back and slugging down the drink in one gulp, the other one coughing and choking from the tiniest sip. Tierra waited for her companion to finish the Guayabita del Pinar. They left without a word to anyone, swaggering like a town bully but trying not to exaggerate, so as to be credible.

When they had mounted Sunny again and trotted away, far enough to be out on the broad flat plain, Tierra kicked her heels into the animal, clucked softly, and the horse shot off, flying like the wind. Danae bounced almost a foot up off the horse's back, but as her fear began to leave her she was filled with the pleasure of the danger. She didn't think about the camp, or her sleeping classmates, or the teachers, or her mother, or anything but that girl she was holding on to and her swift steed. The only thing that mattered was the churning rhythm, the rough but pleasurable rocking, that she was experiencing at that moment. Later, the gallop became less frantic and she had the impression that they had been riding for miles and miles, hours and hours, or years, when suddenly there arose before her eyes a huge row of what looked like dinosaurs.

"Don't be scared, *machita*, those are the *mogotes*. This is the Valle de Viñales," Tierra said, her voice filled with awe. "You should see it in the day-time—at night you can't see the colors, the infinite shades of green."

Danae suspected that she was seeing an unusual sight, that this might never happen again, that she was being brought to see, for one time only, a unique moment in one of the most astonishing landscapes in the universe—and there was no way she could express her emotions. So she was silent.

"Say something!"

"I can't, I don't know what to say . . ."

They rode back in silence, at a full but easy gallop, and they slowed down only when they began to approach the camp. They decided to rest inside one of the tobacco-drying sheds. Danae was flushed with fatigue, and she felt feverish. Lying down exhausted, each girl in one of the huge tobacco-gathering baskets they found, they began to go over their brief lives while Danae ran her index finger around and around in a pool of guava jam that had oozed up out of Tierra's navel. There was not much to tell. Danae moved to her friend's basket and soon the two of them were asleep, snuggled into each other like little chicks.

"Oh shit, wake up! Hurry! It's twenty to five! Jesus! Hurry!" Tierra was whispering excitedly.

Danae's eyes fluttered open. She yawned and stretched her arms without the slightest sign of uneasiness or confusion—she thought she was waking up in her own house, that she had dreamed all of this, so lovely and indescribable it all was, thought all this was happening in a dream and that when she put her feet on the floor she'd be in the bedroom she slept in with her mother. Then the other girl's words registered.

"Twenty to five! Sheesh! I've gotta run! They ring the bell at five!"

"I know . . . !"

"But wait a minute—how the hell do you know exactly what time it is if you're not wearing a watch?" Danae asked perplexedly, panting as they ran across the fields.

Tierra Fortuna Munda had no time to reply. With her two hands she parted some raggedy bushes and cocked her head conspiratorially toward the suddenly visible barracks. They had come out directly opposite the window at the head of Danae's bunk. Danae ran swiftly across the road and clambered inside the building.

Lying on top of her mattress, still wearing her boots, she tried to breathe quietly, tried to calm the pounding of her heart. From up on one of the rafters, a gigantic rat was looking down at her. She avoided looking into those yellow, malicious eyes by covering her face with her pillow. The shrill chirping of the crickets and other night creatures began to fade, and the rising sun began to warm the breeze.

Dear first love,

We're back in the city and I want to tell you that I already miss the beautiful, incomparable experience I had with you in the country. Despite the terrible accident, the death of . . . I don't want to write about that, I still can't talk about it. I hate to even mention death.

But anyway, ever since we left the camp, today at five, all I've done is think about you and me. I know that it's going to be hard for me to get used to the city again, living with my mother Gloriosa Paz, and the grind of everyday reality dropping like a ten-ton truck on my memories. School again! Classrooms, ugh!!!

I rode almost all the way with my head out the window, breathing the good clean air, that indescribable smell of morning near the river. The green plains, glittering with dew. The minute we entered the city I started feeling this terrible, terrible anger and frustration. I can't tell you—I couldn't bear it.

Will we ever see each other again?

We got off the bus at the school entrance. The trucks had already brought the suitcases back, so we were each supposed to go and pick out the one that belonged to us. I went with the others, out of pure inertia I suppose, because I'd left my suitcase with that wonderful smell of papyrus and Persian poetry with you. I had the feeling that I'd forgotten how to walk on pavement, my feet felt too light and the street seemed like a cloud. Gloriosa Paz, my mother, was waiting like any other mother, but I must surely have told you that she's like a windmill when she starts waving her arms around and wanting to smother you with love. She makes such a spectacle of herself—it drives me crazy. Not to mention that she embarrasses me. She wasn't upset with me about the suitcase, she said she was proud of me because I wasn't selfish, and that you can replace anything but your good name. Then she cried. I hate it when Gloriosa Paz cries—it's like somebody's opened the dam. The parents of ——— (I won't mention her name, out of superstition) weren't there, and that made me very sad. Or her suitcase, either, because I'd taken it upon myself to give it to you, too.

Andy Crater Face was all over me, like always, making a pest of himself. You know, I'm sure, that as far as my general public is concerned he's something like my "boyfriend." I let people think that to throw them off—and so nobody will know about the secret relationship between you and me. I swear to you, and I know you believe me—the first in my heart is you. The second, Andy Crater Face, is a delicious trick, to keep anyone from suspecting. I don't suppose you're jealous. I always told you I wasn't going to hide these things from you. Andy Crater Face is a good kid, very in with all the other kids, and he's got a good heart—plus he dances something brutal. Of course his family is kind of common, off the rack, you know, not exactly tailor-made, although revolutionarily pure. You and I are a different kind of couple, complex, and we have to keep it to ourselves, because we *are* a secret.

You know you can come to my house whenever you want to. You can't go any longer without coming to Havana, if for no other reason than to prove to yourself that there's nothing in the world more beautiful than the Valle de Viñales. And so you'll regret that you came to visit me, the way I'm regretting right now that I've come back to this inferno—I should have stayed with you. But as soon as we're adults and can make our own decisions, and I can support myself financially, we'll change this situation.

My love, I know how much you must be suffering from the abuses of the Higher-Ups. I am, too—for you, for me, for your family, for all the problems that we've had to face—but what I don't understand is how those people can still be doing as they please! Although I have the feeling that nothing will happen to you and your family, and that makes me feel better. Justice always triumphs in the end. I *will* convince my mother to let me go see you. You come soon! A truckload of kisses. Your girlfriend.

SEVERAL YEARS PASSED, and from time to time I would receive letters addressed to my goddaughter Tierra Fortuna Munda and her brother Chivirico Vista Alegre. The mailman would pass by, look at my trunk bleeding from its folds and channels, the scars left by the machetes, and wonder aloud to the spirits:

"I don't know why I'm visited by these presentiments. The dead tell me not to deliver this envelope in person, they say it's better to leave it at the foot of this ceiba tree. If the path of the person it's addressed to leads that person to find it, then they'll find it."

And I, of course, did nothing to see that Tierra received the letters. I made no effort because I knew that the sender of them wasn't absolutely sure she wanted Tierra to receive them. The ones to Chivirico Vista Alegre, on the other hand, those I delivered to him personally, not to mention the fact that the mailman was less uncomfortable delivering them to the batey when they were for people—Chivirico, for example—other than Tierra Fortuna Munda, because there was something about Tierra Fortuna Munda that filled that poor mailman with superstition. He would hem and haw and mutter and curse, and swear that delivering letters to a person with a name like that couldn't possibly bring good luck or change the will of her fates.

But to get back to what happened the next morning, the morning after that night when Danae, led by the campesino teenager, sneaked out of the camp and was initiated into the mysteries of the earth—because to tell the truth, what happened all those years afterward is tinged with tragedy and I don't feel like talking about that now—even if it shouldn't be all that hard to guess where this thing is going, I don't want anyone to think I take any pleasure in the somberness of the situation.

So—the morning after the adventure, something hilarious happened. As usual the youngsters in both barracks were awakened at dawn, but this time not long after reveille they heard Patent Leather Director Puga call out:

"Camp, atten-*hut!* Fall in!"

The students realized that something was up; things smelled bad.

When all the brigades had fallen in for the morning formation, Director Puga and the other teachers stood before them. Margot Wrangling's fangs were dripping a poisonous-looking green mucus, and Mara Medusa looked as though her head was about to burst open like a volcano and spew out lord knows what, she was so mad. Her forehead was as furrowed as my trunk. Puga cleared his throat into his fist and then crossed his hands behind his back. He couldn't keep his legs still for a second; they were jittering ninety to nothing, and his knee was fairly vibrating.

"Anybody know what that is?" And he pointed to the recently white-washed wall of the barracks, now streaked with big broad brown brush marks.

There was no reply; all the girls shook their heads no.

"I woke up this morning, came outside to smoke a cigarette, and I noticed that strange decoration that the painter had put there. On his own, of course, I said to myself, because nobody asked my opinion and I didn't give anybody authorization to put abstract art on the wall of these barracks. So I went to find the handyman, and he said he didn't know a thing about it. I came back. It was still fresh, like it had just been done—I touched it, and it felt like shit. I smelled it, and it smelled like shit. I tasted a little bit of it, and it tasted like shit—Shit, I said to myself, this is really shit! So I want whoever did this to take one step forward. I want to tell you, whoever it was, that you'll do better to come clean now than if we have to find out for ourselves who it was."

Patent Leather Director Puga waited for the students to react. The longer they stood motionless, the more furious he got.

"All right, since nobody has the intestinal fortitude to step forward, we'll wait for the results of our investigation! And it won't take long! In fact—look, here it comes, and with excellent results, judging by the smile on Noel the Nuisance's face."

Noel the Nuisance was almost running, with a grin of happiness spreading from ear to ear. He was waving a stick in the air, with some sort of bundle—it was hard to tell just what it was—hanging off the end of it.

"Here's the evidence of the crime!" Noel the Nuisance crowed.

Director Puga made a gesture of impatience at that goofy beanpole of a crime fighter.

"Just the facts, Private. What did you find?"

"It's panties, sir, and they're full of shit."

The camp erupted in hoots and gales of laughter.

"Don't try to be funny, Private. Report."

"Well, I followed your orders, sir—"

"You better have . . ." growled the director.

"I made a search of the area, sir, all around the camp, and the only thing I found that seemed out of place was this, sir, a pair of panties full of fresh shit. I thought it was a bag of treasure or something, you know, because it was kind of lumpy. But when I turned it over, using this stick here, it was all covered with flies, sir, and they swarmed up all over the place, and the smell unstopped my nose, and me with a chronic head cold . . . So to, uh, sum up, sir, this is a pair of panties, and they're full of fresh shit, and they must belong to one of the girls here, and the shit is exactly the same color and texture as the shit that appeared on that wall early this morning, sir."

"So it's sabotage," Margot Wrangling mused aloud, taking a close look at the suspect underwear. "Aha! I discovered a clue! Look, some writing! Quick, Noel the Nuisance, go wash 'em out, I have the feeling we'll know a lot more about who did this when we can look at these panties clean!"

Noel returned, his face twisted in disgust, with the more or less clean article still hanging from the stick. Softly, he read out the name written along the elastic of the panties—and as he read, he turned livid with shock and delight.

"Danae Duckbill Lips! There, behind Irma the Albino!"

Danae had known for a good while that she was found out. She'd recognized the panties, of course, but she'd kept quiet, hoping for some miracle and praying, "Help me, La Milagrosa, help me, La Milagrosa . . ."

"Come here, Private." It was Margot Wrangling, and her eyes blazed. "So, destroying public property. Two demerits, equivalent to going without two meals. And you'll scrub down the walls and paint the outside of the barracks. When you're off! . . . *Duty!* Do you understand? And prepare for a public trial, in which your file will receive a permanent stain, and with your own shit—ha ha ha! . . . Now, Private, tell us what your intentions were in destroying state property." Margot Wrangling was going a little overboard. Mara the Wheezer and Director Puga looked on in shock at the quivering wrinkles and the froth at the corners of her mouth.

"I'm sorry . . . I had diarrhea, I couldn't make it to the latrine, I wanted to get rid of the panties, so I . . ."

"Enough! *Enough!*" The teacher-guide slapped the girl.

"Stop, Margot. It's not like she murdered somebody . . ." Patent Leather Puga caught the enraged woman's arm in the air as she was about to slap Danae again.

"I'd make her fill a hundred bottles with ants and then draw a circle on the ground and turn the bugs loose. She'd have to keep those ants from crawling outside the circle. And if even a single one of them got out, I'd expel her from the camp, of course, to start with, and put it in her record. But first I'd give her a chance, with the ants . . ." whispered Mara the Wheezer, proud of her judiciousness.

A Big Party, and Sucking Face
with the Manatee

When you attack, it's tentative! When I attack, I mean it!

COME ON, RENATA the Physical, *vieja, no seas pendeja, mamita, vamos.* No goin' wussy on me, now. It's down in the last shower—here, I'll find it—I made it two weeks ago. Bullshit, nobody's gonna find out, unless you tell 'em, that is. Here, run your hand over it, feel it. *Coño, niña,* it's two huge holes, I can't believe you can't feel em. 'Course I had to close 'em back up again; no, it wasn't easy, that's the truth—I used some wadded-up bread, some boiled sweet potato, two or three pieces of that hemp rope all unraveled, and I made two plugs and fitted them in . . . Here they are! *Ave María Purísima,* just stick your finger in and—*plop!*—they're outta there. Now, one for you and one for me, and I brought the razor blade in case we have to make 'em wider, excavate, you know. 'Course we can't make a twenty-four-inch TV screen here because if they catch us we won't live to tell the tale. Can't go *too* far. I'm warning you, too, the first thing you've gotta do is shut your mouth, just brick it up; you don't want 'em to know we're in here spying on 'em . . . Shh, it's the Mummy and Busy Hands. Just keep your eyes open and your mouth closed. Concentrate on that monster pair of baseball bats. Don't worry, nobody but us knows about this Technicolor, Technismell, Technitouch movie theater—

live and direct from Boys' Town! Wow, boys take a long time to piss, and then all that dripping and the *whippety-whippety* at the end when they shake it, and the loose drops everywhere. You'll see, now they'll start kissing each other, like any other couple, nothin' new. I didn't know these two liked to show their equipment like that. I'll tell you, life without heavy equipment is no life at all. Whoa, girl, what a tongue! That's right, slurp it. *Slp slp slp, slsh slsh slsh.* Half-staff, half-staff—ah, now the flag is rising! Oh, look at 'em sword-fighting. Now they've traded weapons. Ooh. *Pero díme una cosa, tú,* doesn't it hurt when they squeeze their thing like that, those two big hairy, sweaty balls? That's the one thing I don't like about guys—their balls, those hairy things hanging down like that, like one of those medieval leather pouches, you know, but without any gold doubloons or whatever you call 'em. Ugh, you can have 'em as far as I'm concerned, I don't like hairy balls or a hairy back. Now hair on the chest, that I love, it's so manly, so virile, it's sexy as hell, all those little curls you can make around your finger . . . *Ay! Santísima,* look, there's some white stuff on the end, both of 'em! Girlfriend, *focus!* You must be as blind as a Renaissance turtle. See now? Don't talk so loud, they'll hear us. *Alabao,* that Mummy is a sword swallower—*coño,* and without even breathing hard. So *mira,* I gotta be honest with you, I, just on the spur of the moment, very spontaneous, I mentioned to a friend of mine about these holes I made . . . which I learned are called gloryholes, how about that? Which makes us a couple of gloryhole freaks, eh, *chica*? . . . So . . . what was I saying? If I can't remember, it must've been a lie, eh? Oh yeah, so this buddy of mine told me that every night he comes to the latrines with some other guys, he didn't say how many, hundreds of 'em, though, I think. They come to fool around. You know—*do* it. What, do I have to draw you a picture? Ri-i-i-ight. So anyway, we agreed to a friendly exchange of holes. He asked me if I could invite a girlfriend of mine, a *close* girlfriend, right? Of course I'm pretty careful, so I said, Listen, I'll try but I can't promise anything. I don't know if I'll have any luck with my *cúmbila* Renata the Physical, because she's a tad . . . you know . . . I just don't know if she'll do it. No, dude, no way, don't even think about it! With Venus Putrefaction, Carmucha Women's Shelter? Not with either one of those phonies. The girl with the most balls is Renata the Physical, I told him, which is why you're here, sharing my secret. *No seas boba,* I know I told you that you and I were the only ones that knew about the peepholes, but what difference does it make if there's three of us instead of two? The bottom line, *mi cielo,* is that if you don't say yes, if you don't want to go through with it, then I'll ask Danae Duckbill Lips, who is a girl with true grit, as I once heard somebody say—plus, with that mouth, she's a natural. I've heard people say she's hanging with spirits, with that antediluvian Big Foot, the phantom of the barracks. Not me, I won't have anything to do with all that espiritista bullshit. 'Course it's true she's tight with those guajiro eyesores, I figure she's probably screwing one of 'em—you can tell your friends that I, Salome the Satrap, saw it coming—and I am a force to be reckoned with, my dear. So—ready? I recommend that you either stick your mouth to the hole or your anus. I begin things with my mouth, then I move on to the second phase, maximum danger. Never in front! Your vagina is pure gold—sacred! The deal is, we're supposed to scratch at the peepholes—let's get this show on the road, eh? *scrch, scrch,* like two prisoners trying to communicate with the outside world, or just plain escape, but not us, what we want is to stay for all eternity, mouths at the ready. Psst, psst, okay boys, the worship of false idols has begun. Let's start oiling up our machinery. That's right, fellas. *Okra, okra, makes the gumbo go down slick, okra, okra, you can use it on your stick.* Oh, if my daddy only knew what a star pupil I'm being here in the School in the Country! And you're not far behind, Renata the Physical! When it comes to fun, you're the *man!* The one we oughta bring is Irma the Albino. Can you imagine that stick in the mud with her mouth or her ass stuck to a gloryhole and her eyes turned back in her head when they slap that lead pipe to her? No, oh no, my two-by-four from the Quick-'n'-Easy Lumber Yard, my dream in pink marble, don't start goin' liquid on me yet. Slow down, Renata the Physical, you're getting mine too excited—mine is not as laid back as yours is, *chica.* Listen, by the way, I heard something about Danae Duckbill Lips and Andy Crater Face—I heard they were out squeezing the juice out of Andy's sugarcane stalk in the plantain field the other night—I mean, is that nasty or what, foolin' around when you're surrounded on all sides by future platanutres? I'm telling it like I heard it, but I'm actually not so sure—I figure she probably gets it on with Crater Face but that something else is going on, because there are also those who say that that innocent-looking little cookie is messin' around with one of the guajiros. The other day she ran off and was skinny-dipping with one of those freaks over at the truck farm of horrors, and ate pork wrapped in banana leaves and roasted in a pit. She came back about an hour before sunrise with her chest out like she was some big explorer coming back from safari in darkest Africa. And smiling like the cat that ate the canary! I could just taste those fried pork rinds, I'll tell you. Yep, that was last Sunday after the visit, after her mother had left—she managed somehow to escape off to the hut those guajiros live in. Hold on, girl, let's change places, my jaw is numb. And changing the subject, too—I don't remember who it was that told me she saw a manatee. Oh no, not that way, you don't want to do it like you're scraping the corn off the cob. Don't tell me you don't love it! Look at me and learn, girl—you spread your cheeks with your fingers, but first you spit on your fingers, like this, a good gob of spit. It hurts at first. Actually, it hurts the whole time. Oh, I remember who was talking about that manatee. It was Fermín, the one that was going around saying I was just what he'd been lookin' for. How wrong a man can be, my love. Yes ma'am! One and the same, Adenoids, who knows how to write a love letter, let me tell you—these kind you don't sign, you know—Your Anonymous Admirer? Ay, I love the earthiness of the country, don't you? Can you imagine, swearing on his mother's vagina that he'd seen a manatee this big? I'm telling you, when they were giving out brains and God said *Come forth,* that kid came fifth. And anyway— aren't manatees supposed to be extinct? Whoa, this one came forth, too! What about his neighbor, did he leave a load in your intestines? All right, now it's our turn, right?

When you attack, it's tentative! When I attack, I mean it!

WATCH OUT, THE GROUND is covered with maggots, tapeworms, pinworms, you name it. All of a sudden I got the urge to shit a barbed-wire turd the size of the Capitol building, a zeppelin that'll iron out every wrinkle in my anus, *chica.* Ha ha, ho ho, hee hee—hilarious, saying "anus," how refined that sounds after we had ourselves a screw worthy of that porn movie *Doin' Your Duty.* That's not its real title but nobody remembers the real one, and it fits, so that's what everybody calls it—*Doin' Your Duty,* because it's about this woman that works full time with her feet in the air and her cunt wide open, waiting for hundreds of guys to come in—and girls, too, by the way—and do just anything with this woman, screwing her and cumming on her face and tits and all over her and doing everything else to her, so she's covered with piss, shit, earwax, boogers, spit, menstrual blood, even used tampons, scabs, you name it—the most disgusting thing you ever saw, which is why it's called *Doin' Your Duty,* right, because people *do their duty* on her! Renata the Physical, will you go to the latrine with me? I don't like to do number two alone at night in the dark. I'll tell you, that was great, as good as in a five-star hotel or better. While those other idiots are getting all prettied up for some cultural activity, we're out here riding bareback, in an all-out architectural orgy. Hold the curtain for me if you will, so I don't feel so alone and abandoned. Jeez, this smells like shit! I'm going to try not to talk so much so I don't breathe this stench in through my mouth. Don't go, Renata the Physical, the worms are hungry, they're so excited about this shit they're about to be served that they're wiggling around all over the place. I'll tell you, there's excrement bubbling up down there that's been there for fifty years. Don't move an inch, now, *chica.* Just look at the eyes on those worms! I'd almost call 'em little vampires, and look how their little tongues are licking their chops. Yi, it's slippery around the edge of this hole. Ay-y-y-y! A cave-in! I'm falling! Don't turn loose of me, Renata the Physical! Hold on to my hand! Oh no! A-a-a-agh! I'm drowning! *Glg-glg-glg-glg . . .*

YOU KNOW WHAT they say: When the manatee's on the move, something's bound to happen. Well, although the ceiba tree hadn't said anything bad was going to happen, I rushed up out of the river. But that was far from the worst—the pain in my chest was killing me, a stabbing, throbbing pain. Moss, constellations, and crawfish were running off my body with the water, plus the little snails that stuck to my skin as I was passing by a little stand of coffee trees. The journey didn't seem as long to me as it had other times at night. The closer I got to the camp, the more the music drew me in. I could hardly breathe. Not just because it's almost impossible for a manatee to breathe out of the water (although I am a manatee under the spell of and protected by the ceiba tree, the royal palm, and the spirits that live inside their trunks), but also because the excitement of the prospect of fun took my breath away. It was the night of twenty-one thousand sighs.

When you attack, it's tentative!

By this time the ceiba tree, the royal palm, the parrot, the owl, the hutia, and several other animals that live in the woods and underbrush—and I, of course—were following the personal histories of the various members of the brigades. We knew that something bad was coming, but the ceiba tree, our mother, has always believed that one should let life be the one that calls the shots, for life is filled with enigmas—any sudden intervention on our part might just make the situation worse. Which is why we had all decided to watch and wait. Play a tiny little part, maybe; put just our finger in, perhaps, but that was it—just the bare minimum. We feared most of all for Tierra Fortuna Munda, the child enlightened in the mysteries of nature, but we told ourselves that fate couldn't be so drastic with her and that there was always her god-mother, the ceiba tree, who would do anything—what she would do, none of us could foresee—to be sure she suffered as little as humanly possible.

I heard laughing and hooting not far off. Bestial guffaws. *Tears follow close on laughter,* I thought. The ceiba tree knows that I can be very pessimistic, and speak my mind about it, to boot. It's noisy when a cetacean decides to get somewhere on land; I've worked on my body so it looks a lot like a little girl's, or a dwarf's. I have some lumps on my chest that could well be called breasts, although they don't have nipples; my tail has not quite perfected its imitation of the daring, pointed-toe feet of classical ballerinas; and yet I wasn't wallow-ing, or waddling, or walking, or running—I was *flying.* So fierce was my desire to see what would happen that night—and what, I ask you, seeing that the lights of the mess hall were all off and there were so many youngsters dancing, could keep me from blending right in with them and shaking my amphibian booty?

From over by the latrines I could hear some sick-sounding whispering going on. I have a sharp ear, because right after that I heard this noise like a muted crash and then yelling like crazy, so I detoured over that way, where a girl's voice was calling for help:

"Help! Hel-l-l-l-p! Salome the Satrap fell in the hole in the latrine and is drowning in shit! Help!"

If I hadn't been hovering around the neighborhood like a big manatee moth, Salome the Satrap wouldn't have lived to tell the tale, because with all the racket they were making over in the mess hall nobody would ever have heard Renata the Physical's screams of terror or come to the aid of her friend, who had fallen into the shit-pit.

Down inside, the hole was literally crawling with a sea of yellow maggots as fat as your little finger, wriggling around in all that excrement, and in the middle of it I could make out bubbles produced by the girl's desperate attempts to breathe while submerged in all those feces. I am extremely fastidious about my personal hygiene, and I couldn't bear Salome the Satrap, but there was nothing to do but save her, and since I'm a very special manatee, favored above all others by the gods, I can not only swim but also fly, walk, and run at great speed (as I've demonstrated). I rushed into the latrine like gangbusters and was immediately met by that horrendous, stinking sight. Renata the Physical was trying to rescue her classmate with a pole from the clothesline, poking it around in the spot where Salome the Satrap had disappeared. So I girded my loins, took a deep breath, and dived in headfirst. My head bumped into the top of Salome's skull, so I wrapped my body around her and dragged her to the surface. We bounced up into the air (a heroic manatee), both of us covered with new, antique, and reproduction diarrhea, mud, worms, and every kind of microbe and bacillus and disgusting thing imaginable. Salome the Satrap had almost suffocated. I shoved her into one of the showers. Renata the Physical couldn't believe her eyes when she saw me, but she fainted anyway. I turned on the tap and the trickle of water made all these little circles on Salome's skin, finally revealing the scratched and scraped entirety of it. My mouth-to-mouth resuscitation helped bring her around. Then I had to revive the other one by dousing her with cold water. When Salome the Satrap opened her eyes and they came to rest on me, a manatee, she almost dived back down the hole in the latrine.

"I can't believe it. Renata the Physical, it's the manatee . . ." she whispered out of the side of her mouth, trying not to move her lips.

"Yeah. Pretty awesome. It saved you. I couldn't do it by myself." Physical batted her eyelashes like an idiot.

I made certain they were both out of danger, then devoted a few moments to having a shower and making myself presentable with some little flowers woven around my neck and waist. And then I flew off, disappearing into the warm air, toward the place where the drums were beating. Oh, I loved the serene sound of the flute, the melody of the guitar, the elegance of the violins, the voluptuousness of the maracas and the güiro.

The mess hall was full, full, full—not a single person had stayed behind in the bunks. I managed to hide behind a big vat of boiled milk so I could see everything without being seen. That night was the big fiesta, with musicians brought in from a camp nearby. Puga, the one the ceiba tree calls Patent Leather, was announcing that the guests had volunteered to offer their services, their knowledge and their art, FREE OF CHARGE! to the campesinos and youngsters working on the farms, who of course were also volunteers. We were then informed that these were not just musicians but writers, actors of the stage and screen, musicians, and singers, all of whom had left the city, their comfortable homes, their families, to join the collective effort. It was with great dedication and energy that they were ready to give the very best of themselves—their art. That's what Director Puga said, and everyone believed him, even I, a manatee given the gift of immortality by the magic and friendship of a ceiba tree and a royal palm. Even I, a manatee who has witnessed so, so many lovely stories turn out badly.

Still excited, still roistering, the nymphs and ephebes had their dinner. In comparison to previous nights, the meal was relatively luxurious: boiled sweet potato, unwashed and therefore grayish flour, a few strands of canned meat. There were not a lot of cans, given the number of diners, and to give everybody a decent portion the cooks would have had to turn into a kitchenful of Christs and multiply not bread and fishes but greasy Baltic meat and gristle. Plus tonight they had to add in all the artists and whatnot—who were contributing their creative genius, it was true, but also pulling up a chair. The bread truck hadn't shown itself all day, so half-green sweet potato replaced the bread. And since they hadn't managed to get their hands on what the authorities called cola-flavored soft drink, what the youngsters called brake fluid, they created a strawberry-flavored drink, the color and taste of which made you think of that sore-throat medicine Aseptil, or that antiseptic stuff, Timerosal. The dessert consisted of burned tomato custard accompanied by some kind of thick, hard-to-swallow jelly.

Night fell cool over the countryside, and a group of the guests who had finished eating early started fooling around on the drums:

> *Dear mother, this letter I write you*
> *to tell you your son is so blue,*
> *so lost and alone in this jailhouse,*

that I hardly know what to do.
And weeping tears of rage and grief
and tears of mourning, too.
I do not cry out of fear for my life,
for a grown man shouldn't cry.
Only for you do I cry these tears,
a mother no more, nor a wife.
When I arrived that morning
after being out drinking all night,
I saw my pa abusing my ma
and I stabbed him in a fight . . .
Oh, son, he says, what have you done,
your granny was my ma.
Daddy, when you grew up a man,
you took and married mine
and swore to be faithful and kind.
So now I have no daddy, now I have no ma,
now I have no one to love me
when the night's so cold and alone.
Mami, don't cry, save your tears,
don't cry, and always wear your brassiere.
I'm not afraid of big tough bullies,
even bullies with knives,
'cause the blood of big tough bullies,
I've spilled many a time.

Migdalia, don't be cruel,
lend me your boyfriend till tomorrow.
Pancha, don't be cruel,
take me with you to Havana . . .

Louder and louder rose the honeyed echoes of the singers, faster and faster went the song, until the revelers fell back exhausted. In a while, one of them had the brilliant idea of connecting the camp radio to the speakers Director Puga had lent for the occasion, and suddenly the voice of that romantic late-night announcer Pastor Felipe, the famous disk jockey with the cinnamon skin and eyes the color of emerald sugar-cane squeezings, was heard, flooding his listeners' ears as he crooned his famous lead-in: *NOCTUR-NOOOO.* The musical show that began when the nine o'clock cannon shot went off across the land, the most listened-to show in all of Cuba, began its broadcast with a melancholy ballad by the duo Juan and Junior . . .

Danae was one of the last to take a tray; she headed over to one of the concrete tables, skeptically studying her food. Emma the Menace scooted over to make a space for her. On the other side of the wide table sat a man of forty-something who was running a big bent aluminum spoon over his tray to get up every single bite.

"I don't like sweet potatoes," Danae said, pushing the tray away, and the man went on the alert; his eyes devoured the food that apparently was not going to be touched.

"You keep not eating, you're gonna get tuberculosis." Emma the Menace pushed the tray back in front of Danae.

"Pff. I stuff myself on weekends—you saw what my mother brings me."

"Yeah, which is also why you get the shits you get, not to mention the wet farts and the silent but deadly ones that smell like rotten eggs. Worse than Venus Putrefaction," scoffed Carmucha Women's Shelter. "You've already gone through my whole forty-five days' supply of kaolin and anti-spasmodics."

"I'm not the only one. Venus Putrefaction's mother comes in loaded up with stuff, too."

"And why exactly do you think we call her Putrefaction, because she shits night-blooming jasmine?" Migdalia Fake Eyelashes shot back.

Brigida the Imperfect was having an animated conversation over at the table with the teachers and brigade leaders. The girls and invited guests had the first turn in the mess hall, before the boys, who were waiting impatiently. Starving, standing outside getting dew all over themselves, they started banging with their spoons on their canteens. Alicia Machine-Gun Tongue had been in the infirmary for days, with food poisoning from a fish with ciguatera she'd eaten.

"Let's hurry up there, ladies, the gentlemen are growing faint from inanition!" ordered Director Puga, clapping his hands three times to hurry them along.

"What does that mean?" asked Danae Duckbill Lips, chewing abstractedly.

"What?" replied Pancha Flatfoot socratically, fixing her with her eyes like a hypnotist or basilisk, flecks of sweet potato at the corners of her mouth.

"That last word he said, in-a-ni-what?"

"In-a-ni-tion, girl, it's like starvation," Emma the Menace, proud of her erudition, replied.

The forty-something was listening with amusement, but his eyes never left the dried-out sweet potato.

"Now that I think about it, I haven't seen Salome the Satrap and Renata the Physical in a while. Or Irma the Albino either," said Pancha Flatfoot, who then immediately added: "So are you gonna eat that sweet potato or not?"

Danae shook her head, but she had noticed the interest shown in the tuber by the man sitting across from her, and she answered Pancha Flatfoot with her eyes fixed on him:

"Last I saw her, Irma the Albino was nursing the rats; the girl's brain is fried. As for the Satrap and Physical, at this hour they're no doubt nursing themselves, on a couple of baseball bats this long," and she held her hands about a foot and a half apart.

Everybody laughed and made further filthy comments, at the same time lunging for Danae's tray, to grab the sweet potato. Emma the Menace came away with it, but Flatfoot hit her hand from underneath and launched it into the air. Danae caught it on the fly and started racing around the long table. When she got to the other side, she plopped down alongside the man, using him as a shield against her pursuers. The man looked uncomfortable; he scooted his backside along the hard concrete bench. Danae put the sweet potato on his tray, and he made a gesture that not even he could believe—no, no, no thanks.

The girls went away, laughing and talking uproariously. Mara the Wheezer and Margot Wrangling looked up and called loudly for quiet, but then immediately went back to their pleasant conversation with two black, muscular dancers with shaved heads who looked like nothing so much as statues carved from ebony. I, a discreet and well-behaved manatee, was still curled up behind the vat of boiled milk, my eardrums on maximum, my eyes peeking around one side of the large cooking pot.

Danae Duckbill Lips insisted, and the man finally stuck his fork into the tuber. She watched as he ate. He hardly chewed; he wolfed down the sweet potato like a person who thinks the food is going to be taken right out of his mouth, which was why he suddenly choked, coughed, and turned as red as one of the sugared tomatoes for dessert. Danae passed him her canteen with the strawberry-flavored drink so he could wash down the chunk of food that had gone down the wrong way. Smiling, nodding his head in gratitude, he turned to her and thanked her, which was the opening Danae had been waiting for, to unleash her curiosity.

"You're a . . . singer?" she ventured.

"Oh heavens no, I'm a playwright, or was, I'm not sure anymore . . ."

"But what we need here is music, you know, people who can sing . . . So we can dance and have some fun . . ."

"Oh, you'll enjoy my play, I think. It's the story of some teenagers, you'll see, something like you . . ."

"They didn't tell us actors were coming—to the country!? God help them!"

"They didn't tell us, either, exactly . . . um . . . although we were more or less expecting it . . . yes, we had an intuition . . . a sneaking suspicion, you might say . . ."

From the tone of his voice, Danae knew the man was being ironic, but she still didn't understand.

"What's your name?"

"Danae, but they call me Danae Duckbill Lips, because of my big lips . . ."

"*Danae weaves the hours gilded by the Nile . . .*"

"You know that poem!"

"And the poet."

"My grandmother knew him, too, but she would never introduce me to him. I saw him a lot of times by accident because every once in a while when he was taking his walk he'd walk under the balcony of my house. I used to make fun of him, because he was so fat. I didn't find out it was the same person until a long time after that, when I saw a picture of him. My grandmother was friends with the lady that cooked for him. She always said he was not to be disturbed. You know, my grandmother's dead now, died of kidney cancer and also a black ball that got lodged in her throat. Nelly, the cook, says that the poet writes all day long, every day, rocking in a rocking chair with a caned back. She says he puts a board across the arms of the rocking chair to write on. Is that right?"

The man nodded, his face glowing with happiness at finding an admirer of the famed poet in that godforsaken, run-down camp.

"Lovely to meet you." He put out his hand to her. "My name is Ruperto, or it is now; I used to have another one but it bored me. Now I am both *I* and the reincarnation of a playwright who died hundreds of years ago. Thank you so much for the sweet potato. I was sliced down the middle, wounded in my soul, and lost in the shadows, as the Sapphires used to sing—tossed, cracked, split, shaken, and well stirred, as I myself might put it. I'll see you again in a while, I'm going to go wash off this tray now, brush my teeth, and come back for the performance. Adieu."

The man certainly talked different than any other man she had ever known. She rescued her tray; the remains of her dinner had been eaten by the other girls. She followed the stranger to the washbasins, but he had gotten far ahead of her and she lost sight of him in the dimness of the ill-lit wash area. On the way, she ran into Andy Crater Face.

"So have you heard, beautiful Duckbill Lips? The infirmary is packed full of the dead and injured—well, at least the injured, I was kidding about the dead. But cheer up, some of them are half dead. They brought in Renata the Physical and Salome the Satrap, with asthma both of 'em, and one of them with maggots all over her, even crawling out her ears—she went headfirst into the latrine, the worms practically had her for dinner. They say that if it hadn't been for a manatee that suddenly and mysteriously appeared and jumped in and saved her, she wouldn't be around to tell the tale. Nobody much believes all this, you understand, but since the other girl was a witness . . . They also say that Big Foot was roaming around last night, over around the girls' barracks. That true?"

Danae Duckbill Lips shrugged her shoulders and kept straight on toward the wash basins, but Crater Face was not deterred by the girl's indifference.

"So, then, Flipper Lips, any comment?"

"I've told you not to get fresh with me, Andrés Crater Face. I'm not one of those girls that you're used to pawing over." She stopped and glared at him.

"Yeah, but why don't we meet tomorrow out in the plantain field? When will you say yes, my love-lump? You love to chow down on those sliced steak and grilled onion sandwiches my mother brings on Sunday, you're all goo-goo eyes with me *then*. But the other six days you metamorphose into a spiny urchin. Shit, I bet even Kafka, with his cockroach, couldn't win your heart."

"You listen to what I'm going to tell you, Andy Crater Face. I told you I like you; we'll probably start being like boyfriend and girlfriend, but don't start pulling on me or getting all swellheaded because that's the worst thing you can do, I can't stand a slimy slug drooling all over me, and that's what you're turning into—we'll see who's more Kafkaesque than who . . ."

"Then I can harbor some hope, dream of a brief interlude in the plantain field tomorrow? . . ."

"Yeah, yeah, sure, of course you can. The password will be *Danae weaves the hours gilded by the Nile* . . . Don't forget it." She walked off thinking delightedly that he could wait for her sitting all comfy-cozy on the cold ground with pillows under his ass so he didn't get hemorrhoids.

Or maybe, who knew, she'd change her mind and go.

"*Danae* wha—? . . ."

She liked him, there was no doubt that she liked Andy Crater Face. He was funny and she liked boys who made her laugh, but her heart was set on another person. Although it was scary and she was mostly pretty hesitant, it was time to get a boyfriend. It would be so great to get back to Havana and be able to tell people that she'd fooled around with anybody she felt like in the country, the farm and all the mangoes, as the saying went. She needed a boyfriend, a kid to squeeze in the movies, do a little French kissing with when they got out of school so she could drive her girlfriends wild with envy, a guy who'd defend her against that gang of boys in Cristo Park that had started out raising her skirt when she walked home from junior high but not long ago had graduated to putting a knife to her throat just to take away a lemon ice that she was walking down the street licking with all the lecherous gluttony in the world. She was sorry to lose the lemon ice—the line to buy 'em went around the block four times at least—but she would've been a lot sorrier to lose her life, so she handed over the cup in less time than it takes the cock to crow.

Cocks crowing—how she was going to miss that, the crowing at sunrise, when she got back to the city. *Oggundaddié! Kikirikí!* She remembered very little about the city, almost nothing. Just on Sundays, when Gloriosa Paz, her mother, came to visit her, like all the parents, then she was flooded with memories which at other times were locked far, far away in a distant part of her brain. But there was one thing about Gloriosa Paz, her mother, that distinguished her from all the other parents. She got to the camp before anybody else. She was one stubborn early riser. Before 4 A.M., she would already be parked in front of the barracks, leaning on the ceiba tree. She looked like a bird of ill omen, a vulture, with that *sleeveless coat blacker than the soul of the man who sent you poor kids here,* as Gloriosa Paz herself would say, *I look like a damn buzzard in this coat, but at the hour I have to leave home it's cold as hell, the transportation is awful, I have to change buses like six times to get here.* She would be bundled up as though for a war, with about ten different layers of clothes on—she'd always been a cold-natured woman. Her arsenal included several small portable stoves, so she could lend a cook fire when other families, not so well prepared, asked, plus the bottles of kerosene or alcohol that went with them. Her back would be bent, and according to her, her spine was just like an *S,* totally twisted out of shape, from having to carry the two big sacks of food and utensils that she plundered in order to satisfy the needs of her daughter and half the camp. Turtle steaks that made Danae want to throw up from just smelling them, long loaves of bread that she'd devour in three or four hours, hard-boiled eggs that disappeared into her mouth in hard-to-believe quantities, dozens of pizzas that Danae would keep in big empty cracker tins after having scoffed down two or three and passed out several among the other kids, including the teachers—for whom her mother had the most profound compassion, because nobody came to visit them. Gloriosa Paz also brought potato or plantain chips wrapped in brown paper, yellow rice with fish or chicken, depending on what Gervasio could steal at the restaurant where he worked, soda crackers, saltines, and little round María cookies excellent for a person's digestion, pastelillos of Russian beef or guava, Soyuz 15 croquettes that set records for staying "up" in space because they stuck to the roof of your mouth and you couldn't get 'em down again—these, her mother had to stand in line over at the café for seventy-two hours to get—twenty jelly rolls, ten boxes of sponge cake, about fifty slices of layer cake, some of those long crunchy cookies like fingers covered in chocolate, chocolate bars, cream cheese (for these last three delicacies she had to stand in line for nine hours in Parque Lenin). There were thermoses of lemon or vanilla ice, thermoses of pop, that soft drink they sold at the "ten-cen'" on Calle Galiano, finger sandwiches with deviled ham and cream cheese spread from the one on Obispo. Del Monte fruit salad. Thermoses of coffee. "Cowflops," which were those guava danishes from Perico's on Calle Obispo. Fifteen cans of condensed milk, some cooked in a double boiler till they turned to "mud," some straight. Thermoses of tea. Strawberry, vanilla, and lemon sherbet. Thermoses of yogurt. Pound cake from the bakery next door to the Castillo Farnés. And then there were the aspirins, acetaminophens, tampons, and bath soaps, the laundry soap, the Fab, the shampoo (half a bottle, so the ungrateful child wouldn't waste it), a change of work clothes freshly washed and ironed. Times were better—not great, but not so bad as before. Oh, the eternal obsession with food and the other necessities of life! Eating and possessing. Food and things. Only a person who has been hungry and lacked even the essentials of life can understand this phenomenon of hoarding, the desperation to eat that is not gourmandizing, not unbridled epicureanism, for gourmandizing requires a palate, an appetite, though in excess; it is a love affair with food. Only the person who has owned nothing, who has survived with the bare minimum, can understand the fierce desire to have, which is not avarice, either, but another kind of sickness, a sickness that gradually—second by second, year by year—eats away at a person, his or her immune system, until the human being, or Cuban being, is at last turned into an inert shell of body and mind. A piece of garbage.

It broke your heart to see that woman standing there so early in the morning, like a big half-frozen doll or puppet or scarecrow. The whole camp made fun of Danae Duckbill Lips' mother.

"Your mother is kinda rattly in the coconut, Danae Duckbill Lips. She's been wandering around out there for hours, humming that song in English, or what she thinks is English—*ay deed eat ma-a-a-ay oo-we-e-e-ey!* What, did she manage to slip her keeper?" With these, or similar, words, Emma the Menace woke Danae every Sunday.

She couldn't stand her, just couldn't deal with her—Danae was mortified by Gloriosa Paz, her mother. She herself loved to sleep till noon, and the only day of the week she could do that was Sunday, which was when her mother, Complicate-Everything-to-the-Point-of-Chaos Gloriosa Paz, decided to get here before dawn. Danae Duckbill Lips was at the age when teenagers dream of murdering their parents.

"Don't be upset with me—if I sleep any later I miss my connections."

Danae *hated* for her mother to visit her. She didn't even want to remember that someday she was going to have to go back to the city. Her mother was the prime evidence that a place as horrible as the city existed. Everything about her stank of sticky asphalt, salt spray polluted with the smoke from boats and factories, the tar from the docks, rancid grease, spoiled milk, sawdust, cat piss, dog turds . . . you name it. Of course, Danae didn't want Gloriosa Paz to come visit her on Sundays but at the same time she wasn't about to turn away the food, the things her mother brought her. Or did for her, because all day Gloriosa Paz, along with the other mothers, would stand over the washbasins and wash the dirty clothes that had accumulated all week long. That was truly a relief, because the uninterrupted hours of work hardly left the youngsters a chance to breathe and sleep.

"There's a pair of panties missing."

"Yeah, I know, I had to throw 'em out. And thanks a lot—I got a demerit because of you. I shit in my pants and they found out who it was because you embroidered my name on every goddamn thing I own."

"And if I hadn't it would all be gone by now."

The sun had turned to soft orange and the fields were tinted a golden sepia, but the mother was still chattering away. Families were gathered together in separate clumps, so as not to have to share their food. Over there, next to a '54 Dodge, Andy Crater Face's parents were gobbling down big sandwiches of roast pork and onions. Andy's father had traded a guajiro a few bars of bath soap for the pork. A few yards away, Irma the Albino's mother and little sister were finishing off big cups of mamey milk shakes; they had the cups upended and were tapping them on the bottom to get out the last drops. Emma the Menace was arguing with her little brother, who she claimed had been cheating at a game of dominoes they were playing with her aunt and uncle. The camp loudspeakers began to broadcast all kinds of foreign languages spoken backward. It was the signal that the day was over—tapes run backward to drive people crazy, so they'd go away.

Gloriosa Paz, Danae's mother, was like a locomotive at full speed, asking idiotic questions and complaining—Danae was too thin; it was the truth, she bet she'd lost twenty pounds in just these few days; the sun had dried out her beautiful skin and left wrinkles as deep as the furrows in the trunk of that ceiba tree; she'd brought a toothbrush so she could use it on her fingernails; the soles of her feet were like shoe leather, all callused and yellow-looking; lord, her hair was so burned and dry it was just terrible, and those split ends!! . . . But what disturbed her the most was that vagueness, that far-off look in her eyes, the way she wouldn't even look at you, the tiredness in her face, the big green-and-purple bags under her eyes.

The loudspeakers went on haranguing the camp in Czech bleated backward.

"Don't you want to go back? I can get a certificate from a doctor friend of mine. Mario the Tender's father got him out that way, and another girl from Río Verde, too . . ."

"But the rest of the story is that Mario the Tender had to go through the biggest embarrassment of his life. They called him every name in the book—faggot, flake-out, you name it—and they put bullfrogs in his bed, threw rocks at him and almost killed him, and he'll probably get kicked out of school. But even if they don't expel him, he'll lose his right to go to the university. Even if he's a brain in everything—which he is— the best in every class—"

"Life is more important than that—it's so important that every minute of your life you feel you're being true to yourself. Is it true that one of the boys in this camp wrapped his arm in a wet towel and broke his own arm so he'd get sent home? And that another one pulled out a perfectly good tooth? I don't want that for you."

"I'm perfectly fine, Mamá. Don't stick your nose in where it's not needed." The daughter got up off the thick root of the tree where she was sitting and left her mother still soliloquizing. She did what she did every Sunday after eating—she went to take a nap. "Let me know when you're leaving. I'm in the barracks. I can't talk to you anymore."

"You seem so grouchy since you've been here."

Now the loudspeakers had gone from Czech to Hungarian, and still backward.

She had changed, she could feel it; she was so filled with doubt and uncertainty. Which side were the good guys on, and which side the bad guys? Was her mother a bad guy or was it the teachers? The Higher-Ups or the guajiros? Who was telling the truth? Where *was* the truth? She decided to go with the flow, act on her intuitions. Tierra Fortuna Munda was her friend; she had taught her the beauty of trees. Danae believed adults lied, some more than others. But Tierra didn't lie. Tierra told the truth. She treated others as others treated her.

The loudspeakers were chattering through the Russian and Bulgarian primers, from back to front.

She returned to the mess hall with a strange weight on her feet that was not big glops of mud—there was a slowness about her that was unusual for her. The performance had started. She sat in back, on the floor with the other musicians and artists and writers, who were waiting their turn to entertain the students.

> LALO: That fear again? In this world—and you need to get this through that thick skull of yours—if you want to live you're going to have to do a lot of things, and among them is forget that fear exists.
>
> CUCA: Easier said than done!

Even the melody of the leaves and branches rustling in the breeze had stopped; the frogs had suspended their incessant croaking; the birds perched on the eaves of the zinc roof were avidly watching every movement. Night and nature had become an immense stage, and every particle of them was caught up in the play being acted out upon it. Even the audience's breathing seemed part of the play's text. We were all waiting expectantly to see what the outcome would be of the story of two teenagers who had murdered their parents, because that was what the play was about. Danae looked for the playwright in the crowd, the man she had given her sweet potato to, but she couldn't see him.

The intermission came. Her eyes searched the shadowy areas of the mess hall, where the dim lights didn't reach, and that was how her gaze came upon me, a manatee dripping with perspiration, half hidden behind a big vat of milk. She rubbed her eyes to be sure she wasn't dreaming. I gestured in the friendliest way I could, to tell her that the man was outside, smoking and gazing at the stars. And so she would believe in my existence. She crept outside on all fours, stood up, and went over to the author.

"Jeez, I think I saw the manatee! Either that or I'm seeing visions. How about you? You must be bored spitless with your play."

"No, but scared. I just received news that a close friend of mine has died, an extraordinary man, and I can't do anything, I'm a prisoner and I'm not a prisoner. They say my place is here . . . Don't say anything, don't feel like you have to find something to say. Ah, the dream of the manatee!"

"I know about death. My grandmother died like two months ago."

"I'm forty-five years old, and I'm beginning to feel that life is like this . . ." He snapped his fingers. "I'm beginning to look at old people differently. Soon *I'll* be old."

"Don't be like that. We all really like what you write. That play . . . Did you see how quiet we all were, how everybody was watching? I've never seen the people in this camp sit so still. And that silence! It was amazing! Aren't you impressed by that?"

"Honored, yes, or rather shocked . . . It would be lovely if you didn't forget me. It's so nice to leave a mark on someone, for someone to remember you with a little affection and admiration. When you get to be as old as I am today, I'll be *really* old, if I'm still around at all."

"Oh, you will be, your fate is to live forever. I'm going back in, the second act is starting . . . Ey, maybe *I'm* the one that won't reach *your* age. That's life, right?"

Danae returned to her place, but not without first peering into the shadows of the high grass alongside the mess hall. Tierra Fortuna Munda had invited her on another late-night horseback ride. For a while the playwright paced back and forth outside, along one side of the mess hall, then he slipped in unobtrusively through the kitchen door. He plumped down on the floor beside me, stretched out an arm, and his hand brushed my skin.

"I'm thirsty," he whispered, "let me drink from your lips."

I leaned over him and my lips sated the yearning of his mouth.

CUCA (like a police officer): You killed someone?

BEBA (like another police officer): Then why is there so much blood?

CUCA (like a police officer): Do you live with your parents?

BEBA (like another police officer): Do you have any brothers or sisters? Answer me!

CUCA (like a police officer): You wasted 'em, didn't you? It'll be better for you if you talk.

LALO (very vaguely): I don't know. . .

At the end of the play, no one made a sound. The guests—the artists, musicians, and actors—broke into timid applause, and then the youngsters followed. The teachers could hardly express their confused emotions; their faces were rigid, the atmosphere tense. A dancer with a folk-dance company decided to give the party a second start with drums, maracas, guitars, bongos, violins. Slow and sober, the music filled the mess hall, but it remained within. Their breathing had formed a sort of halo, a fog or curtain of mist that prevented the songs from expanding out into the immensity of the plains. The rhythm grew more complex, and the sound crescendoed. And the party was on. More than a collective dance, it was a kind of trance, as though everyone wanted to free themselves from the anguish of reflection, from that enigmatic state that *The Night of the Assassins* had plunged them into.

Danae Duckbill Lips danced with Andy Crater Face. Soon, though, she tired of that pointless party—what were they celebrating? Boredom.

The playwright had vanished, and there was not a trace of the actors, either. Leaning on the door at the entrance to the mess hall, she could make out a roiling pillar of smoke, and then flames immediately shot high into the sky. They were coming from the direction of the batey.

"*Fire! Fire!*" she shouted to the dancers inside. No one heard her, though, except me—at that moment nothing but a quivering mass of manatee, linked to her by fear and anxiety.

We looked at each other, knowing that none of the people inside would react quickly. And that few would be interested in the problem. And that if they were, they wouldn't be authorized to take action. So we two took off running. As we arrived, the campesinos, with the help of the *güijes*, were trying to put out the flames. Danae looked for Tierra Fortuna Munda in the general confusion. The ceiba and the royal palm were puffing and blowing so hard that finally the river overflowed its banks and its water sloshed up all over the batey, extinguishing even the last spark among the charred and blackened ruins. I heard Bejerano say to another member of his family, as he went out to cut and gather palm fronds to rebuild their huts with:

"This is a warning. I came on them with the torches in their hands. Fortunately, they waited until we were all together in Yolandina's house eating. They burned everything else. Yes, there's no doubt about it, it's a warning. It was them, the Higher-Ups, I caught 'em in the act, crossing the beet field with the torches just sputtering and sparking, like the soul of Satan. Tierra! Tierra Fortuna Munda! Where do you think that girl's gotten to? Imagine running off when she's needed most, dadgummit."

> *I am the punto, the song of Cuba*
> *that in the woods and hills did sound*
> *when the mambíses battled*
> *with machetes in hand,*
> *with machetes in hand . . .*

I don't know where that damn noise is coming from, I don't know where I'm going, or even where I've come from. Quiet! Shut that music up! Can't they see our houses are burned down? Can't anybody see that those people want to get rid of us—the eyesores, they call us! And get rid of us for good—do away with us. If I meet up with that Brutus Escoria on the road, I'll cut his head off with one swipe of this machete. A murderer, by god, that's what he is, a murderer! Get back, you weeds! I'll cut down this whole countryside, by gad! And tell them to shut up that devil's music! I won't hear you, devil's song, or hear anything! Ay, I feel like dying! Why was I born to this? Why do I have to put up with them calling me a dog, making fun of me? Why didn't they give me a name like everybody else's? Why did they have to name me Tierra Fortuna Munda? Why am I this me, this air, this sky, this water, this fire, this earth, this moon, this sun? It'd be better if there were just a war.

> Belle, Belle, Belle, Belle—Belle climbs up the hill,
> and if it weren't for that ole Belle, Cuba would not have a hill.

Tierra, Tierra! Where are you!? It's me, Danae, your friend! You can trust me, I've been looking for you. The whole settlement is asking what's happened to you, where you've got off to. Your father needs you, you've got to help me cut down palm leaves for the roofs of the bohíos. I'm not leaving until you all have houses again. Wood, we need wood for the walls. One of your father's friends, a man that lives in town, promised to bring some sacks of cement. Everything that comes, comes for a reason—now you'll be able to build houses that are more solid, better, you know, quality. Concrete is more resistant. Wait, hold it! Stop swinging that thing, stop cutting things down like that—you're all in a fury. Anger doesn't do anything, Tierra. Listen to me. Your name is different—it's pretty, they'll get used to it. And if they don't, screw 'em. You didn't see me thinking it was strange, right? Who's that singing? Who is Belle?

> I have a deplorable habit,
> sometimes even me it embarrasses—
> although I lie down in my bed at night,
> when I wake up I'm in somebody else's.

Belle? Nobody knows, we figure it's a cow. Here, people stick cows with the weirdest names you ever heard of. And not just animals, people too. If you can call us people. Are we? Why do they burn our bohíos? They treat us like animals. I know we're not normal, but that doesn't give them the right to kill us, does it? I can't live like this, Danae. I don't want to leave the place where I was born, don't even like the idea of it. At least not because I'm forced to. Not that way. If I do leave, it ought to be of my own free will. Before this part of the country got so full of people, we were a happy family. My friends were the ceiba, the manatee, the royal palm, the hutia, the sparrow, the fly-catcher, the Zapata wren, the hummingbird, the butterfly, that spirit of the woods that appeared in the shape of a mischievous black dwarf with a big head—everybody calls him the chicherekú. The whole woods and forest and plain and everything. The countryside. The wilderness, because it was a kind of wonderful wilderness. Ay, this pain in my chest! . . . I feel like I'm being stabbed, what a cramp—it's blinding me, I don't understand . . .

> *Belle, Belle, Belle, Belle—Belle climbs up the hill,*
> *and if it weren't for that ole Belle, Cuba would not have a hill.*
> *The bells in the church tower, they say ding, the women, they*
> * say dong.*
> *I'll take the bells any day, caramba,*
> *'cause they ring and they don't do you wrong.*

Who's that singing? It's such a sad voice it gives me goose bumps. And yet the tune is catchy. But the owner of that heartbroken voice must be going through a terrible time. Tierra, why don't you come back to the city with me, and get Chivirico Vista Alegre to come too, and all your relatives, the whole bunch? I mean, I know there are a lot of you, I don't know where I'd put you all, I live in this tiny little apartment with my mother. But I could talk to some people I know. Gervasio would help us, he's really nice, he's a waiter. We could divide you up into people's houses, really nice, decent people. Then we could go see the police. Of course the city is dirty, not in the greatest shape—falling apart sometimes, in fact—in fact, I guess it's a prison of asphalt and garbage, but if you think about it, the whole island is a cage, and the ocean is the bars to it, everywhere you look. Don't get so upset, Tierra, stop pacing back and forth like that, put the machete down—if you keep swinging it around like that, you're going to wind up hitting me. Or hitting yourself. And then where would we be? It'll all work out, you'll see. Calm down. You look like a tiger in a cage with a boa in front of you.

> *Belle, Belle, Belle, Belle—Belle climbs up the hill,*
> *and if it weren't for that ole Belle, Cuba would not have a hill.*
> *Vaya, not have a hill a-tall, e-eh!*

I'm not going to calm down, goddammit, because I'm mad and I don't feel like calming down! Don't you see that they're trying to take away everything that belongs to us, the soul of the forest? Don't you see that they're trying to scare us? They'd be capable of burning us alive to make us leave the batey. You're one of them, too, aren't you? You, too, of course! Miss highfalutin city girl! You're here for a month and a half, nothing here gets you in the gut, nothing here cuts you like a knife—you couldn't care less what happens here! To you, I'm a freak! My parents, my brothers and sisters are just outlandish monsters to you! Do you think I've never seen myself in a mirror, with these six breasts, my fingers all twisted and gnarly? Do you think I like being ignorant and uneducated? That's what you all think, that I'm an uneducated, ignorant half-wit! But I'll tell you, just so you know—I probably know more than you do! I haven't gone to school much, but everything I know, I was taught by the ceiba tree, the manatee, the royal palm, and the güijes! Don't come near me, don't do it! Don't you dare touch me, I'll skin you alive! You're just like them—you're all cut from the same cloth—murderers! Who do you people think you are, do you think you'll be able to bring me under your power like you do the caracoles, rubbing them and putting a spell on them so you can have them in your power? Lissen to th' song a the orishas: We all a us comed ovah th' salt sea, an' we all a us are one, that's what the restless soul of a slave told me through the mouth of the royal palm, and I'm not going to betray it. You are not going to divide us up, no sir! Divide and conquer, that's the motto of Brutus Escoria. Well, he knows what he can do with that!

Belle, Belle, Belle, Belle—Belle climbs up the hill,
and if it weren't for that ole Belle, Cuba would not have a hill.

How can such a happy song be sung with such agony? Come here, Tierra, come over here, I'm your friend. I'm your sister. You can believe me—haven't I shown you that you can trust me, haven't I risked being expelled from the School in the Country by running off to the woods with you? You're the only person I truly love, the only one who's ever given me everything. I can't leave you, and I can't bear to see you this way. The most important thing to me is you, it really is you. Let me hold you. I love you. Let me kiss you. Kiss me. Let's lie down here, the sky is like a wet towel, look, how beautiful, the dew on the grass. You know something? What I like best is taking a nap in between the rows of the tobacco, hidden among the tobacco plants, under the netting, while everybody else is working. Looking up at the sky through the netting that protects the plants and hearing the little feet of insects pattering near my ear, feeling the ants tickling my skin when they crawl on me, the heat and the sunlight that burns my skin. Knowing that I won't be able to have any of this in the city, that it will all be off-limits to me when I get back, makes me so furious I could just explode.

> Out of the thick grove of star-apple trees,
> Above the lovely boughs,
> Flocks of painted butterflies,
> Butterflies flutter out
> Seeking the morning sky.

Where's Danae?! Has anybody seen her? She and I were dancing not long ago, but you know how she gets, the foul mood just comes over her—just because I was dancing a little close, like this, pelvis to pelvis, she whacked me upside the head so hard my ears are still ringing. Brigida the Imperfect saw her talking with the guy that wrote the play, out there outside, uh-huh, uh-huh, that faggoty guy, or the one they say is a faggot, I don't know anything about that. They looked pretty sentimental, out there under the stars—like Fred and Ginger, you know, but with the generation-gap thing. So anyway, I lost sight of her. She ran off with a manatee? Out that way? That's what Irma the Albino says—of course if you're looking for somebody dopier than Irma you'd have to have 'em tailor-made; now she's raising little rat babies. No, honest, I'm serious. What? Salome the Satrap and Renata the Physical saw the intrepid manatee, too! I'll tell you, they're going to have to send the whole camp to the happy farm, *mi amigo*. But anyway, *mira*, where's Duckbill Lips, anybody seen her? Think she's gone AWOL? By which I mean catchin' her z's, don't anybody get the wrong idea, okay? ... No, *mi hermano*, I wanted to apologize, I didn't mean to bug her. If there's still time to say you're sorry, why not do it? I've gotta learn when to keep my big mouth shut, y'know? This mess hall is as hot as your mother's twat, dude. She's probably out there somewhere, living it up, having herself an evening of culcha, reciting poetry, you know. She's kinda the romantic kind, she loves all that loneliness and night and the first light of dawn bullshit. And speaking of the first light of dawn, it's almost sunrise. Have these people forgotten that there's work tomorrow? We're going to be falling asleep between the rows. Me, I don't get my fourteen hours, I'm no good for nothin'. He-e-e-ey! Look, here she comes! How about that! Oh good, I caught her off base! Yep, she's tagged out for taking too big a lead here tonight, and they just may send her back to the lockers, folks! Looks like Duckbill Lips could be out for the rest of the game! It all depends on what she's willing to do for the umpire! Whoa—what's that column of black smoke over there? And what's wrong with Danae, why's she covered with that black soot? Hey, girl, get over here! Where've you been, eh? Are you faking this or what? Where's the fire? You get all sulky on me, I'll turn you in for the reward money, honey, awright?

> *At the line of the ocean lapping the shore,*
> *in the mangrove thickets quaking in the cold*
> *at first light glisten the shimmering rocks,*
> *and their fragrant petals the flowers unfold.*

"Where's the fire?!"—where *was* it, you mean. You people are idiots, a bunch of semiconscious morons. The batey's on fire, the lives of those poor people are in mortal danger, and you people are back here partying, doing all the stupid things you always do—letting your brains get washed with all those idiotic things those idiotic teachers tell you. If you really want to know, Brutus Escoria and his men set the whole settlement back there on fire—fortunately they waited for the whole family to be together eating in one of the houses, in Yolandina's bohío over there. But can you imagine if one of them, or one of the children, had been in their house asleep? They just barely had time to run out with whatever they could carry—basically they lost everything they owned. When I left they were rebuilding. And all because the Higher-Ups want to build a luxury hotel. I hope you can keep your fat trap shut about me going over there. You tell, you'll live to regret it, I promise. I feel awful, really weak, I think I've got a fever—I feel just awful. Hold me, Andy Crater Face, hold me. Protect me, ay, protect me.

I without bitter grieving, without bitter grief,
I without bitter grieving, or guilt that torments me,
watch the clouds, pink and white, blow in from the east,
rampán rampampán, blow in from the east . . .

Despite the bad weather forecast by the weather report, the teachers decided that their pupils should go to work in the fields as usual. I'd barely had time to jump in the river to alleviate the terrible dryness of my delicate manatee skin. Brigades number 9 and 17 were sent to dig up potatoes. Andy Crater Face was happy to work close by his girlfriend. Yes, she had said *yes*, just like that. Out of pity, in an act bordering on the melodramatic, he'd practically demanded it. Now they could be considered formally going steady. Although she had agreed to it in the middle of an attack of hysteria the night before, or in the wee hours of that same morning, when he discovered her sneaking back from the burning batey. She was so nervous, she said so many weird things, and she begged him to hold her against his chest—he was delighted. He hugged her so hard her ribs creaked. She kept crying like a faucet, with all these deep moans and sobs that scared him, he had to admit. The only thing that occurred to him was to ask her:

"So what'll it be—yes or yes? Are we hitched?"

"Yes, yes, shit, yes, yes-s-s-s . . ." She turned and ran off toward the wash-basins, where she stuck her head under one of the taps and wet her hair in the stream of water until she felt as though there were thousands of needles pricking her scalp.

The teacher-guides gave the order to form up, and then they read the weather report to the brigades—today severe thunderstorm and possible tornado in the area, very nearby, near the town of La Fe. Director Puga knew that he had made a mistake in allowing the party to go on until dawn, and that one of the teachers, the one that disliked him most, Margot Wrangling, would probably write up a report, denounce his improper conduct, his going too light on the students. His job was to act as a fire wall, to turn their energies away from partying toward work, and he ought to begin with himself— the first rule for these Schools in the Country was to counterattack by good example. And so today it would be from the party to breakfast, from the smoky café con leche to the morning formation, from the morning formation to the field. Come hell or high water. Until hell freezes over. And even if heaven and earth split wide fucking open. Why, there was no need to worry about what the weather forecast said; they never got it right, anyway. When they said there was going to be rain, the sun was hot enough to fry eggs; when they said there was going to be *a fine day, with sunshine, fair skies, and calm seas*, you could bet your month's salary that there'd be lightning and deluge and the storm surge would wipe out towns and cities all along the coast.

At midmorning, Danae kept the date she'd made with Andy Crater Face, out in the plantain field. He'd been waiting a good while. She lost no time; as soon as she whispered out the password—*Danae weaves the hours gilded by the Nile*—he stood up in the clearing so she could see him. She had no time to waste, if it was going to happen, then let it happen. She liked him; she thought the boy was cute, fun, despite the fact that he always wanted to be hanging around her. She stripped off her clothes, stepped up, and kissed him. While he was returning her kiss, he ejaculated on her thigh—he never even penetrated her imperturbable dry vagina. She wanted a steady relationship, she said, though she had no idea what she was talking about—it didn't make much sense, but she did it so he wouldn't feel rejected, or because she had to say something, or because she was embarrassed to confess that she'd experienced no emotion with the kiss—or maybe she had, she wasn't sure. Maybe she'd been expecting too much. She realized she didn't have time now to think about what had just happened. Her hymen was a bother. She ran back to her row, making the excuse to Andy that the teacher would make her pay if she caught her gone, would give her a dozen demerits, and she didn't intend to go hungry for days because of *him*.

Andy Crater Face felt great, he'd snared a girlfriend, the object of his desire since he'd set foot in that revolting, disgusting camp. And without much effort, if the truth be told. Not that he was planning to replace her anytime soon—this one was serious. He threw two or three potatoes in his rowmate's sack and double that number of glances over at the girl, who was about a hundred yards away. His friend was waving and signaling to him—they were way behind, the last ones in their brigade. Suddenly, the guajiros stopped working; they could sense danger. Nervously, fearfully, they announced that they'd all better be getting back—they could smell foul weather in the air, what was coming was going to be bad. I sensed beforehand that Obón Tanze, the spirit of the sacred fish, was about to emerge in a black pearl of water and loose his wrath upon the world. Just then, the Higher-Ups' car appeared—*Nobody's authorized to stop working, let's move, let's move! Who do you think you are, you lazy bunch of slackers!* The guajiros stood their ground; there could be unprecedented loss of life, they added, their expressions rigid. Brutus Escoria, irate, stubborn as a mule, swatted at the air— nobody was leaving this field, they had to meet the goal and surpass it, and that was the end of the story, so they'd better just get used to it. And by the way, what was Bejerano's daughter doing hoeing, parked over there next to a student? Hadn't they made it clear that no member of that family could mix with the students? That was called privileges, and in this camp nobody could enjoy any sort of personal consideration. It wasn't fair to the other girls. Danae Duckbill Lips, out of that row this minute; demerit number twenty-two for the lucky young lady! Tierra Fortuna Munda would have to leave. None of this sentimental nonsense with these people—could they get that through their thick skulls? Wasn't last night enough for them? Bejerano stared at his daughter; she was wiping her hands on the worn legs of her pants. She obeyed her father and walked away, toward the batey.

> *I hear the murmur of the leaves and the roar of the waterfall,*
> *I hear the wind begin to sigh around my bohío,*
> *and to the strumming of my lyre I sing,*
> *ta-dum, tara-dum, tara-dum, the returning of the dawn.*

I saw it the minute I got to this miserable place—there was going to be an accident. We were still on the bus. Danae Duckbill Lips refused to listen when I expressed my discouraging assessment. I was filing my nails and she was looking in fascination, absolutely enchanted, out the window. Is this *it?*— potatoes and tomatoes? I don't see what's so great about it. I knew things were going to turn bad. Nobody would believe me when I weighed the air—in these camps, there are ghosts *everywhere*. Big Foot, for example. *The decision was unseemly. Unseemly, I repeat, and I record this judgment for history's sake in this diary, which has never left my side since I began to keep it, at the age of eleven. But I talk and talk, which is why they call me Alicia Machine-Gun*

Tongue, and my words are food for the wind. That wind for which we were all almost food today, due to the stubbornness of the Higher-Ups.

We had finished lunch—if you can call it lunch. I know lunch, and that shit was no lunch. We didn't even have the right to go back to the barracks. Director Puga kept yelling in this threatening tone of voice, *Since the party last night lasted till dawn we can't afford to return to the mess hall!* We'd eat in the field, and we'd have fifteen minutes, and then we'd hit it again, "under the sun," as they kept saying. Sun? I doubt it. The sky was blacker than Irma the Albino's fate. The air was heavy, sultry, and it stank, as though everything rotten on the face of the earth had been stirred up around us. The food truck had taken its sweet time, but it finally came. We feared the worst—that they'd forgotten about us again. They solved everything with the excuse that they'd forgotten. My belly was full of forgotten. Bread with tomato slices, salt, sweet potato butter. They were going to make us hate tomato and sweet potato for the rest of our lives.

The trouble started when we were about halfway down the fifth row of the day. All of a sudden the sky turned even blacker behind us than it had been. It all happened in an instant—at first it was a gray whirlwind in the distance, but it was coming toward us at a speed we could not believe. The clouds were in the shape of a big 7 up in the air, and it was raining pellets of celestial rocks. They were shiny, gleaming, brown or bone-colored; my aunt used to call them "lightning stones"; she said that the aborigines had polished those pieces of limestone till they'd turned them into war axes. We heard this deafening roar, like the sky had opened and was sucking up the earth through a straw. Our eardrums popped, and we thought they were going to burst—my ears started bleeding. We started screaming and yelling like wild women, and they told us to run, run from that gigantic monster that was chasing us. We fell down over and over again, got up again the best we could—the wind was throwing us around like dolls. At one point I looked behind me and saw this crimson mass covering the whole sky, from the sky all the way down, and trapped in the center of it were flying bohíos, people, cars, horses, whole tobacco sheds. The last thing I saw was Danae Duckbill Lips and Emma the Menace like two kites going straight up over my head, then sucked into the tornado. There were flickering lights in the sky far off, over by the royal palms. I was pulled up off the ground by the funnel and sent flying off like a rocket, but it seemed like in all directions at once. I lost consciousness when this tremendous weight fell on me and squashed me.

It was a miracle that worse didn't happen in that natural disaster, despite the fact that almost everyone wound up buried in the mud. On the one hand, the relief parties were quick and well trained, the mud was not terribly thick, it was really more like liquid, and a lot of people managed to get out on their own. We came out of it with a few injuries, nothing serious, things like fractured arms, broken legs, bloody heads. The numbers, though, were considerable—of the sixty-five people out in the fields the tornado passed through, thirty-seven were sent home. Me, who had always wanted to get sick— I'd even faked an allergy several times by running stinging weeds and all kinds of disgusting things over my skin—this time I actually got down on my knees and gave thanks for having just been scratched and dented up a little. The infirmary was full and there were not nearly enough nurses and people to go around. Once the scare was past, after two days of well-deserved rest, the ones who remained went back to the farmwork. The following weekend, our relatives didn't show quite the same enthusiasm as at first; mistrust was in all their eyes and faces. Several students decided to drop out, among them Brigida the Imperfect, Salome the Satrap, Noel the Nuisance, and Eduardo Busy Hands. Irma the Albino also wanted to quit, but her father wouldn't support her there. Irma the Albino had to stay, and that was that. Not for long. Danae Duckbill Lips suffered the most from her absence; they were good friends. She was my friend, too; she never ignored me when I was giving one of my speeches, which could be a little incoherent in the beginning for some people, even for me, but in time she realized that fortunately or unfortunately, without my even knowing it, my perorations predicted the future. Danae Duckbill Lips believed in me. That's why at moments such as this I have to stand behind her, have to support her, especially now that everyone is repudiating her. How quickly we become adults!

> *I look upon the blue of the sky, admire the land so green,*
> *I hear the song of the mockingbird and the murmur of the stream.*
> *The tunibamba, the bamba'o, the high clear voice I bring,*
> *Ai-eee!*

Dear first love,

Even though I've sent several letters and gotten no reply to any of them, I've decided to keep writing to you. Not knowing why I do it. I am just determined, I suppose, not to lose contact. What sense does that make if I'm not even sure whether my letters reach you, or whether you've moved? It may be even worse—you may not want to receive word from me.

My life has changed from what it was when we met. Months have gone by and it's now been a year and a half since I was at the La Fe camp. I haven't forgotten you, even though I've never heard from you, or anything about you. My mother, Gloriosa Paz, refused to travel to those parts. You can't even mention the lake to her, where she wasted a whole Sunday trying to find a vehicle of some kind to take her back to the city. She says she has terrible memories of that place; and the truth is, it wasn't easy—I can't say I had the time of my life, either. And now, if I add it all up, I guess maybe I was foolish to think that I could live there forever. Like I don't think you could get used to the city. Gloriosa Paz says everybody has their place. I'm not so sure that I agree, but at least I do begin to see her point.

Gloriosa Paz has taken a husband, as she puts it. He's a bricklayer, or since there aren't any bricks, he's a cement block layer. He's a mulatto, and you can imagine, with how racist the people in my neighborhood are, that he's become the butt of everybody's insults and wisecracks and remarks out of the side of their mouths. People also say that the individual is a switch-hitter, that he may be about half queer. Oral tradition would have it that there are no men anymore, that the ones that don't stand for such things bend for 'em. I don't like him; he's this guy who's got no problem showing up at certain hours—lunchtime, dinnertime—to sit down at what used to be our table, monopolize the french fries or the plantains or the yuca with garlic. And then wham, bam, thank you ma'am, he's outta here again.

Andy Crater Face and I are still sillily in love. I still have the same girl-friends, although my favorite ones are Emma the Menace and Alicia Machine-Gun Tongue. We all went into the next grade and they didn't divide us up into different rooms. All but Irma the Albino, who won't be here anymore, and that scared-mouse of a face of hers. I just can't get it out of my mind. Surely you remember Emma the Menace and Alicia Machine-Gun Tongue; they're really nice to me. Sometimes we fight, but in a day or two we make up. We depend a lot on each other; we borrow clothes from each other to go to parties and things. Renata the Physical got married and never showed up at school again. She works as an usher at the América movie theater.

This year, once again, we won't be spared the Schools in the Country. There was a rumor that there wasn't going to be any more agricultural work by young people; the campesinos complained that instead of being helpful we caused them all kinds of losses, messed up the harvests with our inexperience and lack of love for the land. The first part I agree about, but not the second. I learned to love the land. I respect and love nature, the wilderness, the woods, the forest, the whole thing, and I owe that to you.

I don't actually think there's any use writing you anymore, but I hope someday to get some word from you, even a postcard. I'm in the middle of finals, and I'm counting the days . . . I hope we get to go back to La Fe; rumor has it that they're going to send us to Vivero, near San Juan and Martínez. I suspect that even though that's far from where you are (I looked it up on the map), we could manage to see each other.

I think of the sunrises with you. Sometimes I'm walking along the street and I think I hear that sad voice echoing in the distant hills. I stop, close my eyes, and I can imagine the cart driver, even smell the fragrance of the dawn. Dawn is a beautiful word that we never use in the city.

> With the most ardent yearning
> I turn a gaze once more to the sun
> and in my rustic song I say,
> to the rhythm of my lyre,
> blessed the man in Cuba
> who greets the returning of the dawn.

THE PALM'S IMPETUOSITY, CONTROVERSY, FLAMENCO HEEL-TAPPING

*A*fter the tornado and the rain, there were days and days of terrible stormy weather. An invasion of giant mosquitoes, cockroaches, and bubonic rats appeared out of nowhere, overrunning the barracks, tobacco-drying sheds, fields, everything. But even this natural calamity did not keep us from working like dogs—which is how the teachers and Higher-Ups treated us, like dogs, like mangy dogs. The biggest part of the time we would be soaked, drenched with water; if our clothes dried, it was on our backs, and we barely ate. All there was on the menu, if you can call it that, was rice so dirty it was gray and tomato jelly or sweet potato butter. Because of the rain and wind and storms, the provisions trucks were suddenly conspicuous by their absence—the weather was the excuse this time; there was always some excuse. So I got depressed. I spent a week and a half without speaking to anybody, without making a sound, at least while I was awake. Danae Duckbill Lips was the only one who could understand the state of my emotions. She and I have always been just like this, this close. Her sense of solidarity would be stirred when she saw me leaning against the royal palm ringed with plantains smeared with cacao butter and tied with red ribbon, and she would creep over to me, little by little; after a while, as she lay on Chaw, my raggedy leather jacket, she would get up the courage to speak to me in that timid little voice of hers, half mournful and half respectful, and ask me:

Emma the Menace, what's happening to you? Are you all right? You can come with me to my friends' house, the guajiros'. They're nice people, really, you can't believe all the things you hear about them. They're wonderful. You can swim in a lake that's just divine—nobody knows about it, it's behind the clearing where they live, in a little hidden place, and you can eat fried pork rinds or pork wrapped in guava leaves and roasted like they make it . . . Emma the Menace, I hate to see you like this, so quiet, with your eyelids droopier than ever.

That part about my "eyelids droopier than ever" almost made me laugh; I had to pinch myself to keep from cracking up and breaking out in an attack of hysterical hilarity. Because I do have droopy eyelids, and my depressions do accentuate that. Danae Duckbill Lips was always swearing that this American actress had the same kind of eyes, which were what everybody thought made her look so exotic and beautiful. Danae Duckbill Lips was always a good friend. It's a shame that husband of hers insists on beating her down so much, humiliating her, reducing her to something less than a garbanzo bean. I should go see her, I really should. Oh, I have asthma again, the legacy of all those baths under the irrigation sprinklers.

Anyway, because of all the rain there was a danger that the tobacco would rot; a lot of it was already beginning to be ruined by the blue mold. They moved us to a different field, although Bejerano and his son Chivirico Vista Alegre were still with us. They put us under the netting for the blond tobacco and ordered us to strip the leaves off and pull off all the new shoots. In a few days we were transferred to the drying sheds, where we were supposed to sew the best-looking leaves to the drying rods. Then we would sling the drying rods over our shoulders, shinny up under the roof, and hang the rods across two rafters so the leaves would dry better. Danae Duckbill Lips loved that work, she was an expert at hopping up the ladders like a frog, carrying a rod so loaded down it looked like it was going to break in two—they would bend in the middle something awful—and hanging it up in the rafters. You could see the split and cracked skin on her bony back; she climbed the ladders barefoot.

On one occasion I actually let Duckbill Lips talk me into it and we sneaked out to the guajiros' batey—separately, so as not to be missed. We'd agreed to meet out there; what I discovered was a community of the nicest people, but with such suffering engraved in the wrinkles around their eyes. We ate like there was no tomorrow; it's a miracle we didn't founder; we also drank bottles and bottles of rum. Bejerano and Santa had to dunk us in the lake to sober us up a little before we went back to the barracks. I got to know Chivirico Vista Alegre and his sensual cousins much more profoundly; you could see from a mile away that the kid was dying to jump Danae Duckbill Lips' bones. His sister Tierra Fortuna Munda couldn't hide her jealousy. Danae Duckbill Lips was treated like a queen, and she deserved it; she had been the only one of us recalcitrant student-farmers from the city—god, for us this was torture—who'd dared to cross the border, step over the line, and actually spend some time with them, actually offer them her friendship. From what I could see, Duckbill Lips really wanted those people to believe in her admiration for them, although, also from what I could see, there was a certain uneasiness, a skittishness in her behavior—she seemed to have this way big attraction to the girl with the tangled hair and wise look in her eyes. Tierra Fortuna Munda was definitely first in the exclusive circle of her love. With Chivirico Vista Alegre she would play around (Margot Wrangling would have said she flirted), but you couldn't tell whether the young man had made a crack in her coconut or not—whether she really liked him. I confess that at first I was a little repulsed by the physical defects of the extended family, but little by little I started to find things to like about Chivirico Vista Alegre and his cousins. I kind of halfway fell in love with him. For a long time, months I mean, after we went back to the city and started school again, my mouth (and other parts) would water when I thought about that strange boy with the ringlets in his sun-battered hair, his three green eyes (he had three eyes), his full lips, his hands covered with fingers, his two navels, one just below the other. I never opened up to Danae Duckbill Lips and told her about my crush on Tierra Fortuna Munda's brother. I thought it might interfere with her relationship with him. I suspected that there was something between my girlfriend and the guajiro.

God, how time passes and things change in this fleeting life of ours! When I was fifteen I thought I was immortal, I had no idea how long youth might last—forever, I thought. I wonder whatever happened to those people. My kids also had to go through those Schools in the Country, and they were somewhere close to La Fe, but no matter how hard I tried, no matter how many people I asked, I could never find out anything about that batey and the people that lived in it.

"Oh, compañera, those people moved away, nobody knows where, and people say they died off! Uh-huh, you know, ahem, that whole great big huge family died off, and there's not a trace left of 'em. They were good people, but difficult, you know."

The only one I ever heard anything about was that disgusting Brutus Escoria; he'd married some dykey girl—that's what the drunks in the bar in town told me when I asked, not long after we left. *Yes, ma'am, a bitchy, grouchy, grumpy kinda man-acting woman that gave him five kids, although none of 'em survived the series of epidemics that broke out back then.* Which didn't surprise me—their dying like that, I mean—because after the storm and the tornado and the spell of bad weather, things just went from bad to worse, people and animals dying all over the place—Death making his rounds, you might say, even visiting one of us.

The accident happened the day after I discovered that the royal palm could talk just like a person. I was leaning back on the tree like it seemed like I always was, cogitating on the fact that these forty-five days of School in the Country seemed like an eternity, although at least I'd been screwing like a wild woman, which I would definitely not have been able to do under the close scrutiny (i.e., thumb) of my family. And for no particular reason I reached out and was going to steal one of those red ribbons that was tied around a bunch of moldy plantains painted with lipstick—there were all these bunches of plantains all around the tree. I knew it was voodoo or santería or whatever, but it didn't matter to me, I'd lost my hair clip that I used to keep my hair up off my neck to give myself a little relief from the heat and that piece of raggedy ribbon was just the thing, as a temporary solution, of course. So I pulled off this ribbon, red faille it was, I'll never forget it, and all of a sudden I heard this voice saying, "Don't touch that."

Well, that made me jump. I looked all around, trying to see who had said that.

"No need to look around, I'm right here. I'm the spirit of the royal palm, I live here. It's me that's talking to you."

I looked up into the top of the tree and the palm leaves were waving in the breeze, making a strange melody. Just then an arm emerged from the trunk of the tree, and the hand was clutching a sword. I almost died. I crawled backwards for several yards—I was sitting on the ground—never taking my eyes off that tree.

"No need to be afraid, I won't do you any harm if you don't harm me. Give me back what you took from me."

And out of the trunk stepped this little Indian-looking man, very muscular, almost naked, with just a piece of some kind of rough fabric, dyed red, for a loincloth. Agallú Solá, the father of Changó, the god of thunder.

I put the piece of red ribbon back in exactly the same place I'd taken it from, tied the bunch of plantains up in it again, and said to myself, *Feet, don't fail me now!* Then I took off running back to the camp, like a bat outta hell. Except for Danae Duckbill Lips, they all refused to believe what had happened.

"Emma the Menace is crazier 'n a loon," howled Pancha Flatfoot, who by this time had turned into like a substitute boss and secret dyke.

I was all curled up in Danae Duckbill Lips' bunk, and I could see Irma the Albino. She was holding these little roly-poly rats up to her breast and nursing them. The orphans, as she called them—they had turned into a bunch of colorless rodents with skin so transparent you could see the blue veins through it.

"God, Irma Albino, that's so disgusting! Why don't you let them find their own food? They're big enough not to need you or anybody else anymore. It's dangerous, they're going to give you a disease."

"Don't be an idiot, Emma the Menace. Can't you see I'm their mother now?"

They more they sucked her nipples, the pinker and rosier they got. Her nipples, I mean. They were surrounded by this celestial-looking aureole, like the scarlet circle around the mouth of somebody with tuberculosis. When the animals finished nursing they would crawl off in Indian file and wiggle under the mattress, to go to sleep—the pillow wouldn't nearly cover them by now. And Irma the Albino would go back to being her own milky-white self again, although if possible paler and weaker-looking than ever.

That was the last time I talked to her. Danae Duckbill Lips made signs like to leave her alone, she was incorrigible, there was nothing anybody could do; I realized I was wasting my time trying to talk to her.

"If you ask me, she's started thinking she's a white lab rat," she added, and we had a secret laugh, covering our mouths with our hands.

That night there was a party again, but they didn't bring in any musicians or singers or actors or anybody, they just turned on Director Puga's tape player and we danced with the boys. Andy Crater Face was still totally drooling over Danae Duckbill Lips, and I noticed that they weren't always bickering and picking at each other like they had been. Although the minute Tierra Fortuna Munda showed up, my girlfriend sneaked off with her into the woods. The party lasted just as long as it was supposed to—things had tightened up considerably since that first time. We all went to bed early, and Danae Duckbill Lips came back five minutes before they woke us up.

Mara Medusa announced in that squeaky chicken-voice of hers that the day was going to be cloudy. As the owner and manager of the radio, she was totally up to date on all the stupid things that happened, or *occurred*, in Cuba, including the weather reports. The Meteorological Institute was forecasting high humidity, clouds, and possible heavy winds and strong thunderstorms for the part of the country we were in. A gray day. My teeth chattered just thinking about it. Once again I was getting pain in my joints from the humidity. Ever since then I've had acute arthritis and chronic asthma. But I was shocked out of my suffering by Margot Wrangling's irritating screech:

"Brigade number 9, on the cart! Let's go, we're off to the tobacco sheds, you rattlebrains! On the move, you bunch of dried-out twats!"

Poor fucked-up bitch, I thought.

I loved sewing the tobacco leaves. As a souvenir of my adolescence I keep that huge needle with the rusty eye that a thick sisal cord could fit through. I had gotten to be a real expert—the best—at sewing together sheaves of leaves and stringing them on the rod. Actually, Danae Duckbill Lips and I were tied for the best, although when it came to climbing up to the top of the drying shed she was definitely the champion. In the future, I, like my friend, would miss the camp.

We got on the cart. A rooster crowed, and then another one answered, far away. Mara the Wheezer turned on the radio, and there was a program of campesino music. Justo Vega and Adolfo Alfonso were pretending to have this big argument. Back then I hated that kind of guajiro song where they would make the lyrics up as they went along and sing like nasal-voiced troubadours or something—the *punto*, it was called. I hated *anything* that was like local color or folklore. As time has passed, though, I've become a real fan of those voices; it isn't so much that you care what they sing as that you like watching them walk the tightrope of rhyming against the lines they've just set themselves, thinking they'll never be able to rhyme and make sense at the same time, and then also that particular guitar of theirs, the *tres*, going *chink-a-chink-a, chink-a-chink-a-chink, chink-a-chink-a, chink-a-chink-a-chink-a-chink.*

> *Justo, I want you to tell me,*
> *whether you're ready to sing—*
> *ready to debate me,*
> *and not give an inch.*
> *I want to see you fly up and away*
> *like a bird on the wing,*
> *and then if I have my way,*
> *I'll bring you down to earth again,*
> *the only problem being*
> *if I run out of gasoline.*

The fog made the air heavy. The cart lurched off through the steaming mud, rocking back and forth and jerking and jolting like an arabesque, the wheels hitting big rocks and our ovaries bouncing up to our tonsils. The countryside was shinier and more glistening than ever, and it evoked passions in you, as though your emotions had been embroidered in opaline light by the hand of an angel. The high pennons of the royal palms were tossing in the breeze like long hair, in a dreamlike slow-motion flutter. Now Justo Vega went on the offensive:

> *I'm always ready to debate*
> *without fear and without quarter,*

I'm always ready to debate
without fear and without quarter,
and to let our listeners decide
who gets bread and who gets water.
With our ideas and our voices.
we'll enter the guajiro debate,
giving our listeners their choices
between you and me, mate,
but without any of your swear words
or your off-color jokes,
without any of your swear words
that offend the folks.

The boards in the floor of the cart were jumping around like the keys on a piano keyboard playing jazz. I looked around for the rising sun; I was cold, so I turned my face to the sun's rays. And all of a sudden I felt pellets of mud and clay hitting my face. I asked what was happening, but without turning around; I didn't want to lose the warmth.

"One of the wheels's stuck in the mud up to the axle," Salome the Satrap answered.

What were we going to go? We couldn't just sit there. Should we get down and push? Isn't that how the people in the movies solve this kind of problem?

"No, that won't be necessary," the teacher-guide said, clicking her teeth together. "And it's a little early to be getting so frisky, don't you think?"

I too welcome a clean debate,
without fear and without quarter,
but what I fear may get in the way
is wanting lily-white palaver.
I resent your accusations
that I make off-color remarks
and use bad words and profanation.
I think you're mind's macabre.
You are such a strait-laced fellow,
walking the straight and narrow,

that any word the least bit yellow
has to be totally laundered.
So let me say this just this once,
and not need to say it more,
Adolfo, you are an old woman.
And now— I yield the floor.

Hummingbirds, bobolinks, bugler birds, and blackbirds were beginning to stir—they were fluttering, flying, and diving through the air, and all trying to outsing each other. Uh-huh, I have no doubt that there were emerald hummers and mockingbirds—every kind of bird that lived in the countryside was out that morning in full force. The sound of their music, mixed with the song on the radio, filled the plain, and it sounded like what I heard somebody call it once—an honest-to-god parliament. There was the sound of beating wings, thousands of wings, the snap of wing feathers, so many that at times it sounded like somebody dancing the flamenco, with all those tapping heels, a whole troupe of flamenco dancers all dancing at once on a wooden stage out there in the wilderness. The cart would not budge, and the more the guajiro gunned the tractor, the more the wheel buried itself in the mud.

Sing, sing, as loud as you want,
whatever you like,
sing, sing, as loud as you want,
whatever you like,
but remember our bounden duty here
is to sing what the people like
and make sure that they enjoy themselves
and have a little smile.
Sing fearlessly, and make your bride
the muse of happiness,
let's make the audience split their sides
but with judiciousness—
and be sure the laughs you get
are not at my expense.

We were all holding on to the uprights on the side of the cart for dear life, trying not to fall or be thrown out. The rocking made you nauseous. My blistered hands were sweaty and they slipped on the wood. Danae Duckbill Lips started laughing, Pancha Flatfoot was jumping up and down and laughing, Salome the Satrap was laughing, Renata the Physical was laughing and la-la-ing along with the song on the radio—I suddenly realized that they were all laughing like idiots. *Tears follow close on laughter,* I thought to myself. It was ugly, desperate, stupid, irresponsible laughter. I used to get so sick of all that laughing and guffawing sometimes, I couldn't stand so much unmotivated hilarity—laughing just because, for no reason but to entertain yourself—or to incite yourself to laugh some more. Irma the Albino was behind me, behind *us,* at one of the front corners of the cart. I didn't know whether she was laughing too or not. There wasn't time.

> *I've never been a comedian,*
> *or thought life was a circus,*
> *but I'll tell you, your complaining*
> *is making me right nervous.*
> *To my way of thinking,*
> *you're way, way, way too serious.*
> *What we need here is spunk and spirit,*
> *and to carry out our mission,*
> *what we need here is spunk and spirit,*
> *and quick wit and intelligence.*
> *I'm not saying you have to offend*
> *or act like a circus clown*
> *but what we're supposed to do here, friend,*
> *is show the people a good time,*
> *so stop looking down your nose at me,*
> *and put away that frown.*

Just then several guajiros came up with sticks and pieces of wood and stuff and started to dig and stick wood under the wheels and everything while the driver kept gunning the motor and rocking the cart backward and forward, the engine going *grrrnn, grrrnn, grrrrrrnnnn.* The men stopped and recommended that we should probably get off. Margot Wrangling agreed, but grumbling all the way. The wheel came loose and the cart was saved from the quicksand (or whatever). We got back in and started off again. Off in the distance it looked like the royal palms were rushing toward us, rushing toward a dangerous liaison with our heads.

> Laugh if you feel like laughing,
> guffaw if you want to guffaw,
> laugh if you feel like laughing,
> guffaw if you want to guffaw,
> but I'll have no vulgar trifling
> with my standards of behavior.
> You can talk any way you like to,
> use any words you choose to utter,
> but don't try to justify yourself
> when you wallow in the gutter.
> And also don't try to paint me
> the spoilsport of the debate,
> don't you try to paint me,
> the party pooper of the debate.
> It was from my sainted mother
> I learned decency and restraint.

The cart was moving a little faster now, and it wasn't rocking and bouncing so much, although it still had its moments, with the road so muddy and dotted with pools of rainwater that you didn't know how deep they were till you were in them. And then, to make matters worse, the *ssst, ssst, ssssst* of the mist turned into a roar, an absolute downpour. We'd lost a lot of time, and other brigades had already started working. Mara the Wheezer was nervous about what would happen to us, and protesting against some abstract wrong that had been done to us. *How were we ever going to be workers in the vanguard after that betrayal by nature,* that kind of stuff. Off in the distance I could make out a group of boys pulling up beets and throwing them in burlap sacks. We drove by a field of potatoes. Potatoes, tomatoes, beets, tobacco—I thought my head was going to start spinning from the whirling rows of crops. At night I was constantly having nightmares about enormous tubers, or starving rats gnawing at my breasts. By now the mist had lifted, the sky had cleared, and now the sun was beating down something fierce; we knotted our quilted jackets around our waists.

> It's not that I'm trying to make
> you the spoilsport or party pooper,
> it's you yourself with your long face
> that's making yourself the loser.
> And though you'd like people to see me
> as the butt of your disdain,
> and although you may think me
> vulgar and clownish and vain,
> if I were to pull off some corn silk
> to make me a fake mustache,
> the people would laugh themselves silly
> and fall right on their . . . chairs.

It all happened so fast. Just when it looked like we were going along as smooth as you please, when the potholes were fewer and not so deep, all of a sudden the tractor fell into a second bottomless pool of muddy water. At first it just sort of tilted in; the driver tried to gun the motor, but the hole gave way and sucked in the whole front end of the tractor, swallowing the cabin with the steering wheel and everything. So the cart wound up on its head, vertical in the middle of the road, and we were all catapulted through the air, like *that*! I heard screams, shrieks—

"A cart's turned over, run! The students' cart turned over, run for help! It's killed the girls from Havana!"

I was buried headfirst in a pile of cow manure they used as a fertilizer.

> You try to be so funny,
> so witty, so ironic, so smart,
> you try to be so funny,
> so witty, so ironic, so smart,
> because you think there's money

in prostituting our art.
Set your sights on higher goals,
let the light from above on you shine,
because if you keep on the way you're going,
with suggestive and risqué lines,
you'll spoil the good fun,
the clean give-and-take
of the campesino debate.

This is it, I thought; we're all dead. I opened my eyes. Danae Duckbill Lips was huffing and puffing and shaking me by the shoulders. She saw that I was still alive and vanished again, out of my line of sight. I carefully raised my head. Danae Duckbill Lips, Venus Putrefaction, Migdalia Fake Eyelashes, and Carmucha Women's Shelter were reviving the rest. I noticed that the royal palms were closer and closer, and there were more and more of them, as though they'd been planted in my corneas.

I would never ever pretend to betray
the good fun and clean give-and-take
of the campesino's traditional debate,
the debate that'll give me victory
and light Cuba on its path to glory.
What I deny is the whimsical way
you paint me as I ain't,
and I know for a fact, as sure as I'm me
that you do it knowingly
to fool the folks and also blunt
the points I score against ye.

So then there was all the chaos and confusion that always comes with such a terrible accident. The campesinos, the teachers, and the students from the other brigades nearby ran to help us. The people from the batey brought alcohol, hydrogen peroxide, Mercurochrome, bandages, cotton balls—anything they had in their medicine chests. Tierra Fortuna Munda rode at full speed to the town, but she came back shaking her head—none of the Higher-

Ups showed the slightest concern about us. The girl said they asked, just as calm as you please, whether there were really a lot of people killed.

"We don't know yet," she answered, shocked, forgetting about the driver buried in the mud.

"Then don't make such a fuss—go suck that syphilitic horse you're on, can't you see we're in a meeting?"

> *When you say such things about me,*
> *you insolent little whelp,*
> *when you infer such things of me,*
> *you insolent little whelp,*
> *that's when I hold you in contempt*
> *and think that you're beneath me.*
> *You cast aspersions left and right*
> *on my innate humanity,*
> *when it's you, you blue tobacco blight,*
> *that's lost your equanimity—*
> *in cowardice, you're no better than the hutia*
> *and you're as blind as the three blind mice.*
> *And just as those rodents were given what for*
> *with a carving knife to the hilt,*
> *the same for you is now in store*
> *if you don't confess your guilt.*

The ambulance took its sweet time. Two people, we knew, had died. The driver and Irma the Albino. I didn't see her smile for the last time. I figure she was catapulted out of the cart the second the tractor tipped into the hole with the poor driver. She wound up under the front left wheel of the cart. Irma the Albino was dead. Danae Duckbill Lips, trembling and vacant-looking, made the announcement. Suddenly I could raise my body, nothing hurt—I ran over to where the curious were beginning to gather. Irma the Albino dead. All I could see were her white-white, almost transparent legs, with the greenish blue veins all inflamed. From the waist up, she was buried in the ground. The wheel had cut her body in two. Irma the Albino died instantly. Cut in half. Two stumps like two roses rolled over by a pair of skates.

Danae Duckbill Lips and Tierra Fortuna Munda were holding each other. Tierra's face was rigid, dry, and her jaw was set in rage. Danae's tears cooled the campesino girl's weathered back. The teachers were running around, screaming for some kind of transportation—Anything that moves, *caballero*, this is going to cost us, this is going to be terrible. Poor girl, poor thing. *Ay, ¡qué desgracia!, no tiene nombre.*

Tierra Fortuna Munda leapt up onto Sunny's back, several guajiros returned to their bohíos to get their own horses. Out of the trunks of the royal palms planted in the eyes of every one of us flowed reddish-colored rivers, like the fluid from the thighs of a woman giving birth. Then the ambulance came and all together we managed to set the cart upright again. The rest was just too much to take in. A horrible black swamp. Arteries, mud, panicked terror, the persistent cramps of desperation and paralysis. I wanted to run time backward. As though life were a train and you could go back and forth between the car in front and the car in back.

> *Compare me to the hutia*
> *and to the three blind mice,*
> *but none of that will cause me to*
> *confess that I'm anything but nice.*
> *Such comparisons have no effect on me,*
> *and the only way they might*
> *is if someone in a sweet soft voice*
> *should ever think to compare me—*
> *oh, then I'd have no choice—*
> *to that skinny carcass of yours.*

The word spread, of course. In Havana, parents dropped what they were doing and ran out into the streets, carrying whatever they were holding, dressed however they were dressed, leaving their whole world behind them. Some of them were half naked, in underwear or whatever, slips, Taca-brand shorts, the ones with the long legs—passion enhancers, we called them, sarcastically as you can imagine. Or naked. The news of the accident came on the radio, but they didn't give the names of the people that had been killed. My mother, Carmelina Tagore, heard the news at work. In the store on Bulevár San Rafael. She was wrapping the brassiere of the year for a customer and all of a sudden she heard the news. She jumped right over the counter and ran out . . . and ran, and ran. Didn't stop till she got to the bus station. There were no buses, all that was left was one car, but it was already full. She begged and pleaded, she got down on her knees and put her hands together and appealed to their sense of charity, she explained and explained again—there was nothing else to do, she grabbed a guy in a headlock and dragged him out and threw him on the sidewalk. Then she wouldn't let the car stop until it got to La Fe. The passengers were yelling and screaming and cackling and waving their arms around, but in that henhouse of a public car she was like Righteousness, slapping people right and left. The door opened and my mother, Carmelina Tagore, rolled out onto her knees on the red clay soil of La Fe. The car took off in fear and terror, headed for the open highway. Carmelina Tagore, by the way, was a lot of woman; she had one of the most succulent bodies in Havana. She loved classical ballet and the theater, and once she managed to sneak into an Italian opera, I mean sung by real Italians, that was being performed for diplomats and stuff. She was making her way down one of the rows of seats carefully reserved for the guests of honor when an usher stopped her.

"Compañera," he said (and I'll have to tell you this one in Spanish), "esto es exclusivo para el cuerpo diplomático"—"this is only for the diplomatic corps," *cuerpo* being both corps and body, you see.

So she looked at him, with that backside of hers and that big bosom of hers, her eyebrows all eyebrow-penciled, her quivering lips painted a glorious crimson, and she replied:

"Querido, lo del diplomático te lo debo, porque cuerpo me sobra"— "Sweetheart, I'll get back to you about the diplomatic part, but the *corps* speaks for itself."

And she plunked herself down and enjoyed the opera.

> *And now you've descended to insults vile,*
> *proving my former contention*
> *that not just every once in a while*
> *but as an everyday convention,*

you're a rude, crude, vulgar, illiterate goon
and totally without redemption.

We received orders to "build a barricade," and we knew what that meant: An imaginary concertina-wire fence between each and every one of us, to keep us from "conspiring," as they called it. We called it talking, which is exactly what they were getting at. The silence lasted a week. The reason none of us left was that we had to stay, we had no choice. The teachers lied, telling us there was hope that Irma the Albino would survive. We knew she wouldn't. Unless Dr. Frankenstein came along, that is, and sewed her up with barbed wire. We saw them take out one part of her body, covered in these huge clots of blood, and then the other part embalmed in mud. In the days that followed, we were expected to act like nothing had happened; that next Sunday there was another "cultural activity," a mixer with boys and girls from a nearby camp. Yet there was a silence, a silence that lasted a second and then as long we ourselves have lasted, the whole rest of our lives. Afterward, the days were slow, hollow. Danae Duckbill Lips got drunk on this awful liquor, Guayabita del Pinar, that's flavored with this berry, guayabita, a terrible way to get drunk, and she ran off with the guajiros from the batey. I confessed in an attack of drunkenness that I was in love with several people at the same time, and that I couldn't choose between them because I loved them all the same but at the same time differently. There was a profound silence, but the arguing on Mara Medusa's radio could never be turned off.

That just goes to prove the view
that I've always contended:
you're blinded by rage and jealousy
and your own pretensions.
You say you want a clean debate
without any vulgar dissension,
but when push finally comes to shove,
despite his good intentions
and all of his pretensions,
the saint becomes a demon.
But a demon preaching lo-o-o-ve . . .

One afternoon we discovered hundreds of rats climbing up the trunks of the royal palms. The nights were full of piteous moans and squeaks and murmurs. Then, finally, the Higher-Ups paid us a visit. They did a search and found Irma the Albino's mattress just full of little newborn rats, very similar with respect to their transparency to the deceased. The watchword for the morning formation was changed: *And if death should take us in the battle, let us welcome it.* I didn't want to die. *I don't want to die,* I insisted, speaking to Alicia Machine-Gun Tongue, who looked at me, her teeth chattering. *Nobody wants to die,* she replied, her teeth like castanets. *Nobody's going to die, much less now that this woman . . .* But Irma the Albino *was* dead. She had died. She was never what you might call my favorite person, I'm not going to be hypocritical about this, I thought her neurons were a little slow and that she was disgusting to boot, nursing little baby rats at her own breast, for god's sake. When I first met her she was neat, tidy, very clean and hygienic, you know, even excessively so, and then all of a sudden—*bam*—she changed. She was disgusting, but that didn't mean she had to die so young, and that way— squashed like a cockroach under the wheel of a cart. And then we were lied to. The teachers lied to us; they told us that Irma the Albino was getting better day by day, practically minute by minute. And yet that false news was kind of consoling, in the end.

> *That is a lie, a lie, a lie,*
> *you hypocritical thing.*
> *The only reason I'm here tonight*
> *is to have a debate and sing . . .*

Palm tree, come here. Be right there, I replied. I took a few steps forward and two rude arms reached out to me. We held each other for several hundred years. I, like Danae Duckbill Lips, have a secret friend.

Mira, muchacha, take my eyes, look at the world with my eyes. So I took them. And from a great height I looked out upon the wilderness, the woods, the forest, and I saw the sacred mountain. That was when I discovered a herd of ostriches trotting along, with *güijes* gliding along above them. And Irma the Albino sitting astride the feathered back of one of the birds. She was more translucent-looking than ever; she was smiling, yes, but kind of nervous-looking because she still wasn't quite sure how to handle those invisible reins.

Calm yourself, Justito, my man,
here, have yourself a Valium . . .

Alicia Machine-Gun Tongue didn't stop chattering, muttering, until the day of our departure. I built a wall of silence around myself, a silence as sharp as a hunting knife. Danae Duckbill Lips took refuge in love, in her first love. Or in her first and dissimilar confusions. The other girls also *tried* to fall in love, or at least hook up with somebody; in the end, the secret objective of the girl students in the Schools in the Country was to become an initiate in love, or sex, or both. I was never very clear about it; from the physical point of view I liked several of the machos in the barracks next to mine, but I recognize that I was too demanding in terms of spirituality. Coming to a meeting of the minds or whatever with Chivirico Vista Alegre would have been a mistake. *So get thee behind me, Mistake,* I told myself.

You hush your mouth, why I . . .
Why I . . .

It's true that that controversy continues to haunt and torment; it never stops, it goes on forever—it's *immortal,* like what they say, falsely, about immortality. Although the voices are hypnotic and what they are saying is not bad. I am a royal palm that loves a good time; anybody who wants to get something out of me, wants me to do 'em a favor, all they have to do is invite me to a party, especially one where there's dancing—although I can't take too much of that *son montuno* droning, or that *chiquichín, chiquichán,* that horse-sounding clopping of some of the *puntos.* I like melodies, is what I like . . . but not all dragged out by repetitions. I asked Emma the Menace about her life in Havana and whether she wasn't a little frightened, the way I went on, the perorations of a hysterical tree. She shook her head. I'll teach you to dance the flamenco, I said, in a mad passion to dance, and I set my old roots in motion. You can't imagine the heel-tapping I went through to try to bring a smile to that girl's full ripe lips; for several days her eyes had started watering at the least thing, and warm tears would bathe her cheeks. I'll introduce you to men who hunt caymans, I told her, or crocodiles; you will drink *aguardiente* from my entrails, eat sesame seeds warmed in my gourd bowl, the gourd I read the future in. Aguanillé bongó. *Anda, mi majúa,* my sweet girl, lay your head here on my shoulder, drink *la wámbana,* the water of purification, and tell your sorrows to the jubo snake that wraps about my loins and will encoil you in pleasure if you let him. Let us celebrate, let us find pleasure in drums and joyful noise, see how the conga drum's skin throbs, see how it joins the song and causes us to forget. Do not be troubled, do not be disturbed. Go fish for the silvery little biajaca, to offer it up to the Flag of Power. Aaah, this little girl is crazy about me. Emma the Menace embraced my trunk. Aaaah, this little girl worships me. *Ponme la mano aquí, Macorena, ponme la mano aquí . . .* And she put her hand on me. And I put my hand on her. *Aaah, Macorena . . .* Your fleeing compañera now lives in the woods and wilderness, you have seen her, a dead girl gliding through the air. Have no fear, I protect her. *Aguanillé bongó. Cusubesita mía,* my little darling. Hold me and don't let go.

> *Since you're clearly at a loss for words,*
> *I declare myself the champion!*

Why didn't you go back to the city?

Solavaya, make the sign of the cross over yourself every time you meet a chicherekú. It can't hurt and it might help. Death came so near you, it brushed right past you, and now will come a hard time, a long time of wisdom in which you will become old and somber. Whenever you need me, you have only to find the nearest palm tree and bury your desire, your longing, your wish among its roots. I will hear, and I will look into my gourd bowl and divine your most hidden, secret longings. I miss the voices of that noontime, it was an entertaining argument, very funny, the singers insulting each other, making fun of one another, inventing new ways to upset each other. As you will surely understand, it's hard to get the love of my dreams to ask me to dance. Who would understand a palm tree? Who would dare ask me to shake a leg? I've heard that a poet once said that palm trees are brides-to-be waiting. Waiting for what, for whom? That's a very imaginative lie. A trick to make us believe that we are the queens of adventure.

Why didn't you go back to Havana? The country leaves a deep mark, more scars than nostalgia.

> *Champion! How dare you take that title!*
> *Why, I'm a better man than you,*
> *and I'll prove it in REAL battle—*
> *so come on, put up your dukes*
> *and prepare for your teeth to rattle!*

The palm tree just took fire, all by itself. It was a beautiful thing to see. While the fire was consuming the tree I was listening to a hypnotizing melody—*The Conga snake from Jaruco, it go slithering by* . . . I was standing there awestruck, bewitched by the way the trunk was burning, the crown of fronds, when I realized that Danae Duckbill Lips and Tierra Fortuna Munda were there. *The Scorpion cutting sugarcane, only in my country, compay* . . . Between the two girls, the *güijes*, and me, we almost drained the lake trying to put out the fire. Out of the ashes and the stubble (not that much was left), a god emerged, as though being reborn. He was all dressed in bright red, an androgynous dancing creature that gradually reconstructed the tree, part by part, as he wriggled and twisted his body. The new royal palm turned out more glorious than before. As though the ashes, and the caresses of that god, were just the touches, the perfect adornments, to make it suddenly even more beautiful.

In the center of the girls' barracks, the tent Margot Wrangling had had set up so she could have some privacy was on the verge of collapsing in on itself from the shaking and jolting that was going on inside it. While the brigades planted, picked, brushed the dirt off the plants and seedlings, hoed, picked off suckers, stripped leaves, pinched off flowers, sewed, dried, weeded—in a word, broke their backs working, Margot Wrangling had left the field under the pretext that she wanted to look in and see how the sick boys were doing. She said sick boys, not sick girls.

The four supposedly sick boys were waiting in the mess hall, lying in wait for their prey. The camp was deserted. She went by the infirmary first and saw what she was hoping for, which was that the male nurse was off at the policlinic in town, loading up on medications and supplies. She was surprised that there was nobody in the boys' barracks clamoring for her presence, so she decided to lie down on her bunk for fifteen minutes or so, and she went on over to the girls' barracks. So as not to dirty the mattress, she took off her muddy pants and tight shirt. She lay down in her panties and bra and closed her eyes, as though she were asleep, her hands up behind her head. In no surreptitious manner did Fermín Adenoids, the Mummy Casimiro, Luis the Licentious, and Tin the Man enter the improvised cabin—they acted as though they did this every day. While Fermín Adenoids set about sucking her breasts, the Mummy Casimiro was more direct; he spread her legs and slipped his lovestick into her black hole, which stank of vomited-up shrimp. Luis the Licentious, hovering like a vulture over the teacher-guide's head, introduced his enormous blue-veined tuber into her apparently unconscious mouth, while Tin the Man stood by, whacking at his whacker in preparation for sodomizing the woman playing dead. At no time did Margot Wrangling protest, or even as much as blink, although she did wiggle considerably from the waist down. Judging from the pleasure on the boys' faces, this event was not an infrequent one. And as justification, it might, according to Margot Wrangling, be considered sophisticated group therapy, aided by the science of necrophilia. The Four Horsemen with their Pocketful of Elixir, you might also say.

Dear first love,

I have some pretty unpleasant news to give you, or I think it will be unpleasant, even though your life must have changed a lot too. I married Andy Crater Face, that kid who was always on my tail, trying to put the moves on me. I don't know if you'll forgive me, but I think I really love him. And he swears that I'm what he needs more than anything in the world, that he lives and dies for me. We're very young—that's no big news, I'm tired of hearing that same old song and dance all the time, people accusing us of making the biggest mistake of our lives—getting married when we don't know a thing about it. The truth is, we decided to get married because we didn't have any-place to be together, and Gloriosa Paz, my mother, decided that we should do whatever it was we had to do in our own home and not in some filthy dirty "hotel" room or lying on top of some dirty wall somewhere. Oh, before I forget, I got pregnant. Gloriosa Paz, my mother, was furious, you can't believe how mad she got, but I lost it, the baby I mean, I had a miscarriage, it was so terrible, all this thick clotted blood everywhere, ugh, it was just awful. It's strange, I was in such a good mood all the time, and starving. One morning I woke up with this warm sticky liquid running down my thighs. I miscarried at three and a half months. My uterus was in a bad position or something, backward or upside down or something. Gloriosa Paz is the one that got all the information on that. I'm planning to get pregnant again soon; I love the way it makes you feel, the way *it* feels—you get all round and sleepy.

How's the batey, and our *güijes*, the ceiba tree, the river, the lakes, and your horse Sunny? I've almost lost hope of ever getting a reply from you to my letters, but I keep writing, although I'm not even sure I have the right address. As I've told you before, they sent us to two Schools in the Country after Pinar del Río, but they were so far away from La Fe that there was no way for me to escape and try to find you. I wonder whether you've forgotten your girlfriend, who in a certain way has always been faithful to you? Far down deep inside me I sense that I'm still important to you. I miss your joy in life, your happiness. Your moments of rage, too—you looked so breakable. I read in the newspaper that several families from La Fe agreed to move to the new cooperatives. It was a very short article, didn't say much, and it was not particularly convincing, I must say. Is it true, was it you they were talking about?

Andy Crater Face is just the nicest sweetest boy in the world, although he can have some tantrums that would straighten your hair—he's very jealous and mistrustful. But I swear, the worst thing is that I'm bored and I don't know why. He makes me laugh, but there are mysteries he has no idea of—he's not an accomplice, you know? No, not like you were.

The city is nothing but dead people, and in my memory the countryside still has a tremendous seductiveness. It must be easier for you to erase me from your memory, with all the adventures you have out there, than it is for me to erase you. I don't deny that thinking about that stings my jealousy a little, but I have nobody but myself to blame, right? Gloriosa Paz just came in yelling, and she won't let me concentrate on my letter; she's complaining that she got fired—no, that they sent her to clean bathrooms at a restaurant over on Calle Línea, El Potín, it's called; the administrator got pissed at her. Just because she saw a huge rat in the kitchen and mentioned it to a customer. Which is absolutely forbidden. We're being overrun by rats.

One day we'll come to rescue you—I say "we" because it will be with him, Andy Crater Face. Do you remember that I used to call him Wart, too, because he could be so infuriatingly persistent and there was no way to get him off you? He's changed; he's funnier, as I said before. If the moment when we go to see you is slow in coming, then it will probably be with kids, because I plan to have a lot. All girls, so as not to have to worry about military service or war—although there are those Schools in the Country, what a headache for parents *they* are!

By the way, nothing panned out for me in that respect, so much effort in vain. I didn't manage to go into a career. I wanted to study geography but I didn't make it, even with my participation in the Schools in the Country, even with my good grades, even with my discipline. I wasn't combative enough. It was foreordained. The ones that benefited were the usual Privileged Ones. I told Gloriosa Paz that I'm not going to be bitter about the situation. I'll go to a technical school or be a librarian—as much as I love to read, that would be a good job for me, I think. Anything to kill the boredom.

I hope that I'm still in some little corner of your heart.

Yours always.

(I won't sign the letter so as not to get into trouble.)

SEEN FROM HIGH in the lush crown of leaves, the parties were a bore. I much preferred it when the youngsters were at work. In that, the manatee and I agreed. Not the ceiba tree, though; the ceiba tree was always a lazy-bones; she avoided work whenever she could. She'd accuse me of being a cruel and abusive taskmaster.

You, royal palm, are unfair, encouraging those poor teenagers to let them-selves be so overworked. What did she expect? I love, absolutely love, to work; she loves to idle. Well, I shouldn't exaggerate. The ceiba works, but she is less skilled at warlike things. Now war, lightning, that sort of thing, that's right up my alley. Sacrifice for the cause, that's me. Yet when I give, I *give,* and without asking for anything in return. I gave a huge heap of tenderness to Emma the

Menace, never harboring any certainty that she might love me in return, never knowing whether she would respect me or, on the contrary, wind up taking me for some chattering, prattling piece of vegetable matter. And I should make it clear that I was not disappointed. She loved me like no one else. Youth is pure and total love; later, all that changes. Old age is this—wise immobility, the awareness that one has lost fear. Some time ago I heard a little five-year-old girl say to her mother:

"Life is more important than death because it's harder to live. Dying is easy."

"And just where did you get that piece of information?"

The little girl pointed at her temple. "From in here, from my head." That warm, new little head. In a while the little girl was at it again; she demanded an explanation of love, and it was then the mother who stammered out some silly phrase not entirely free of melancholy, and with no few poetic pretensions:

"Love is living in a constant cloud."

The little girl reminded me of Tierra Fortuna Munda, the ceiba tree's goddaughter, though she is also under my protection. *I know that Tierra will suffer, how do you think I can not know that?* the ceiba tree painfully confessed to me one day, sorry for having taken so much to heart that little girl born among her tangled roots. *Meanwhile,* she added, *let her enjoy these incoherent fragments of life the best she can, and not see what is to come.* Sometimes not even we, the sacred plants, are able to change or deflect the unfortunate events that fate has decreed. Tierra was like a comet on an all-too-well-determined path drawn by a hand grasping the pencil of fate. When Danae caressed Tierra Fortuna Munda's body, the girl's erogenous zones would swell and grow pink and smooth with wetness, her breasts would throb, and from her pores would emerge golden sparks that lit up the constellations.

"Kiss me here," she would say, opening her sex fragrant with gladiolas, oleanders, and wild tulips.

The day before the students were to take their final leave of La Fe, Director Puga decided to give them the day off; the students would be able to do whatever they wanted, but first they had to pack all their things in their suitcases and leave the barracks clean and orderly. That is, in better condition than they had found them. Danae Duckbill Lips looked at Irma the Albino's suitcase; in the chaos and craziness of the accident, the dead girl's parents had forgotten it. So what was she supposed to do with it now? She couldn't just leave it there. She sighed and turned to her own suitcase, lifted back the top, and the fragrance of Persian poetry filled the air around her. She put article after article of clothing in, all folded with meticulous care, and sat pensively for several moments. She closed and locked the suitcase, furtively climbed out the window, raced across the road, and didn't stop until she reached the guajiros' batey.

"Santa, Santa, it's me! Bejerano, it's me, Danae Duckbill Lips! Open up, I've come to say goodbye to you! Tierra! Tierra! Are you in there?"

Santa came to the door with her hair all tangled and a mess, as usual, but her face was yellow, drawn:

"Come in, *m'ija*, we haven't slept a wink. Tierra is burning up with fever, crying the whole blamed night, lying in there like a rag doll. I wrapped her feet in brown paper and ground coffee and I put a piece of brown wrapping paper on her chest, too, with cocoa butter, and—*pff!*—nothing, it didn't work. Chivirico Vista Alegre is all torn up, too, all melancholy because you folks are leaving tomorrow. Bejerano is out gathering curatives, *amor seco* for dysentery and to prevent spitting up blood on account of love troubles, *anamú* in case a freak has got to be aborted, *bejuco uví* to unstop the bladder, *amansaguapo* for the *amarres,* if we were to need a spell, *ateje hermoso* to keep from scarring too bad, *caimito blanco* to give the talismans power, *celosa cimarrona* to gargle with, *helechos del río* that'll give a person clairvoyance, the leaves and bark of *mangle* to purify the blood, it's an aphrodisiac . . ."

Danae left the woman standing in the door ticking off the names of weeds and plants and trees and their various curative and magical powers. She went through the parlor and pushed aside the curtain that separated it from the bedroom. She saw Tierra Fortuna Munda, pale and feeble-looking, lying on a pallet made of dry palm fronds, her immense eyes fixed on a piece of sky framed by the off-square window. Kneeling beside her, Danae kissed her lips and held Tierra's body to her own, trying to draw out the fever.

"If you weren't sick I'd ask you to take me to Viñales to see those *mogotes* right now, in the daytime. I don't want to leave without seeing them in the daylight."

"There's nothing wrong with me, just a fevered soul because you're leaving. I don't want you to go. Don't go."

Danae pulled the tousle-haired head to her, kissed the lice-infested scalp, and slid her hand up under the girl's shirt to caress the mammalian row of teats.

"What are those two doing in there so quiet?" Santa said loudly from the front porch. "Vetiver root for massages, *palo cachimba* to keep the whirlwind from coming back, *rompezaragüey* for *despojos,* for a good cleansing of the spirit . . . Why, *niña mala,* what are you doing out here at the door dressed up like a highwayman with that temperature that you've had!? You bad girls—answer me, where the devil do you think you're going dressed like that? Tierra Fortuna Munda, you just wait till Bejerano finds out you've stolen that horse, as weak as you are!"

Danae helped Tierra saddle Sunny, then put her foot in the stirrup and swung up on the horse. Then she pulled Tierra up behind her, astraddle the horse's rump.

"And you're going to let that city girl turn herself into a decal on a black willow tree, and you in the bargain? *Alabao!*" But she saw that a smile had lit up her daughter's face, and she didn't worry anymore.

They rode for hours. Danae held the reins the entire time, though guided by Tierra, who was holding tight against her back. Her smell impregnated her skin, her breathing warmed the back of her neck, her pelvis rubbed against her buttocks.

"See those green mounds, those cone-looking things up there that look like sleeping dinosaurs half lost in the fog? Those are the *mogotes,* that's the Valle de Viñales," Tierra announced in a weak voice.

"There's nothing like it, I've never seen anything like it in my life. Tierra, Tierra, you don't know how much I'd like to live there forever, disappear with you into that place!"

"From far off it's wonderful. But it's not a place you can live. It's just to look at, to savor with your eyes."

They dismounted from Sunny and left the horse grazing on fresh green grass while they sprawled on a hilltop to invent the future.

"We are never going to see each other again," said Tierra Fortuna Munda with a sigh.

"If you can't come to Havana, I'll come here."

"Will you write me?"

"Like a girlfriend to her first love."

And they laughed as they rolled down the hill. A huge branch came between Tierra and the rocky abyss. Danae rolled on top of her. Tierra pulled up a weed and as she chewed on the stalk she made another embarrassed confession:

"I've hardly gone to school at all. You know I hate school, but I do know how to write, I learned my letters with my cousin Santoral al Dorso. My handwriting is not good, or my spelling, but you'll figure it out . . ."

"From the echo of an ivory war horn, *mi amor,* or the noble conch, or even smoke signals . . . Here, I'm leaving you the key to my suitcase, you're inheriting the Persian suitcase and everything inside. I don't need it. You can also keep Irma the Albino's things—she needs them even less, poor thing."

She removed the necklace of false lapis lazuli beads that the key was hanging from and tied it around Tierra Fortuna Munda's neck:

"Keep it as a talisman. Don't lose it."

Dear first love,

Just a little note after so many letters lost in oblivion and so many events that have happened in my life. I am sitting on a bench on the Paseo del Prado; I've brought my daughters here to play. Yes, I have two daughters, Ibis and Frances. They're eight and six. I was working in a neighborhood library; they transferred me on supposedly good terms, but actually I got thrown out. My services were no longer needed due to the books I was recommending to the customers, most of whom were students. Today, and as of only about two and a half weeks ago, I work in the office at the Marriage License Bureau in the Palacio de Matrimonios, which is right across the street from the Paseo del Prado where I am now. I'm a clerk. I type out the marriage certificates. People get married so they can have more bread, beer, irons, sheets, pillows . . . There are people that get married, divorced, and married again just so they can buy double in the special newlywed store, and all this to-do in less than a month.

My husband, Andrés, was laid off. He's apparently going to be able to get work in a microbrigade, building one of those horrible buildings whose greatest aspiration is to be a chicken coop. As you can see, our situation is not easy. I'm the one that's been supporting us. My in-laws' retirement is like a joke; what they get a month, two people couldn't live on for two weeks. And my mother is even worse off. I've started doing people's fingernails at night, painting them and all. I taught myself to do manicures, you don't exactly have to have a doctorate to do it. It allows us to breathe, at least, and keeps the rope from around our neck . . . I'm afraid it's getting to Andy; yesterday he hit me—he had never done that before.

I shouldn't tell you my troubles. I don't know where to send this to you, there's no way even for me to know whether you're still alive. Not knowing, it's hard on me . . . I'm so tired of waiting for something I don't understand. I should leave you alone, although this afternoon it's you I need most in the world. Today is sunny and cool, there's a salty breeze coming in from the north. Yesterday it rained the whole goddamned day . . .

The Mandinga Chicherekú and the Amulet

𝒯HE LADY WHO sat down beside her, the one who got on at the last station, was nice; she never stopped telling risqué jokes about old people who wanted to die while having sex. She looked to be quite a bit older than Danae, fifty-something. Although a natural blond with wavy hair, she had not yet had to resort to dyeing it, since there was not a trace of gray. She had brown eyes, liver spots on her skin, and an unpleasant black hole caused by tooth decay spanning her two front teeth, but the owner of the repugnant teeth was very pleasant. She told Danae that she'd been born in La Fe but for many years had lived in Havana, married to an agronomist. She came back to her hometown fairly regularly, whenever her vacation time from work allowed, plus the days she got with medical certificates signed by doctors she managed to pay off; she came to see her family, a ninety-year-old grandmother with a mind still as sharp as could be, her mother, still young but with hardening of the arteries, and a prolific bunch of brothers and sisters that had given her she didn't know how many nieces and nephews.

"My father died of prostate cancer last year. It was terrible because it lasted so long, his suffering I mean."

Danae observed the woman at length, wondering. Now she had a clear objective, which was to go in search of Tierra Fortuna Munda. Might this woman be her? But she had not the slightest idea how Tierra Fortuna Munda might look as an adult, and although the woman had only five fingers on each hand, she might have had plastic surgery. Was it her or not? Danae asked her name, pretending to do so out of good manners. Disappointment. The woman answered that her name was Rapsodia Imblú. If she'd had plastic surgery, she might also have changed her name.

"And your father?" Danae asked uneasily.

"Oh, him, what a scatterbrain. I told you, he died of prostate cancer last year, it was horrible. He was divorced from my mother, but he came home to die when the doctor threw him out."

"No, no, you already told me that. I meant your father's *name*."

"Esperanzo, his name was Esperanzo, may he live in glory and in the grace that God has surely bestowed upon him . . . It's a strange name, but I'll tell you, the one they gave my third brother is stranger still—Lenin de los Santos, imagine. Isn't that enough to ruin a youngster's life? So just think, I got the best name of the lot. At least my name reminds people of that famous piece of music. When I was a girl I roamed this country from one end to the other, every day it seems like, almost . . ." She swept her hand, holding a palm-leaf fan, at the woods and thickets that were rushing by. "I was a caution when I was little, outdoors all the time, there wasn't a door or four walls that could keep me in. The train tracks were my world. Do you know the sleepers are still wood? They've never changed them, or of course the train either. I would hop along with one foot on each side of the rail, hopping along and at the same time singing out the names of all the kind of trees they had made each sleeper out of—sea hibiscus, cedar, Haitian mahogany, San Domingo boxwood, bay cedar, balsa, walnut, weeping willow, black willow, hicaquillo, cypress, tropical pine, Caribbean pine, corozo palm, sierra palm, white cedar, naked Indian, wild tamarind, jiquí—on and on, like a hobo girl, riding the rails like in the old days, that was what I'd be pretending, until the engines would practically be on top of me . . . it's a miracle I wasn't run over and turned into grease. Oh, the things you do when you're a kid . . . "

"I was here once when I was young, at that age when you hate your family, you want to be free, that time when you're not quite a teenager anymore but not quite a full woman yet either. It was during a School in the Country . . ."

"Oh, so you know this area! . . . It's not the same to visit as to be born here, of course. A person can see from a mile away that you're not from around here, but I'm sure you left friends . . ."

"Yes, I have very fond memories of a friend from back then, a girlfriend of mine, but I never saw her again. I came back to Pinar del Río to other Schools in the Country, every year, in fact, but never to any place as dense and thickety as La Fe . . . Her name was, or is, Tierra Fortuna Munda. She belonged to a batey, pretty far from the town, that the Higher-ups had stigmatized. You ought to know about that, it was that big extended family that the parapsychologists and all kinds of scientific researchers studied. They did experiments on them and everything . . . Sisters and brothers lived together as man and wife, cousins with cousins, I don't know whether you knew about them, they were—"

Rapsodia Imblú didn't let her finish. With something of a tragic air, and giving a long sigh, she took her hand and filled in the blank:

"—No offense, but freaks. I mean eyesores, just as ugly as they could be, but with minds that were very advanced, very superior intelligences. People said they could bend forks by just looking at them, that the palms of their hands bled or that oil came out of them, or that fruit juice came out of their navels . . . I knew that family. They all died. Fertilizer poisoning. Don't look at me like that, with that face like a calf with its throat cut. Tierra didn't. No, not her—she was the only survivor. She married a real son of a bitch that she hated with all her might—Brutus Escoria, an opportunist with too much power and way too much evil in him . . . ."

"I know who you're talking about."

"A loco, and dangerous. They had five children, and all of them died from one epidemic or another. She signed up for that terrible war in Africa, wanting to die. She always wanted to die, I suppose because of the complexes she got from being born the way she was, plus she was a little masculine-acting, too, you know? But she didn't get killed. When she came back, Brutus Escoria had moved off to Havana with a high-priced whore, one of those that have been all over the world and always wind up here, because where else would people pay them the attention they get paid here? Brutus Escoria got promoted. So Tierra was saved. She . . . now, nobody knows where it was that she had her operation, but one fine day we realized that she's not only gotten rid of that husband of hers but also the spare parts of her body. She didn't have six fingers on her hands anymore, but five just like anybody else, two breasts like any other woman, although they say that her navel still runs guava jam, can you believe that? Ugh."

"Where does she live?"

"Where else? Out in the woods."

"But that could be anywhere. The woods go on forever."

The other woman threw her head back to free the back of her neck, dripping with sweat, from her thick mane of hair.

"Well, that's true. You'll have to walk a long way if you want to find her, and prepare your throat, because yelling won't get you much out in that wilderness. Ask for the help of the chicherekú—that Mandinga with the look of an owl does so love to find a problem for himself to get into, he's sure to help. You could hire him to yell—if you can manage to teach him to talk, ha ha ha, hee hee hee oh, I tell you . . . That Mandinga chicherekú has been trying to learn to talk for thousands of years; he's the dumbest spirit of a black man that ever lived."

The train stopped at the old station. Danae figured it had changed very little in a hundred years. As the woman gathered her things to get off, Danae said goodbye to her. When her feet touched the platform, a chill ran down her spine: Where was she going? Why not stay on the train to the end of the line, then go back to the beginning, then back to the end of the line again, and so on, back and forth ad infinitum? She didn't want to get off, but she already had, and the train would stop for only five minutes. And there she was, there was no way out now, the train was beginning to move, black smoke filled the station—the faces that were most exposed to it were covered in black greasy soot. She'd have to walk into town, she told herself, imagining the pain of the open sores on her feet. The only people who'd gotten off were Rapsodia Imblú, the guy with the rooster that had deflowered the young woman with the pus-covered legs, an old man with a burlap sack over his shoulder, and her. Rapsodia Imblú had walked off very quickly, and was now a good distance away. She steered clear of the guy with the rooster. She decided to go up to the old man.

"If I remember right, the town is far."

"Two hours away, not a minute more or a minute less. I'm going that way, if you want . . ."

Danae took that as an invitation to walk with him. Rapsodia Imblú was disappearing down a dirt path, almost surely leading to her relatives' bohíos. The guy with the rooster took a road a little broader, dappled with golden sunlight. In exactly two hours she and the old man arrived in the town. They went directly to the bar, their throats parched, an acrid, sharp smell of sweat hanging about their bodies. Danae thought she recognized the bartender from when she was here so many years ago.

"No, you're mistaken there, I'm his son. And *that* drunk is the son of Sappy, another lush that you probably ran into back then, and that one way over there is the son of Lousy, which was another one of the sots that was in here all the time when my father ran the place, and that was a long, long time ago, back when frogs had hair. Like father, like son. I'll tell you, as the tree is bent . . . Rum or firewater?"

"Firewater. Even if it's hot, it's still water."

"Down there all the saints help . . ." Sappy's son came out of his stupor and made that incomprehensible pronouncement.

"How might I find Tierra Fortuna Munda?" Danae inquired.

"*Ay caray,* a shitload of years ago I was best buddies with her brother Chivirico Vista Alegre; if he'd listened to me, he wouldn't've bought the farm like he did. Don't eat that cabbage, *chico*, Chivirico, I told him. You know those people are lower than snakes, I mean think about it, *compay,* they sprayed that pesticide around here that's pure sulfuric acid . . . I warned him, *ayyy,* what a fucking pity . . ." This was Lousy's son, barely able to keep his head up.

"He's been sitting at that table snoring for twenty years, just trying to make it from one hangover to the next," explained the bartender. Then he added: "You can find Tierra Fortuna Munda in the woods, near where that camp called La Fe is, over by—"

"I remember where it is, I can go straight to it by memory." Danae thanked the old man, who was knocking back his fourth shot of firewater, for having led her from the miserable train station to the bar, and then she started off for the lake.

First she passed by the town's beauty parlor and asked them to wash and cut her hair—not too short, just shoulder length or a little shorter. She also asked where she might bathe and freshen up. The younger girl rolled her eyes. The girl with more experience, acting more friendly, murmured, "There ain't a hotel here—at least not yet. You can use our shower, if you don't mind the way it looks. It's back behind the latrines. I don't have no soap, but I made up this kinda gel thing with ylang-ylang flowers and sandalwood, smells real good and it's refreshing. I put in some menthol and arnica."

Danae was grateful. Under the trickle of water from a fiber cement tank warmed by the sun, she felt as though her skin were peeling away from her body in long strips. How long had it been since she'd had a bath? At least not like this one, not like she felt now, so conscious of each and every part of her body.

The hairdresser was kind enough to put a bottle of the homemade bath gel in her pack. They invited her to sit down with them for coffee, which she was served in a metal canteen that was dented but clean. They also set delicious honey-drenched *torrejas*, the Caribbean French toast, before her. She remarked what a wonderful coincidence this was; for years she'd been dying for some *torrejas* dripping with honey. They asked if she had relatives in town. No, she replied, just a friend, but then for some reason she made up a name; naturally, neither of them had ever heard of the person, and they looked at each other in puzzlement. When she left the beauty parlor she felt like a new woman, fresh out of the box—or maybe even with the cellophane still on it. Then she walked and walked and walked, without resting, slipping and stumbling when she came to rocky ground. The sun beat down so hard that within minutes she was sticky and smelly again.

After so many years, the geography had changed considerably, the plants and trees and weeds had become harsher and more perverse. She walked for three days, lost, bathing in the water that gushed from the feeder pipes or sprayed in tiny diamond droplets from the sprinklers, eating tomatoes, oranges, and guavas. She slept in run-down tobacco-drying sheds, like in the old days, certain that her presence there would attract Tierra Fortuna Munda. It was hard to find the camp; it had pretty much been demolished, and in its place she discovered a gate with a sign announcing that a luxury hotel was to be built on this site—although according to Rapsodia Imblú that plan had been around for decades and would probably be around for several decades more, since the land was too unstable, too loose, for heavy construction. Then she remembered the ceiba tree, and her eyes scanned the area. It was nowhere to be seen. She wandered around for a while, and an enormous hole made her suspect that it had been taken out by the roots. Nor could she see any royal palms anywhere around. Later, she would find out that on the afternoon the inhabitants of the settlement were poisoned and died, the royal palms had begun to bend under their own sadness, and that finally they had withered away from grief. Their fronds were now buried in the tangle of the undergrowth.

The fourth sunrise was gloriously white, misted with fog and sparkling with dew. Flecks of yellow pollen stuck to her eyelashes. Standing in the door of the drying shed, Danae almost gave up any hope of finding Tierra. She thought she'd have one last dip in the lake and then return to the train station to wait for the train, another train. Or the same one, but on the way back.

She played and dallied all morning on the bank, skipping stones at an imaginary target. She waited for the sun to rise off the horizon enough to warm the water. Then, naked, she ran all around the bank and into the fringe of woods. She had to keep herself from eating yuca raw. How wonderful it felt, running around naked with nobody, absolutely nobody, to see her—all by herself, alone, at last! Delirious with happiness, she jumped into the lake, waded out until her foot no longer hit bottom, and then swam out to the center. There, she ducked her head under, and held her breath as long as she could. Yalodde, mother of rivers, help me find Tierra Fortuna Munda! ¡O milagro querido!

The Mandinga chicherekú at the bottom is death, the manatee and I, come, dive deeper, a little deeper. The manatee with its abused-little-girl body. Every least little bit of good and evil all mixed together—the girl who'd had the accident, Irma the Albino, Santa, Bejerano, Chivirico Vista Alegre, the whole big family, the güijes, the spirits of the forest that sleep by day and play at night. Every little bit of it, you big ugly woman you, Mandinga chicherekú, don't hold your breath, let your lungs fill with fresh sweet water, moss, roots, fish, frogs, and crawfish washed in by the sea, furtive creatures lurking in their shells, silvery guppies, biajacas. Ten pounds of shit in a five-pound bag. Mandinga chicherekú, every least little bit of good and evil mixed up together in one big jumbly mess.

From a distant radio came the voice of Luis Carbonell, "the watercolorist of Antillean poetry," famed interpreter of *Oh Fuló, oh Fuló, that sweet black woman Fuló!*:

> *Juana Pérez, espiritista,*
> *Juana Pérez, so spiritual,*
> *Juana, she cures whatever ails you*
> *with water from the well.*

Danae felt a sharp, shooting cramp in her back, another spasm in her legs. She was almost paralyzed with the cramps, but she still had the strength of her arms. She pulled upward, into another dimension, up, up, toward the surface. Her head emerged, blue from lack of air and the hard struggle, crowned with the long tentacles of water plants and tiny, silvery, wriggling fish. She could hardly make out shadows, so filled with mud were her eyes. She'd better rest, be still, calm down, calm down, let herself go, float, drift along until the cramp passed. Ugh, and the water was so cold it squeaked. In the deepest part of the bottom she had bumped into the manatee:

"Get on my back," it said, clearly pronouncing each syllable, "you're still young, don't let yourself get all carried away. Heroines that commit suicide—you *never* read anything about *them*."

She recovered her strength, the cramp passed, and she began to swim. On the bank she gathered her clothes and got dressed, still wet, and then plunged deeper into the woods.

"Tierra! Tierra Fortuna Munda!" she shouted like a madwoman. She laughed at the idea of looking for her where there was almost no chance of finding anyone. Little by little the forest swallowed her body; her silhouette blurred and faded. But some hope remained that she would reappear.

Danae rubbed her eyes with the back of her hand. It was a vision. It resembled the Virgen de la Milagrosa, and it was waiting for her in the brightly illuminated center of a clearing. It was a woman, sitting with her back to Danae, her hair neatly combed, and one might almost say properly dressed. Crowned with the sun's rays and with a serpent coiled at her feet. It was her.

"Tierra!"

She turned her head. Her face was harsh, her forehead furrowed; she was lost in a daze, or a daydream. Danae approached her with uncertain steps, levitating.

"It's me, that girl, Danae Duckbill Lips—do you remember me?"

"Of course, I've been watching you for days. Why have you come?"

"It's me, I'm here, I'm not a spirit. I came to love you."

"*Alabao*, you're almost . . . you've hardly changed at all, maybe not so skinny. And I'm supposed to believe you?"

"I'm old, but you, you look just the same. I wrote to you."

"Oh really? I never got your letters."

"I did, I swear. I swear I love you."

"Don't swear. Here, sit down, drink this." She held out to her a gourd calabash filled with rum.

"I don't drink . . . well, but this time . . ." Danae's hands and arms were trembling like the wings of a hummingbird.

Tierra studied her out of the corner of her eye.

"Did you hear? My family got poisoned with a pesticide—nobody knew where it came from—since they couldn't run us out, they poisoned us. It was Brutus Escoria that planned it. He waited for my old man to plant a field of cabbage and he sprayed it with that stuff. They all ate cabbage like it was manna from heaven, except me. Terrible, they didn't die right away, oh no, that was too easy! They were paralyzed, like vegetables, for months, the children, the old folks, the women, all of them. So they carried them off to some secret hospital somewhere where they do brain studies and they grafted slices of pituitary glands from stillborn babies on 'em. They did experiments on them, in other words, and they died by the handfuls. The details were never clear. Me, they made me go to school. A *live-in* school. Brutus Escoria promised to visit me on weekends; the only way to get out of there was to marry him. I married the person I hated most in the world, to buy my freedom. I went through nightmares, terrible things, with that man. Every night I had to listen to him brag about wiping out the batey. Then he'd beat me up and rape me. The nights seemed like they would never end. It was horrible. I had five children with him; they died from epidemics that no doctor ever knew the origins of. Two years later a group of soldiers came looking for cannon fodder for a war, and I stepped forward. But I got out alive. As you see, I'm still here. I came back safe and sound. Well, not quite sound. I was wounded. I got an emergency transfer to a hospital in some country, I don't even know where, and they put me back together and when I came out of the anesthesia they had cut off all the what they called 'excess' parts of my body, the parts that other people didn't have. And when I got back here I found out that Brutus Escoria was living with a whore in Havana, one of those high-class whores they have there, since he'd been promoted to head up some office in some important ministry or other. That was a relief, I couldn't have gotten better news. Since then I live with my solitude; I built my own bohío in a place nobody can get to. In-ac-cessible. People think I'm crazy, that I'm a homeless person or some kind of lost soul from purgatory or someplace, wandering around, on the verge of extinction."

"I had more or less heard about what you just told me . . . Did they cut down the ceiba tree?"

She smiled mischievously, conspiratorially.

"No, the ceiba is right near where I am, just like always. We protect each other."

"Why don't you come to the city with me?"

Tierra shook her head, though without much conviction.

"What about you? What's your life been like?"

"I told you about it in my letters. I got married, too, to somebody you met, Andy Crater Face, the one that used to pester me all day long to be his girlfriend, the kid in the School in the Country. Hm, you don't remember. We had two little girls—I say little, they're teenagers now. I left all that, just up and left, to come out here and find you. No, no, no, don't misunderstand . . . I love him, but I'm sick and tired of the same thing, day after day. Go to the office, mop the floor, cook beans, go get the girls at school, wait for him to come home from the microbrigade to talk about how there are no bricks, the cement never seems to get delivered, the construction on the building is going nowhere. It was *us* that was going nowhere. I got sick of living like I was a robot, or some brainless ambitionless dimwit, like there was nothing more to life. I wanted to go back to the point where I cared what I looked like, for him, you know, so he'd think I looked nice. We've had serious problems, nothing to wind up in the crazy farm about, compared to your problems they were nothing, but we'd fight all the time, even hit each other. We were going to wind up killing each other. I can't say that I don't love him. But I can't stand the state of silence he subjects me to. I figured I'd find you and ask you if we couldn't live together . . . I'm sure that Gloriosa Paz would let us live in her apartment; it's small, but if two can live there, three can."

"What about your daughters?"

"Don't ask about them for now . . . I guess they'd be with us during the week and with their father on the weekend. Where three can live, five can . . . It's irrational, I'm sorry . . . I ought to check first with the others, they're the ones that will be affected by all this. My plan isn't very sensible . . ."

"It's strange, you've come at a moment when you're sick of your life and I'm sick of mine . . . But what if you change your mind and want to leave me and go back to him?"

"That's a risk."

"Yes, it's dangerous. I hope that at least you could pay for my train trip back." She laughed thrillingly, throwing her body back on her elbows, her thick hair falling away to reveal an elegant neck the color of chewed tobacco.

Danae noticed that Tierra Fortuna Munda was still wearing the necklace of false lapis lazuli beads, with the key hanging from it.

"Our amulet . . ." She reached out and gently stroked the rusty key.

"I've never taken it off."

Tierra drew Danae to her, kissed her eyes, and then her mouth moved from her eyelids to her cheeks, to her neck, rose from her chin to her lips. Her tongue snaked out, and Danae's tongue met hers. She unbuttoned her blouse and her breasts filled Tierra's hands. Danae caressed two vertical scars where the extra breasts had been, on the torso of the woman with the forehead starred like a gar's. Her hands touched the hard, erect nipples; she pinched, then nibbled. She lowered her mouth to Tierra's navel, where a stream of guava nectar was forming a small liquid mirror, and she licked at the sweet quicksilver. The fragrance of oleanders and gladioli opened her nose, her entire head. She licked and sucked at her corolla, her mount of Venus became a red, open temptation, glorious with black seeds and oozing fresh papaya liquor. And thus, making love to one another, they spent two weeks. Hardly speaking. Looking at one another, caressing one another.

·　·　·

SHE CLUNG TIGHTLY to Danae's arm, shrank behind her, seeking protection as they pushed their way through the crush of the train station. She was mistrustful of the city, wary, although the salty breeze off the bay, smelling of tar, cooled her face and brought her a pleasure she had never quite felt before. At least they had escaped the eternal yelling and shouting of the passengers on the train, the crowd at the station. She came from a place of silence, she hated the noise of wars and cities. Of the first, she had considerable experience, because of her participation in several battles; with respect to cities, she clumsily kept an enormous number of details at arm's length. Handling money, for example—she didn't understand the first thing about large bills. How did one get on a bus and pay? Asking permission or for help sounded ridiculous. Danae patted her hand affectionately. They walked arm in arm along Calle Égido to the Parque de la Fraternidad. Danae told her that when they got to more or less the center of the city they needed to let go of each other's arm, so people wouldn't talk or, worse, openly make unkind comments that were meant to be overheard by them. Two women flaunting their intimacy would not be viewed with approval. Tierra was taken aback by this remark; she didn't like what she had heard. Weren't they going to live together? They'd certainly be giving people something to talk about. Her veins were practically boiling from the heat, her eyes sought the relief of trees, leaves, branches, a cooling shade, but all she saw was a dry, miserable treetop just peeking up over what Danae explained to her was a building where they had Spanish dances sometimes, the Rosalía de Castro Society. She sensed a strange shadow behind her; it was not the manatee, or the hutia, or a garter snake, or a bullfrog, or a porcupine or a rhinoceros or a bull; they turned their heads and realized that it was a guy braying, snorting, salivating, frothing at the mouth:

"*Ay, mamis, qué culos más ricos*—I'd like to get you two in that doorway over there right now and chew the meat right off your backsides, and then suck right down to the marrow of happiness!"

Tierra had only heard such gross vulgarity from the lips of Brutus Escoria. She hunched further into the shelter of Danae's body.

"Oh yeah, *mamita*, you don't know *how* much a little girl-girl action turns me on!" the slobbering animal insisted.

Tierra quickly released her friend's hand, but Danae insisted, she took her hand again, in a sign that she couldn't care less what that troglodyte thought. He stumbled off to the right down Calle Muralla while they turned to the left, looking for the Parque de la Fraternidad.

Tierra could not suppress a cry of pain and shock when she saw the ceiba tree imprisoned behind an iron fence. She cried out a prayer to her god-mother, the ceiba tree who had aided in her very birth. In the forest, her farewell to the sacred tree had been a brief but emotional one, as had her farewells to the palm, the manatee, the chicherekú, the box turtle, the hummingbird, and the *güijes*. Danae smiled and pointed out the Capitol building to her.

"They say that years ago, when guajiros would come to Havana, the first thing they'd do would be take a picture with the Capitol building behind them."

Tierra shrugged her shoulders, made a face; she didn't understand what possible interest such a thing might have. The Capitol looked big and ugly to her, with those limp, straggly royal palms standing before it like an unkempt honor guard. A stupid-looking landscape; she decided not to say anything, so as not to hurt her friend and hostess's feelings. She studied Danae out of the corner of her eye; she was an attractive woman, although her eyes had become melancholy. She needed to dye her hair, which was full of split ends despite the recent haircut, and it would probably do her good to put some makeup on the dark circles under her eyes. As they were walking, she had noticed that almost all the women used eyeliner, lipstick, powder, some color on their cheeks. She personally liked Danae just the way she was, natural, but she could understand that her husband might not have been so crazy about a woman who had pretty much let herself go. As she was observing her mouth, her rounded shoulders, her eyelashes—in a word, her friend's mortality—she realized that she had not stopped loving her. She didn't care—pretty or not, love, being truly in love, was a matter almost of caprice. Of course if there was one thing she had learned in the war it was that when a woman wants a man to obey her orders, before she says a word she needs to put on her war paint. She'd learned that, all right—she'd made it all the way to captain!

Sitting on a stone bench at the bus stop, they enjoyed the waning of the day and the coming of evening, which seemed earlier than usual. The buses gave no signs of life and the rest of the frustrated passengers decided to head out on foot for their various destinations. The two women were left alone in the darkness. It was Danae who dared rest her head on Tierra's lap.

"I can hardly believe that we're together after so many years."

Tierra bent her body over her and kissed her—her eyes, her swollen, fragile lips, the blisters from the sun. Hours and hours passed; there was not a detail of their lives that they didn't minutely recount to one another . . . and at many silly little things they would laugh like turtledoves.

"So is this bus of yours coming or not?" Tierra asked, smoldering with love.

Danae, lost in thought, did not immediately reply.

"You know, I'm not sure, maybe I should take you straight to Gloriosa Paz's house . . . No, no. I think it'll be better if you come with me and we'll talk to Andrés and the girls. They might just as well meet you now."

As she finished the last phrase their faces were illuminated by the headlights of an old '54 Dodge that was turning the corner toward the Paseo del Prado. It was a public car, a kind of communal taxi. It wasn't hard for the driver to guess that the two women were waiting for any kind of transportation that might come along, and he congratulated himself for having taken a detour off his usual route. Even from the outside, it was clear that not another mosquito would fit into the car, but the man braked and insisted. Danae managed to get in by pushing with all her might against a heavyset woman with a no less broad-faced little girl on her lap. Beside her there was an old man who looked as though he sold candy on the streets, and he had a child on his lap, too, the son of the octopus-bodied woman. Then, next to the window, there was a lawyer—he had the insignia embroidered on his pocket. He was wearing a Mexican guayabera and was just lighting a cigar. Nor could even a mountain climber pile onto the front seat. A young woman with her hair in an extravagant chignon and wearing a long dress of pink chiffon was sitting on the lap of her boyfriend, who was wearing a white suit—they had just gotten married at the Palacio de Matrimonios. Between them and the driver sat the mother-in-law, also in a white suit, and complaining.

"*Alabao, ave María Purísima*, I can't breathe in here! There's not enough oxygen for a woman to breathe! Listen, driver, you couldn't fit a flatworm in here, not so much as a paramecium. The lady that just got in is enough, forget about the other one, let her stay. You couldn't fit her in here with a shoe-horn. No sir, just let her stay."

The others joined in the white whale's protests. So Danae put her foot down—if they didn't let Tierra in, she wasn't getting in either.

"Let's don't be premature, *chica,* we can work something out here. I'll make you a deal—if you come with me now and pay double, I'll put a rocket in the exhaust—just kidding! But I can do my whole route before you know it and you and I will come back and pick up your friend . . . We both win—I make my profit and you two get a ride."

"I can't leave her alone here! Why don't I pay you double and both of us will wait for you here?"

"And they say people aren't as gullible as they used to be . . . Not to men-tion that I might find a passenger that'd pay triple. You really think I'd come back? You'd better take the deal; I'm being honest with you today, sweetheart, and it's not every day I can say that. Your friend is not going to get bored, right, *mi bulunga?*"

Danae and Tierra looked at each other. Tierra blinked and nodded imperceptibly; Danae should go.

"I'll wait for you. If I could wait for all these years I can wait two or three hours longer."

Danae's hand slipped from hers. The unique, unforgettable hand of Danae, like a glove kept as a souvenir. A sound of rusty sheet metal as the car door slammed and the '54 Dodge, in a tribute to its long-suffering engine, rolled away in a cloud of black smoke. Danae turned and through the rear window saw Tierra's silhouette, blurred by the fine mist off the ocean that hung in the air. As she stood there before the ceiba tree, it was as though the roots of the magnificent tree were springing from her head. Danae gave the address of Gloriosa Paz.

The Dodge drove down street after street, its windows fogged over with smoke and soot mixed with the air's humidity. The obese woman's jaw never stopped; she licked big flat lollipops and chewed taffy she'd bought from the old man who was doing her the favor of carrying her child on his lap. A short time after getting in the car, Danae had realized that this was the same cellulite-ridden fat woman, the same children, and the same old man that she had spoken to at the train station as she was leaving for La Fe. The other passengers, she had never seen. At a stoplight, she saw the same men cross the street, carrying the same mirror, as the ones who had walked between her and the flamboyán five weeks ago when she had been fleeing the city. This time the mirror was framed in a gold frame, and on the gleaming golden wood there perched a brightly glowing hummingbird. The hummingbird, they say, is the patron of omens and of happy lovers.

Suddenly she emerged from the dreamlike state she had been living in since she found Tierra on the banks of the lake. She needed to solve this problem as soon as possible; she wanted so much to hug her daughters, take care of them again. She couldn't go on with this without talking to Andrés first. *Not today,* she thought, *I just can't talk to him today, but I can at least see the girls for a few seconds, I'm dying to give them a big kiss.* She asked the driver where his route took them. What a coincidence, they were going to go right past the corner of her house. It would be a question of just stopping for a second, giving the driver some more money so he'd agree to wait, running upstairs, holding their little bodies tight against her chest, trying to explain to them that this time she couldn't stay, she was so sorry, but she'd be back in a few hours to explain the situation and take them home with her—they would be living with their grandmother, her, and a friend whom she loved as much as life itself. For twenty pesos the driver acceded to her pleas, although he made it clear that he wasn't going to wait forever.

The *iyaguoná,* the bride of the *santo,* the lady dressed in white with a turban embroidered with silver thread, reappeared. It was the same person, or spirit, that had given Danae the seat beside her at the train station so she could talk with her a while. The car stopped at a stoplight and she crossed the street carrying a bunch of gigantic sunflowers in her skirt held up to make a kind of basket. She was moving as though in slow motion, and she turned her head slowly toward Danae inside the car, her eyes glowing with a strange peace. A yellow shawl covered her shoulders and a wide blue cloth with long fringe was tied around her waist. Danae noticed that she was wearing the key to the suitcase around her neck, the amulet Tierra Fortuna Munda had held on to so zealously for so many years.

All it took was those few seconds to get the message. All it took was for her eyes to meet the eyes of the *iyawó.* Child, you are marked for danger. Child, watch your eyes. Child, you must not argue, no matter what may come.

Child, the knife is on the prowl, circling and circling and circling around your neck. Child, offer Oshún violins and teach language to that contrary little black man, that Mandinga chicherekú, the little prince, the ghost with the skin of a goat. Mocombo Forifá Arikuá went off to the woods to find his walking stick, to find his scepter of power, and he met a spoiled little girl, such a difficult little girl, worse than that Muchángana that went off to war. *Aaay,* but that little girl is the direct daughter of the ceiba tree, who conceived her by grace and bore her through the vulva of a woman. *Aaay,* that little girl had been chosen to put the ritual candles at the foot of the ceiba tree. Tierra Fortuna Munda, that is her name, and she must spill the blood of the goat, a ceremony forbidden to women, but she is different, she has been crowned by the *santos,* and at her bidding the clay vessels shall sound. She possesses the potent scepter, oh compañero, oh brother, oh daughter, oh the okobios transformed into little devils. Daughter, you must hold up the gourd, drink the rooster's blood, revive sprigs of basil in holy water, rub them in from head to foot and repeat: *Fragayando yin, Fragayando yin* . . .

This is not a thing for women, or until not long ago it wasn't, but they say that María Teresa Vera was the first woman to sing in Abakuá, that's what people say . . . Cry, *hija,* cry as you dance, for weeping and dancing are signs of life. That's why this island cries while it dances. Ay, my lovely one, my sweet one, my heart is on crutches, but my loins are free.

Un Embácara, the judge who punishes, will take pity upon you, and upon those you love. You, my daughter, hold in your hands the salvation of Tierra—do not hesitate to do battle for her. Hail to the sun, hail to the moon, hail to the constellations and the planets, hail to the universe. Hail, hail, light and progress, and take mouthfuls of *aguardiente* and spray it from your mouth onto the trunk of the mother, the ceiba, for she asks it of you. Pray the prayer to purify the air around.

Gracias, Madre, for this sacred space for thought. Madre, illuminate, guide, and protect those who enter here. Gracias, Madre, for your safety and protection. Those who come with evil thoughts and dark emotions shall not cross this purified threshold. Godmother, cleanse their minds and draw us to the friends that we most love. Gracias, Madre, for peace.

Mandinga chicherekú, open the door, *carabalí.* My da-a-a-aughter. *Bulunga, caray.*

Danae shivered.

"Ave María, that was the Gypsy that possessed you! Cross yourself," joked the driver as he watched the twisting and writhing of the woman's head through the rearview mirror.

Danae bent her head back and exposed her throat to the light. She closed her eyes, in a trance, and the sweat traced honeyed streams from her temples to her chin and from her chin to the hollow between her breasts.

Don't go back home. Are you crazy? said the Mandinga chicherekú, who had learned to talk only because Danae had so fiercely wished it. *There are things that happen that shouldn't happen. You are mad, girl. This is not the time to go back home. Your husband is capable of doing just about anything. Don't go back, beautiful girl. I tell you this, I who am a specialist in souls as black as coal. He is not a bad man, he is not evil, but he is resentful, and indignant, and a man disgusted is the most unpredictable thing there is.*

I AM THE DARK light of the city, and I am going to tell what might have become of those two women. What might have happened but didn't, though it did on so many other occasions with so many fevered women who defied the patterns of behavior laid down by their society.

What might have happened was that Danae got to her house, longing to see her family, wanting to resolve her problems with her husband, while Tierra was anchored on a cloud . . .

YOU KNOW HOW it was, Swan, you know me better'n anybody, you and I have been buddies for oh god a lotta years now, a shitload of years, and you know that I loved her, *compadre,* I adored her like I've never adored anybody else in my whole fucking life. But shit, Swan, she asked for it, she brought it on herself, there are fucking chicks that there's no help for. I told her, *Stay,* I told her, *don't go.* You know how it was, I don't need to tell *you* how it was, *mi compay,* I can't explain what happened, but I fell in love with her, first time I looked at her, them there eyes, you know what I'm sayin'. You know how I called you on the telephone, feeling like shit, the day you fucked up Gizzard's big toe, I sent up an SOS then, remember how I called you, man, late that night. You knew right away I wasn't callin' just to be callin', you better than anybody know that I don't beat around the bush, I just spit it out—Danae's gone, man, I can't find her anywhere, and you told me, you were so damn sure, man, She'll turn up, you said, You just wait, she'll turn up, she's probably just getting you a pair of horns fitted in a bar somewhere—No, *mi cúmbila,* she's not running around on me, I said, that chick is pure and wholesome, you can see that she's one of those that doesn't get all twisted around and corrupted, and in a little while you called me back, I was asleep, and that time you got me to thinking, you sure got me thinkin', *mi compay,* messed my head up real good that time, so for three weeks I suffered like a mule, for three weeks she was off somewhere, god knows where, man, out of it, completely *gone,* it's not easy. So that same morning she called, before you did I think, I don't remember, my brain's like mush, man, and she gave me all this metaphysical crap, this bullshit about needing some time and some space, man, it was like some shit out of philosophy, man, I didn't understand a word of it. Then every once in a while after that she'd call to talk to the girls but she wouldn't leave an address, or even say where she was, and this is not like el Norte, you know, up there the police can trace a call, but not here, here the fucking lines get bugged for other very special reasons but not just because your old lady ups and leaves you, you can't just go down to the station and tell 'em your old lady has taken the train, because then it's *you* that everybody in the neighborhood is talking about—although the news spread, I'll tell you, that goddamn Beneranda, you can't tell her *any*thing, man, you'd think she'd throw a line to me and the girls, but no, she's out spreading the news all over the neighborhood, makin' me out to be this pendejo, man, and taking Danae's side of course, I'll tell you. Thank goodness I had you, man, nobody's gonna pull your chain with this shit, man, no way you're gonna believe the shit people were sayin', 'cause you know what *really* happened, man, which is that she comes in after three weeks of livin' the good life, she comes to the door, which was wide open because of the heat in that fucking apartment, and not a breath of air stirring anywhere, man, so she sticks her head in the door, the fucking bitch, says hi, real sweet an' soft like nothing'd happened, and the girls ran out of the bedroom so fast you couldn't hardly see 'em, *Mami, mami, mami!* crying, what a spectacle, *mi asere.* The folks had already come back from Cincinnati, so imagine, I had to grab my socks and be a man in front of them, you know, *mi compañero,* and not cry at night or anything. And my old man says, She'll come back, she'll come walking in that door and get down on her knees and ask your forgiveness. The old lady, now, the old lady wouldn't say anything, the old lady *never* gave her opinion, man, not one word about her daughter-in-law, and you know, Swan, you know that I've been faithful to that woman, I mean at one point I'd have loved to put it to Belinda, man, that girl that had the hots for yours truly, man, the one that was chasing all over for me, she was just about as good as it gets, too, man, plus she had family in the Community that got her all the clothes she wanted, she dressed something incredible, man, and with all that, I never jumped that chick's bones *once*, man, never, never once scratched my wife with the thorns off that rosebush, you know, I was a virgin for her, a virgin for that bitch, and never, as the record will show, man, and as everybody knows and will tell you, never did I do it with anybody else either. And I'm a man, Abakuá, I ain't lyin' to anybody, you can absolutely take my word when I say that, *mi asere,* I ain't trying to impress anybody—I was wiped out, *mi bróder,* it was all I could do to drag myself out of bed in the morning while that bitch, that bitch, that . . . *bitch,* man, was out there . . . So she comes in the door, just kind of sticks her head in the door like somebody stickin' their head in the picture in a home movie, you know what I'm sayin', *mi amigo,* and "Hi," she says, and the girls start cryin' and goin' on, you know, that's normal, they're just little girls, man, teenagers, I mean, she's squeezing 'em, cryin' her crocodile tears, they're all goin' on, man, puttin' on this show, because Mami, too, man, my old lady, too, and even Papi was sheddin' tears like you wouldn't believe, dude, cry me a fuckin' river, okay? my old lady and old man, who'd just gotten back from el Norte, boy they missed it, did they ever miss it, but they came back so cool, man, no stress, no worries, they were just as cool as a couple of ninety-year-old cucumbers, you know what I'm sayin'? and then—*boom, bam, bang*—they both fell apart on me, my old lady's blood pressure goes through the ceiling, my old man gets palpitations, he's having trouble breathing, on account of that ungrateful bitch, man, it's a miracle they didn't take the long road to glory right then, I'm telling you, *compay,* it's a wonder they didn't check out for good, it wasn't easy, man. So then before anybody could draw a good breath she just comes out with it, no preparation at all, man, *I don't have time, Andrés, I've gotta go get somebody at the Parque de la Fraternidad.* So? I say, what's that to me? and the girls go all wonky and weepy, they could tell the chicken was about to fly the coop, you know what I mean? kids and animals have a feeling about stuff like that, man—but she goes on, We'll talk about it tomorrow,

Andrés, all right? I beg you, Andrés, shihee shihah, Andrés, let's not start, let's act like civilized people, all right? *Civilized people!* she's sayin' that to *me*, man, Swan, *mi asere*, you know how I waited for that woman, man, if you were lookin' for anybody more civilized than me you'd have to have 'em custom-made is what I say, I didn't deserve *that*, man, I deserved better than that, because she manipulated me, dude, she stuck the knife in and then she twisted it, *mi hermano*, she slipped that sucker in my back and made chopped gizzard outta me, man, and I *loved* her. Shit . . . I loved her . . . don't doubt that for a minute. She was the one and only, man, she was and *still is* the one and only, it was like an eternity with her, thinking about her, from the minute I saw her I couldn't get her outta my head, man, and for her to do me that way—*Listen*, she says, she's got her hands on her hips like Who do you think you are, mister? *Listen*, she says, *if you don't calm down, Andrés, I'm leaving right this minute, so stop shouting, I'm sick and tired of it, d'you hear!?* And that's where you came in, remember? just when I grabbed her by the hair and almost busted her skull against the window, and she got lucky she didn't go through that window and take off flying through the air, too, *compañero*, and if she didn't it was because the girls stopped me, they were hanging onto me and crying and carrying on, and that was when you came in, and by then there was so much blood it looked like a car wreck in that apartment, man, I don't remember much about it, in detail, you know? the fine details, but they say that that was when I grabbed the screwdriver and popped her eye out, the one she kept in the drawer of that Singer sewing machine of hers—the screwdriver, I mean, Swan, man, *you* know what I mean—and ain't it just my shit luck, man, and hers too, that that screwdriver was lying around the house that night—and all of a sudden she was yellin' *Tierra, Tierra, help!* like a crazy woman, *He-e-e-lp! Tierra, I love you!* Yes, sir, fucker, you heard it right—*I never loved you*, she says to me, *I made a mistake, it's her I love, Tierra.* Who?! says I, fuckin' pissed as hell, man, who?! and I tried to murder her, I admit it, man, I did, I tried to cream that bitch's potatoes right there, man, and you couldn't get her out of my clutches, either, not you or anybody, because I was going to tear that bitch apart with my bare hands, man, and that's when I lied to you, Swan, 'cause it was me that grabbed that knife and stuck it in my side—aw shit, look at this, man, look at what this bitch did to me, man, call that shrink cousin of yours, Swan, quick, before she kills us all. And that's where she made the mistake of her life, dude, because while she had one hand over that hole in her face where her eye went, blood gushing out everywhere, with the other one she was feelin' around all over the place, on the furniture and everywhere, trying to find something, her eye, man, can you believe that? and she finally found it in between the cushions on the couch, man, and she had the good sense to stick it in her pocket, can you imagine the cold-bloodedness of that bitch, man? carrying her own eye around like that? and then she starts screaming *Yes, yes! I'll murder you all!, I'm going to slit your throat first, Andrés, and then bring me the heads of my daughters on a platter, and then I'm going to fry these old goats in their own fat,* that was when she had that fit, you tried to control her, but she was like a wild woman, until you floored her—*bam!*—a knockout, and she's out of service, and you grabbed that damn telephone, *Go ahead,* I said, *estás en tu casa,* and you called Mazorra, let me speak to Kiss-Ass, you say, the son of the mayor of Pinar del Río, yeah, the *doctor,* not the patient, tell 'im it's his cousin . . . Yeah, hey, wassup cuz? Listen, I'm sorry to bother you, man, but I've got a case here, you won't believe this, man, the wife of a buddy of mine, she's gone berserk, man, totally over the edge, you know? nutty as Mr. Peanut, *mi hermano,* and my friend's put her eye out, there's blood all over the place, it's an honest-to-god emergency, man, we need an ambulance bad, the chick skipped out, left home and whatnot, quit her job, left her kids, husband, inlaws, and it looks like it wasn't for another man, dude, it was for another *woman,* awright? somebody named Peerless or Hairless or something, I don't know, but it's a disaster here, man, but the worst part of it is that *mi compay* is a decent hardworking kind of guy, you know, so we need to do something quick here, and I know you can help us out, I'm counting on you . . . No, right now she's kinda unavailable. Out like a light, actually, KO'd in the fourth, under deep anesthesia, man, I tapped her, you know? and you know me, you know I know how to use my fists, man, and if she comes to, I'll give her a kiss on the chin again, man, I mean if she's already missing an eye she'll never miss a few teeth, right? That's what you said, Swan, *viejo,* you were bitin' down on that receiver, man, like it was a chicken leg—the girls panicking, especially Ibis, she's the one that's traumatized the most about this whole thing, I'll tell you, man, Frances was always on my side . . . Anyway, the ambulance came before the cops did, and when the cops finally got in the house I made up this story that the unfortunate matter was being handled by the shrinks, you know? that the poor thing was pathological, had been for a long time, that she got this way pretty often but this time she kinda went overboard. You know I loved her like crazy, Swan . . . it's a miracle I didn't strangle her, man, her doing that to me— I mean I lived to make that bitch happy, man, I did everything I could for her, me out there laying those goddamn cement blocks like a fucking slave, man, *chacataplón, chacataplón, chacataplón, chacataplón,* no, *chico,* you don't do that to a man . . . it's a disgrace is what it is, man, because when I met her she was *nothin'*, this little mouse of a girl, in the Schools in the Country she'd scarf down these steak sandwiches my old lady brought me, but she acted like a fucking princess, man, taking these little-bitty bites like *Oh, my mouth is so dainty!* Well, I'd like to see what her mouth's like now, man, after you fixed her choppers for her. And her eye, too, man . . . I tell you, she's just lucky I didn't run her through the meat grinder and have her for supper . . .

I INTRODUCE MYSELF once more—Good health to you, *ekobios,* I am the sensitive light of the city. The events might have occurred in the following way, as they had occurred with other women. I am Mandinga chicherekú disguised as the sensitive light of the city.

Danae might have been sitting next to a gray, grimy window, and she might have been wearing a long white shirt with arms much too long, so that they could be tied around her to pin her arms behind her back in moments of crisis or spasms. Danae might have been able to look out on the same landscape she had been looking out on for the last twelve years, a ceiba tree with yellowish leaves, a royal palm red in the sun, a dusty road that ran along one side of the property, men and women wandering aimlessly around an empty piece of ground, an old garden, now dead and dry, but still holding in its memory the fragrance of oleanders, gladioli, and jasmine; half-ruined statues, symbolizing the four seasons, spring, autumn, winter, summer, might still have been standing there.

Danae might have registered things in her memory without chronological order; she might have been staring into space.

One afternoon the Nice Nurse might have whispered in her ear that someone wanted to see her. No, it wasn't a visitor from outside, it was a patient in the other wing of the hospital who had recognized her. A very old gentleman who couldn't get around except in a wheelchair.

"He always points you out to me, but he asked me not to tell you his name. He wants to see if you really haven't forgotten him, like you promised once, a long time ago."

Danae might have been led to the large, echoing room reserved for the people of most advanced age. He would be off in a corner, curled up in a wheelchair, his hands trembling, his body wasted away, nothing but skin and bones. Danae might press her palms to her temples. She might start to cry, because while she tried to remember she might once more realize that Gloriosa Paz, her mother, had died of pneumonia two years ago. Childhood would have ended with the death of her mother. Who was that man with all those refined, handsome-looking wrinkles? Could she possibly know someone so old?

". . . *In this world—and you need to get this through that thick skull of yours—if you want to live you're going to have to do a lot of things, and among them is forget that fear exists.*" The slightest hint of an ironic smile, almost a smirk trying hard to be a smile, might pass across the old man's face as his tremulous voice recited those words.

"Ruperto!" Danae might exclaim, and the Nice Nurse might decide to leave them alone with each other. "You're here too? *Alabao,* oh, wow, this really is a surprise. Years ago I was a librarian, I found all your books, published abroad. I've read you! The last thing I ever expected was to run into you—and here, lastest of the last!"

"Another proof of what a small world it is, eh? Well, from that camp where we met they brought me here, and I've never been able to escape. Until just two months ago they kept me incommunicado. See, for certain high-ranking people I'm just a madman, even if for others I'm a genius. That's the way history always works. At first I wrote—secretly, as you can imagine, smuggled my manuscripts out any way I could, friends, you know . . . It was very hard—a true martyrdom. Now they look the other way—of course, I don't have as many compromising things to tell anymore. But what about you? What kind of mistake did *you* make for them to declare you insane?"

"That's exactly what it was, a mistake. I'm here by mistake, I swear to you. I married a man I shouldn't have, had two children, which I'm not sorry for. I think I loved him, I still love him. Affection is funny that way, you can go on loving your hangman. Later I realized that my true love was a woman, I fell in love with a woman, like me, a woman, can you believe that? Before you realize it, you've gotten so mixed up and confused. I hid it from myself, I didn't dare . . . I didn't have the courage to accept it . . ."

"Ah, that's something I forgot to warn you about that night. The problem of being a woman. The moment a woman steps over the line, the word once was 'transgresses,' *puf!* Power loses it—we might even say it goes nuts. An imbalance has been created, and so Power must restore it. A woman does something grand, and they immediately put a man above her to try to mute the splendor of her work. And if she commits an actual error, they decapitate her. From you, to take the nearest example, they have taken an eye—a bad joke, but as you will understand, we shouldn't be wasting time beating about the bush. It was him, I suppose."

"Yes, him, my husband."

"Is it glass or your own?"

"It's my eye, I picked it up in time, but of course it lost mobility, it's just there . . ."

"Did you have to fake many orgasms?"

"No. Well, a few . . . . A lot."

Danae might change the subject by referring to that encounter in the camp at La Fe.

"And you—look at you!"

"You were right, I was fated to live forever, if this is what you call living. I've lasted too long—I who always felt I was going to die the next day. Aaaah, it's such a bore, having to be so old . . . These days I console myself that at least I have been able to confirm what a French friend of mine told me once: death is nothing, it's just the weariest of wearinesses, the last weariness . . . Aaah . . ."

He might yawn, the mouth like a tunnel might frighten Danae. The open mouth like that suitcase she had taken to the School in the Country when she opened it and from the inside, from the wood, a fragrance of Persian poetry wafted up to her. The old man might suddenly become a suitcase, that arborescent suitcase, his legs and arms the flowering branches, his belly the inside of the case, and that insistent fragrance of Persian papyrus might creep into the labyrinths of her memory . . . While Ruperto, or the suitcase, might stretch out to sleep, or die, she might take off running. She might run through the cold, dirty hallways, the male nurses after her. They might not be able to catch her, because when she took off on these races through the hallways no one could manage to stop her—she would run like a deer. Finally they might corner her at the end of one of the hallways, hit her over the head with a black rubber pipe, tie her arms behind her back. They might give the order to lead the sick woman to the electroshock room. Two jolts of electricity a day might not have been enough—it might well be clear that the dosage would have to be increased.

> *It was a night of full and silver moon, with lightning and with thunder, that a fine and cultured gentleman set out with his coach and coachman. He was dressed in white from head to toe, with a medal on his breast, and as he passed the four corners he was stabbed three times in the chest. "Open the door, my darling, for I am wounded to the heart; three times the man has stabbed me, and this life I must soon depart. It is a hard thing he has done, and a hard thing I must do, for I leave you here to weep alone, and our unborn baby too."*

"At some point a very long time ago I knew a girl that was called Renata the Physical. I don't remember her face or why she'd been given that awful nickname . . . Yes, I was fifteen . . . Yes, Emma the Menace would squeeze out the blackheads on my nose and throat, and on my back too, and I'd do the same for her. We would do that for hours on end, all those noontimes in the hot sun . . . Yes, I had a mamá like everybody else . . . Yes, she loved me with a love that was pure and disinterested, a mother's love . . . Yes, I wasn't able to tell her goodbye . . . Yes, I didn't say goodbye to anybody . . . Yes, I squeeze my jaws together, bite down on this hard thing, it's like a horse's bit, a piece of wood, it breaks my teeth, makes my gums bleed . . . Yes, I'm a good girl, delicate, faithful . . . Yes, my mind does not exist . . . yes, or my body either. . .Yes, I don't exist . . . Yes . . . yes . . . yes. . . *Mandinga chicherekú, Mandinga chicherekú* . . . Yes, Agugú, and the mischievous spirit of a newborn little black baby, seven months in its mother's womb, a little ebony doll, earn your soul and defend me, your heart beating its wings, the size of a big owl moth . . ."

THE SENSITIVE LIGHT OF THE CITY

*W*HAT FOLLOWS IS also what might have happened. The sensitive light of the city might wash over Ibis, who would be on her way to work; the young woman might have left her children at the day care center, the Children's Circle, knowing that today was her mother's forty-seventh birthday. July 11. She had always liked those numbers, seven and eleven. In *charada*, the mystical significance of dream images. There were *charadas* all around the world. In the santería *charada*, Angayú was eleven and Yemayá was seven. In the Cuban *charada*, matchbox was eleven and excrement was seven . In the American one, mechanic shop was eleven and socks was seven. In the Chinese one, rooster was eleven and seashell, seven. In the Puerto Rican one, money was eleven and bird was seven. In the Texas *charada*, horse was eleven and hog, seven. In the Indian *charada*, rain was eleven and sleep was seven. In the Aztec *charada*, factory was eleven and mariachis, seven.

She might decide to put out of her mind the many images associated with eleven and seven in the various *charadas* and go buy something sweet to give her mother for her birthday; her mother loved *merengues*. She might have walked from the variety store on Galiano, which was closed for repairs, to the "ten-cen'" on Calle Monte. The emaciated man behind the counter might say how sorry he was, that day they wouldn't be receiving the ingredients they needed to make sweets. She was the one that was sorry; she would have wasted all that time and energy walking, and she might run to catch a bus at the bus stop at the Parque de la Fraternidad. And she might make that journey for nothing, to catch nothing but her breath at the end of it.

At the corner, somebody might have been selling ferns potted up in little pots; a plant might just perk up her mother. She might buy the fern, her nose might sniff at the cool humidity of the plant as she walked along, looking at that fountain across the street there, la Fuente de la India, which was what people called it because it portrayed a woman wrapped in a marble tunic, sitting on a sort of throne, her left hand holding a cornucopia spilling out pineapples, mameys, plantains, soursops, star apples, mangoes, papayas, or perhaps just flowers and little river rocks. The Indian Bounty was accompanied by four elegant dolphins. When she was a little girl, she liked to compare her mother to that woman with a face that was sensual even within its prison of marble.

Her mother might be forty-seven today and also might be crazy, locked up in Mazorra.

Her sister might be flying around the world as a stewardess.

Her father might have married again; his new wife might be that stuckup whiny girl who had gone to school with her sister Frances, that Marilú, the daughter of Salome the walleyed librarian, the one they called the Satrap when Salome and her mother were in school together. It was very possible that Marilú had given her father two boys, who might be almost the same age as Ibis's kids. Andrés, her father, might have moved into the new building that he and his microbrigade buddies might finally have finished building. An eyesore of god-awful fiber cement, a typical microbrigade project, a cancer on the face of the city. From which her mother, sister, and she might give thanks that they'd been saved—to think that he was building that concrete monster since before she'd been born! There might have been some possibility of living there, back when her mother was still healthy. Then the family most probably fell apart, shattered, exploded.

Ibis might walk along thinking that she ought to buy a bunch of olean-ders, or gladioli; her mother might spend hours smelling them. Last time, she had eaten them—she had torn them off the stalks, some with stalks and rib-bons and all, and stuffed them into her mouth by the handful and chewed them and swallowed them. Ibis might have taken a cream-filled cookie out of her purse and started to put it in her mouth when she might have seen a beg-gar woman with her eyes fixed on the hand-cookie trajectory toward the mouth.

The beggar woman might have been sitting on the low stone wall with her back to the ceiba tree, so that it might look as though the roots of the tree were growing right out of her head. The woman might make brusque, stac-cato movements, but Ibis might daresay she did so with a certain savage dis-tinction. It might be clear that she was starving. Two youngsters might pass by and throw stones at her, and call out mockingly:

"Hey, crazy lady! You and that tree quit talking?"

Ibis might go over to her and hold out the package of cookies to her, and she might take it, pretending to be calm, disguising her anxiousness to eat, never taking her eyes off the younger woman. By now she might be a gray-haired woman, older than her years; behind the wrinkles and the dirt one might be able to see a beauty that was still pure, utterly unlike the urban sort of beauty, and it might make her different from the other homeless women wandering the city. The woman might study Ibis's features as she gnawed at one of the cookies.

"Incredible how much she looks like her!" the woman might mutter, half to herself.

"Me? Look like who, if I might ask?" Ibis, curious, amused, might ask.

"Bah, what difference does it make? She disappeared into that pearl-gray-painted taxicab and I'm still waiting for her . . . I've been very constant, very patient . . . for a long time . . . . Maybe she's trying to convince her family . . . Anyway, thank you, appreciate the cookie."

Ibis might tenderly caress the wild-haired head; the woman might not pull back from the warm touch. Ibis might think about her mother, might tell herself that when all was said and done, she was lucky to have been admitted to the insane asylum. With all the crazy people wandering the streets, at least she had the consolation of being cared for and stabilized. She might take away her hand and the other woman's eyes might flutter open—she might have closed her eyes in a kind of bliss. The bus might not come, might seem never to be going to come, and Ibis might begin to grow impatient.

"It's only natural, nothing ever comes by here, not even shade," the disheveled woman might remark. "Listen, I sell poisons, you want to buy one? Nobody gives a shit about poisons, but maybe you'd be interested."

Ibis might shake her head. She might remain silent for ten minutes or so, trying to forget the beggar woman, but she might not be able to control herself much longer.

"Excuse me, I don't usually come to this bus stop—have they changed the route, do you think?"

"I don't think there ever *was* a route here!" The woman might laugh uproariously.

A second group of teenagers might pass by, walking toward the pre-university school, making fun of the dirty beggar lady, and they might also yell insults, throw stones at her. The woman, on her knees, might start praying and singing to the ceiba tree. From the trunk there might emerge a box turtle, and the turtle and woman might embrace one another and hop around the foot of the tree. They might not stop hopping and skipping and singing until the figures of the youngsters had grown small in the distance.

Why not help her mother to die? On several occasions she had asked her to.

"Ibis, *hija,* I want to die. Find a way for me, there must be a way, a poison that doesn't leave any traces."

"Don't be silly, Mamá, how can you think that I would ever let you commit suicide?"

But what if Ibis decided to buy the poison from this abandoned madwoman? And why would this street person want to live and her mother not? Maybe this poor mentally ill woman twisting her filthy hair into ringlets around the index finger of her right hand while sucking the thumb of her left hand like a baby might still harbor some hope of a miracle, a blinding light that would illuminate and clear her mind, while her mother might have lost even the consolation of thinking a miracle possible. One afternoon, while she was snacking on cactus, she might have asked Ibis:

"My mind is gone, isn't it? Blown? All burned out? Before, I held on to some hope that it wasn't, that it was all just some kind of bad dream, a joke ... Now, I don't know. It's like blackouts, up here, in this shit-for-brains I've got ..." she might say, tapping her knuckles on her head.

A '54 Dodge, painted pearl gray, might turn the corner as though coming from the Partagás cigar store. The beggar woman's eyes might sparkle with expectancy. The car might pull up in front of Ibis; it might be packed full. Alicia Machine-Gun Tongue and Emma the Menace might stick their heads out and yell at Danae Duckbill Lips' daughter.

"Ibis, get in, come with us! It's your mother's birthday, we're going to visit her!"

"I know it's her birthday—you think I'd forget? I was waiting for the bus ..."

"Oh, sweetheart, it's been years and years and years and *years*—since frogs had hair, as I once heard somebody say—since they moved the bus stop—and can you believe they haven't put up a sign to tell people! Just beautiful!"

"Are you going to buy the poison or not?" the beggar woman might ask.

"Are you coming or not?" the driver might ask impatiently.

A very fine drizzle might begin to fall, and from the asphalt of the street a sickening steam might begin to rise. Ibis might take her leave of the old beggar woman with the promise that she would be back sometime soon, maybe next week—maybe next week, she might repeat, not very convincingly. Poor neglected thing, no family, and clearly crazy. Ibis might think she could present her case to the hospital, maybe even manage to get her admitted. At least her mother, being a patient, wasn't in any danger. Imagine, the way she suffered, thinking about mere danger. She might detest the doctors who attended her, might want to kill herself. Ibis might refuse to help her die. Ibis might stop to think—she might have a moment of uncertainty. Tierra Fortuna Munda. Tierra Fortuna Munda. Tierra Fortuna Munda. Why in the world might Ibis be repeating those words, which meant nothing to her either together or separately?

Then, if all this had really happened in this tragic way, as it has happened on other occasions, Danae might have written a moving letter:

Tierra, my beloved Tierra,

How old I feel every time I write you or think about you, think about us as teenagers, riding Sunny through the Valle de Viñales. Of course I *am* old. And sick. Very sick. If someone were to tell me this minute that I might be able to find you, to see you, I might actually hesitate. I wouldn't want you to see me this way, all wrinkled, skinny, crazy, and with just one eye. Today is my forty-seventh birthday—it's a lot, but it's nothing. It's hardly anything when you compare it to how long I yearn to live.

The bed I sleep in is so hot, so hot—I never stop sweating, it's disgusting. The pillow smells of medicine, of that glue—they call it gel—they put on my temples when they give me the electroshock treatments. I spend more time plugged in to that machine than to reality. I've turned into some kind of clock-radio, or lamp, or battery charger. When I'm lying down, my only land-scape is my toes, wiggling around like little midgets that won't stay still, want-ing so bad to free themselves from my body. Or I stare at the circles of yellow pee on the sheets. I still haven't been able to learn what the objective of lock-ing me up in here is, what the reason for it might be. Oh, yes, the doctor thinks I need to rectify my behavior. I'm paranoid, schizophrenic, aggres-sive—very dangerous. I attacked Andrés, my husband, with a knife—or a fork, I don't remember, nothing serious, a scratch on his side. Apparently I threatened to decapitate my girls and walk down the street with their heads on a platter. I must have been crazy. I don't remember any of that.

My mind blank.

My mind black.

My mind no color at all. Like a still lake, inhabited by silvery little fish flit-ting here and there . . .

That's no excuse for him putting out my eye.

I'm like a story that I'm telling myself, little by little, or that other people are telling without my permission.

The mistake was not telling you that I loved you from the beginning, when we were teenagers, when we met. Tierra. What a mamey—that's what people used to say when somebody was really nice, so-and-so, whoever, is mamey.

Mameys, when you cut them in half, open their red flesh to your eyes, the glistening seed in the middle like the surface of a mahogany desk that some-body has just finished polishing, but the flesh, ay, the slices of the mamey, dis-solving in your mouth, that unique fragrance, like vegetable and meat all at once, the flavor that lies on your tongue like a sweet secret. When I think about freedom, it comes to my mind in the form and flavor of the mamey. Your skin, Tierra, had that same delirious drunken flavor as the mamey. I would kiss the throbbing brown skin of you, my lips would get all dry wait-ing for your slippery saliva, I thirsted for the guava jelly in your navel or the coolness of that winelike liquor between your thighs, or the thick mamey milk shake in the orifice of your vagina.

The mistake has to have been not accepting our love from the beginning, but I didn't even know I loved you that way, so firmly and mysteriously. So *womanly*.

I didn't know a person could fall in love that way. With another woman. Like yourself, like myself. And so dramatic in her passions.

The mistake was continuing to send those letters, *Dear first love, Dear first love*, as a way of disguising it, covering it up, so Gloriosa Paz, my mother, wouldn't find out, so the girls at school wouldn't start suspecting us, know our weakness. And I was never open with Andrés, either, I was never honest with him. He didn't deserve my trust. Or maybe he did, maybe I've been too hard on him. How could I have been such an idiot, writing you that way, without speaking clearly, without having the courage to make a decision?

You, of course, must have thought I was joking, fooling around, or even making fun of you. Or that I was just a bored city girl entertaining herself. In my letters I never said anything that would let you truly know, nothing to make you come to me. Just that greeting, *Dear first love, Dear first love*, and the stupid way I'd end them—*Love, . . . Kisses, . . . Yours, . . .* like in some triv-ial, perverted game. A whole stack of letters that invariably talked about the same things—stupid. And that's how my whole life has been—a piling up of stupidities. I am a hoarder of stupidities. Oh, the letters . . . what good did they do?

What good! Why, they never even reached you! You told me so yourself. The letters were never delivered to you. Thank goodness. It could have been worse.

I'm almost asleep, with that whistling inside my brain that cuts me in two dirty halves. I should never have left you in the park, next to the ceiba tree. The tree planted in your head. Growing like a miracle.

I don't know who you are or why I'm writing you or why I'm thinking about you, Tierra Fortuna Munda.

Oh, I know! I was coming back from somewhere in the country. I got home, stepped through the door, and said hi. The girls were studying in their bedroom. Andrés was sitting there in an undershirt, combing and recombing his greasy hair. Leaning on the windowsill, looking down at the street, were my in-laws, having café con leche. It was so terribly, suffocatingly hot. I said hi again, and he swung around—angry, furious to hear my voice saying hi so calmly a second time. Ibis and Frances ran out of their bedroom with their arms out to me, laughing, smiling, shouting, you could see how happy they were to see me. My in-laws didn't say boo. And then it started. According to what he started yelling at me, I'd been away for several weeks. According to his insults I should be ashamed of myself for being a whore, a bad mother, a bad wife, humiliating him and the girls and the whole family, what a disgrace, what a fucking *whore* I was . . . I felt something cold on my face, my eye jumped out, I stuck my finger in the hole, it was hot.

I had just left you in the Parque de la Fraternidad. And once more, I couldn't tell you—Tierra, I love you. I've always been embarrassed to express my emotions, even to the person who was supposedly the first to have the right to know them.

This bed is so goddamned hot. The Nasty Nurse has tied down my hands and feet. I am *restrained.* She is injecting a pink liquid into the vein in the crook of my right arm. She thinks I'm going to try to escape. Which I might. That's enough—I need to go back to my house, my mother—my own home, with my daughters and you, Tierra. That's enough, please, get me out of this red-hot oven of a mattress. How wonderful it would feel to dive into a lake, or stand in the water gushing out of the irrigation feeder pipe. Enough, please, I can't breathe.

Last night the *güijes* visited me, the spirits of the wood. We galloped down the Gívara hill, in Vueltabajo. Irma the Albino was there, too, trying to convince me to go over to a dance at Bejerano and Santa's bohío.

And who *are* those people?

I found out that my mother died. The terrible thing about it is that I don't remember her face. Her eyes were dark—black, right? I will never again be able to hug Gloriosa Paz, or smell her hair, such thick hair she had, and it smelled of figs. Figs? But ha ha ha, I've never seen a fig tree in my life. Or have I? A fig tree, a flamboyán, a box turtle . . .

This image belongs to another person, not to me, not to me. It's a little girl that looks like a boy, running around, skipping and hopping and carrying on, her clothes all raggedy—dressed like a boy, too, a regular tomboy, racing through the woods, through the underbrush, waving a machete in the air, trying to defend herself against the people that are chasing her, the bad people. The Higher-Ups. She's shouting *Fire! Fire!* The flames are devouring the cane field. The girl is running at the speed of a hallucination, and the abuser is about to catch her. There he is, he's grabbed her, they're struggling, he hits her as hard as he can. She doubles over in pain, her thin body almost breaks in half, like a leaf of grass, a vine cut with a knife, a stalk broken off by evil fingers. This image is not mine. I don't recognize these figures. The girl, the one calling for help, is named Tierra. Tierra Fortuna Munda.

I hate to dream. We sick people shouldn't dream. The suffering lasts even longer and is more intense, and then I can't control it. Ay, Chacumbele, rescue me.

Sleep, you have to sleep. That is my daughter's voice. Have you finally brought the poison? But why not? Why the hell won't you listen to me? Why won't you do what I ask? You have no respect for your mother, do you? The day I die, you'll see, your childhood will be over. Yes, it's blackmail. The eternal blackmail.

Rest, you've got to rest. What is that, Ibis, darling? A pot of flowers. And who are they for? Why haven't you brought me what I want, which is the poison? It's my birthday. She says I'm forty-seven years old today. I suspect I'm more than that. If she says so, I shouldn't argue. And those two women with you, who are they? Introduce me, have you forgotten your manners? Emma the Menace and Alicia Machine-Gun Tongue, friends from when you were young.

Oh, yes, of course, how wonderful, I'm so glad to see you. Leave me alone with my daughter for just a minute if you will. Just go outside there a second, please. I beg you. I need to look at her, look at her a little. Before I die.

Where's your sister? Traveling. Visiting the pyramids in Egypt. And what about your father? With that bitch of a wife of his, I imagine—she's already had the second boy. And what about Gloriosa Paz, my mother? Mamá! How many times do I have to tell you that she passed away two years ago?

Tierra Fortuna Munda. Tierra Fortuna Munda.

I say that name over and over again, hundreds of times.

Mamá, will you tell me once and for all what those three words mean, what relation they have to each other?

I should keep my mouth shut. If I keep talking they'll take me to the insane asylum again and lock me up in that padded cell. The doctor will speak to me very gently and calmly. And oh so slowly. An injection, he'll say, he'll order an injection of something. The electroshock therapy is essential, he'll smile. And time marches on . . . No, I shouldn't call attention to myself. The vein in her neck throbs as the needle pricks it. You are in good hands, señora. Your daughter has told me that when she is alone with you, you repeat the following phrase: Tierra Fortuna Munda. Is that the name of a person, an animal, a place, an emotion? Is it a vision?

Not to mention that I don't understand the first thing about that phrase, myself. Tierra Fortuna Munda. Nor do I want to be taken for a fool. Or for a ride. Another injection, the doctor says with that face of his like a rotten soursop. Listen, Doctor, I'll tell you—Tierra Fortuna Munda is fate, understand? He smiles: More pills, six a day. Move along, patient. Step forward, private.

The ambient sound becomes conversations broadcast by loudspeakers in several unrecognizable languages, apparently spoken backward.

My poor brain is full of loudspeakers . . .

It was a night of full and silver moon, with lightning and with thunder, that a fine and cultured gentleman set out with his coach and coachman. He was dressed in white from head to toe, with a medal on his breast, and as he passed the four corners he was stabbed three times in the chest. "Open the door, my darling, for I am wounded to the heart; three times the man has stabbed me, and this life I must soon depart. It is a hard thing he has done, and a hard thing I must do, for I leave you here to weep alone, and our unborn baby too."

There, there, go call my friends, ask them to come back in. Emma the Menace, Alicia Machine-Gun Tongue, you can come back into this nauseating, sickening room. Lie down with me on this burning bed, the fakir's bed of nails, the nonflying carpet—the heat, my god. Jesus, the heat. Who'll take pity on me and give me a cigarette, a coffin-nail, huh? We stopped smoking, it was so expensive, and you shouldn't smoke either, your health is not good and you know how bad it is for you, for your mind. If you've got bats in the belfry already, imagine how you'll be with smoke in it! All right, all right, leave the advice for another day if you don't mind. There'll be plenty of time to fight. Entertain me. Tell me a story, and try not to make it up as you go along.

Ay, Danae, *mi amor*, do you remember when we'd go to the Schools in the Country and run off to the Roncali lighthouse, on Cabo San Antonio?

Of course I remember. Just as clear as day.

This is a letter and she will never know.

WHY IS IT called *tierra* and not *tierro*?

Why is it called *tierra* and not *tierro*? Why is it round, like two breasts sewn together, like the two halves of an orange—a *naranja*—or the belly of a pregnant woman, and has never had any phallic tendencies, even while it was first forming? Why do we say *naturaleza*, in the feminine, and not *naturalezo*? Why did the old poets prefer to write *la mar* and not *el mar*, the way most people do today? Why is it *la noche*, night, *la madrugada*, dawn, *la soledad*, solitude, *la ternura*, tenderness, *la felicidad*, happiness, *la luz*, light, *la luna*, the moon, *las constelaciones*, the constellations, *la voz*, a person's voice, *las caricias*, caresses, *las flores*, flowers, *la melancolía*, melancholy? Why would it seem that the really poetic words are in the feminine? But that's nonsense. *Mentira*, lie, is feminine, and that's not so poetic. And there are lots of poetic words that are masculine: *el cielo*, the sky, *el alba*, another word for dawn, *el misterio*, mystery, *el deseo*, desire, *el parto*, childbirth, *el bien*, good as opposed to evil. And speaking of evil, that's masculine in gender, *el mal*, and so is power, *el poder*. Although we shouldn't forget *el querer*, loving, a word that belongs to the strategy of desire. And also has a little bit of goodness in it. *Bondad*, goodness, is a very pretty word, and very feminine—it's conjugated in the feminine. On the other hand, *muerte*, death, which is feminine, no matter how she gets herself up to look attractive and profound, could she ever seduce anyone?

As I think about these things I gradually become younger, the names reappear, although then they run away again—run away like escapees but also like water, into the sudsy, stinky leftovers scraped off the plates. I hated to wash dishes, it's awful, but I truly abominate the other household chores. I don't think it's worth squat, being an excellent housewife. I do what's necessary, what I can; I don't know how to sew a button on straight, never learned to crochet. I do weave, though—thoughts, useless thoughts, that won't keep you warm in the winter or cool in the summer. My grandmother was a girl, a young woman, an adult, an old woman, and then she died like everybody else—and nobody knew the difference. And my mother repeated the cycle. And now I am on my way to being old. All of us are. Neither my mother nor my grandmother were housewives of world renown. They knew how to weave stories—that is, by telling them they unraveled their lives.

Old age. Before, I liked to behave cool and aloof toward old age. For several years now, though, old people have inspired the same tenderness in me as newborns. Except that newborns come from death and have forgotten it, while old people are moving toward it but have never managed to remember it. Is it possible that that's the way it is, as easy as that? Do we really come from death? Bah, we might just say that to console ourselves, to keep us from thinking that we're wasting our time, or maybe it's that that's what we *ask* ourselves, since it's more a question than a statement, maybe on that side of the unknown it's not a question anymore, it's a certainty, since it's *almost* clear to us, the fact that we are coming from life, when actually we arrive from nothingness. If in fact we come from anywhere. But nothing is nothing, so nothing*ness* must be the *essence* of nothing, and so therefore it can't be a *place*, a *where*. Who's to say that we aren't always leaving, going away, that everything is not an eternal departure, à la Novalis? So instead of coming in we'd be going out? Instead of saying hello, instead of introducing ourselves, we should be saying goodbye? Then, instead of saying *you were born on such and such a day,* we could turn the phrase around, the meaning of the phrase, and say *you died on such and such a day.* And that might not make us sad; on the contrary, it might make us sincerely and honestly happy. And the day of our death might be more than anything the birth of mystery. What if the true meaning of life is that we are eternally departing, undertaking a journey toward a new mystery? I used the adverb "eternally"; I hate adverbs because of the physical and mental space they occupy, and the word "eternity" gives me a fever, because although it's lovely it just takes in too much.

So anyway, I was saying that old people fill me with tenderness, as for example when I hear them give their opinion about any old thing, however ordinary—war, for instance. War, *guerra,* another ugly noun that's feminine. Here I am thinking and talking nonsense; we will never know whether we're on the verge of war at this very second. Old people start telling their terrible experiences of slaughters, the horrors of war, remembering the multitudes killed, the children left orphans, the maimed and injured, the ones that just disappeared. Huge areas of land wiped clean, annihilated. Forever. Do you suppose that the earth, as a planet, is going someplace in the universe, or returning? Could it not be that our daydreaming has led us to imagine the path it is taking? Is the earth being born or departing, do you suppose? "Universe" is a frightening yet also touching word—filled with enchantment, yet it's masculine. *Uni-verso.* One and verse. Poetry, though, *poesía,* is feminine.

So anyway, old people keep giving their versions of things, their advice, going off toward death on us yet filled with their old people's confidence, believing that we who are staying behind on this earth will not repeat the errors, the outright disasters, committed by our forebears. Poor naïve old folks! And here we are, breaking our promise, stubbing our toes hundreds of thousands, millions of times against the same philosopher's stone, putting our foot in it up to the knee, up to the middle of the earth. Old people are so old it breaks my heart. To think that I'll be like that someday, very very old, if I'm lucky and don't die first. In this struggle like a game of dog-eat-dog. Just that simple. And fatal.

My mother got old overnight. And that next morning, when I woke up and saw how old my mother had gotten, I put my head on her breast and I cried. *Ay, Mamá, don't die without me, wait for me. Oh, wait, let's enjoy this a little longer.* And then, all around me, everybody, absolutely everybody, had suddenly gotten old. Even my first daughter, the minute she was born. *But look at her,* I said to myself, *she's a toothless old woman, her skin's all wrinkled, her hair's thin, she's making incoherent little whines and whimpers just like a woman in the last stage of hardening of the arteries.* My daughter nursing at my painful breast, like a freak, a mystery that bleated. My mother nursing at my other breast. My breast swollen, red, my nipple with some kind of rash, like the earth when preparations are being made for war.

Then this lady, an older woman who'd been through several pregnancies, heard that my pains hadn't ended with the childbirth. This was quite a shock for me, but for her it was no big deal. *Mira, niña,* she said, *your problem is, your milk is curdled, the milk doesn't want to come out because you've got such a lot of it and your milk ducts are narrow* (I pictured myself as some kind of factory filled with pipes and gears all out of whack), and she went on, *Take a comb with big teeth, and stand under the shower, nice and straight, so the water falls right on your breasts, and comb along your breasts, away from your body, toward your feet, and let me know what happens.* And right away the milk started flowing, the ducts unclogged, and my breasts stopped hurting. The lady gave a little smile and very softly said, *The person that won't take advice doesn't reach old age.* When I had my second child I thought that first experience would help me. Forget it. Everything was different—different pains, different vomiting, different cramps, different spasms, there was *nothing* that was the same. Nor was that other little girl the same as the first one, although she did have the face, skin, feet, and all the other features of an old woman.

Do you suppose we really think about the fact that old people don't seem to be in any hurry to do anything, or get anywhere, or any hurry about *anything*? Why should they, when you think about it? Then why are we, who are desperate to be young, always rushing? Maybe because we're so anxious to get to that unknown place. Or to knowledge that we don't have, which once you have it, it's too late. Old people look so serene, they behave so properly all the time; it makes you kind of envy them. No, it's not envy, it's that it makes you love them, makes you want to cuddle them against you so they won't go away, so they won't get to that other unexpected place. Does that other unexpected place exist, do you think? There's no other place. We float from life to life, or from death to death. Maybe we're totally wrong, maybe the *real* objective is precisely to be wrong. Or to be on a perpetual journey. By train? All profundity turns out to be superficial. Every afternoon I sit somewhere and watch the old people in the parks, feeding the pigeons or the sparrows; old people love to sit all by themselves—all by themselves except for the birds, preferably pigeons, as though the old people were going to fly off with them into infinity. Old people sitting on benches, leaning on their canes from centuries past, laughing, loving to laugh, defending their laughter, as though the rictus of death were going to snatch it from them and they sensed that, though without ill will. Not "sense"; sensing things is for young people. As though they *knew* it, were absolutely sure that death hated laughter. As though their whole lives they had been old. There is a difference between old men and old women; old women laugh when there's need for it, while old men laugh about everything, like lovely old fools.

Most nights, I dream about my grandmother howling with laughter. I wake up with my heart in my mouth. In my dream, I see myself carrying my daughters to meet her. She is very frail, very crestfallen, like during those days just before she died. My older daughter, Ibis, is the spitting image of her, at least when she was a little girl with sparkling, mischievous eyes, so blue that you'd almost be afraid that one morning they wouldn't open. When she was first born, my older daughter looked just like when her great-grandmother was a dotty old lady, so wrinkled you thought she was taking her last breath. My second daughter, Frances, takes more after her father's side of the family.

In this dream, I'm going to visit my grandmother, and suddenly she becomes very happy, because I'm whispering words of love that I always refused to say to her before—out of embarrassment, lack of time, neglect, or just because I was a hateful granddaughter, and disrespectful. Because I thought my grandmother was going to live forever. Because my grandmother was always on my case, and a miraculous lady to boot, a real in-your-face kind of grandmother that bugged you just enough that it was easy to forget that you loved her the way you loved nobody else.

My mother warned me: *Your grandmother will go away forever and you'll never see her again, and you've never thanked her for all the things she's done for us. It's hard to believe that you act so heartless with her, like such a cold bitchy little thing—she's the one that raised you, you mustn't be so thankless.* My mother didn't suspect that I didn't want to face that woman who was becoming more and more a stranger to me as she lost strength and her mind faded, this woman who left drops and smears of blood everywhere she went, who hardly slept because all that time she was dying she would call out for somebody to dump pitchers of ice water on her head, because the heat was taking her head off, sawing her head off at the neck . . . It was unfair for her to suffer like that, but I didn't have the courage to face the fact that she was dying; my grandmother's illness cut me in two, I had to become indifferent. That was my mask. I was still a child, I suppose, and I trusted in miracles; I trusted that she would be saved by a miracle. The miracle that would not allow her to leave us.

The afternoon before she died, I decided to go see her. She was sitting in the green rocking chair, that rocking chair that she wouldn't let anybody else sit in, that she had rocked me in so many times when I was a baby, cooing at me, spoiling me I suppose, teaching me and rocking me to sleep at the same time. She had her feet tucked up under her; she had kidney cancer and that position seemed to relieve the pain. We found out about the cancer afterward; she had hidden the papers the doctor gave her and would never let us take her to the hospital. After saying hello to me she sat in silence for quite a while. Then she got up, pulled herself up with great difficulty out of that rocking chair, like a two-year-old learning to take its first hesitant steps. She went to the kitchen and brought me back a pastry, a *pan de gloria,* and then she took me by the hand and proudly showed me her little patio, its floor wet, dwarf ferns in little pots, the plants a little droopy and tired-looking from the lack of air and space. She pointed to a cage where she had a white rabbit. It was a tremendous surprise to me when she took it out of its cage; I don't know where she got the strength to pick it up. A roly-poly white rabbit with red eyes. She pronounced a prophecy:

"I want to give it to you. I bought it at Monte y Romay not long ago. It's yours, take care of it. It will love you as much as I do." We laughed at that, at the idea that a rabbit would be able to love as much as a human.

I repeat: Apparently as old people reach the end of the end, down where the story of their adventures starts petering out, they start being fascinated by laughter, and they begin to love to laugh, all the time—absolutely guffaw. My grandmother, however, gave the impression that she had thought quite a bit about laughter. She kissed me; her kiss stank of rotting blood, sick skin scraped dry. I was repulsed. I didn't kiss her back. How I've regretted that lack of sympathy, of simple humanity—that arrogance on my part!

My grandmother flickered out the next day—she died not of despondency as she had predicted she would die, but rather of a mystery that burst inside her. She coughed up a ball of hair, black. It might have been the goiter; she had a goiter. And maybe that was why her kiss smelled like a skinned rat.

But that afternoon when I left her house I went back to my own, and to do that I had to cross I don't know how many wide streets and avenues with that rabbit in my arms. I was still a little girl; I didn't really have much idea of distances. No bus driver would let me get on with such a monster animal. As I was approaching the Parque de la Fraternidad, the rabbit started thumping and squirming; it was hard for me to hold it. I was just going to cross the street from the sidewalk in front of the Capitol building to Calle Teniente Rey when the rabbit kicked out of my arms, jumped into the street, and started running like crazy, with me right behind it. I just had time to hear the screeching of the tires. I looked over toward Parque Central, the car was already right on top of me, fortunately it was just a bump. At the same moment as my mother says my grandmother started turning really serious, gravely, gravely serious. The next day she coughed, or burped, spit up, and died. The end of life for her was that filthy hairy black ball, vomited up out of the region of all passion, all those kisses—her mouth.

A clerk in the bookstore next to the Supreme Court managed to catch the rabbit and he was kind enough to bring it to me, while other people had carried me to the sidewalk and were wiping the mud off me to see if I was badly hurt. It was just scratches. I was scared for the rabbit, that squirmy, soft creature in my arms; I thought it might get aggressive. So, to keep it from escaping a second time, I dug my fingernails into its fur.

The rabbit was locked in my room, tied to one of the legs of the desk, for a year. After a year, it had wasted away from the martyrdom, the imprisonment. Its red eyes flickered out and it spit up a hairy black ball, identical to my grandmother's. But I had never managed to make it love me the way she did; the fire in its eyes was always the flame of panic. Its eyelids fluttered closed, the way old people's do. Its heart said "Enough." Its heart, which detested tenderness.

At that moment I missed my grandmother because she was mine. Today, though, I miss everything that dies, that abandons us, everything that can't be saved. Do you suppose the earth is like that—unsavable? Life is that way. Unsavable. "Salvation" is another word in the feminine. We say *Así es la vida*, "That's life," not *el vido*, masculine. Or *lo vido*, which would be like a pun, a terrible combination of "that which lives" and "emptiness." But we do say *olvido,* oblivion, or that which is forgotten. *Nacimiento* is a masculine noun; it means "birth." I had a friend once—she's the only one, the only friend of mine I've never stopped loving—whose name was Tierra Fortuna Munda, and I don't know where she might be right now, when I'm thinking of her so intensely, as though I were thinking of myself.

A mystery: Might it be "Goddess," in the feminine, instead of "God"? That friend of mine that I've never forgotten asked me that one warm morning.

I'm thinking all this so as to escape with as little on my conscience as possible. A person is born to flee. I am constantly thinking, so as to give myself courage and entertain my mind with these absurd thoughts. I have thought about all this a great deal, so as to *wish to be able to love,* that line from Fernando Pessoa that I read so much in that School in the Country. So much thinking, just to arrive at a line of poetry that has already been born, *nacido,* and even forgotten, *olvidado!* So many times around the bush just to be able to make up my mind to flee! Flee, fly, run away forever—is that an advisable solution? *Forever* sounds so terrible yet at the same time as obvious as *never.* I will *never* turn back. That is what I am thinking now as I flee: I will not set foot on this ground again, I will never again yield. I know that I have learned, out of habit, to love all that I am abandoning. But I don't want my obligations, my "duties," to turn into slavery. What I need is for my duties, my obligations, to not stop being pleasures; I need to live with dignity. If I were to concentrate less on the density of words, it might not be so hard for me to be a little more decisive about my escape. My *possible* escape. "Flight" is a fascinating word. Written or spoken, all by itself like that, *fuga,* it's either an unfamiliar line of poetry or an unknown flower, an intrepid animal or wild beast. Look, you people out there, try it, say it: *flight. Fuga . . .* Ineffable. . .

"Beauty" and "poetry" are women—too much women, if you ask me. "Love," at least the love of *amor,* sounds like a man, smells like a calf fetus. "Miracle" is androgynous. As *milagro* it's a masculine noun, but it's used for women's names, so it has that smell about it, too, the earthy smell of the sugared sex, a cave with stalactites and stalagmites of hardened honey. Maybe someday I'll reread *Daphnis and Chloe* as naively as when I was a teenager. I don't know why now I associate a phrase from that old book with that song by Nino Bravo that was such a hit during the time of the Schools in the Country—could I really be that frivolous? That song I hummed to myself so much back when I was a teenager: *Standing next to the door of love I found you, my love, and I kissed you, my love, and now all my dreams have come true, my love* . . . Is my memory failing me? Could it be that I actually read *Daphnis and Chloe* at the time? No, no way, I read it a long time after. It must be menopause, or all those jolts to my head. I'll never be myself again. I am freezing in this heartrending agony that comes over me when I remember my youth. I loved you and I still miss you, dear Tierra Fortuna Munda. Please, you people, stop hitting me in the head.

To a Slender Shoot, I Most Liken Thee . . .

*H*ow was it, you ask, that the arm of justice at last wielded its sword? I alone can tell. I, La Milagrosa, the Miraculous One. For in my state of mystical presence, having been brought once more to life by the royal palm and revived by the ceiba, I am much more alive than dead. If you people only knew, if you had any idea how hard it is to solve problems from the realm of the immaterial. A lot of people would have called for Danae and Tierra Fortuna Munda to be burned at the stake. But not me. I was not going to allow anything terrible to happen to them. And so they were saved, and I helped them defend themselves.

Tierra was not so lost and adrift and abandoned that evening at the bus stop across from the Parque de la Fraternidad, waiting for the bus that never came, as you might think, and the wolf is not as fierce as people say he is—or as he'd like people to think he is. What I mean is that Andrés did not put out Danae's eye nor was Danae taken off to Mazorra, that horrific hospital.

It's true that there were certain problems, certain inconveniences, certain obstacles to a happy ending, because there was no way Andrés was going to just let things go, just like that, bye-bye nice to meet you, and certainly not when it came to a woman, a *woman*, mind you, taking his wife away from him, and right under his nose, so to speak. Double humiliation for a man. He—there is no doubt about this—he would much rather she'd left him for a man like him, or a worse one, if possible.

That evening, or really just dusk, the sun had barely gone down, the taxi driver drove along dropping off his passengers one by one, and the last person he dropped off was Danae, who got out at the door of her building. The man repeated his conditions: he'd wait for ten or fifteen minutes *maximum*, so make it quick. Then they'd go back to the park and pick up her girlfriend and from there they'd go to Gloriosa Paz's place.

Danae ran up the stairs two at a time, her heart in her throat, her hands like ice. Excited at the prospect of seeing her family, fearful of the reproaches that she knew would follow, filled with guilt (yet radiant) for having lived three weeks of such intense happiness, disconcerted at not having the slightest idea how to present the new situation, the decision to separate from her husband, take the girls to go and live with Tierra Fortuna Munda. She was lucky not to run into any of her neighbors on the stairway, because she wouldn't have been able to hide her feelings and she'd have blurted out her story right there, to the first person she met.

As she stood, her heart pounding, before her door, her mind was racing—it's now or never, she thought. No time to think anymore; she put the key in the lock. The house was in perfect order, as though she'd never left. And to think she'd been beside herself, imagining how helpless they'd be without her!

Her mother- and father-in-law were sitting at the table, each holding a glorious big cup of café con leche to their lips. It was a miracle they didn't choke when they saw her, because their eyes almost jumped out of their sockets and they froze in mid-slurp, the *sssslllrrrppp* still hanging in the air, no idea what to say or how to react. The radio was on full blast, as usual, and the television too; with all the noise you could hardly hear the girls playing pattycake in their bedroom.

"Hi," she said. It was all she could get out.

Andrés recognized her voice and shot out of his parents' room. He looked thinner; he'd apparently just gotten out of the shower because his hair was dripping wet and he looked all fresh and talcum-powdered. He was wearing a white undershirt, new, and a pajama bottom that was also new, no doubt bought in Cincinnati by some of her in-laws' relatives. She was self-conscious about what she must have looked like, after the long hot trip, but she also felt the impulse to throw herself in his arms, ask his forgiveness, forget about Tierra Fortuna Munda, and leave everything just as it was, not throw away this moment when the two of them could still look at each other with tenderness.

"Danae!" It was him that ran to her, pulling her to him, kissing her eyes, then her lips. He was passionate, weeping.

She responded to his touch. The in-laws, convinced that the reconciliation would be nothing less than triumphant, very affectionately greeted their daughter-in-law and immediately went off to their bedroom, closing the door behind them.

It was Ibis that discovered Danae and Andrés in each other's arms.

"Frances! Frances! Mami's here, it's Mami, she's come back!"

"Mami, Mami! Oh, we've been so lonely without you!" cried Frances, unable to hold back a moment's bitterness.

The girls clung to their mother and she knelt to hug them, eyes brimming with tears. Then she raised her eyes to her husband's face; he was less unsure than at first, less hesitant, and in fact looked like a man delighted to have won a boxing match.

After a few moments of hugs and kisses, Danae realized that the clock was ticking, and she held her daughters back away from her.

"I have to go get a friend of mine that I've brought with me. She couldn't come over here because there was no space in the taxi—"

Andy's face lost its self-satisfied smile; suddenly it was serious, doubtful. She realized that this wouldn't be easy, but she had to go on.

"—Then I'm going straight to my mother's house. I'm moving in with Gloriosa Paz. I need some time . . . Frances, Ibis, could you go in your room for just two minutes? Papi and I need to talk."

"No, the girls are going to hear whatever you have to say. You two just stay right there."

"Have some consideration, Andy, don't make this harder than it is."

Ibis and Frances gave signs of wanting to skulk away, but their father stood between them and the hall that led to the bedroom.

"They're staying."

"All right. I didn't want to say it this way, but if there's no other way, if you won't give me any other choice . . ." She waited for some weakening on his part, some change of heart, but he didn't react. "We're going to get a divorce, Andy. I'm going to live with my mother, her apartment is small but I don't have anywhere else to go, and I think we'll be all right there. They're coming with me." She motioned toward the girls. "In a few days, you and I will do whatever needs to be done legally to share custody . . ." She paused, twisting the strap on her backpack. "One more thing, before you find out from some-body else. I love this woman who's come with me. We're . . . we're lovers."

Andy was not expecting that, oh no, not that. It was then that he ordered his daughters to bed, immediately.

"No, wait. I haven't finished. You wanted them to hear this, so they'll hear it," Danae went on very softly but firmly. "Tomorrow the whole family will meet, if you agree, here or in Gloriosa Paz's house. I've made up my mind."

"Tell me this is a joke. Tell me this is all some sick kind of joke. No, no, you've never been able to tell jokes, you're terrible at it, nobody ever likes those stupid jokes you tell . . ."

"It's the truth. Do I look like I'm joking?"

Andy stepped back, jerked back as though he'd been slapped, and then with one blow he knocked her to the floor. Frances and Ibis started crying hysterically. They didn't know which side to be on, their prostrate mother's or their enraged father's. Their grandparents came out to try to calm things down.

"Son, son, get ahold of yourself, you don't want to make things worse. We couldn't help hearing, the walls are like paper. Let her go, she's not worth your getting in a mess for somebody that's already made up her mind—"

"Get away from me! Get away! If she thinks she can do this to me in my own house, she's got another think coming!"

Danae, recovered, picked up her backpack from where it had landed after the punch and went to say goodbye to her daughters. He stepped between them, but Ibis went unhesitatingly to stand with her mother.

"If you're calmer tomorrow and you're willing to, we'll talk . . . Ibis, be patient, be patient for my sake, sweetheart. Stay here, I'll explain everything to you later, this is not the time . . ."

"I understand everything, Mamá. I'm going with you."

"Yeah, go with her—you're both cut from the same cloth!"

Andy was shouting and throwing anything he could get his hands on that belonged to his wife—a lamp given them by Gloriosa Paz; a reproduction of Goya's painting of a dog drowning in the sand, one of Danae's favorites; a music box with a porcelain ballerina; a plaster angel; a fat Buddha; a plastic Virgen de Regla bought at El Rincón; a Spanish doll with straight black hair, the only doll his wife had owned as a child; old record albums from the past; hard-to-get editions of books as well as paperbacks; the pots and pans they'd bought when they first got married; souvenirs; knickknacks . . . An entire life flushed down the sewer of rage.

"Papá, stop, calm down, please, Papá! I'll stay here with you, Papito!" Frances was whining and whimpering pitiably, hanging on to the tail of her father's T-shirt.

Danae tried to stop the man, but every time she stepped toward him she received a shove, an elbow. Once he spit in her face.

"Get out of here! I want you to just evaporate, I can't stand to look at you! Go! Get out of here, you bitch!"

"Andrés, I can't leave you this way! Don't you see the harm you're doing to our daughters?"

That he heard. He suddenly stopped shouting; his last words remained on his lips. He pretended to think and then, stepping toward her, standing so close to her that she felt his breath on her face, looking her straight in the eye, he said between clenched jaws:

"No, Danae, you left me and I was patient. Nobody but you is screwing up your daughters. It's you that ran off without even telling us. You cheated on me, and I swear by these two girls' lives that that is going to cost you. Don't think you're going to just waltz out of here and everything's going to be roses."

She heard a shrill whistle downstairs, then the honking of the '54 Dodge, and she realized that she'd been upstairs long enough to try the driver's patience. She took Ibis by the hand and tried to convince Frances, who ran in terror to take shelter behind her grandmother's legs. Danae's heart turned suddenly to stone; she turned, walked out, slammed the door behind her, and she and Ibis ran down the stairs. She didn't have the heart to show the girl how guilty she felt.

The breeze off the ocean cooled her face and she realized that the worst, or at least what she'd figured would be the worst, was over. She touched her aching jaw, saw that it wasn't broken, although her face had started swelling. The taxi driver whistled as he drove, but he never took his eyes off Danae in the rearview mirror. She waited for Ibis to ask some question. The little girl kept her face glued to the window so that her mother wouldn't see the big teardrops that were running down her cheeks. Danae felt a huge sense of relief; she breathed, and her chest, that *box of whimsy*, as Tierra Fortuna Munda had called it, responded with an asthmatic, oppressive wheeze.

She found her just as she'd left her, sitting on the marble bench with the pigeon shit all over it. The ceiba tree, her backdrop, growing from her head. Tierra Fortuna Munda smiled questioningly; the presence of that third person whom she guessed to be one of her friend's daughters made her feel self-conscious and uncomfortable, and reduced her, she felt, to the role of intruder.

"I'm sorry it took so long . . . we decided that Ibis would come too. This is my daughter Ibis . . ."

"How are you, sweetheart?" She wanted to give her a kiss on the cheek, but Ibis turned her face away and responded icily.

"All right, ladies, let's be on our way," chided the taxi driver, again impatient.

> *Self-interest and love*
> *had a pulling-match one day,*
> *and though love was strong*
> *self-interest won the day.*

At the sight of Danae's face, Gloriosa Paz's surprise turned to alarm. She was flustered, and she began to do several things at once: she tried to soothe the bruises with Agua de Florida, made coffee, started a pot of beans, tenderly caressed her granddaughter's head, remarked to Tierra Fortuna Munda how hot it'd been—anything but talk about the elephant in the room with them. Finally she couldn't contain herself any longer:

"Danae, I can't stand it, I've got to talk because I don't know what else to do. Your husband called before you all got here. I know everything. You know that I try to have an open mind and I try to understand . . . and of course your relationship, I mean, um, your new relationship . . . with her . . . who I'm very happy to have here, after so many years, don't misunderstand me, heavens, we're so glad she's here to visit . . . visit. But I mean of course it's not a visit, is it? Danae, I want you to understand, I feel like this has just been dropped on me, like bang, you know? and at my age it's not easy to, um, accept this situation. What will the neighbors say? My friends? . . . But above all, your daughters. I don't think you've thought this through very well, the consequences . . ."

Tierra Fortuna Munda lowered her eyes and pushed back the cup of coffee.

"I think I'd better take a walk," she suggested.

"No, just stay there." Danae put her hand on her to hold her back, then turned to Gloriosa Paz. "You're insinuating that we won't have your support, that you won't help us . . ."

"Let me think, Danae. For the time being you can stay here; we'll see about later. You're my daughter and she's my granddaughter and if that's your decision, and if she, your daughter I mean, supports you, then I can't very well do any less, can I? . . . I'm behind you, but later on don't say I didn't warn you. Your husband is threatening to destroy you . . ."

The next day, Danae tried without success to locate Andrés. Her mother-in-law answered coolly, saying that her son was out making some "very delicate" arrangements, as she put it. She wouldn't let Danae speak to Frances— as a mother, Danae didn't deserve it, she'd lost the right to call herself the girl's mother, and she should just be prepared to suffer the consequences, because although in a moment of distraction on their part, just dropping their guard for a single second, they'd made the grave mistake of allowing her to kidnap Ibis, she could be sure that they would get her back. The mother-in-law's voice was threatening. Danae and that friend of hers had better be prepared, because they were going to be ruined, brought to their knees, reduced to rubble. They were no better than scum!

"YOUR HONOR, THIS woman is a disgrace to society. The immorality of her actions is clear. She left her job, abandoned her family to enter into a lesbian relationship with a deserter from the heroic war which an entire people had undertaken and for which so many heroes offered up their lives. I will also show you evidence, your honor and ladies and gentlemen of the jury, that this woman is a drug dealer. Cocaine, to be exact. In her house, more precisely in the drawer of a Singer sewing machine owned by the accused, her husband found a package containing two kilos of pure cocaine. We have conducted an investigation into this discovery. The accused naturally denies any relationship to or knowledge of the contraband that was found, a normal reaction by any person confronted with clear evidence of his or her guilt. Your honor, ladies and gentlemen of the jury, given the gravity of this case and the clear weight of the evidence, we ask that the guilty party be given the maximum sentence allowed by law: death by firing squad."

How easily that phrase "death by firing squad" rolled off his tongue.

The courtroom was filled with police. Family, only the accusers—Andrés, his parents, Ibis, and Frances, too terrified to understand the seriousness of the possible verdict. When the prosecutor made his argument, raised his left arm and waved it in the air like that famous character in the Brazilian TV series *Roque Santeiro,* his Rolex gleamed for all to see. A lascivious spot of foam appeared at the corner of his mouth when he pronounced that fatal phrase "death by firing squad." Bloodbath, they called him, because of the number of innocents he had sent off to that very fate.

"Citizen Tierra Fortuna Munda is also accused, your honor—and what a name!—of military conspiracy and desertion, complicity in the trafficking of illegal substances, disturbing the peace and public order, kidnapping, and corrupting the morals of a minor. This last offense, sir, would have occurred had we left the daughter of the first accused in the hands of those two ... women," the prosecutor observed.

Danae, in handcuffs and standing before the court, was looking down at the floor. Tierra Fortuna Munda, likewise immobilized, never took her eyes off Danae, trying to give her courage even if only by telepathy.

The defense attorney had behaved absurdly, stammering excuses, wiping his forehead. He had not even managed to learn his clients' names. Clients whom, as one could clearly see, he took no interest whatsoever in defending. Quite the contrary: it was against his professional interest to defend them. He had argued only that since the crimes committed were a threat to the world's security, he, unfortunately, on this occasion had to assume the role of a person standing in defense of those who, from his point of view, it was not possible to pardon or find innocent—he was forced to call them "unregenerate." So he was this close to calling for the death penalty himself. But he controlled himself, justifying that control with the argument that he was carrying out the mission the Revolution had charged him with, looking after the interests of his clients and he asked that the sentence be reduced—softened—to life in prison without parole.

Danae bit her lip and big tears rolled from her eyes all the way to the hard rubber flip-flops that all prisoners were required to wear. Tierra hardly blinked. The courtroom was swept by a murmur of general approval. The prosecutor took up the accusation once again:

"Maximum sentence for Tierra Fortuna Munda: death by firing squad."

At that, Ibis and Frances began to cry. They had understood. And from their breasts, sunflowers sprouted. Their deep wail of lamentation filled the courtroom. And it was then that I decided to make my entrance. I, the peacemaker. I, La Milagrosa. The bride of the *santo, hija de las Mercedes.* She who purifies and who labors for peace. She who is envied by the orishas. Daughter of Obbatalá, the magnificent mother.

No more bloodletting! I cried, and the room froze. *No more torture of innocents! Bring in the witnesses, stand back, make way for the witnesses! The real witnesses, not the ones that have been paid off. Enough of backstabbers and betrayers! Now the victims will speak!*

Dead silence. You could have heard a pin drop. I myself, however miraculous a miracle worker I might be, was impressed by that collective hush. I was expecting a firefight, cannons, war. I expected to be hit by a rocket attack, but they were finished, they had no strength left. They were just throwing their little tantrum there, kicking and thrashing in their own doo-doo.

The first person to testify was the time of the city, the fleeting hours of adolescence. Years passed before our eyes, and we were able to see the entire history of the accused, Danae, her personal history from birth to the moment she was sent off, obligatorily, to perform agricultural labor far from her home, separated from her mother, for forty-five days every school year. The time of the city's testimony was very forthright, true, and compelling, despite the fact that it was narrated in blank verse, and everybody knows that the authorities are allergic to epics and allegories, they get like food poisoning from decent poetry. But when at last time, whose metaphysical personality was based on the exhaustive chronology of events, rethought its testimony and started speaking in rhymed couplets, a magical aura filled the minds of all those present, and they were hypnotized by the testimony of this exceptional witness.

Second came the music of the city. One would have to say that it was pretty tragic to hear the music of the city testify about Andrés and the abandonment, especially when attention was called to the disparity between Andrés's accusation and his wife's true offenses, if in fact there had actually been any. *Cumbaquín, quin quin, cumbacán; cumbaquín, quin quin, cumbacán; cumbaquín, cumbacán, baquín, bacán,* and both the judge and the members of the jury almost started dancing right there, because they were most certainly moving their shoulders and their legal backsides in their seats. The witness, or "deponent" as I heard one of these legal types call her (music I mean, which is a feminine noun), called for order and demanded that each person return to his or her place, she had not finished her statement. It was probably music that gave the essential piece of evidence. That brick of cocaine found by Andrés, the confused husband, did not belong to Danae, but to her neighbor, Matilde, who had left it with Danae before she fled her home for the small village of La Fe. Matilde had planned to be clean if the authorities made a search of her residence. Danae hadn't wanted to inform on her neighbor. She was, in fact, assuming the responsibility for a crime that she had not committed because she did not want to send someone to the firing squad because she had turned informant on them, and because she apparently had this martyr complex. Oh, she was the stuff of legends.

And speaking of stuff and speaking of legends. One of the most compelling and moving statements was made by the legendary arborescent suitcase, which was made out of *stuff* so wonderful that it not only had the fragrance of Persian poetry but had, after all these years, come back to life as a powerful tree (having once been a writing desk in another incarnation). It was that arborescent suitcase which had prevented the transition between the city and the country from being too traumatic for the youngster Danae once was. It had helped the teenager adapt, had imparted knowledge to her by way of that fragrance we were speaking of, that faint perfume of Persian poetry that had always awakened in the girl a wondrous, constant curiosity about the beauty of nature, life, love, and poetry.

Thanks to the arborescent suitcase, an entire panoply of sensations opened before Danae's intelligence, refining her sensibility and endowing her with a taste and respect for that poet who had written in the solitude of distant Havana nights:

> *An innocent—no, innocent of being innocent, awakening*
> *innocent.*
> *I do not know how to write, I have no idea of Persian poetry.*
> *Can the person who does not know Persian know anything*
> *at all?*

Very beautiful, very grand, but the lines echoed in the chamber like a bunch of lead daisies tossed in slow motion to a penful of starving pigs. No active member of the forces of authority was moved—why, they didn't so much as twitch. Which was not the case of the accused, however, or the girls, or the witnesses. And I do believe I saw Andrés' eyes begin to redden, and he did everything he could to stanch the emotion in the slippery hollow between his eyelashes and his eyeball.

Then the totally unexpected occurred. Suddenly the floor split open and the ceiba tree emerged from the entrails of the earth. Oh, Madre. Mother of mothers—all kneel before her. Blessed mother. Through the windows streamed an opaline light. White light illuminated the face of Tierra Fortuna Munda; electric sparks sputtered across the woman's body. The ceiba reigned. Embrace me, my queen, Tierra whispered. Sweet goddaughter, the ceiba called to Tierra, beckoning her to come, approach, take refuge in the lap of her roots. She made a hollow at the foot of her trunk and there prepared a soft throne. Tierra was crowned with basil leaves. An honor guard of hutias and owls stood by. The sun descended upon her head and the moon resided in her womb.

I give you powers, my daughter. Resolve this matter. Call upon the manatee, the royal palm, the Mandinga chicherekú, the sun and the moon, the sensitive light of the city and the countryside, and bid them multiply your strength. Become, now, that which we dreamed you were to be: the angel that upholds the resurrection. Take back that which belongs to you, the gift of truth.

To a slender shoot, I most liken thee. She recited the forbidden line from Sappho.

And every inch the great lady, the ceiba tree vanished the way she'd come, drawing her roots into the deepest recesses of the mystery, leaving Tierra Fortuna Munda suspended and trancelike. Levitating in sacred ascension.

Suddenly the courtroom began filling with amniotic fluid. The sticky liquid then became salt water, sea water, and the audience, the jurors, the judge, the prosecutor, the defense attorney, everyone but I, La Milagrosa, and the accused, mutated into fishes—swimming inside an enormous net, their faces showing clear signs of fear and anguish. The waves subsided, little by little, and became almost transparent, and then became the flowing waters of a river. The manatee breached, dived to the bottom, and carried the half-drowned and exhausted Danae and Tierra Fortuna Munda up to the surface once again. Danae was surrounded by white flowers as she floated, a languorous Ophelia. But Tierra emerged and coughed, taking enough oxygen into her lungs to breathe. She dived in again and swam as deep as she could, down to where the black waters tugged at her feet. Prisoner in a cage of mirrors, a cage, moreover, filled with sharks, Tierra Fortuna Munda did combat with the monsters of the sea until she had slain them and flayed them, one by one, and the bloody water clouded her sight. She experienced hallucinations. And then it was Danae's turn to awaken from the spell, from that momentary death which had been sent to her by the dark and negative fairies. Obeying the order of the manatee, her guide, she descended into the sinister depths. There she took Tierra Fortuna Munda by the hair of her head, and as though lifting loose a treasure from the clutch of the seaweed, she tossed her beloved upward toward the stars. The river was sucked down a hole in the morning star.

Bolts of lightning, peals of thunder, and the royal palm ripped through the roof, rising into the center of the courtroom, and there it demonstrated its power by changing into a golden sword and then returning to its upright plant form. It spoke a name:

"Matilde. Step forward. And confess."

The neighbor stepped forward, placed her hand on a Bible, swore to tell the truth, the whole truth, and nothing but the truth.

"I am guilty—no, guilty of being guilty, awakening guilty. But I am not the only one that's guilty. If I am good for anything it's as a scapegoat. I'm guilty, I'll repeat that so there's not the slightest doubt about it. Danae had no idea what was in that package. All she's guilty of is being a naive goose. She agreed to do me the favor, the way she had so many times before, for different reasons. I didn't act alone, there's somebody higher up. His name is Brutus Escoria. I've wanted to testify ever since this trial started, but he wouldn't let me. Apparently so as to destroy the woman who had once been his wife, or rather his victim: Tierra Fortuna Munda. He's a man with hate in his heart, and has been since time immemorial. He has manipulated us all, even Andrés, because it was him that made Andrés start this trial against his wife."

Tierra Fortuna Munda descended from the moon, gliding like a seagull. So it was him. So it was him who was pulling the strings, while he sprawled all comfy in his big armchair, behind the two-way mirror so as not to be discovered. Him, the man who had exterminated her entire family.

In the navel of the royal palm a crater erupted, and the consequence of that was an earthquake and a hurricane at the same time; hundreds of dead bodies were flung out from the epicenter, and as they were blown by the true breeze of life, their skin fell away, and out of what remained dripped a gelatinous substance that turned into *güijes*—dead bodies transformed into spirits of the woods and rivers. With their heads like straw-thatched roofs, their navels oozing guava jelly, they filled the courtroom with a greenish phosphorescent light. One of them came to stand before Danae:

"I'm Irma the Albino. I am protecting you, as La Milagrosa wished me to do. Have no fear."

And she flew up to perch on one of the leaves of the royal palm.

A group of *güijes* parked themselves next to Tierra Fortuna Munda. You should have seen them: the way they danced and played and fooled around and laughed would make the meanest man alive just break out in big smiles. They were giving a demonstration of the happiness they hadn't experienced in life.

"We are your family. I'm Bejerano, your father. This is your mother, Santa. And there are your brothers and sister, although I can't tell them apart because we all just look like *güijes*."

And finally the Mandinga chicherekú shot like a rocket out of the mouth of the crater. And that little black man started to dance, why, I've never seen such dancing in my life. First he'd imitate that amazing way owls move their heads, you know, turning them all the way around and moving them back and forth like those Balinese dancers? And then he'd creep along like a box turtle or crawl like a snake, like the jubo, scurry like the hutia, peering all around, whistle like a hummingbird, warble like a wren in the Zapata Swamp, scold like a blue jay, strut like a peacock, trumpet like the bugler bird, caw like the red-tailed hawk. And wiggle his backside, oh that backside . . . The Mandinga chicherekú now has a voice, and as he wiggles he uses it:

"When the lie is revealed, all that remains is to pull aside the curtain."

And the curtains were drawn aside by *güijes* both diligent and party-loving, swinging and swaying to the rhythm. The two-way mirror shattered into a hundred million pieces. Behind it, in the chair where Brutus Escoria was supposedly sitting, before an electronic panel like an astronaut's, there was the decomposing body of a gigantic rat. One eye was still half open. In the evil glow of that eye, Danae recognized the gaze of that rat who had spied on her from the rafters of the barracks in that far-off School in the Country.

I, La Milagrosa, the Miraculous One, couldn't contain my emotion, and knowing that with the triumph of those under my protection the pain and grief had ended, I fainted into the divine arms of the Mandinga chicherekú.

You never saw so much paper flying as in that courtroom when time, after testifying, stepped down from the stand and resumed its usual course in the testimony of Matilde:

"I am guilty—no, guilty of being guilty, awakening guilty. It's my word against yours, against yours, Brutus Escoria. Danae has always been a good mother and good wife. We shouldn't be accusing her of anything, unless it's of falling in love and thinking that love stands still, unchanging. Tierra Fortuna Munda is not a traitor, as you've been made to believe."

But although Andrés felt tremendously relieved, freed from the pangs of conscience he had suffered at sending the mother of his daughters to the firing squad wall, he was not all that happy when the judge brought his gavel down and declared both women innocent. Andrés' face fell, his eyes dropped, and he started toward the door. Right on his heels came his parents, who were also embarrassed to have lent themselves to such a shameful charade. Ibis and Frances ran to their mother.

Tierra Fortuna Munda, though, walked over quickly and put her hand on Andrés' shoulder, in a sign of reconciliation. He turned toward her, surprised.

"We have to talk," she said.

Then they retired into the shadow of a huge filing cabinet. Meanwhile a shaft of the sensitive light of the city shone gaily on the protagonists of future stories.

"Andrés, I love Danae."

"So? So do I. But there was never a sense of adventure between her and me. That's the only thing I can reproach myself for. Now the challenge is yours, I pass the baton to you—don't drop it."

"No, Andrés, love is not an obstacle course."

"Oh, no? *Coño,* look who's talking! How many obstacles have been put in your way?"

"But I won. Love is a mystery that we must keep alive."

"Don't be so sure. That's such a cliché it makes me want to laugh."

THE GOLDEN DUST of the sensitive light of the city drifted in the air. Around the Supreme Court, people were acclaiming the victors—or rather victresses, feminine. Danae thought she caught a glimpse, among the crowd, of a mirage from her childhood—she saw a cottony white rabbit with red eyes scurry between the legs of a little girl. Tierra Fortuna Munda, who had been talking to Andrés and was some distance behind, took advantage of her friend's momentary confusion to step forward and take her hand. A warm hand trembled in a harder, callused one. They were cheered as heroines, but such raw enthusiasm—vehemence—was unsettling to the modest lovers.

Frances and Ibis watched the two women admiringly. Andrés decided to move away from his daughters, so he made a path for himself through the crowd, waving to the girls and telling them that soon they'd all get together as a family and talk calmly about what had happened. Gloriosa Paz was in a chapel filled with candles, giving thanks to La Milagrosa, her mother, to whom she had never stopped praying tongue-twisting Our Fathers since the old lady's death two years ago.

Tierra Fortuna Munda was terrified at all the commotion. She closed her eyes and asked one last favor of her godmother, the ceiba tree. And at that, the golden dust of the light swirled around them in a dense golden cloud and led them off to a solitary spot, not very far away, beside the Fuente de la India. Tierra Fortuna Munda and Danae kissed each other's lips. A torrential downpour fell, washing away all the dead and yellowing leaves.

And only a few understood that phenomenon, though its origin would be talked about for years and years. The storm lasted for weeks, lashing the city with its power. But one must note that the next day, at the foot of the fountain, an amazing sight was seen: somehow, miraculously, two ceiba trees had grown up, their trunks wound tightly around each other. And since that day their roots have been venerated by the faithful, who come as though in procession to receive the eternal blessing of nature and of love, this blessing symbolized by walking three times around the trees. Lovers make vows of peace to time, tossing tarnished coins into the air.

Paris, January 1999

TRANSLATOR'S NOTE

A myriad of voices inhabit and tell the story of *Dear First Love,* the story of a young woman and of Cuba itself, all of Cuba. The voices are those of teenagers, of young adults, of parents and other mature people, of old people (women, mostly), and of the dead; they are the voices of city-dwellers and countryfolk, of Bureaucracy and Nature, of Guile and Simplicity, of Sordidness and Poetry, of the profane, secular world of Marxist-Leninist-socialism and the mysterious, sacred world of santería. They are the voices not only of people but also of natural phenomena and human artifacts—the Golden Light of the City, the Time of the City, the Arborescent Suitcase, the Ceiba, the Royal Palm. . . . And Zoé Valdés has given each of the characters (and beings and inventions), each of the strata, each of the spheres and worlds its own way of speaking, its own vocabulary, its own story. This is not a solo performance, it is, as Zoé Valdés says, a chorus—even, perhaps, if I may be allowed the apt cliché, almost a symphony, with movements in which the tempo, the mood, the idiom changes from section to section.

As Danae, the heroine of this novel, moves from the city to the country, the flatness and hardness of the novel's language and imagery shifts, becoming richer, softer, more poetic. The city, we might hazard, familiar as we are with so many city/country novels, is the sphere of materialism—socialist materialism, of course, but also the hard materialism of concrete and asphalt and heat and scarcity, the materialism of "getting by"—while the country is (with exceptions, for Zoé Valdés is no novelist of the starry-eyed persuasion) a realm of greater exuberance, greater abundance: At the simplest level, though the people are poor they have more food to eat, and a richer and more nourishing variety of it, than the government seems to be able to command for its "volunteer" workers. (Why, the very navels of these country people ooze marmalade!) But aside from that abundance, the country is also the realm of the spirit, or spirits, plural, a place one might call animistic, pantheistic did it not already have a name: It is the locus of santería.

Santería is that religion, that fusion of African and Catholic beliefs, which is and has been practiced by the country people of Cuba since the early years of slavery on the island. Once its faithful were almost entirely blacks, the children and grandchildren of slaves, and almost entirely rural, but today it has spread through the population—or at least bits and pieces of it have—so that it reaches, as Zoé Valdés shows us, even into the Higher-Ups such as Brutus Escoria, who are mostly white, and even into the city. And with the spread of the religion went the spread of the religion's vocabulary, its mix of Spanish and African words, its adaptation of Spanish to santería purposes. But those purposes, let it be noted, are not to invoke the dark, malignant force that Brutus Escoria espouses, not that threatening, voodoo-sounding and therefore possibly Haitian manifestation of the merging of the two cultures, but rather a life-affirming force, for santería is a religion of protection and nurture and comforting that is embodied in the grand Ceiba (one of its highest deities) and the Royal Palm, who will go to war, but only in the defense of love.

But let me stop there, for the task of the translator is not to interpret the novel for the novel's new readers in its new culture, but to transport the language—or languages—of the novel across the chasm of incomprehension in as faithful a way as possible, not breaking any of the merchandise, not spilling any, and not, certainly, adding any extra baggage to the load. And in this translator's view, that faithfulness entails reproducing, in so far as possible, the idiosyncrasies of the original style (or styles): its several registers and mixtures of registers, its peculiar vocabulary, sometimes—when it becomes "specialized" in some way—its peculiar terminology, the particularities of each character's speech, the slang, the stiltedness, the awkwardness, the occasional eloquence, the naturalness of human speech and expression in all its varieties.

But it is not only the characters of the novel that speak in differing ways; the novel itself runs the entire gamut of registers, from lyricism to vulgarity, from the sublime to the scatological. Zoé Valdés has always written forthrightly—more than forthrightly—about the body and its secretions and excrescences. She shares with Thoreau and Whitman, perhaps, what more than one critic has called an "excrementitious vision of the world." This is a vision that sees that only out of rot, out of excrement and ickiness, can new life come. And just as Zoé Valdés is clearsighted about the sublimities of love, she is clearsighted about the fetidness associated with the cycles of nature. It is as refreshing and haunting a vision in her as it was in Thoreau, Whitman, and a writer such as Juan Rulfo, whose grotesque situations somehow prefigure Valdés' own.

In all this I have tried to follow Zoé Valdés' lead, and I hope the novel's readers in its new culture, its new language, will find that each voice is, indeed, a slightly (or enormously) different voice. Zoé Valdés' intention has been to avoid homogenizing the richly varied and many times even conflicted culture (both societal and literary) she is writing in and about. I have felt I was bound to do no less, even if I have had to "invent" or hybridize one and another of those modes of expression. I hope the novel's readers will derive as much pleasure from the results of the experiment as I did from the process.

Andrew Hurley
San Juan, Puerto Rico
January 2002